KNIGHT'S RANSOM

ALSO BY JEFF WHEELER

The First Argentines Series

Knight's Ransom

The Grave Kingdom Series

The Killing Fog
The Buried World
The Immortal Words

The Harbinger Series

Storm Glass
Mirror Gate
Iron Garland
Prism Cloud
Broken Veil

The Kingfountain Series

The Poisoner's Enemy (prequel)
The Maid's War (prequel)
The Poisoner's Revenge (prequel)
The Queen's Poisoner
The Thief's Daughter
The King's Traitor
The Hollow Crown
The Silent Shield
The Forsaken Throne

KNIGHT'S RANSOM

JEFF WHEELER

47NORTH

Text copyright © 2021 by Jeff Wheeler
All rights reserved.

Published by 47North, Seattle

www.apub.com

Amazon, the Amazon logo, and 47North are trademarks of Amazon.com, Inc., or its affiliates.

ISBN-13: 9781542025294
ISBN-10: 154202529X

Cover design by Shasti O'Leary Soudant

Printed in the United States of America

In Memory of
Daron Septimus Wells

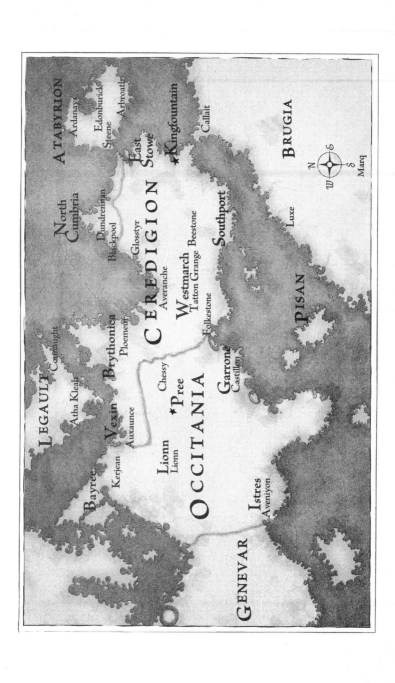

Documenting the history of Ceredigion has far exceeded the ten years I'd predicted it would take. I began with the reign of King Severn Argentine and have gone backward to document his brother Eredur's reign. Attempting to go back even further, I realized it would be nearly impossible to discover more than scant details about the reigns of the first Argentines. Due to unrelenting civil wars and conquests between neighboring kingdoms, I found very little information in the palace archives, and what I did find I thought to be inaccurate in the extreme. Because the first two Argentine kings bear the same given name, the elder was called Ursus and the younger Primus. I believed they were their names but have now been proven wrong.

This much I have been able to cobble together from the scraps of history left to us these many centuries later: After the destruction of Leoneyis due to a massive flood, Occitania began to impose itself as the dominant kingdom in our world, and a new dynasty was established that persists to this day—the house of Vertus. The first Argentine king, Devon Argentine, came onto the scene after his grandfather died without a male heir. Devon's mother, who claimed legitimacy to the throne through her father, was preempted from taking it by her nephew, one Gervase Hastings, who seized the Hollow Crown for himself. His rule was marked by bitter contention among his nobles, fueled by King Lewis the Wise of Occitania. The two relations clashed until the kingdom of Ceredigion nearly ceased to exist. But when King Gervase began to sicken, he finally agreed that Devon Argentine would take the throne and unite the realm.

Beyond these few words very little has been passed down. But in my research, I happened to visit the kingdom of Legault, where I discovered a most interesting document in the archives. It was a copy of the journal of a young woman who lived during these turbulent times, an heiress of Legault whom King Gervase held in Kingfountain to guarantee her father's loyalty. As I read it, I was immediately struck by how the events from the past mirror so closely our own days.

—Polidoro Urbino, Court Historian of Kingfountain
(during the reign of Andrew Argentine)

I'm only eight years old, but I swear everyone here at the palace of Kingfountain is an eejit. I listen to the servants worrying all day long, not over rising loaves of that awful-tasting pumpernickel bread. No, they're worrying about how long King Gervase can hold on. Of course, they should be worried. He's a fool eejit too. Gah, I wish I were back in Legault. This land is about as backward as a tail-headed cow. But alas, I cannot go back. I'm held as ransom for my father's good faith. I miss my da, who's a good sort, even though he's a noble from this land. I love that he taught me to use a bow as well as a sword. None of the other girls here know the first thing about either. They simper and buff their nails with stones to make them prettier. They can't stand me or my hair. Or my tongue. I say what I feel. That's what a Gaultic girl does. There's a lad here, though, another hostage like me. Poor little runt. I've been here months longer than he has, so I had to show him everything. He's Lord Barton's younger son. His name is Marshall, but I call him Ransom because I think it annoys him. He kept staring at me hair when we first met, so I nearly clogged him in the head. But he's not an eejit. Not like the others. After I asked him why he kept bothering about me hair, he said it made him think of autumn leaves when they change color. The other girls laughed at him when he said it. I clogged them instead.

—Claire de Murrow, Princess of Connaught
(which is in Legault
. . . and living in Kingfountain, even though I don't want
to be here)

PROLOGUE

Murdering a Child

King Gervase set the goblet down but didn't release the stem. It was already past sunset, and he had a splitting headache, which even the wine had failed to quiet. He felt his left eye begin to twitch. He hated when it did that, especially when someone was looking at him. Particularly the way Lord Gilbert was looking at him, with a little bit of sympathy and a greater portion of contempt.

"What did you say?" Gervase asked, tightening his grip on the stem of the goblet.

"My lord, he said he won't relinquish the castle."

The pounding in Gervase's skull felt like a smith's anvil. The words were incomprehensible through all that noise. "Lord Barton won't?"

"Yes—Lord Barton. He's strengthening its defenses as we speak." Gilbert had a sheen of sweat on his brow, and his tunic was mud splattered. Clearly he'd just ridden all the way from the Heath and up the hill to the palace.

Gervase stared at him in disbelief. "He gave me his sworn oath that he would relinquish that castle. He had no right to build it, no royal permission, and it is close enough to pose a strategic risk to the royal castle at Beestone if he finishes it. Yet he has proceeded anyway, bold as you please, and the only reason I didn't raze it earlier was because of that nagging whelp and his army!"

"That's the one, for certain," Gilbert said, rocking back on his heels. "He's defied you *again*, my lord. His loyalty may shift like a weather vane, but he's betting on Devon Argentine winning this conflict. We can't let Argentine use that castle as a stronghold. Nor can we let open defiance from such an insignificant lord go unpunished." The middle-aged noble stepped forward and planted his palms on the dining table in Gervase's state room. "You can toss a coin in the fountain of Our Lady to pray Barton will come around, but I'd wager that coin he'll be supping with Argentine before the end of the month."

"B-but I have Barton's son," Gervase said, his voice suddenly strangled with emotion. "I have his little brat as a hostage."

The look in Gilbert's eyes was cold. "I know, my lord. Which leaves you with one choice: you must kill the cub to tame the bear. John Barton clearly doesn't believe you will execute his son. You must prove him wrong. If you don't, you will lose every bit of leverage you have with the other hostages. You think Archer will still stand by you? He dotes on his daughter, but he's not afraid of you. None of them are. Because they don't think you have the spleen to do the hard thing. Prove them wrong, my lord. Or give that empty crown to Devon now and save us more needless bloodshed."

Gervase saw the palms on the table turn into quivering fists, saw the knuckles bleach white with the strain. Lord Gilbert had no soul left. This civil war had destroyed not only the morale of the men—it had destroyed the men themselves. No one was faithful. Everyone wanted to see him fall. He shut his eyes, unable to bear the accusing look coming from the other man, his distant cousin, who had lost sons of his own in the conflict.

"You have to," Gilbert said dispassionately.

The words echoed within the clanging noise of his brutal headache. Gervase Hastings, King of Ceredigion. He'd loved the sound of it twenty years ago. Now it was a curse. He should have let someone else claw after the prize. Even with his eyes closed, he felt his eyelid twitching still.

So be it. His enemies thought he was weak. He had to prove them wrong. The thought of that innocent boy's face came into his mind amidst the hammer strokes. When Gervase had brought the boy, Marshall, to Kingfountain, the child had held his hand as they walked the main corridor of the castle, something children did out of a natural instinct of trust. The memory of that touch plunged a knife of despair into his heart. A little groan almost came out, but he stifled it, knowing it would further unman him in Gilbert's eyes.

"Your Majesty," Gilbert said evenly, his voice like chunks of ice from Dundrennan, that distant stronghold Atabyrion still held. It should be part of Ceredigion, but he hadn't the strength to win it back. "What are your orders?"

Gervase opened his bloodshot eyes, lifting lids that felt swollen. A dull pain sizzled in his abdomen, and his heart clenched with dread. He glared at Gilbert. "What does Barton call that castle again, the Heath?"

"Aye, my lord."

"We leave at dawn for the Heath. Send the trebuchets tonight and my riders to protect them. When they get there, tell them to start building a gallows within sight of the walls. We'll hang the boy first. Then the sire."

He picked up his goblet of tepid wine and nearly choked trying to get his next sip down. Gervase knew he wouldn't sleep that night. He might never sleep again if he followed through with the plan.

A cheer went up from the men as King Gervase of Ceredigion rode up to the war camp encircling the cursed keep. It was nearly midnight, but he hadn't wanted to stop along the way. The Heath lay due west of

Kingfountain, although not far enough west to be in the borderlands, where he'd fought so many battles—of will and of might—with both Occitania *and* his rival for the throne. He was saddle sore from the ride and grateful to see his people had already put up the royal pavilion for him. The banner of House Hastings hung limp from a pole in the central spoke of the tent. Limp, how fitting. Wherever Devon was camped that night, there was probably a little breeze to rustle *his* standard. Curse him.

The knights of Gervase's mesnie dismounted and began preparing for his arrival in the tent. Squires tended the horses. Gervase loved his mesnie, these men who had fought with him and for him for so many years. Yet the sight of some of the younger faces brought back painful memories of those who had died. How many from his original mesnie were left—five or six? His brain felt like bread pudding. He couldn't think straight. Although he mourned the loss of those who had come before, these knights were young and ambitious. They'd tied their hopes to him, for a lord owed his mesnie rewards for their faithful service. Some had defected to the Argentine brat, but those who had stayed were loyal. Tried and trusted. He cared for them as if they were his own sons.

After dismounting, he limped toward his tent, tugging off his gauntlets as he went. Of course he'd ridden to the Heath fully armored. Even though his men offered him protection, he couldn't risk an ambush or a Gaultic archer skulking in the woods with a longbow, just waiting for an opportunity. Gervase didn't have the manpower to rid the woods of bandits and thieves. Every boy age fifteen or more was fighting on one side or the other. He caught a glimpse of Marshall Barton as he approached his pavilion and quickly went inside.

Lord Gilbert was there, wearing a hauberk and gloves but no battle armor. As a couple of knights hastened to remove Gervase's armor, he grunted and looked to Gilbert. "Did Barton do anything when he saw the siege engines coming?"

Gilbert pursed his lips and shrugged. He folded his arms, looking at one of the burning lanterns. "His men saw us building the gallows today. It's right in front of the camp, my lord. He thinks you're bluffing. He's not sent a single word."

From the way he said it, it was clear Gilbert thought so too.

The buckles were undone one by one and the straps loosened, helping Gervase breathe properly again. He was getting too old for this nonsense, even though he was only in his fifties. The ache in his chest was worrisome.

"Thank you," he said to the nearest knight, Sir William. "Get some food before coming back. I need to speak privately with Lord Gilbert."

"Aye, my lord," said Sir William and promptly obeyed.

Once the tent was clear except for the two of them, Gilbert gave him a studying look. "Have you lost your nerve, my lord?"

"I brought the child, didn't I?"

"What if the mother starts wailing from the battlements? I wouldn't put it past Barton to arrange for something like that."

Gervase snorted. "I suppose he might. The blackguard."

"He's cunning. And he's testing you. They're all testing you."

Gervase looked away, feeling his courage wilt. How could he do this thing? A child should not be held accountable for the sins of his father. And yet the bonds of family were the strongest inducement at his disposal. Money could be replaced. Lands could be conquered. But a son . . . a son couldn't be raised from the dead. Only in the fables of the Fountain did things like that ever happen.

The pallet and blankets had been laid out, and Gervase was weary enough he thought he might actually fall asleep after not sleeping the night before. This game of warfare vexed him.

"Tell me now, my lord. Are you going to go through with it?"

"I will, I swear on the Lady." He turned and faced Gilbert. "On the morrow, if Barton doesn't open the gate and surrender the castle, I'll hang his son and then send the body back to the mother by trebuchet."

He clenched his hands into fists. "Tell him what I said, Gilbert. Tell him he *dare* not test my patience any further."

Gilbert nodded coolly. "I will."

Before the candle burned halfway out, before the pit-roasted capon on his plate was consumed, before Gervase could even finish his first cup of wine, the reply came back.

Barton would not yield the castle.

And so Gervase could not sleep that night either. With a cloak shrouding his body, the King of Ceredigion walked through the camp, trailed at a distance by his most trusted knights. Soldiers watched the wooden pickets in case Barton tried a night attack. Gervase hoped that he would. Such an action would bring the fight where it belonged: between him and Lord Barton. But after hours and hours of waiting, the sun began to stir behind the clouds, and the end of night approached. Gervase hadn't even attempted to sleep, and his eyes felt chalky with grit and irritated from the campfire smoke.

Men roused from slumber, the camp beginning to churn with life. Fresh logs were tossed onto fires, and men rubbed their hands over the leaping flames. Gervase found himself staring at the tent where his hostage still slept, but as the shadows were driven away by the sun, his gaze shifted to the gallows, fashioned from one of the trebuchets. A rope hung from it with a noose at the end. A barrel to stand on was positioned beneath it on the turf, both wet with morning dew.

Everything seemed like a dream. No, it was a nightmare. Gervase refused an offering of bread to break his fast and took up his position by the gallows. And then there was young Marshall Barton, smiling and holding the hand of Lord Gilbert, who led him toward the king. When Marshall saw Gervase, his smile brightened, his expression a marked contrast to the malice on his companion's face.

"Do I get to go home to Papa today?" the child asked innocently.

Gervase's throat clenched. He stared at the boy, his brown hair and hazel eyes. "Not today, lad," said the king, trying to wrestle the words out.

"But that's his castle," young Marshall said, pointing.

"Aye, it is. I just wanted to get a better view of it."

"It is a pretty castle," said the boy. "But it's not as pretty as Kingfountain."

It felt like one of the hot coals from the fire lay sizzling in Gervase's chest. It was painful, a slow torture of agony. "Do you miss Kingfountain?"

"Aye. Can we go back soon?"

He saw a soldier wipe away a tear, turning his face from the scene. Gilbert's eyes blazed with fury. His expression showed he thought Gervase was daft for talking to the boy before killing him. He looked determined to march him up to the barrel and do the deed himself. But no, there was a soldier who'd been paid to do the deed already standing by the barrel, holding the noose in his hands, which hid it from the boy's sight. The man looked greensick but determined.

Gervase's stomach clenched. Was he going to be sick?

"I want you to stand on that barrel," said Lord Gilbert, releasing the boy's hand and putting his own on the boy's shoulder instead. "You'll see your father's castle better."

"Oh," said the boy and started walking toward it.

Gervase thought he would choke. He gazed at the battlement walls, clearly visible in the morning haze. And yes, he saw soldiers standing there as silent witnesses. No sound of wailing had begun. Did Barton's wife know what was to happen? The coward probably hadn't told her anything. He would likely lie and say he'd been given no warning.

Someone stifled a groan. The whole camp was as quiet as death. As the boy reached the barrel, he was lifted up by his executioner. The boy stood on tiptoe, one hand above his eyes to help him see better.

Gervase stared, his throat dry and clenched. Then he saw one of his knights, the youngest of the mesnie, Sir William Chappell, turn away from the scene. He was so young he still had a few freckles across the bridge of his nose. The knight pretended to cough to stifle his tears.

Gervase looked back at the barrel and watched the hangman put the noose around the boy's neck. Marshall shifted enough to glance at the king. He looked confused, and there was a little spark of worry in his eyes.

Lord Gilbert nodded to the hangman to kick the barrel.

"Stop," Gervase said, marching forward suddenly, his heart sizzling with unbearable pain. "Stop, or you'll hang next!"

The hangman backed away from the barrel, eyes wide with surprise and mouth grinning with relief.

Lord Gilbert whirled on him, eyes blazing. "If you do this, you'll lose. We *all* will! Think on what we've already lost!" For an instant, the king thought Lord Gilbert might defy him and kick the barrel himself.

The boy, Marshall, lifted the noose away from his neck with trembling hands. Many of the men were weeping openly, and the boy was clearly frightened. Even if he did not understand precisely what was happening, he knew something was terribly wrong.

The king reached the barrel and gripped the boy by the ribs, lifting him up and setting him down on the dewy turf. He knelt beside the child and took his hand, afraid at what he'd almost done. What he'd almost allowed himself to be persuaded to do. The hollow crown sat in a chest in his tent, but he still felt the weight of it. Would King Andrew have ever stooped to murdering a child? Even the child of an enemy?

Never.

The boy gave a quizzical look to the king kneeling before him.

"Did you get a good view, Marshall?" he asked.

"It-it was . . ." His voice trailed away, and tears gathered on the young man's lashes.

The boy's father had rejected him. Gervase stared over the lad's shoulder at the small castle and the men hunkering at the walls. That meant the child was forfeit.

"Let's go home," said the king in a kind voice. "Let's go back to Kingfountain. I'm your father now."

Four years now. I've been at Kingfountain for four years. But the king has died, and now there is no more requirement to hold a hostage for obedience, so we're all going home. I'm finally going home to Connaught. My homeland. My true people.

It hasn't been all bad, though, and I have to admit I'll miss the books. I love reading the histories, even if they're full of a bunch of nonsense about Fountain-blessed lads and lasses. I prefer the Gaultic tales of the Aos Sí and the barrow magic. The stories my mother told me before she died of the pox. The only people I'm sorry to leave are the Gaultic under-cook, Siena, and Ransom.

Looking back on it now, it's obvious that King Gervase sowed the seeds of his own downfall when he wouldn't murder an innocent child. It caused a row with the last lords supporting him. And then his only son choked and died, poor sod. With his wife and heir both dead, what else could he do but give the kingdom to Devon Argentine, the Duke of Westmarch? He caved to the inevitable and declared Argentine his heir, and wouldn't you be amazed? The rebellions stopped at once.

Now King Gervase is dead too, poor sod, and today is his funeral. His corpse will be plopped in a boat coffin, they'll shove him into the river, and down he'll go over the falls by the sanctuary of Our Lady. I thought it more than peculiar the first time I witnessed it. They think we in Legault are a superstitious people, but they throw coins into fountains hoping for favor. I nicked one once when I first came here, but the servant who caught me made me put it back and warned me if I was caught again, I'd get tossed into the river too. After that, I always made sure no one was watching.

Da is finally taking me back to Legault today. I can't wait to be home and go hunting again with him. I won't miss the prattling chatter of the court.

It's a glorious day.

—*Claire de Murrow*
Palace at Kingfountain
(on the death rites of a king)

CHAPTER ONE

A King's End

It was the Gaultic girl's fault that everyone had come to call him Ransom. She'd meant it as a joke at first. She did like to tease, and for some reason, she liked teasing him the most. But the name had stuck, mostly because everyone in the palace knew the story of how he'd nearly been hung from a trebuchet in front of the walls of his father's castle. His father had gambled with his life, shrewdly predicting that the king wouldn't go through with his threat. And he hadn't. For which Ransom was deeply grateful and deeply hurt.

It was a breezy day, and so the words of the deconeus were difficult to hear as he rambled on in his liturgy, the prayer over the dead. Ransom crossed his hands in front of himself, standing still, even though he had the urge to crane his neck and try to get a better view. Everyone at the palace, servants and all, had gathered to witness the occasion. King Gervase's stiff body lay in a canoe on the edge of the royal docks. His cheeks were gray and looked nothing like the man in the flesh. Yes, the body bore a strange resemblance to the man he'd known, but he didn't look the same without his smile, which he'd always reserved for Ransom and Claire—of the dozen or so hostages of varying ranks—or the laugh lines around his eyes. Near the end, there wasn't much the king could smile about. But he had always taken time for his son, Ransom, and

Claire—a walk through the royal gardens, a pretend duel with wooden swords, or a sweet from the kitchen. He'd seemed lighter at those times, happier.

Ransom's heart ached with loss. The king had been a true father to him. Tears stung Ransom's eyes, but he willed them back and blinked quickly. He wouldn't lose his composure, not in a crowd. Not when *she* might see him.

Ransom blinked quickly and shifted his gaze to where Claire stood side by side with her father. The man was a giant. He was huge, thick, and the sword belted over his chain tunic was nearly even with Ransom's chin. She looked like a tiny thing in her father's shadow, but she was a little taller than Ransom, and he was taller than most of the boys his age at the palace. He was taller than any of the new king's sons, who all stood dutifully by Devon and his wife, Emiloh, although the youngest was fidgeting. They were younger than him.

His gaze went back to Claire's hair, which looked deceptively brown in her father's shadow. Her hair had always fascinated him. He'd heard that many in Legault had hair the color of pumpkins, but Claire's wasn't like that. Its color seemed to change throughout the day, the brighter light revealing shades of crimson. She turned her head, as if she'd heard his thought, and caught him looking at her. He quickly looked away, but not fast enough because he caught that teasing smile again.

The wind died down, and the deconeus's voice reached Ransom's burning ears.

"May his soul find solace and rest in the depths of the Deep Fathoms. And may the stains of blood from this terrible war be washed away, giving us peace in our noble realm at last. The Lady hear us."

Everyone in the crowd murmured in agreement. "The Lady hear us."

His stomach lurched as the knights of King Gervase's mesnie, wearing their gleaming armor, knelt and lifted the poles arranged horizontally beneath the canoe. He glanced at Sir Will Chappell, who was tall and strong and had an expression of determination. Ransom wished he'd been allowed to be part of the funeral guard. But he wasn't even a squire yet, and that duty belonged to knights.

The strong men hoisted the canoe and marched slowly, solemnly, to the edge of the dock. The deconeus of the sanctuary of Our Lady turned around to face it, a black cloak fringed with silver fur covering his pale gray robes. The new king and queen wore similar mourning garments.

Ransom breathed in through his nose, watching as his king was carried to the edge. The roar of the falls was muted today, as if the waters themselves were paying reverence to the man's remains. The knights stood at the edge, sunlight flashing off their metal armor. His heart yearned to be one of them, to join a mesnie and take part in battles, fighting for the honor of a great lord. But whom would he serve? His hopes for the future had shriveled right along with Gervase. After his son's death, Gervase had finally allowed his depression to overcome his health. Over a few months, Ransom had watched him burn out, a candle snuffed by the darkness inside and around him.

The knights at the back of the canoe lifted their poles higher, while the knights near the head lowered theirs, creating a ramp. Ransom flinched as he heard the canoe scrape against the poles, then splash noisily into the churning river. Everyone strained to see it, which blocked Ransom's view. A child closer to the front pointed. That was considered rude at such a solemn event, but it was one of the new king's sons. His mother, Emiloh, put his arm down and gave him a quiet but gentle reprimand. Ransom looked away. He could not bear to look at that family for all the resentment it stirred. Why couldn't Devon Argentine have been content being the Duke of Westmarch and Count of Averanche? Why had he been so greedy?

Many nobles had fled to the camp of Duke Devon before it was over. Every week had brought news of another defection. Ransom had watched the toll it had taken on the king's health.

Ransom knew when the canoe had gone over the falls because of the collective gasp that could be heard from downriver. It came from the throats of the thousands who had gathered on the bridges and on the island sanctuary to view the spectacle. The sanctuary of Our Lady had been built centuries ago on an island that split the falls of the river straddled by the ancient town of Kingfountain. Ransom was one of the lucky ones who'd attended the funeral at the palace of Kingfountain, because he'd lived there for years.

But not any longer. The new king had come, along with his supporters and his large brood of children, and the butler had told Ransom there was no longer room for him. He would need to leave Kingfountain after the funeral. It was probably the worst day of his life, he decided. Claire was going away as well, to Legault, something she'd talked about nonstop for days.

The crowd of nobles milling around the dock began to disperse now that the ceremony had ended, but Ransom didn't feel like leaving yet. Some people patted his shoulder in sympathy as they walked by. Everyone knew that he'd been like a son to King Gervase.

As more people left, he started walking out to the dock. The dull roar of the falls was a constant murmur. He'd miss that when he returned to the Heath.

What was he going to say to his father? To his mother? The tangled feelings in his chest were too much for him to unknot. Anger, resentment, sorrow, loss. Grief. That was the biggest one, all thick and dark and brooding in his chest. As he neared the edge, he saw Sir William standing there, arms folded, gazing down at the river.

The knight had taken an interest in him since that fateful day by the trebuchet. When Sir William glanced up and noticed him, a sad smile flickered on his mouth.

"Come to pay your respects, lad?"

"Aye, Sir William." Ransom stood by him, gazing at the rush of waters. It was too beautiful a day for a funeral. Where were the rain and thunderheads that had lowered over Kingfountain for what seemed like months? It was almost as if the skies had reflected the sadness of King Gervase. Were they now reflecting Devon Argentine's feelings? He'd won in the end.

"I'll miss him," said the knight. "He was a fair master. A good lord."

"He was." Ransom sniffed. "Where will you go, Sir William? Have you found another mesnie to serve in yet?"

"Not yet. Be grateful you're not a knight right now. The king left us each a sack of silver livres, but they won't last for long. It's expensive keeping a horse. And armor and weapons."

"I wish I were a knight now," Ransom said, unable to comprehend what William meant.

"You will be, no doubt about that. You're more than a head taller than other boys your age and stronger too. You could pass for fifteen instead of twelve. No, you'll be a knight within five years, or I'll eat a goose's liver raw."

Ransom smiled at the jest. "Where will you go?"

Sir William looked across the river, his lips pursed. "I can't go home. Have an older brother, you see. You wouldn't know anything about *that*, would you, lad?" He chuckled, and Ransom grinned.

"Yes. My older brother is Marcus. I only have one sister." A poke of sadness stabbed him. His siblings hadn't communicated with him since that day by the castle of the Heath. He'd heard nothing from his family, except for a few letters his mother had written to him. He felt some loyalty to her because of that. He had written to her only twice, most recently to inform her of Gervase's death. In truth, he had hoped his parents would come to the funeral, but they hadn't seen fit to show up. He doubted his homecoming would be a happy one.

"The oldest gets it all, and sisters get a dowry. My father has four sons, one daughter, and two girls in wardship. No, I've been thinking about riding to Occitania."

Ransom stared at him in shock. His feelings were dangerously close to outrage. "You're going to try and serve King Lewis?"

"No! Of course not! The king has been sponsoring some tournaments in the town of Chessy. He wants to keep his men-at-arms in good training while there aren't any wars to fight. If you win a tournament, the reward is high. It's not just for swordplay and lancing a target, but for demonstrating knightly virtues on and off the field." He shrugged. "I don't trust or support the king, but I think it's wise to reward traits you expect in your warriors. Maybe I'll find a new lord to serve while I'm there."

"Can I come with you?" Ransom asked. The prospect was more compelling than returning to a family who didn't want him.

"You want to get your brains dashed in already, Ransom?"

Ransom hadn't heard Claire approach, but there was no mistaking her lilting accent, which she'd striven to maintain despite her many years at Kingfountain. He loved listening to her talk, even if some of her words made absolutely no sense to him.

Sir William's smile broadened, and he turned his head. "We may be standing too close to the edge of the water, lad. She's just the kind of sprite who's liable to shove one of us in."

"You're more likely to trip and fall out of sheer clumsiness, Sir William," she said with a saucy smile. "I was rootin' for you not to drop your end of the pole too soon. It would have been ghastly dropping the king's body back on the dock, wouldn't you say?"

Ransom thought her irreverent humor inappropriate considering the moment, but she could get away with saying anything. She was especially sassy with the palace cook, but that had never stopped her from being given a buttered roll or a ripe peach. One time she and Ransom had climbed a tree so high that they were both afraid to come down and had to yell for a long time before a gardener found them. He'd chided them for their foolishness, but that hadn't stopped Claire from climbing the very same tree the next day.

"I tried my hardest, demoiselle," the knight replied.

"Good, Sir Knight. I'm grateful they didn't trust Ransom here with such a responsibility. That casket looked heavy. I'm not sure he'd have been up to the job."

There was that provoking smile again. How she enjoyed teasing him. Near the docks, he could see the crimson hue of her hair on full display. Some of the breeze caught a few strands and brought them across her face.

"I wouldn't have dropped it, Claire."

"We'll never know now, will we?" Her dress was a pretty shade, not quite blue, not quite green, with a crisscross bodice over a pale blue under dress. She tilted her head a little and looked at Sir William. "So you're off to Occitania to clash swords all day? Heed my advice and hide in the shrubs until the other men have bashed themselves silly, then come out fresh and win the day."

"Hide in shrubs?" Sir William asked with a chuckle.

"And you, Ransom. You're going back to the Heath to see your da." Her look softened a bit. "I'm sorry. Not even I can find humor in that. Your family may not have bothered to visit you, but at least you have one. I'll miss seeing ye both here at Kingfountain. But I'm grateful to go back to me mother country."

"What about your father's estate at Glosstyr?"

She tossed her head. "Who cares about Glosstyr when he can rule all of Legault!" The way she emphasized those words told him what he already knew—her heart beat firmly and fastly for her native land.

"If he doesn't want Glosstyr anymore, I will take it," William said.

She crinkled her nose. "Are you trying for me hand, Sir Chappell? I'm only twelve. Give me a few years yet before showing your ambition so nakedly. You're embarrassing yourself."

Ransom sputtered out a laugh, knowing that it wasn't William's intent, but she was a vixen with words and could turn someone upside down before they knew what had happened.

"You know he didn't mean it that way," Ransom said.

"Don't I, though? Isn't that what all you young ruffians want? A wealthy heiress to wed? Thankfully, I get a choice as me mother was Queen of Legault. She chose me da, so I get a choice too. All the women of Legault get to choose who they marry and whether to use their mother's name or their father's."

"Are you so sure?" Sir William said, his cheeks flushed from their banter. "What if King Devon decides to conquer Legault? He could change the laws."

"I'd like to see him try," said Claire with a knowing smile. She glanced over her shoulder for a moment. "Well, my da is giving me a stern look, which I suppose means he wants me to stop having a little fun with you two gooses. Fare thee both well, Sir William and young Ransom."

"Young?" Ransom challenged with a grin. They were the same age after all.

"I was going to say short Ransom, but I thought that might hurt your tender feelings. Fare thee both well. I'll likely never see you again. 'Tis a pity, to be sure, but only because neither of you are brave enough to hazard a trip to visit *my* mad kingdom."

With that final insult on her lips, she tossed her mane of brilliant hair and started back to her father, who stood at the far end of the dock like a block of granite. Lord Archer was an intimidating man. He'd served King Gervase until the end, mostly out of duty and partly because his daughter had been held as ransom for his loyalty, although it had become obvious no harm would come to her in Gervase's care. Now that Devon Argentine was king, he was turning his face away from Ceredigion to the greener country called Legault.

Partway down the dock, Claire turned back and waved good-bye to them both. Her smile was genuine.

Sir William folded his arms. "Whoever marries that lass has no idea what they're in for," he said in an undertone.

＊

When we arrived at Glosstyr, they made such a fuss. The streets were crowded, and the shouts and claps were quite noisy. Truly, I wasn't expecting flower petals to be rained down on us from the battlement walls. Da rode ahead, waving occasionally to the masses. I'd not expected them to cheer for me, yet they did. Mothers were weeping, as if they'd been fearing for me life all along. I don't understand it. I wasn't ever in any danger. If King Gervase had threatened me, I know as right as rain that Da would have cut off his legs and made him walk to Dundrennan on the stumps.

The people of Glosstyr surprised me. I was a little girl when I was last here, and I only remember pining for Legault. I've some affection for them now. Still, I'm anxious to be on our way after the feasting is done. Glosstyr has my father's people, but I miss my mother's homeland. The clans of nobles have been dueling each other these many years for the proxy right to rule after Da returned to Ceredigion to support Gervase. All told, it's a mess. But I love them anyway. My people are on an island kingdom as old as the world. A kingdom with standing stones and unperturbed forests that are older than the legends of King Andrew. There is magic deep in its bones. I can't wait to be back. But for now, I'll share a part of my heart with Glosstyr.

—*Claire de Murrow*
Glosstyr Keep
(the long journey home)

CHAPTER TWO

The Heath

Upon the death of the king, Ransom had been given a small purse containing thirty silver livres, the pick of one of the rouncies from the stable, and a training sword from the palace smithy. Thirty livres would not last long, but it would be enough to bring him home. It was a kindness of Sir William that he offered to ride with Ransom to the Heath, which was on the way to Occitania.

Ransom chose the horse Gemmell. The horse was too small to be a destrier, but he had the endurance and fearlessness of a warhorse. He had an easy nature, and although Ransom had ridden him many times on hawking expeditions with the king and his son, the horse had never once bucked him off. Gervase's son, Bertram, had been a true friend to Ransom during his time at Kingfountain. His accidental death had truly been a tragedy.

Ransom and Sir William rode side by side, with a packhorse tethered behind them, carrying the knight's armor, two lances, and the rest of his baggage. The roads were still considered dangerous, but they'd passed about a half-dozen soldiers wearing King Devon's badge, the Silver Rose from House Argentine, riding back to Kingfountain. Sir William had commented that the new king had started sending patrols through the realm. A good sign that peace might be established in some of the lawless parts of the kingdom.

After a full day's ride, kept at a leisurely pace because of the packhorse, they arrived at a fork in the road.

"Your father's castle is yonder," said Sir William. "It's been a few years, but I remember all the yellow broom growing in this area. That's why this place is called the Heath."

Ransom's nerves had been increasing along the journey. He wished there were a way he could have stayed at Kingfountain. His parents had never asked for him back, and he wasn't even sure what they would say when they saw him. Still, he felt he owed his mother a visit, and the desire to see her pulled at him. Besides, he knew thirty livres would not last long in Occitania, and he did not wish to be a burden on Sir William.

"Do you want to spend the night?" Ransom asked. "It will be dark soon."

Sir William pursed his lips. "Sorry, lad. I wouldn't want to abuse the right of hospitality. I fought against your father during the war." He shook his head. "I'd rather sleep in a meadow. But there's a village farther on, closer to Westmarch. I'll try my luck there and avoid an . . . awkward confrontation."

Ransom expected his parents would honor the right of hospitality, but he wasn't sure enough to press the matter further.

"Well, Sir William. Good luck on your travels. I hope you reach Occitania safely."

"I'm wearing my hauberk under the tunic just in case," he said with a grin. "Your older brother, what was his name?"

"Marcus," Ransom said.

"Your father's name is John? That's a common name in Ceredigion." Ransom nodded. "Aye."

"Well, he sired you, so there must be some good in him." He winked at Ransom. "You're a good lad. I'm glad to have known you. If I had any prospects, I'd take you on as my squire right now."

Ransom felt a keen ache in his breast. "I'd still go with you."

Sir William sighed. "I know you would, lad. And I'm sorely tempted. But I don't have the money to start a mesnie of my own. I have no lands, no income. I have to prove myself all over again to another lord. But I promise you this—if I come across a situation that requires a strapping youth willing to work hard for very little money, I'll be sure to mention your name."

Ransom grinned at the banter. "I'd come."

"Your prospects are brighter than you think. Maybe I'll come looking for work from you in a few years. Go to your father. And give your mother a kiss, even if it embarrasses you. Do right by her, and she'll do right by you."

"Thank you. I will."

Sir William straightened the fingers on his right hand, cocking his thumb, and then tapped the thumb against his left breast twice, an informal salute between two knights, one they did as they passed each other on the road. It was a sign of respect, and although Ransom was much younger and didn't deserve the tribute, he felt the honor of it catch fire in his chest. He mimicked the gesture, and Sir William nodded to him and continued down the road.

Ransom watched him for a moment longer, wishing he could follow. Sir William was a true knight and more of a brother to Ransom than Marcus had ever been. The brothers had never been playmates— Marcus was four years older, and he'd always gone off with Father on his duties as head of the estate.

"On, Gemmell," Ransom said, shifting in the saddle.

The steed obeyed and took the fork in the road. The road cut through a light grouping of yew trees, and Ransom kept his eye on the thick branches, hoping no thieves lurked there waiting to rob him. But there was nothing beyond a few wagons and small encampments. After clearing the rise, a meadow of yellow broom opened before him, along with a view of the castle his father was still building. The years had added to its height, but there were still some timbers framed along the walls along with ropes and winches for hauling stones to the higher towers. It seemed a small village had been built up around the base of the keep, with two dozen or so wattle-and-daub houses made of timber and mud. Living in the shadow of a castle provided protection, but these seemed to be skilled workers, not farmers. A few pens with sheep and goats could be seen, and the road was riddled with ruts and puddles.

No one took notice of Ransom as he approached, his horse's hooves thudding in the dirt. He saw workers on the walls, many laboring vigorously despite the lateness of the day. Carts with cut stones and timbers were brought up the road to the main oak door of the castle. Ransom joined the flow and proceeded to the gate.

When he got there, a sentry halted him. "What's your business, lad? You here looking for work with Lord Barton? We got enough guards. Too many if you ask me, and you're too young."

Ransom stared at the man, not recognizing him or anyone else.

"I'm Lord Barton's son," he said, his voice suddenly squeaking. He cleared his throat.

The sentry looked at him incredulously. "You're not his . . ." Then his voice trailed off, and his eyes widened with surprise.

"I'm Marshall, the second eldest," Ransom said.

The sentry's eyes bugged out. He grabbed the other sentry and shoved him. "On your way, man! Marshall's home!"

Night had settled over the keep, and a crackling fire lit the hearth. Ransom sat on a bench, his stomach full of venison and carrots and bread aplenty. His younger sister, Maeg, stared at him as if he were a particularly interesting stranger. She was probably seven or eight and shared his coloring, but it was clear she didn't remember him well. She stared at Ransom the way he used to stare at Claire—interested but bashful—at the beginning of his stay in Kingfountain. Thinking about her brought back the awful reality that he might never see her again.

His mother, Lady Sibyl, had greeted him with relief and surprise and many tears. But his father, Lord Barton, hadn't appeared yet, and neither had his older brother. Both, his mother had told him, were directing stone masons on repairs for a tower wall and roof.

The food he ate was tasteless as he awaited their return. Finally, noise from the front of the castle announced their arrival. The two hunting dogs, Manx and Moor, lifted their heads and began whining. Ransom's stomach clenched with worry as he rose from the bench to greet his father. His mother and sister also rose.

Lord Barton was a big man and a stern one. He'd lost an eye in one of the battles of the civil war and wore a patch over the socket that had a lead ingot sewn into the leather. His hair was mostly gone, but he had a scraggly brown beard streaked with gray. He had big arms, a short temper, and a slightly menacing look.

He paused at the threshold for a moment, looking around the room in confusion before his eyes settled on Ransom. When they'd last seen each other, Ransom had been a child. Now he was nearly the size of a man.

"The runt sprouted," his father said with a gruff chuckle. He strode into the hall, claiming it with his outsized presence. Behind him came a broad-shouldered young man, one who also had a wispy beard. The father and son had clearly been hammered from the same forge. Ransom's appearance had always favored his mother, although he had his father's bulk.

The brother gave Ransom a wary look, a warning look.

"Hello, Father," Ransom said, grateful his voice hadn't broken again.

"'Father' is it?" said Lord Barton. "Now you claim me, after your true father is dead?"

"John," said Lady Sibyl, her voice drenched in pain, "our son was a hostage."

"Did you ask to come back to the Heath, lad? Or were you, as I've heard, happy to eat from the king's table? What do you call yourself, lad? The name *I* gave you, or the name you were given there? We've heard all about you, *Ransom*."

The young man's guts twisted with dread and humiliation. He didn't know what to say, how to respond to the utter lack of love or concern coming from his father. A stifled sob made him turn his neck, and he saw tears dripping down Lady Sibyl's cheeks. Maeg was hiding behind her mother's skirts, looking at their father with an expression of fear.

When Lord Barton relinquished his son to the king's custody, he had clearly barricaded his fatherly feelings behind a wall of stone. Ransom had known enough to dread his return—his father had not been affectionate before the incident at the Heath, and he'd certainly made no overtures since then—but even so, he'd expected more. He'd expected *something*. Filled with shame and anger, he was tempted to dash out of the hall, fetch Gemmell, and ride hard after Sir William. But he'd parted from the knight hours ago, and he had no idea how to find him.

Lord Barton sniffed and went to the table, searching for something to eat or drink. He turned his face to Ransom, the lead ingot flashing in the firelight. "Best to put it bluntly. I have nothing for you, lad. I've been loyal to Devon Argentine for years, and someday I hope he'll make me an earl. But that title would go to Marcus, along with the Heath. All of it. I have a little dowry for Maeg too, but building this castle has cost me everything." He grabbed a goblet and filled it, taking a long, slurping drink. "You brought a horse, I saw. A nag, by the looks of him. And that sword at your belt is cheap. Gervase didn't reward you very much, did he? May he drown in the Deep Fathoms." His voice throbbed with bitterness. "I've nothing for you, lad, and given the state of things, I may be called upon at any moment to help defend the realm again. There have been skirmishes with the Atabyrions up in the North, and Brugian ships have been marauding our southern coast since Gervase died.

"You can stay the night. I'd grant that hospitality to any stranger, for stranger you are. In the morning, be on your way."

Ransom's throat felt thick with tears, but he refused to show emotion. He nodded to his father and went by the hearth, pretending to warm his hands. The flames fed his anger. He still remembered being that little boy, brought to stand on a wooden barrel in front of the Heath. He hadn't truly understood what was going on, although he remembered being afraid. Someone had teased him later that his father hadn't wanted him, that he'd left him to die, and Ransom had punched the boy in the mouth. He wanted to punch the rock wall beside the hearth, but he didn't. He stared at the sizzling flames, the red tongues lashing the logs.

Lord Barton began to talk again, addressing his wife and then his son, giving instructions about the work that needed to be done. He slurped down some more drink and made a fuss about the poor quality of the venison the woodsman had caught in the nearby forest. After he was done eating, he left, saying not another word to Ransom before going.

The sound of steps came, and Marcus joined him near the hearth. "You can sleep in my room if you want," he said in a low voice.

Ransom turned and saw the look on his brother's face. Was it guilt? Ransom didn't trust his tongue, so he simply nodded. Marcus left the hall, and his mother and sister quietly did the same. A few servants came to start cleaning up the mess of the meal. Some bread and gravy were tossed to the hounds, and Ransom squatted down and rubbed both of them while they noisily ate.

The great hall was so tiny in comparison to Kingfountain. Everything felt small and tight, like a stone dungeon. His seething emotions calmed, but the resentment he felt cut deep. He couldn't wait for morning. He'd leave first thing and try to find Sir William. He'd learned some Occitanian at the king's court and thought there might be ways he could be of service.

He sat down and leaned against the wall near the hearth. The stone was warm against his back. One of the dogs, an older one he'd known as a child, came up and curled up next to him, the wolfhound laying his muzzle against Ransom's leg. He smiled at the dog and scratched his ears.

After a while, once the castle had quieted down, Ransom heard footsteps on the floor rushes. His mother entered, looking around for him for a moment before noticing him on the floor.

"Marshall," she said, gesturing for him.

He rose and approached her.

She had a paper with a waxed seal in her hand. Her eyes were red from crying, but her mouth was firm and determined. She handed the missive to him, then showed him the name written in ink on it, ink which had soaked into the paper. *Sir Bryon Kinghorn—Castle Averanche.*

"What is this?" he asked his mother.

"Sir Bryon is my cousin," she said in a low, emphatic voice. She hooked her hand around his neck and pulled him closer. "Averanche is part of King Devon's lands. It's a castle near the sea. You must go there, Marshall. I've asked Sir Bryon to take you into his service. This letter will be your introduction. If you start training now, you could be a knight in five years. Since my husband won't train you, my kinsmen shall." He took the letter in his trembling hands, and she held his face and kissed him twice. "You're a Barton, but you are also a Chaworth." She kissed him once more. "And you are *my* son. Be as loyal to Sir Bryon as you were to the old king, and you will go far. Loyalty, my son. That is the true coin of the realm. Will you do as I ask?"

The gratitude in his heart was overwhelming. "I will, Mother. Thank you." And he kissed her back.

A knight is more than just a warrior. Anyone can hold a sword and swing it about. Anyone can be taught to sheathe a lance in a ring suspended from a wooden post. Anyone can sweat and bleed. Yet most of the young men who desire to become a knight fail. The skills of sword and shield are useful in times of war regardless, and it's helpful for a person to know how to obey orders, even if they grumble about them. But a true knight is a leader of men. That is the heart of what a mesnie is, a group of knights with one leader.

Before someone leads, they must first learn to follow. And following is a difficult skill. It's not one taught in the training yard or on a horse. When me da gives an order, he's obeyed. I don't know how he earned it or what he went through to achieve it, but he is a true knight, a true leader. King Gervase was not. He wore a famous crown, and yet men did not obey him. Da doesn't talk about his time as a youth serving under his uncle. I've asked. He won't tell me, and a dark look comes into his eye when I press.

—Claire de Murrow
Glosstyr Keep
(watching the boys play in the training yard)

CHAPTER THREE

Averanche

The wax seal of his mother's crest had gotten Ransom past the gate and into the great hall of Averanche castle. It was evening when he arrived, and the raucous noise coming from the trestle tables indicated that those enjoying the food were both hungry and well acquainted with one another. Ransom followed his guide, the castle's silver-haired steward, past rows of sullen men, most with broad shoulders and grizzled beards. They looked like knights. Another row was full of enthusiastic youths who boasted of their achievements of the day and clashed their metal cups together in raucous toasts. The knights ate together. The youths ate separately. All the noise came from one side until a bear of a man with a balding pate and scruffy beard rose from the bench and shouted, "Enough of this racket!"

The thunder of his shout quieted most of the lads, but Ransom heard some of them laughing still.

One of the young men at the table stood out to Ransom, for he wore a very fine tunic, one with intricate patterns threaded into the fabric. It was a prince's costume. His hair was the color of dried thatching, and he was the only one at his table who wore a decorative gorget collar over his tunic. All of the boys at the table had smudges of dirt on their faces, and some had bruises. The fair-headed young man turned as Ransom was escorted past, his eyes blue and penetrating. He said something to those at the table, and suddenly four sets of eyes followed him the rest of the way. The fancy-dressed youth gave Ransom a mocking salute with his cup and a grin full of open contempt.

Ransom had been eager to meet Lord Kinghorn, but his stomach suddenly twisted with worry. After passing through the great hall, the steward took Ransom down a torchlit stone hall. The smell of the sea, which he'd enjoyed as far as the castle walls, had been completely quenched by smoke from the burning pitch in the torches. Averanche was an older castle, one built along the coast between Westmarch and Brythonica to defend against invasions by land or sea.

The steward came to a stop in front of a heavy oak door and knocked on it firmly before pushing it open. The scrape of the door against stone could be heard, and they stepped into a room lit by oil lamps, not torches. A windowed porch door lay open, allowing in a fresh breeze. It was a private study, one with a writing desk full of papers and leather-bound books. There were books everywhere, in fact—some stacked on end tables, a shelf haphazardly cluttered with them. A stand by the hearth held four swords of differing sizes.

Lord Kinghorn sat in the chair behind that desk, a neglected meal on the table before him, and he was coughing violently into his fist. Ransom saw the unfolded note with his mother's broken seal on the table atop other papers.

"Here is the boy, Sir Bryon," said the steward, who then stood by the door.

Interrupted in his coughing fit, the large man gestured for Ransom to wait as he took a sip from a bronze chalice. Ransom hadn't been sure what to expect, but his mother's cousin was quite a bit older than her, his gray hair combed back from his forehead. He had broad shoulders, the physique of a warrior, but there was something interesting in the love of books on display throughout the chamber.

"Pardon," said the man in a wheezing voice. "The smoke from the . . . the torches . . . I can't abide it. Come in. Come in." He gestured with a stern smile, waving Ransom in. He coughed again, a deep grating cough that did not sound like it was from the smoke. The hearth had no fire lit within it.

The nobleman gazed at Ransom, who stood across from the desk. "Look at you, lad. So you are the one I've heard so much about." His eyes were penetrating but not unkind. He looked serious for a moment, and then a smile lit his face. "Good-looking. You seem sturdy. I wish you had been free to come here earlier. Most of the young lads training are only twelve, and you're at least fourteen."

Ransom paused, not sure whether to interrupt, then said, "I'm twelve, sir."

Lord Kinghorn's eyebrows lifted. "Twelve, you say? I wouldn't have believed it. You'll be taller than the rest your age. Well, I'll take you in as Sibyl requested. You didn't ride to Averanche in vain. You're my kinsman. I don't have space for you, but not every boy who has agreed to train will make it." He sniffed, his expression darkening, and another violent fit of coughing took over. Ransom waited patiently.

After regaining his power of speech, Lord Kinghorn looked at Ransom again in his keen way. "While you were hostage to King Gervase, did you do much training? You wear a sword, but can you use it?"

"I did, I have, I mean . . ." Ransom was embarrassed by his stuttering, so he tried to calm his nerves. Lord Bryon seemed like a respectable fellow. "I did train, sir, with the king's knights."

Lord Kinghorn shrugged. "I suppose we'll see, won't we? I will say this, Marshall, that is your *real* name, is it not?"

"Yes, sir. But everyone calls me Ransom." Although the nickname had grated on him at first, as it was meant to, it now reminded him of Claire and his life at Kingfountain. He wondered if she had reached Legault yet.

"You might grow to hate the name now that you're training to be a knight. A ransom is something one knight pays to another for sparing his life. Depending on the value of the knight, the payment can be quite steep. One of our lads is the eldest son of the Duke of North Cumbria. He would fetch a high price were he to be caught."

Ransom wondered if the boy he'd seen in the great hall was the son. "The Duke of North Cumbria is Lord Wigant." He was embroiled in an endless war with Atabyrion, attempting to drive them out of the North, and had never had men to spare for King Gervase.

"The same," said Lord Kinghorn. "His son, James, is worth more than the rest of them combined in terms of wealth and prestige." The nobleman's eyes narrowed. "But not in skill at arms. I'm willing to take you in, my boy, but you must prove yourself if you want to stay. Because you are my kinsman, I will have my captain work you harder than the rest. I do the same for James. I have no favorites, and I will not have it said that Lord Kinghorn bestows favors or honors that are undeserved."

Ransom swallowed, his stomach squirming again. "I came here to earn it, my lord." Unfortunately, his voice quavered a bit.

"Good. Many of the rowdy youths you passed to get here will not become knights. As you know, there are many orders of knighthood. With some, you must buy your way in. Others honor certain achievements. I am a Vox knight, my boy. Have you heard of it?"

Ransom shook his head no.

Lord Bryon leaned back in his chair, the leather squeaking as he shifted, and steepled his fingers. "'Vox' is an ancient word. It means *voice*. At this castle, you will learn how to fight, to ride a destrier, and you will also learn languages, taxes, and ceremony. But the most important thing you could learn here is to listen to the voice."

Ransom felt a prickle go down his back. He looked at Lord Kinghorn with confusion and interest.

"The voice of the Fountain," he said. "One becomes a Vox knight by making a pilgrimage to a holy site. I have done so, and yet I have still not heard the voice. That is why I have all of these." He gestured to the books. "My efforts continue."

Ransom felt a little tremble at the words. A giddy excitement began to form inside him. Some deep part of him said that Lord Kinghorn could be trusted.

The first week of training at Averanche castle was the most difficult and enjoyable thing Ransom had ever done. Every night he went to bed sore. He had blisters on his hands from climbing ropes and swinging staves and swords. His legs ached from climbing obstacles, and he'd earned a few bruises in the practice yard. Captain Baldwin was the bearlike man who had shouted at the younger pups to be silent the night Ransom had arrived. After a few days of rough training, even the simple food they were given began to taste delicious. Baldwin was in charge of training the youths, and he fulfilled Lord Kinghorn's instructions with relish, always making Ransom and James Wigant, whom he mockingly called Jack, work harder than the rest.

Ransom could tell the duke's son had taken an instant dislike to him. He didn't know why, other than that James was the unofficial leader of those in training, and everyone usually deferred to him. Ransom was the only one who could beat him in the training yard— and he did it regularly. Did James resent him because he didn't let him win? Could he not abide being defeated by anyone else?

James had several young men who acted as his personal guard, as if he were already trying to form his own mesnie. On the fourth day, the members of his gang started going out of their way to elbow Ransom in the ribs or shove him without cause. No, there was a cause. They were acting on James's orders. Ransom ignored the subtle abuse, always done when Baldwin wasn't looking. One day, the other boys goaded Ransom into telling the tale of how King Gervase had spared his life.

The duke's son listened with interest and then scorn, and at the end of the telling, he said, "He should have launched you from the trebuchet. I would have."

The mistreatment drove Ransom to work even harder, but the abuse became worse, and he didn't feel he could go to Lord Kinghorn and complain.

It continued into the second week and the third. Ransom felt he was earning respect from the other boys, but none of them tried to befriend him. James had taken to mocking him during dinner, but Ransom refused to rise to the bait. Some of the other boys looked away in discomfort when it happened.

It was during the fourth week that an incident happened in the training yard. Baldwin had matched up Ransom and James with heavy two-handed swords, which he said were popular with knights in Occitania. Baldwin called them bastard swords because they were longer than the ones knights in Ceredigion typically used and required two hands, thus precluding the use of a shield.

Ransom found the weapon intuitive and natural considering his size and strength. Every time James came at him, he blocked the other boy and knocked him back. It felt as if the sword swung itself, and while it was heavier than the wooden practice blades, he didn't get tired as they confronted each other. James became more and more frustrated as the two of them continued to spar.

The weight of the sword tired out James, but Ransom felt as fresh as he had at the start of the day. A thrill went through him as he warded off his adversary's relentless attacks, parrying each strike. When their blades locked, Ransom used his greater size to throw the young man back, and James stumbled and went down, earning some involuntary surprised chuckles from some of the boys.

James lifted his helmet visor, his eyes full of hate and rage.

Baldwin saw the look and stepped between them. "I think that's far enough. Hand your blades to me." Ransom, though breathing fast, didn't feel winded at all. He'd loved the feeling of handling the sword with both hands. He lowered the blade and handed it to Captain Baldwin before raising his visor. James panted heavily, his brow drenched with sweat, and clambered to his feet.

Ransom felt a prickle of warning that the other boy might attack him now that he was defenseless. He didn't know why he felt that, but it was a shuddering sensation that went down to his toes. Ransom held James's gaze as if to meet the challenge he had not yet made, grateful he still wore a hauberk, bracers, gauntlets, and a helmet.

James bent over, gulping down air, and gave Ransom a deadly look.

"Hand it over, lad," Baldwin said, extending his free hand for the weapon, the other clenching Ransom's sword.

James paused for a moment, but then handed over the weapon. The prickle of apprehension faded.

"Get some food," Baldwin said. "I know you boys are always hungry. Ransom . . . stay behind a minute."

The other boys wandered off, but a nervous silence followed them. Their normal banter had been muted. Ransom struggled to get the helmet off and was grateful for the fresh air.

Once Baldwin and Ransom were alone, the bearlike man said, "That was fine swordsmanship, boy. It felt like I was watching the knights go at it. Well, except for one of you." He chuckled. "I worried that Jack might go after you there at the end. He was pretty upset."

Ransom felt itchy from the sweat and the armor. He held the helmet in the crook of his arm. "He doesn't like to lose," he replied.

"No one does, lad. But it's time you started to."

Ransom blinked in surprise. "You want me to lose to him on purpose?"

Baldwin chuffed. "Is that what you thought I meant? No, boy. I think it's time you started training with some of the knights. You've been here but a month, and you're already better than all of these boys. Granted, they might not be trying very hard, but I'll daresay that

Jack was. He couldn't touch you. Which means you won't continue to improve. I want to see you cross blades with someone better than you. Someone clearly better. It'll hurt, boy. I won't lie to you. Not many lads your age can handle a bastard sword for long, but I think you can. Prove me right."

Ransom smiled and nodded in gratitude. "Thank you."

The captain chuffed again. "You won't be thanking me tomorrow, trust me. Now, take off your armor and go get some food before all that's left are peas and butter."

Ransom grinned and hurried off, going to the worktable the others had already abandoned. He tugged off the gauntlets and unbuckled the bracers and guards. While squirming out of the hauberk, he smelled himself and the sweat he'd worked up. They all stank at the end of the day. Ransom went to the water bucket and took a satisfying drink and then hurried away from the training yard while Baldwin put the weapons back in their proper places. He was a fastidious man, the captain.

Ransom jogged around the corner and down the length of the castle wall in the courtyard. He passed the rear of the stables where the horses were kept and thought of Gemmell. When they started to work with their lances, he'd be able to ride again.

A flash of warning came to him, just in time for him to start raising his arms. The staff struck him hard across the front, smashing into his forearms and knocking him down on his back. When his head struck the cobblestones, everything went dark for a moment.

A ship has been found willing to take our household to Legault. Da had chartered with another captain who turned out to be as thick as manure but only half as useful. He'd proposed setting sail, even though there seemed to be a squall on the sea. Da may not be a sailor, but a good man giving bad advice is quite often more dangerous than a nasty brute giving bad advice. That captain was acting the maggot. Da says we may not return to Ceredigion for a while, as if that would bother me. Best to be out of the country while the new king establishes his court and gets used to the burden of the hollow crown. He'll be rewarding his friends with all the plums in his new orchard. Since Da served King Gervase, albeit without much enthusiasm, he doesn't expect any of the delectable fruit. No, Da will prove his worth as soon as someone pokes the royal nest with a stick, and men-at-arms and knights are needed to fight. Course, he may have to prove himself even sooner. Many in Legault aren't keen on having a ruler who isn't Gaultic-born. Some people only listen to forged iron after being clouted on the head.

—Claire de Murrow
Glosstyr Keep
(final entry before embarking on a journey to my true home)

CHAPTER FOUR

The Sound of the Falls

hen the boot struck Ransom's stomach, it hurt and made him gasp for breath as it woke him. Another solid blow to his spine followed, and he knew he was in trouble. With his eyes squinting from the pain, he couldn't make out how many there were, but there were at least four. Maybe five. They'd caught him blind with that staff, and his arms still throbbed from absorbing the blow.

"Bring him into the alley," snarled the voice of James Wigant in an undertone.

Two of the lads hauled Ransom up by the arms to drag him there, where only more pain and humiliation awaited. Sweat had already soaked his braided tunic from the workout in the yard, but he felt something sticky on his brow and saw red in his left eye. Breathing was a challenge, but he managed to suck in some air despite the pain.

Surprisingly, Ransom felt no fear. The pain faded quickly, and his mind suddenly became as crisp as the air on a winter's morning. The thumping of his pulse in his ears slowed, and it almost sounded like a rush of water from the falls outside Kingfountain. Was it a memory? Whatever it was, he buried himself in it, remembering the power of the falls, the beautiful and violent swath of waters that had taken away the canoe bearing his king. An image flashed in his mind of that canoe, of the still corpse that lay inside. The love he'd felt for Gervase thrummed in his heart.

Ransom found his feet and shoved one of his assailants into the edge of the wall before they could drag him into the gap of the alley. The young man grunted in pain and let go. With his newly freed hand, he clenched a fist and punched the other fellow who was restraining him in the jaw, dropping him with a single blow. Ransom lifted his head, feeling one of his eyes swelling shut, and saw three more in front of him, including Wigant's heir. A look of surprise flitted across that usually smug face as Ransom tackled the duke's son into the alley wall.

The two slammed into the side of the stables, and horses inside began to complain noisily. James's head slammed back into the wall a second time before the others grabbed Ransom and yanked him away. He saw the staff coming toward his face and ducked at the last moment. The blow that had been intended for him struck one of the others instead, making the youth slump to the ground. It was a boy named Bart who held the staff, and Ransom charged him. They wrestled with it a moment before Ransom flung him into the side of the stables.

James tackled Ransom onto the cobblestones, and his fist collided with Ransom's skull twice. The pain was jarring, but Ransom still felt that odd, invigorating sensation. Despite his injuries, he felt full of energy. Brimming with it. He rolled to one side, and James barked in pain as his fist hit the stones instead. Ransom twisted and managed to kick James in the stomach, knocking him backward. That gave Ransom the chance to make it back to his feet, and suddenly he sensed someone behind him—Bart with the reclaimed staff. The sensation came too late, though, and the wooden weapon slid across his front and pinned him to Bart's body.

"Hit him! Hit him!" Bart shouted in his ear.

Another youth, Delbert Finn, arrived first and began hammering his fists into Ransom's stomach. Strangely, the blows caused no pain at all. It was like all the hurt was being forced into a small corner of Ransom's mind. After the fourth blow, he still felt nothing, so he rocked his head back into Bart's face and then shoved forward, freeing himself. Delbert gaped in surprise before Ransom punched him in the nose so hard the lad fell to the ground in a heap.

James stared at Ransom in alarm. Four other boys lay sprawled in the alley. His henchmen had all lost the will for this fight. James pressed his wounded hand against his own chest, his face betraying both cowardice and hatred.

Ransom breathed hard, but he didn't back down.

"You served the traitor king," James seethed. "He stole the hollow crown. You don't deserve to be here."

Ransom had no words. The accusation of King Gervase being a traitor sent a bolt of white-hot anger into his mind. He rushed forward and knocked James down, pummeling him over and over. Blood oozed from the broken nose. Finally, Ransom stopped. He found himself kneeling on James's body, hand cocked back for another punch, which he did not deliver. The lad was thoroughly defeated.

Ransom rose and turned around, fist still poised to deliver another blow. The other lads shrunk from him. One was crying. He studied their faces, one by one, meeting their eyes and delivering an unspoken warning. If they ever tried that again, he would not restrain himself. He tasted blood in his mouth.

The pain he'd boxed within his mind began to squirm free. His arms and fists ached. So did his torso and back. There would be bruises—oh, there would be many bruises! There were five of them in all, including the duke's son writhing on the ground. Five against one. Ransom couldn't believe he'd beaten them all. He shouldn't have been able to do that. The rushing noise of the falls receded. A seabird squealed in the distance, reminding him that he was in Averanche, not Kingfountain.

He walked out of the alley, trying not to limp. Everything hurt, but the satisfaction that he'd not been thrashed by Wigant and his henchmen filled his mouth with a sweet taste. It felt wonderful.

Even though it hurt.

※

Ransom leaned against the battlements, his arms resting on a blocky merlon as he stared out to sea. The sun was setting in the west, and the spire of a sanctuary caught his eye along the western coast—Our Lady of Toussan, off the shores of Brythonica. If he looked to the east, he saw St. Penryn. As he glanced from one to the other, he felt drawn to them. Now that the fight was over, he'd cleaned himself up, and his entire body ached with pain, he wondered if he'd need to seek sanctuary in one of those places to keep the duke's son from killing him.

Regret throbbed inside him, as insistent as the pain in his arms. He breathed out, and his chest hurt too. A breeze ruffled the air, bringing that briny scent from the ocean with it. His nose hurt. Although his left eye hadn't swollen completely shut, it was trying to, and he could only squint from it. A dull ache in his back reminded him that sleep would not be easy this night. Well, it wouldn't be easy for any of them.

The knowledge that he'd knocked down a duke's son stoked the ill feelings roiling in his stomach and chest. James's father was Duke Wigant of North Cumbria. The duke of the North. Ransom was a second-born son who had served a king who had long since fallen out of favor with the people because of the endless civil war. Perhaps he should have let the other boys thrash him. But with that thought came a defiant clench of his jaw. *No.*

He heard boots climbing the stairs leading to the defenses. Was it time for the changing of the guard? But as the steps came closer, he recognized the sound of the stride. It was Captain Baldwin.

Ransom couldn't hide his injuries, so he just stared at the sea and pretended he couldn't hear the other man approach.

Baldwin reached him and leaned against the adjacent merlon. Ransom could see the stripes of gray in his mostly nut-brown beard. They stood there awhile, silently, gazing at the rippling waters before they turned into waves that came crashing against the sandy shore below.

"You don't look so bad compared to most of the other lads," said Baldwin finally.

Ransom sighed. "Am I in trouble, Baldwin?"

The grizzled man chuckled deeply. "You might say that. Sir Bryon wants to see you. Now."

Dread wormed through Ransom's stomach. Bleak thoughts had made him so sick to his stomach that he hadn't eaten anything yet. He followed the captain away from the battlements and down into the castle, all the way to the private chamber of his mother's cousin. He hadn't been there since his arrival. None of the other boys had ever been summoned to see Lord Kinghorn.

Baldwin knocked on the door, and they heard a gruff command to wait. After a moment, the door opened, revealing James Wigant. He had bruises on his temple, several cuts on his face, and his nose was absolutely swollen. He looked at Ransom and flinched, blinking quickly, before he marched past him without saying a word.

What could it mean?

Ransom glanced at Baldwin and motioned for him to go in first.

"Oh no, lad," chuckled the captain. "You're on your own."

The sick feeling in his stomach increased, but he walked into Lord Kinghorn's study, smelling paper and leather. The man was standing at the windows, gazing out, not seated behind the desk as before. He coughed lightly into his hand. He looked stern and serious, his expression making Ransom fear the worst. He paused halfway into the room and, unsure of what to do, simply stood there. The door closed behind him.

Lord Kinghorn turned to face him. "Would you like to tell me what happened after practice in the training yard today?"

Ransom squirmed inside as he considered how to respond. What had James already revealed? Had he accused Ransom of attacking *him*?

"Not really," he finally said.

His answer caused Lord Kinghorn's eyes to narrow. "Do you think it is appropriate to take out personal enmities behind the stables?"

Ransom wished he were anywhere else but there. "No, my lord."

"What do you think the Duke of North Cumbria will say when he's learned his son was . . . humiliated so?"

Ransom felt his ears start to burn. He said nothing.

"Well?"

Again, he went with the truth. "I don't think he'll be pleased, my lord."

"Do you think *I* am pleased?"

"No."

"You're wrong."

Ransom, who hadn't been able to meet Lord Kinghorn's gaze, suddenly lifted his eyes. The older man's mouth quirked into a smile.

"I've been waiting for someone to humble that little braggart," said Lord Kinghorn. "I've known for some time how he treats the others. I almost sent him back to his father the week after he arrived. It would not have been politic to do so, however, not without a formidable excuse. You've given me one, and I could send him on a palfrey back to his father tomorrow."

Relief flooded Ransom's chest. He let out his breath, realizing it had been pent up.

"Why didn't you come to me earlier?" asked Lord Bryon.

Ransom clasped his hands behind his back. "I didn't want to tattle."

"But you saw how he treated the other boys?"

"Yes. But he's a duke's son."

"And why do you think he was sent to Averanche, lad? Why do fathers send away their sons?"

The words reminded him of his own father, who'd sent him away within minutes of his return to the Heath. Where would he be if not for his mother? Anger and resentment began to throb in his heart. He looked away.

"How can I expect you to know that?" Lord Kinghorn said with some compassion. "I'll answer you myself. Before a horse becomes a destrier that can be trusted in battle, it must be broken. It must be trained and hardened to withstand the chaos of war. I wish we lived in other times, lad. But we don't. In a few short years, you will be joining that chaos. Whether you live or die will depend on your training and your will to survive. I cannot shield you from the horrors of it. I must prepare you for it. So must I do with Lord Wigant's son and the others. I must make men out of boys." He stepped around the desk, his eyes earnest and sincere. "What you did today took the courage of a man. War is not fair. It is not holy. It is a brawl between men who fight for those they serve whether or not they believe in the cause, just like James's friends did today. Sometimes you know your enemy, and others you're surprised by a betrayal in the midst of a battle. A knight must be ready for any circumstance. He must know when to fight and when to back off. And when it's time to fight, he must fight with everything he has and is, knowing that his enemy will do the same. One will prevail. The other will die or be held hostage for a price. What happened today was the lesson I've been waiting for."

He stepped even closer, his eyes fixed on Ransom's face. "I just wish, my boy, you had come to me sooner and told me what you'd observed happening with the lads. I am your liege lord. Your master. Remember who you owe your loyalty to. Your peers, yes—they deserve a portion of it. But the lesson I wish you to learn is that your first duty is to me. To your liege lord."

He looked at Ransom pointedly until the young man nodded in agreement.

"Yes, my lord. I'm sorry if I have caused trouble for you. Are you going to be sending James away? Back to the North?"

Lord Kinghorn smiled. "No, lad. From this day onward, you will be sharing his room, his companionship. I've told him he must eat with you and no others, train with you, spend his off hours with you, *and no others*, until I'm satisfied he's learned his lesson. He's a stubborn young man. This might take a while."

Ransom's stomach dropped to the floor.

"In other words, I'm going to use you to break him."

✕

I can't believe it has been so long since I wrote the last entry. Time has rushed on nineteen to a dozen. Maybe I'm having trouble reckoning the last five years because they've been so hard. When Da arrived in Legault, he had naught but trouble. Every day brought a new test, a new challenge. When our boat landed, a mob sent by a rival lord tried to abduct me, and we had to put out to sea again to avoid capture. That was only the start. Men who owed Da homage refused to bend the knee, complaining of sickness, a death in the family, a broken toe. What did they take us for, eejits? None of them wanted to be ruled by a noble from Ceredigion, even though he'd married the daughter of their king. Aye, these years have brought us much trouble and great expense.

Finally, after three years of such nonsense, King Devon Argentine sent a message to Da, offering to help settle the peace. Da is a proud man. He never would have asked for help. But the king saw that if one of his vassals lost his holdings in Legault, it would prove a bad omen for the future of the court of Kingfountain. He sent Duke Wigant of the North to assist. Since the king had helped the duke repulse the Atabyrions, he owed him a favor, shall we say. With Duke Wigant's help, those knaves who opposed Da sued for peace and swore fealty to him as they ought to have done when we first arrived. The duke told Da about his eldest son, James, who was training to be a knight in the duchy of Westmarch. I think he meant to win Da's favor and possibly my hand. I am seventeen after all. But Da told him that any man who tries to woo me must first prove himself worthy of me. Lord Wigant praised his son overmuch, bragging that he'd be knighted soon. I'm not keen on being attached so soon. Wigant's son might be the best of men. But then again, a man rarely is.

—Claire de Murrow
Connaught Castle, Kingdom of Legault, the Fair Isle

CHAPTER FIVE

The Drums of War

James let out a long, exaggerated sigh and let his book thump shut. Ransom tried to ignore his companion as he peered at his own book and tried to work out the translation in his mind. It was difficult translating a book where every other word had three possible meanings, all of which he had to keep juggling in his mind as he conjugated the correct declensions.

"I'm tired of reading this rubbish," James said to him. "Let's go for a walk on the beach."

Ransom read the passage aloud, "*Evaunt il lout mitre ensemble il lapel la mort le veil auters.*"

"Your accent is terrible, Ransom. Like gobs of moldy cheese in good wine. It goes like this, *Ebaunt il louez mi très ensemble, il appelle la mort de le veil reigne.* You really need to work on your old speech."

"I know, but it doesn't roll off my tongue like it does yours," Ransom replied, a little jealous that no matter how hard he worked on the language, it didn't come naturally to him. "That's why I'm practicing."

"Let's go for a walk on the beach instead. I promise I'll speak nothing but the old tongue on our way. It would be like practicing. If we're lucky, we might even get in a fight. Come, this room is stifling me!"

Ransom wouldn't say that he and James were friends. But Lord Kinghorn's wishes had been fulfilled. They were no longer rivals, and indeed, they had learned from each other. James continually tried to best Ransom in feats of arms and never could, but his ability with languages, laws, and strategy had proven to be equally valuable. They had been together every day since that fateful ambush by the stables, and while neither young man cared for the other, they did share a mutual respect. The two of them made, it turned out, a formidable team. More than once James had told Ransom that he'd be willing to take him in as a household knight once he was permitted to create a mesnie of his own. It was an offer he'd be a fool not to consider, yet he didn't trust the man who'd made it. To serve a man was to pursue his ends, and Ransom doubted he would ever agree with James's choices.

Looking down at the page with its calligraphic writing and colorful artwork drawn by a scholar's hand, Ransom wondered whether he should rebuff James's request for a jaunt down by the beach.

"Come on!" pleaded the duke's son. "I'll even start the fight. And you can win it."

Ransom put a leather marker in place and gently closed the book. "You're not eager to go out there because of some fisherman's daughter, are you? I think I'd rather hear a flock of gulls squawking than listen to you try to woo another woman."

"Like anything, wooing takes practice, Ransom. Better to practice on a peasant maid than a princess."

"I'll keep reading, then," Ransom said, opening the book and looking down.

"I was joking, Ransom. Joking. Besides, it's already past sunset, and the fishermen have all hauled in their catches by now. The beach is probably empty, awaiting the tide to come in. You know you don't want to sit here reading until the candle burns out again. Let's go outside!"

Ransom hung his head. Sometimes he detested James. Sometimes he tolerated him. But it would never fail to bother him that the education on knightly conduct passed between James's ears without once getting snared in a cobweb of thought. Honor, duty, loyalty—those were only words to the duke's son. *Virtus.* James could say it elegantly, the accent and inflection perfect. But his actions didn't match.

Ransom shut the book again, and James thumped his palm on the table excitedly and rose. "Finally! He relents! I promise, no wooing, even if we stumble across the mayor's daughter bathing in the public square. I'll look away as *you* would, and we'll ignore all temptations of the flesh. I promise on my honor as a duke's son."

Ransom didn't believe the oath, but then again, he knew James didn't either. The two fetched their cloaks, buckled on their swords, and left the room. The smoke-hazed corridor was commonplace to Ransom now. He'd been in Averanche for five years, training to become a knight. He was still half a head taller than James and a full head taller than the other lads, but they'd all grown from gangly youths into more rugged young men trained in the arts of war. Ransom could ride Gemmell through the obstacle course, collecting rings on his lance, better than any of the other students, as well as half the knights who served Lord Kinghorn. While James wore a longsword at his waist, Ransom wore a bastard sword, and he was able to beat Sir Toby at least half the time now. That first year had been a form of torture, but every once in a while, Ransom could hear the rushing of the falls. At those times, the sword seemed to swing itself, and Sir Toby would end up on his back, wide-eyed and startled by his sudden display of skill.

Ransom didn't know why it happened, and he couldn't control when it did, but he relished how it made him feel when the other knights stared at him with respect.

At the rear of the castle was a porter door, a thick oaken door with two crossbars. It led to the beach behind the palace. The guard, a man named Harper, lifted the crossbars to let them out.

Heading down the stone steps at a jog, James suddenly broke into a run, determined to beat Ransom down to the bottom. It goaded Ransom enough to take the steps two at a time until he caught up. James kept close to the palace wall before it connected to the cliff wall, the steps continuing down to the beach, and Ransom didn't want to pass him for fear James might shove him off in a fit of pique. He decided to ram James into the cliff first, and the two nearly tumbled the rest of the way down the steps. Ransom reached the bottom first, but they both arrived laughing.

"You shoved me," James said between his chuckles. "That wasn't very honorable."

"I didn't want you pushing me off the steps," Ransom countered.

James looked at him. "The thought did cross my mind. Are you a Wizr?"

"There are no Wizrs anymore," Ransom scoffed. "Only in the legends we read about. Now, you promised you'd only talk in the old speech. Go on."

"I did promise, didn't I? But you don't think I *meant* it?"

They began trudging through the sand, accompanied by the hiss of the surf on the beach. The smell of the seawater enveloped Ransom as they walked. The entire beach, including some of the stone steps, would be buried in water within an hour or so. Ransom had come to know the seasons, the telltale signs of the advancing tide. It fascinated him how the pattern changed from day to day, but they were safe for a while still.

Clumps of seaweed and driftwood logs littered the beach. The sun had set, but there was still enough light to see.

"Do you have ambition, Ransom?" James asked after they'd walked and joked for a time.

"What man doesn't? I know you have plenty for both of us."

"I do, it's true," the young man replied, chuckling. "I'll inherit Dundrennan. That's to be expected. But an inheritance won't satisfy me. That is just an accident of birth. I have four brothers and two sisters.

I did nothing to be born first. How many siblings do you have? Just a brother, right?"

"An elder brother. I have a sister as well."

"Is she pretty?"

Ransom gave him a wary look, and James spluttered with laughter. "Look at your face! Trust me, she's safe from my evil designs. Is the sister older or younger than you?"

"Younger. She's thirteen."

"I was just curious. No, I have my ambition set on Lord Archer's daughter."

Ransom felt a little tightening in his chest, just as he did whenever James bragged about the assistance his father had provided hers in reconquering Legault. The thought of James marrying Claire de Murrow made his insides feel rubbery and twisted.

"Being the Duke of North Cumbria isn't enough. You want to be Duke of Glosstyr too?"

"And why not?" James said. "The king's power increased when he married Lady Emiloh, the Duchess of Vexin. One could argue it was what helped him win the hollow crown."

"Is that part of your ambition as well?" Ransom teased.

"I don't want to be a king. Well . . . I'll take that back. I wouldn't mind being King of Legault. Sadly, Father says the women in that kingdom can choose who they marry and only their heirs become kings, not by marriage. What a strange notion. Our fathers should be allowed to settle the matter as has always been done. Alliances are a powerful tool."

Ransom kept his expression uninterested and gave a little shrug. Inside he was seething.

"Have you met Lady Claire? You used to live at the palace. Didn't she?"

"We were both children," Ransom said, trying to conceal his growing discomfort.

"So you have met her. It's a wonder you've never mentioned it before."

Like I would ever share my heart with you, Ransom thought. Indeed, he'd gone to great pains to avoid any such discussion in the past, which was the very reason James did not know. Eager to steer the conversation to safer waters, he said, "Do you think your father might not have other plans for you? Atabyrion has always been a threat. You might be asked to marry one of those savages."

"Of course, that's another option. But the King of Atabyrion's *savage* daughter is more of an age with your younger sister. I . . . I'm not interested, although it does happen. No, I think the Fair Isle sounds more to my taste. I wish I could have helped my father's knights subdue those disloyal rogues. I could have met her then. Father said her hair is a peevish color, but I probably wouldn't mind that too much . . . considering the gain in wealth and prestige."

Ransom saw a wave snaking toward them. The tide was coming in faster. "Do you want to head to town?"

"You want me to stop talking about Lady Claire!" James said, his eyes flashing with excitement and mirth.

"No, the tide's coming in."

"You're jealous. Admit it."

"Why would I be jealous of a stewed prune like you?"

"Because you're an eel skin."

They traded barbs the rest of the way to town, each insult more outrageous than the last, intended to make the other snicker and break countenance. When they arrived at the market, Ransom put his hand on James's shoulder.

"Look," he said.

"What? The mayor's daughter is bathing after all?" James said, then let out another laugh.

"No. Look. The knights from the castle are all here. There's Sir Gordon, Sir Beckett, Sir Jude."

James blinked in confusion and looked around in surprise. Yes, the knights had all gathered in the market with full purses. Some were looking at swords, others at saddles. The noise of the market was rowdy with so many customers at once. Normally, it was a much more sedate affair. James looked at Ransom in surprise, and they both approached one of the knights.

"What is it, a holiday?" James asked Sir Jude.

The knight gave him a serious look. "You don't know? Where have you lads been?"

"We were walking on the beach," Ransom said.

Sir Jude's gray eyes were firm and without humor. "A rider from Kingfountain just arrived. Brugia has attacked our southern shores. We're leaving in the morning, lads."

"Where?" James asked, his eyes brightening with eagerness.

Sir Jude frowned at the duke's son. "War isn't a tournament, boy. The Brugians landed at the cove at Folkestone, in Westmarch, near the border with Occitania. They've invaded our kingdom." His cheek twitched with anger. "We're going to kill the dirty sots."

Gemmell wore a plate guarding the flank of his nose, and a chain skirt had been spread across his withers. While the pages cinched the straps on the chain mail, Ransom inspected the shoes himself to make sure there were no rocks or loose nails. Finding one, he called over the blacksmith, who arrived with a little pin hammer and fixed it.

The knights had already left before dawn, and it was up to Captain Baldwin to prepare the young men like Ransom. The weight of the armor didn't seem to bother Baldwin, and the chain hood covering his head and neck gave him a menacing look. He had a sword strapped to his waist and a mace on his other hip.

"No, no!" Baldwin shouted at a page. "Pull harder on the strap! We don't want Jack Wigant falling off his courser before we reach the edge of town! I've taught you better than this. Fix it!"

Ransom looked at James's courser, which was a much finer horse than Gemmell. But then again, all his things were finer.

As James approached in his finely crafted armor, he grinned at Ransom. "Finally. We get to use what we've learned. I'd be more nervous if we were facing Occitanian knights, but Brugians aren't to be trifled with either. Are you nervous?"

"Shouldn't we all be?" Ransom replied, trying to get some moisture into his mouth.

"With your skill? I wouldn't be worried. I'll try not to stay in your shadow. I want to wet my sword on this campaign. Think of it, Ransom! We could be knights when this is done!"

"It could be a trick," Ransom said. "A feint. Folkestone is near the border. What if Brugia and Occitania have formed a secret alliance? We could be riding into a trap."

"This is where your skill with a bastard sword doesn't help you at all," James said. "Brugia and Occitania are mortal enemies. Besides, Occitania won't dare attack us because the duchy of Vexin would be poised to strike at Pree. The queen will protect her husband's interests. Trust me, this is just the Brugians' attempt at a land grab. Folkestone used to be one of their ports, long ago. They lost it. They want it back so they can harass Occitania more. They think Devon is too distracted at Kingfountain to protect his borders. They'll learn the hard way he fights for what is his."

"You sound pretty sure of yourself," Ransom said. He itched beneath his armor, but there was no way to scratch it, so he endured the discomfort.

"As I said, politics is my domain."

"I hope you're right."

"Of course I'm right. I'm a Wigant. By Our Lady, I've been waiting for this!"

Ransom thought it strange that the young man should blaspheme the Lady when they were all in dire need of her blessing.

"Jack! Ransom!" Baldwin bellowed. "Stop being cuttlefish! Mount your maggoty horses already!"

A messenger arrived from the court of Kingfountain. Da must leave and return to Glosstyr at once. There's been a skirmish in Westmarch, and King Devon is summoning his vassals and preparing to repulse the Brugian invaders. There is no Duke of Westmarch still, for the king holds that title himself and hasn't yet invested it in one of his four sons. There's talk that his eldest, his namesake, will get it, and that the next youngest brother will inherit his mother's duchy in the Vexin. But they are young lads and still training to be knights themselves. They're not ready for war.

Da is concerned about leaving me at Connaught castle, but I've told him it will be better if I stay to defend it while he's gone. I'd love it if some half-mad Gaultic noble tried to siege us. Maybe that's one of the reasons Da doesn't want me to stay. So I won't provoke a fight. I wouldn't do that, obviously—I'm no fool eejit. But I won't run from one either. It will take time for him to summon men in Glosstyr.

Meanwhile, King Devon is sending his faithful knights in Westmarch into battle. Ransom is probably one of them. I haven't seen him in five years, yet I still remember him. I hope *he doesn't do anything headstrong or barmy. War is a deadly game. Even the best players are caught unawares. Don't be an eejit, Ransom Barton. But I wonder if you can help yourself.*

—Claire de Murrow
Connaught Castle, Kingdom of Legault

CHAPTER SIX

Knights of Averanche

he countryside of Westmarch was lush and beautiful, but the heat that built up within Ransom's armor stifled him. None of the soldiers wore helmets, though these were within easy reach, as were two ash-wood lances fixed within saddle harnesses. Farmers and other travelers cleared the road for the knights as they rode through, but Ransom had never felt dustier in his life.

They reached the village of Menonval, where Lord Kinghorn and the full company of his knights were billeted for the evening. Their horses were all secured in front of the mayor's manor, which had the look of a castle but lacked any fortifications. Two rounded towers flanked the main door, a double-wide oak structure that wouldn't stand long against a battering ram. The towers were brick and had cone-shaped peaks. The walls, constructed of wood and mud, were highly sloped with soot stains and ivy creeping on them.

Ransom and the others dismounted, and a page hurried up to take Gemmell's reins. Captain Baldwin gave some orders to the youths about caring for the horses. Ransom was surprised to see the other war horses had not yet been stabled, but perhaps the mayor lacked sufficient space for them all. One by one, the young men entered the building through the huge oak doors. Ransom was weary but excited to join the knights he knew from training. Sir Jude was leaning against a wall near the entrance, a scowl on his face. Sir Gordon and Sir Beckett were at hand as well, along with several others. They all had serious, concerned expressions. Despite the blazing fire in the hearth, there was a distinct chill in the room.

Lord Kinghorn stood in the center of the room, his helmet resting in the crook of his arm, his eyes somber.

Something was wrong.

Captain Baldwin pushed his way in, past the young men, and immediately noticed the mood.

"We've arrived, my lord," he said gruffly. "Why does everyone look so greensick? Is there a plague in this village?"

The lord of Averanche didn't smile at the attempted jest. "You arrived not a moment too soon, Baldwin. We've not been here long ourselves. A courier from the constable of Westmarch arrived shortly after we did to warn the mayor."

"The constable?" Baldwin asked, eyebrows furrowing.

"Aye. The Brugians evaded his army. They've penetrated deeper than expected and intend to go farther yet, keeping us guessing as to their intentions. Their advance should reach Menonval soon. We're all that stand in the way of them pillaging the countryside."

The news explained the somber expressions on everyone's faces. Ransom felt a prickle of apprehension. He wanted to ask how many were coming, but he didn't want to seem a coward. He wasn't afraid to face their enemies. This was what he had spent years training for. He wanted to go back and mount his horse, worried that the enemy would arrive while they were standing around.

"Bad tidings," Baldwin said. "What will we do?"

"I've had counsel from my knights," Lord Kinghorn said, "but I'd hear your thoughts, old friend."

The captain sniffed and adjusted his belt. He was a big man, and he'd been in many battles during the civil war. "This is the king's home duchy. I reckon he'll want us to defend it on his behalf. Let's fight the maggots."

Lord Kinghorn smiled. His eyes wandered over the young men who had just arrived. Was he worried about them? His face betrayed no emotion.

Ransom couldn't hold his tongue. "Let's meet them on the road, my lord. Show them the stuff we're made of."

The remark earned a knowing smile from his kinsman. "Aye, lad. That's what we'll be doing. We were waiting for the rest of you to catch up so we could go together. We don't know how many of them there will be, and neither do they know our numbers. They've dodged a confrontation so far, seeking to raid and plunder along the way. Finding us in Menonval might be a surprise to them. With any luck, it might cause them to turn heel and flee." He approached the young men and put a big hand on James's shoulder. Ransom looked at his companion and saw determination and a hint of fear in his eyes. Good. James no longer saw this as a game. "The road is being watched, and we'll leave shortly. But not before we've taken a moment to invoke the Fountain's blessing. Today you fight with knights of the realm. Today you will face your foes as knights yourselves. Kneel."

Ransom's heart flared with surprise and the warm glow of anticipation. It was an unexpected honor. They each felt they'd earned the rank, but it had to be given and only by one who had authority to give it.

As one, the young men Ransom had trained with dropped to a knee before Lord Kinghorn. Ransom had seen the knighting ceremony as a boy when King Gervase had granted the honor to some of his men-at-arms. But that was at the palace of Kingfountain, amidst pomp and decorum. Trumpets had blared. The thing he remembered best was the way each knight had been struck across the cheek as part of the ceremony. The blow was known as the collier.

Lord Kinghorn crossed his gauntlets in front of him and bowed his head. "May fortune shine on us this day. Grant us courage and determination. Banish our fears. We fight in the name of our king, His Majesty, Devon Argentine, defending our land, our homes, and our most precious treasure . . . our families. Let us do no murder, speak no falsehoods, and stand bold before our enemies. In the name of Our Lady we pray. Amen."

"Amen," came the united response. Ransom felt a chill go down his spine. In his ears, far away, he heard the murmur of the falls outside Kingfountain.

Lord Kinghorn went to James first. "James Wigant, heir to the duchy of North Cumbria. I bestow on you the order of knighthood. You are hereby permitted to kill in the king's name, the sin be on his head and not yours. Prepare to receive the gift of the collier." James clenched his jaw, tightened his fists, and Lord Kinghorn backhanded him across the face with his gauntlet. A little cut tore at James's cheek, followed by a dribble of blood. The look of shock on James's face shifted to anger, and then satisfaction. The blow hadn't knocked him down.

Lord Kinghorn looked at all the young men kneeling, one by one. "The collier is a symbol. It is the last blow you will receive without being allowed a reprisal. If any man strikes you hence, you have the freedom to strike back." He held up his finger, which gleamed in the torchlight. "But while a knight *may* strike back, a true knight will yield that right. He will resist. It is a token of Virtus to be able to exact revenge and to choose mercy instead."

He approached Ransom next. "Marshall Barton, son of Lord Barton of the Heath. I bestow on you the order of knighthood. You are hereby permitted to kill in the king's name, the sin be on his head and not yours. Prepare to receive the gift of the collier."

They rode south from Menonval. Ransom's heart burned with pride at the honor bestowed upon him. Lord Kinghorn's gauntlet had struck his brow, but it had not bled. The small pulse of pain he'd felt was nothing compared to what he'd endured in the training yard. Excitement to face the enemy coursed through him. He nudged Gemmell's flanks to increase the horse's speed and passed Sir Gordon on the road. They were all knights now, of the same rank and station. Sir Gordon glanced at him in annoyance, but Ransom didn't care. He'd beaten Gordon many times in the training yard. And the desire to be at the front of the ranks was overpowering.

Ransom passed another few, gaining on the leaders, which included the surly Sir Jude. Trees grew on the right side of the road before it bent, offering a blind spot to hide the presence of the Brugian knights. He felt certain a trap was waiting for them there, but it would have felt impudent to say so given that the others were so much more experienced. Surely they knew better than he did. Still, if there was to be trouble, he wanted to be in the thick of it. It almost felt like he *needed* it.

Soon he'd passed all but three other knights. When he tapped Gemmell again to quicken his pace, he heard Lord Kinghorn's stern reprimand.

"Barton! Get back. Let these knights pass!"

The reproof stung his feelings and made his cheeks flush with shame. He loosened his grip on the reins, allowing the older knights to pass him, and Sir Gordon offered a smirk as he passed by. Ransom's ears were burning inside his helmet. Wasn't he a knight too? He was so humiliated he dared not look at Lord Kinghorn's face.

James reached Ransom and slowed a bit. "So anxious to die?" he asked with a provoking smile.

Ransom seethed, but he didn't say anything. Now that the younger knights were catching up, he allowed himself to increase his pace again, passing in front of James and the slowest of the older knights. He expected the skirmish would start as soon as they reached the trees.

But there was no skirmish. The road bent around the woods and continued toward a distant bridge. Farm fields lay around the woods, with locals using small teams of horses in their labors.

The bridge wasn't far. A few buildings, mostly barns, sat off the side of the road. His feelings still raw from Lord Kinghorn's reprimand, Ransom focused his attention on the road and the bridge. Light flashed off metal in the distance. His insides began to squirm.

"They're guarding the bridge," Ransom said to himself. He felt a pulse of warning, a sickening realization that the fight was upon them. His anxiety quelled as the familiar rushing sound of water filled his ears. He reached for one of his two lances and pulled it out of its saddle pocket.

"Oy!" shouted Captain Baldwin. "What are you doing!"

Ransom could barely hear him over the tumult of his heartbeat and the rushing noise in his ears. The knights in front of him reached for their lances as well. Ransom kicked Gemmell's flanks.

"Easy, lads," Lord Kinghorn ordered. "Don't rush. Save your strength."

As they came closer, Ransom saw the knights guarding the bridge had a different style of armor, with helmets and nose guards that covered the tips of their noses. Each had a long, narrow shield bearing the colors of Brugia.

They charged at Lord Kinghorn's men.

"Ready your lances!" Lord Kinghorn shouted. "They're charging us!"

Ransom's heart thundered in his chest. He already had his prepared. Their steeds began to snort in anticipation of the violence. Gemmell's nostrils flared, and the beast let out an otherworldly shriek. Ransom tried to swallow, but his throat was too tight. Men began to shout, spewing not words but emotions.

Then the battle cry started. "Averanche! Averanche! Averanche!"

Ransom began to scream it himself. He spurred Gemmell forward, wanting to be one of the first to engage. The two forces collided in a cacophony of sound. Ransom's lance shattered on his opponent's shield, but the force of the impact knocked the other knight clean off his destrier. Ransom discarded the broken lance and dodged a lance coming straight for him, nearly coming off his own saddle as he did so. It missed. He grabbed his other one, couched it in his arm, and pressed forward into the next rank of charging knights. He spotted a rival, adjusted his aim, and went straight for him. The lance caught the man in a vulnerable spot, the edge of his breastplate, beneath the arm, and killed him instantly, sending the knight down to the dust-choked ground. Ransom pulled his weapon free, using the length of the lance to block another man aiming for him. The two horses nearly collided, but they passed each other instead.

Ransom found another Brugian facing him and spurred Gemmell on. The two struck each other, and Ransom's second lance shattered against the knight's. They whacked each other with the stumps, Ransom managing to club the man over the head and unseat him before the tide of battle swallowed them both up, like the surf on the shores outside the castle of Averanche. He heard the battle cry being shouted still. Disoriented, he turned and saw many of Lord Kinghorn's knights had gathered in a circle. They were fighting with swords now, their lances used up or useless at such close proximity. Horses trampled fallen men, flailing their hooves against armor. Knights fell and didn't get up again.

Ransom wrenched his bastard sword out of its scabbard and charged into the fray. Chaos reigned supreme. It felt like they were outnumbered by the Brugians three to one. The enemy was everywhere. A knight slashed at Ransom from behind, and the blow glanced off his armor. He twisted in the saddle and engaged, battering the knight so hard the man fell off his horse and added to the bodies already on the ground.

The rushing noise of the waterfall drowned out the cries of battle. Ransom spotted another enemy and pressed into him, knocking him from his horse too. Then another. And another. He could not keep track of how many foes he'd conquered. A war hammer came at Ransom's helmet, but he managed to deflect it with the flat of his sword and used the hilt to return a blow to his enemy's helmet. Despite the grueling pace of the battle, he felt no weariness, no exhaustion. He felt alive, in complete command of his emotions and his situation. Gemmell heeded his every thought, guided by pressure from Ransom's knees instead of the reins. Another knight fell. Then another.

Ransom felt a broken lance batter against his sword arm. The knight facing him hadn't drawn another weapon, or perhaps he lacked one. Ransom grabbed the bridle of the man's horse with his free hand and yanked. The stallion reared in pain, spilling the knight onto the ground, and then backstepped and trampled him.

A ringing blow rattled against Ransom's helmet, but it didn't stun him. He turned, saw a knight with hate in his eyes strike out again with a flanged mace. He only had time to lift his armored elbow to absorb the blow, the feeling of metal clanging against metal ringing through him. But it did not slow him down. Ransom, pivoting his bastard sword, nudged Gemmell, and struck the knight in return. A look of surprise crossed the fellow's face as the sword bypassed a gap in his armor, the blade piercing the metal chains of his hauberk. The knight slumped forward in the saddle, resting on the armored neck of his destrier, and then, face contorted with pain, rode away. A moment later all the Brugians were riding away.

Ransom turned in his saddle, surprised to see so many dead sprawled on the ground around him, as if he and Gemmell were an island amidst a sea of wounded and dying. Lord Kinghorn raised his fist into the air, and a triumphant shout began to rise up from the knights of Averanche.

Again the battle cry sounded. "Averanche! Averanche! Averanche!"

Ransom shouted it until he was hoarse.

Lord Kinghorn lowered his fist, looking at Ransom. There was a strange expression in his eyes. He was grateful, yes. But there was also a hint of fear as he stared at his young knight and all the dead piled around him.

It was a fear that wormed its way into Ransom's own heart.

As soon as Da left for Glosstyr, it began. A noble by the name of Purser Dougal came to visit Connaught with a large escort. That was the word he used. And with a name like Purser Dougal, it's no surprise he turned out to be a complete maggot. I barred the gates and lifted the drawbridge. He demanded the right of hospitality for himself and his men. I did give him a warning before I fired an arrow at his horse. The castellan thought me a bit brazen, but why by the Aos Sí would I invite an armed knight and his retinue into my father's castle mere days after he left? Lord Purse-Face was angry. He made some threats that Da would not be coming home. I think this attack from Brugia is more than it first appeared. Like in the game of Wizr when you move a piece to draw attention from your real aim.

—Claire de Murrow
Connaught Castle, Kingdom of Legault
(the Isle of Dissembling Eejits)

CHAPTER SEVEN

The Game of Wizr

Ransom paced within the barn, stomping on the dirty straw as he went, but nothing could quell the feeling of unease that thrummed inside him like a taut bowstring. Gemmell nickered impatiently, and he gave his trusted steed a knowing look.

"We have orders, Gemmell. Be patient."

The rouncy tossed his head in response and kicked up some straw.

The barn door was open, offering a view of the road toward Menonval, which wasn't far. The family who owned this barn had evacuated their farm after the fighting broke out the previous day. The Brugian knights had retreated but then charged again with even greater numbers. Lord Kinghorn had held the bridge, however, limiting how many horses the Brugians could get across, and the knights of Averanche had won the second conflict.

Sir Beckett had died during that skirmish, along with four other of his cousin's household knights. But many more of their enemies lay dead. The wounded and those who'd been captured during the fighting were being guarded in a barn in Menonval, watched over by the townsfolk. From the captured men they'd learned the size of the Brugian host that had landed in Westmarch. It wasn't a raiding party. It was an army.

And it was bearing down on them still.

Until the king sent relief, Lord Kinghorn would hold the road to Menonval. He'd sent a knight to relay information to the king's couriers, but no support had arrived yet.

One thing Ransom appreciated about his cousin was he always asked his men for counsel before deciding his next move. He had asked his knights what they would do if they were the Brugians and a group of knights blocked their path. It felt like a game of Wizr, only they had no view of the enemy's position at the moment.

Ransom had been assigned to guard another road leading to Menonval, on the south. James and others had been assigned to watch in other locations. If anyone caught sight of the enemy, they were to raise the alarm, and the rest of the force would converge. But everyone agreed it was more likely the attack would come again at the main road because that was where the bridge lay.

The drone of flies and the musky smell of Gemmell's manure became irksome, reminding Ransom of his first year at the castle in Averanche's mucking stables. He wondered why Lord Kinghorn had sent him to watch this road and not kept him with the main body of knights. Everyone seemed to look at him differently since the first battle the previous day. Their eyes held a mixture of fear and respect. He'd killed more Brugian knights than any other warrior serving Lord Kinghorn. Ransom hadn't even tried to count, but others had done so for him. He felt strangely excited for the Brugians to attack again. Yet that very eagerness worried him. And so did the look in Lord Kinghorn's eyes.

The clop of hooves came from outside. Gemmell snorted again, hearing it too, and Ransom hurried to the stone-framed window of the barn. The shutters were open, letting in a warm summer breeze. He saw the colors of Brugia, the glint of sunlight off metal armor. His stomach clenched with dread, and he ducked out of sight.

With his back against the wall, he breathed out slowly, trying to calm himself. The Brugian knights were taking his road after all. And he was totally alone. He held up a hand soothingly to Gemmell, lest the horse betray their position with an ill-timed snort. The knights were trying to tread carefully, but it felt like a crowd. He heard a few snickers, the garbled tongue of their people as they bantered with one another. He recognized a few of the words, but James had always been better at languages.

He was supposed to raise the alarm—something that would, in this case, ensure his death. But if he did nothing, they would hit Lord Kinghorn's knights by surprise. He blinked, trying to tame his rampaging thoughts. One of the knights might search the barn anyway and discover him cowering by the window. That wouldn't do. He steadied himself, trying to quell the rising panic. He was part of Lord Kinghorn's mesnie, wasn't he? He'd been knighted. He owed loyalty to his lord, no matter what the personal consequences.

Ransom quickly went to Gemmell, grabbing and donning his helmet, and then stepped up on a chopping block he'd used to dismount. Gemmell nickered in anticipation, sensing his master's change in mood. He had no lances, so he unsheathed his sword and gripped it tightly in one hand. He could hear the tromp of knights outside the barn, heading toward Menonval. Ransom licked his lips, casting a thought toward Claire de Murrow, realizing he'd never see her again. He pictured the curious coloring of her hair, the slightly mocking smile on her youthful face.

A strange feeling rippled through his soul. Then he heard the distant churn of the waterfall of Kingfountain. He pictured King Gervase's body, stiff and gray, hefted in a canoe atop a row of staves. He thought of Sir William, who had been part of the guard who had honored the dead king. No one would be there for Ransom. He'd be buried near a barn.

But he would die in pursuit of his duty. There was honor in that.

Clenching his teeth, he raised the visor of his helmet and nudged Gemmell to the door. For an instant, the world went still. He felt and heard his own heartbeat. As his steed reached the open door of the barn, he saw the Brugian knights spread out before him, blocking the road and stretching far into the distance. A knight pointed an arm at him. Someone shouted in warning.

"Attack!" Ransom screamed, hoisting his sword into the air as if he were leading an army himself. "Attack! Averanche! Averanche! Averanche!"

He slammed his visor down and kicked Gemmell hard, leaning forward in the saddle as his steed burst forward. He was on the enemy knights in a moment, clashing swords with the first of them. Gemmell shrieked in the fury of battle, hooves flailing. The rushing noise of the falls filled Ransom's ears as he toppled one man off his charger. Then another. Whipping around, he screamed the battle cry again, brandishing his blade. Some of the knights had turned and started to ride away. Others converged on him. Ransom fought like a madman, butting into his foes with his knees. He felt steel blades hammer against his back, his arms. Still he fought, lashing out at anyone within reach, slicing through greaves, striking with the butt of his bastard sword, using Gemmell as a weapon too. He saw Gemmell take a bite out of another horse.

Thunder rumbled. Ransom thought that strange since the sky was so blue. He clashed with another knight, disarming him in a single blow, and the man kicked out of his stirrups and leaped off his horse, scrambling in the dust to get away. A blow struck the back of Ransom's helmet, hard enough that it should have dazed him. It didn't. He turned and caught another attack, blocking it with his blade.

And then he saw Lord Kinghorn riding toward him at a full gallop, surrounded by the knights of Averanche. The thunder he heard wasn't from the sky, it was from the hooves of his companions. Ransom felt a spark of hope. Maybe he wouldn't die this day after all. A burly knight bore down on him. The man looked strong, and he wielded his weapon well, but Ransom felt no fear. He thrust his blade into the man's helmet.

"Averanche! Averanche! Averanche!" called the others as they descended like eagles to strike their prey. The Brugians broke ranks and fled.

The constable of Westmarch was a knight named Dyron Rakestraw. He had been a knight of Devon Argentine's mesnie for many years and many seasons. Although Lord Kinghorn was older, the constable outranked him, and now that he and his men had arrived, he was in command. He had also summoned both Lord Kinghorn and Ransom to call upon him, a fact that made Ransom feel both anxious and excited as the two stood opposite the constable's command tent. The guards posted outside it opened the door and bid them enter. As they did so, Ransom took in the well-lit interior of the tent, which had luxurious fur rugs and a hefty camp cot for its occupant.

"Ah, Bryon, well met," said Dyron with a broad smile. The man had a bushy beard and close-cropped hair. He was a giant of a man, comparable in size to Captain Baldwin. "Is this the lad, then?"

"Yes, this is Marshall Barton," Lord Kinghorn said, introducing Ransom.

The constable rose from his stool and tapped his thumb against his left breast twice, the same salute William had given Ransom all those years ago, although now he had earned it. His cheeks flushed as he mimicked the gesture.

"Greetings, lad. You're the one they called the King's Ransom. I saw you at Gervase's funeral. You were a stripling then. Look at you now. You'll be big, like Lord Barton, I'm sure. Not done growing yet." His bushy eyebrows were nearly as expressive as his eyes, showing his sense of humor. He turned again to Lord Kinghorn. "He's the one who stopped the ambush earlier today?"

"He is. Stood alone against the front line of knights."

"Impossible," chuckled the constable. "When did you knight him?"

"Yesterday. He's earned it."

"By the Lady, he has! I wanted to tell you so myself. Well done, boy. We were closing in behind the Brugians, trying to harry them before they could get to you. Tricky devils, they are. Kept feinting and pretending their host was somewhere else. But they thought they were facing the full might of the king's army, so they tucked tail and retreated. Think we have them surrounded now, but they might try to slip back to Folkestone and escape. Or they may try leaving through Occitania. Can't be sure which road they'll take."

"What would you like us to do?" Lord Bryon asked.

Ransom was keen to hear every word. He still could not believe he'd been invited to visit the command tent. He tried to keep from smiling like a fool.

"How many have you lost in this action?" Rakestraw asked.

"Eight knights. Five more wounded. The rest are pretty battered, but we're ready to fight."

"Good. I need fighters right now. Glosstyr is coming, but he won't arrive for days."

Ransom's chest pulsed when he heard that name. Surely Claire wouldn't be with him, but her father would hear about his exploits on the battlefield. Perhaps he'd tell her. He felt soreness across his body and knew there'd be bruises, but he was ready for another day of fighting.

"Tomorrow, it might be over," Rakestraw continued. "I want you to keep holding that bridge and blocking Menonval. Don't let them get past you. Watch for a full retreat. It's night, but I can't count on them sitting still when they can move without being seen. No one in camp sleeps tonight. Everyone must be alert and ready with a sword in hand.

That means you too, young Ransom. Stand watch with the stars in the sky. Even a bear caught in a trap is dangerous. Be wary."

"Of course, Dyron," Lord Kinghorn said. "Is the king coming?"

"Is the king coming?" guffawed the constable. "He's at Folkestone hoping to catch them there in case they try to escape that way."

Ransom wondered if he would get a chance to meet the king again before the fighting was over. Although he'd felt bitter toward Devon Argentine after King Gervase's death, he knew Lord Kinghorn had served him loyally in Westmarch. Judging by his cousin's character, he thought he might actually come to respect the first Argentine king, even if his loyalty to King Gervase kept him from liking the man.

"Well done, Bryon. You've trained them well."

As they left the tent, Ransom breathed in the fresh air. Although he mourned their losses, he felt good about himself, about the events of the day. In his heart, he hoped he had proven himself enough that Lord Kinghorn might consider taking him into his mesnie. Normally, after a young man was knighted, he was sent back to his father, having earned the status he'd set out to achieve, but Ransom doubted he would be welcomed at the Heath.

"I'm sorry you've lost so many men," Ransom said as they walked side by side back to their horses.

"Thank you," his cousin replied in a distracted way.

Ransom risked a look at the other man. Lord Kinghorn's expression was brooding, and he decided not to speak again. They mounted their horses and rode back to the bridge where the other knights of Averanche awaited them.

When they arrived, Lord Kinghorn gave orders that no one was to sleep, which earned some groans and grumbles from the tired men who had fought hard that day. The mayor of Menonval had brought food to eat, so Ransom enjoyed the remainder of what was left. Then he was given his orders to patrol the area during the night, looking for signs of the enemy, but the others felt confident the Brugians had retreated.

Ransom did his night sentry duty without complaint, riding Gemmell at a leisurely pace. The stars shifted in their nightly dance, and the moon finally rose. With his visor up, Ransom smelled the night air, feeling a little chilled beneath the layers of armor, but it wasn't cold enough to produce mist from his mouth when he breathed.

After a time, weariness started to settle on Ransom, who had not rested since the battle earlier. He took the side road and passed Sir Gordon, who was on his way back from his rounds. They nodded to each other in passing. Farther down the road, Ransom saw the barn he'd hidden in earlier. He decided to give his steed a little rest and thought the barn might be a good place to conceal himself again and watch from the window. The farmer and his family still hadn't returned and probably wouldn't until the threat had passed. As Ransom rode up, he saw the scuff marks in the ground where the battle had raged. A few broken links of mail were scattered here and there. The bodies had been dragged away by the townspeople earlier.

Ransom leaned forward in the saddle, resting his arms on Gemmell's neck. The sky to the east was just beginning to brighten, although dawn was still a ways off. Ransom almost dismounted and walked Gemmell the rest of the way to the barn, but he thought that might not be a good idea. He guided his rouncy to the dark void of the open doors and smelled the straw.

As the shadow of the barn fell on him, he breathed in again.

And smelled sweat.

A prickle of warning went down his spine. He reached for the hilt of his sword. But before he'd drawn it from the scabbard, he saw movement in the shadows as men on foot rushed him. A man with a pole and hook appeared at his side, and he felt the snag of its tip pierce his shoulder guard, gripping the metal chain links beneath it. They swarmed Ransom, trying to get him off his horse.

One of them brandished a knife.

Word has arrived that the conflict ended, and abruptly too, I should say. I don't think poncy Lord Dougal had time to return to his little stone hut before a courier from Da arrived with word that he was on his way back from Glosstyr. King Devon's forces have already routed his enemies in Westmarch, it seems. Mayhap it was a test of the Argentine king, to see if he would defend his lands with iron or feather. The answer was iron. Apparently the knights of Averanche did some noble feats and withstood the full brunt of the Brugian army alone. So everyone is returning to their castles. Many knights from the Brugian order of St. Felix will be ransomed for a hefty sum, making the defeat all the more ignominious. I love that word. "Ignominious." I found that one in an ancient record on the shelves in Kingfountain. I wish knights were trained in matching wits as much as they're trained in matching swords.

Another courier just arrived bearing sad news. Lord Barton is dead. When first I saw the note, I dreaded it was news of his son, Ransom. But it was about the sire, not the son. He died in an accident while trying to leave his castle to *join the king's war. Ransom's brother is now the master of the Heath. Poor Ransom. Maybe I will send him a letter. Would that I could do more to ease his pain.*

—*Claire de Murrow*
Connaught Castle, Kingdom of Legault
La Victoire *(an Occitanian saying)*

CHAPTER EIGHT

Broken Knight

The soldier with the knife tried to jam the blade into Ransom's thigh, but it deflected off his armor. He tried again, his face a mess of rage and hatred, and this time the blade slid beneath the groove of armor but was stopped by the chain leggings beneath.

Ransom knew he was in serious trouble. The man with the pole and hook yanked hard, and Ransom had to grip the saddle horn to keep from toppling backward off Gemmell. His horse snorted and flailed his hooves, knocking back a man who grasped at his reins.

Squeezing his knees, Ransom tried to direct his horse to turn in a circle. He had to turn Gemmell around to the exit. He had to get out.

A spear struck his side, again deflected by his armor. He brought the pommel of his sword down, and it broke the haft of the spear before it could shove him off his steed. Gemmell thrashed, buffeting a man and knocking him down. Ransom could feel no rush of water as had happened in his previous battles. The sensation of being in command of himself, of his weapons, was gone. He felt hollow inside, an empty cauldron.

He was truly alone, surrounded by enemies.

He heard some of the men grunt in the Brugian tongue. The only word he could make out was *kill*. Ransom thrust down with his bastard sword, killing a man who stood too close, but the man with the hook was persistent. He yanked even harder, and Ransom felt his armor twisting, bending, exposing his back to the blows of his enemies. A battle axe struck his side. He felt pain in his ribs and worried the blade of the axe had pierced his armor.

This would end badly for him. He still fought to turn Gemmell full circle, and his field of vision was obscured by the darkness of the shadowed entrance to the barn. Another yank on his armor by the accursed hook rent it further. He felt the night air seep through the leather and links, which were now punctured and open.

Someone threw a dagger at him. He felt the blade hit his back, but he'd turned at the last moment, and it struck metal instead of leather. He struck another man with his blade. Unfortunately, it wasn't the fellow with the pole and hook, who followed the turn of the steed and kept wrenching his pole to wrest Ransom off his horse.

More shouts, more blows. Ransom felt something strike his helm. It rattled him, making him dizzy. But he was finally facing the right direction. Someone grabbed his arm, but Ransom hoisted the man off his feet and launched him atop the saddle before his strength gave way. The man squirmed, trying to get free, but Ransom swatted Gemmell's flank with his sword. His rouncy charged, knocking aside two men who had moved to bar the exit. The horse screamed, a deathly, horrible cry as it charged. Both men were flung aside. The man with the pole and hook was dragged by the horse as they left the barn, but he let go. Ransom felt the loss of weight on his back and realized he was free. The man on his saddle horn tried to grapple with him, but Ransom clubbed his skull with the pommel of his sword. He flung him off and heard the impact of his body hitting the road.

Ransom's heart raced as dread and relief battled for dominance in his chest. He'd almost been killed by the Brugians, but he'd made it free of the barn. He leaned forward, gasping for breath, experiencing a dull emptiness in his chest. A void. It was eerie and frightening. He'd been utterly alone during that fight, weakened in a way he couldn't explain or identify.

Gemmell slowed from a gallop to a trot, snorting, grumbling, heading back toward Lord Kinghorn's encampment. Ransom stroked the rouncy's neck as he leaned forward, grateful the horse had saved his life.

"That was close, Gemmell," he panted. "That was much too close."

The trot ebbed even slower, as if the rouncy's strength was flagging more than Ransom's. That was most unusual for him.

"Almost there. Come on. I'll get you some oats. Hmm? Does that sound good? We're both tired tonight." His gaze lifted to the horizon, watching the sky slowly brighten.

Gemmell slowed and stopped. Ransom sat up, worried, and lifted the visor of his helmet. He looked backward, seeing the barn in the dim light. His arms trembled with exhaustion.

"What's the matter, boy?" Ransom whispered, rubbing his gauntleted hand across Gemmell's neck again.

He could feel the muscles of the beast quivering. Ransom kicked loose from the stirrup, afraid his horse might collapse and pin him to the earth, but he didn't dismount. If he got off the horse, he might not be able to get back on it again, not without help. He looked back again, wondering if the Brugian men-at-arms could see him.

Gemmell grunted. It was a different sound, almost a wheeze. Ransom did dismount then, his instincts telling him something was very wrong. With his visor up, from the perspective of the ground, he quickly found the horse's wound. Gemmell had been speared by one of the soldiers.

"No," Ransom said, aghast, gazing at the animal's bloody flank. There was a trail of dark blood in the road. The steed swayed, trying to steady himself. Ransom had seen wounds like this after the first battle. The horses hadn't survived.

Gemmell swung his neck, and his huge eye looked at Ransom. He looked afraid.

Ransom shook his head in disbelief. He'd trained with Gemmell for the last five years. The horse had been a gift from King Gervase. Pain bloomed in his heart. He heard sounds coming from the barn. He looked back and saw the men-at-arms were stalking up the road toward him. At least eight men, each holding weapons. Did they know his horse was wounded?

Gemmell knelt down, thrashing his mane and letting out an unearthly shriek. The animal's suffering wrenched Ransom's heart. The eye stared at him almost pleadingly. For a moment, Ransom just stood there, sword still in his hand, while tears of anger and anguish seared his eyes. Keening, the animal lay down, and Ransom knelt beside him. He didn't want to deliver the mercy blow, but the spear thrust had probably been fatal from the start. If he wanted to live, he needed to move, and he could not, would not, leave Gemmell behind to suffer. Tears streaming down his cheeks, he delivered his trusted horse from its anguish.

Ransom rose, debating whether he should let the men-at-arms reach him. He wanted to kill each and every one of them. But the emptiness inside him deepened. He knew, in his core, that if he waited for them, he would die. So he trudged away, leaving behind Gemmell and all his coin and gear, walking back to the camp a defeated man.

It was dawn when Ransom reached the bridge to Menonval. Sir Jude was posted as sentry and saw the beleaguered knight arrive, armor twisted and bent, dragging his sword with him.

"What happened to you, lad?"

"Ambush," Ransom panted. "At the barn."

Sir Jude whistled sharply, drawing attention from others. Other knights approached, their expressions showing concern and disbelief at seeing Ransom arrive in such a condition.

"How many?" Jude demanded.

"About a dozen. Men-at-arms, not knights."

"They caught you alone?"

Ransom nodded, too exhausted, too grieving to reply.

"Come on, lad, let's get you to Sir Bryon."

Gripping Ransom's arm, he hastened him to the command tent where Lord Kinghorn sat on a stool, eating some breakfast with the mayor of Menonval. Lord Kinghorn's eyes were bleary from lack of sleep, and when he saw Ransom's state, he rose from the camp stool in alarm.

"What happened?"

"Ambush, my lord," said Sir Jude. "At the barn."

"The same barn we fought at yesterday?"

Jude looked at Ransom, who nodded.

"Jude, take five knights and go scout the area. They may be stragglers or perhaps they're simply lost. Secure the barn and report back."

"Aye, my lord," said Sir Jude. He released Ransom's arm, offered a salute, and left.

The mayor looked pityingly at Ransom. The mayor had been supplying food and relief to Lord Kinghorn's knights. He wasn't obligated to do so, but it was wise to feed the men you counted on for defense.

Lord Kinghorn walked around Ransom in a circle. "Your armor has been severely damaged, lad. Are you injured? I'm not sure if any of this blood on you is yours or from the previous battles."

Ransom was weary, but he didn't feel pain. "I don't think they got through."

"But you were struck with repeated blows. There are dents everywhere."

"I know," he answered, wishing the mayor would leave.

"Go get some rest," Lord Kinghorn said.

"Our orders were to stay awake," Ransom said, looking at him.

"You're exhausted. I'll have someone tend your horse. Go get some sleep."

Pain bloomed in his heart. "Gemmell . . . my horse . . . is dead."

Lord Kinghorn looked crestfallen. "Indeed, that's a shame. I'm sorry, lad. Losing a horse is a terrible blow. A knight isn't a knight without one." He put his hand on Ransom's shoulder. "Get some rest. Take some food. Here. Have the whole platter."

"I'll not ruin your breakfast, my lord," Ransom said. Truly, he wasn't hungry.

He went to his tent and struggled to take off his armor, eventually succumbing to the need to ask a page for help. It took a while, and when he saw it laid out before him, all bent and misshapen where the soldier with the hook had snagged him, he frowned and realized the cost of repairing it would be tremendous. When he was finally unencumbered, he flopped onto his bedroll and shut his eyes.

He was asleep in moments.

When he awoke again, he heard the grunt of horses outside the tent. His head felt dull. That feeling of emptiness persisted. He rubbed his cheeks, feeling the stubble there, and glanced at the set of broken armor. Grabbing a water skin, he took a little drink from it and realized it was nearly empty. He rose, pulled on his damaged hauberk, then buckled on his sword belt. He left the tent and found the men breaking up camp. Most of the tents were down, and pages were stowing the gear. He saw his companions, his fellow knights, joking and laughing with one another.

Mace, one of the boys he'd trained with these last five years, approached with a friendly smile. "We won, Ransom! The king's army struck the decisive blow. They captured the Brugian lord who was in command before he could escape." He grinned and patted Ransom on the back. "Sorry about your horse, though. Everyone feels bad about it. Oh, and Lord Kinghorn wanted to see you when you woke."

"Thanks, Mace," Ransom said. The news of the victory was welcome enough to help settle some of his grief for Gemmell. He walked back to Lord Kinghorn's tent and went inside. Lord Kinghorn was talking with James. The duke's son still wore his armor, and it looked spattered with mud and other signs of the fighting. He nodded to Lord Kinghorn and then glanced at Ransom.

"By all means, you may return to Dundrennan if you wish," said Lord Kinghorn. "You acquitted yourself well, Sir James. And you brought back six captured knights you can bargain with for their ransoms. Two additional horses as well. You've done well on your first campaign."

"Thank you, my lord," said James meekly. "I've learned a great deal serving in Averanche. Given this latest conflict, I think it's wise to return to my father and begin to assume my new duties."

"Indeed. I agree. I will send my recommendations in a letter to your father as well."

"I would be honored if you'd do that for me. Thank you, my lord."

"Very well. You may go."

James gave Ransom a sidelong look as he left, offering no nod or smile as he did so. He departed the tent. Ransom approached his cousin.

"Sir Jude found your steed on the road," said Lord Kinghorn. "The Brugians who attacked you were skulking in the woods. They were all caught. Most surrendered, but a few defied and were executed. Lord Rakestraw sent word that it's over. We're finished here."

Ransom was relieved. "I'm glad of it, my lord."

Lord Kinghorn frowned. "Sir James is returning to Dundrennan. I think you heard that, did you not?"

"I did."

"Well, you are both knights now and can do as you please. There's no easy way to say this, lad, but your father, Lord Barton, died in an accident. They were riding hard to join the king's army, and his horse stumbled. He broke his skull when hitting the ground, died a few hours later. Your older brother is now the lord of the Heath." He pursed his lips, looking deep into Ransom's eyes. "I'm sorry, lad. I know you and your father were not close. It grieves me that any son should not reconcile with his father before his demise. May he find rest in the Deep Fathoms."

The news was unexpected, striking Ransom hard in the ribs. What made it worse was the realization that he'd grieve more for Gemmell and dead King Gervase than he would for his own father, who had never shown him any consideration, let alone love. His stomach clenched, and he struggled to master his emotions. But the events of the past days had hardened him, much like the oaths he had taken. He pressed his lips together tightly, squeezing his hands into fists.

"I think you owe it to your mother and your sister, at least, to return to the Heath and pay your respects."

The numbness filling Ransom's chest didn't subside. "Thank you for telling me, my lord."

"I wish my bad news did not end here. Best to let it out all at once."

"There's more?" Ransom asked in growing concern.

"Ransom, I admire your skill at arms and the leadership you've shown. Without your conduct yesterday, we may have been overrun and suffered a dreadful defeat. But you also worry me, lad." Something in his eyes shifted, and there was that look of fear again. Not fear of Ransom himself, precisely, but fear of what he was capable of.

"I don't understand."

"No, of course you do not. I must put it bluntly. Young men react very differently when they are called to lift arms against their enemies. Some become greensick and vomit. Some become fearful and never want to fight again. It is not easy on a man's soul to take a life. You killed in the king's name, as you were ordered to do. But I fear you enjoyed it too much. You had no regard for your own safety. You were reckless, Ransom. And what happened to you at the barn is a manifestation of that recklessness. You could have been killed." He frowned again, shaking his head. "As a result, you lost your horse. Your armor is ruined and can only be fixed at great expense. You don't have the money to do this. You took no hostages, and therefore will earn no ransoms, even though your nickname should have reminded you to consider it. In short, lad, you are a liability. I took you in because your mother is my kinswoman. I paid for the cost of your armor, your food. The cost to repair your armor, to purchase another horse must come from somewhere. It is not right or proper that I, your liege lord, should incur those expenses again."

Ransom's eyes widened with surprise during the speech. He'd set out to earn honors for Lord Kinghorn, to do him proud, but he had shamed his master by putting him in this situation.

"You're not a boy anymore, Marshall. But a man. You've proven it during this campaign. I would be honored to have you in my service someday, for I believe you will learn from this."

"Some . . . day?" Ransom croaked out.

He'd hoped that day might arrive now.

"Aye. I must start training new knights to ride in service of the king. I've lost several men during this action, and some of your fellows will earn positions in my mesnie. I offered one to Sir James, but he was too proud to accept and has decided to take his winnings back to Dundrennan with him. Now that the duke has claimed Dundrennan as his own, they have need of more knights to fortify the North. I could save you from this calamity, Marshall. I could pay for your mistakes out of my own coffers. But in doing so, I would dishonor you and myself. A knight must bring to his lord more than the costs of his employ. If I took you on, it would not be prudent. Yet still, even now, I hesitate. I *want* to help you. Something in me whispers that I should not. It's the voice, lad. And I swore an oath to obey it, even when it pains me to do so."

Ransom was so crestfallen he feared he might start crying. But he refused to do so in front of Lord Kinghorn. "I see," he whispered thickly.

"No. I don't think that you do. Some wisdom only comes when we've looked back on it after a good while. I wish you the best in your future, Marshall. If you can rectify your situation and desire to come back to Averanche, you are welcome. For now, I will ask that you not return with us."

The blow struck Ransom's heart painfully. Feelings of resentment and worry battled inside him like two furious knights.

"How am I to leave, my lord?" he asked. "My horse is dead."

"One of the knights gave me a palfrey as a gift out of his winnings. I will give it to you, although you cannot ride him into battle. It is not suitable as a warhorse. You have skills and abilities, Marshall, that would be valuable. Perhaps your mother will furnish the funds you need. I don't imagine your brother will."

"He won't," Ransom replied darkly.

"The palfrey is stabled with the mayor of Menonval. You may seek him there. My advice is to find a blacksmith willing to repair your armor. Maybe you can work for him for a season to pay for the cost. I'm sure you'll think of something."

"I'm sorry to be a burden on you, my lord," Ransom said.

Lord Kinghorn shook his head. "You have courage, son. I'm sure it will all work out in the end."

Ransom nodded and left the tent, feeling ashamed of himself. His insides twisted with agony, regret, and the humiliation of his situation. When he stepped outside, he saw Sir James standing there, not hiding that he had listened in keenly.

"Walk with me a moment," James said, nodding his head for Ransom to follow.

He did, and the two companions walked away from the tent. A little spark of hope lit within Ransom's heart. James Wigant was the son of a duke. He'd proven a reliable companion, and while they were very different in temperament, they'd come to respect each other.

Were they friends finally? He wanted to hope, but something about the situation worried him.

"You heard what happened?" Ransom asked him.

"Of course. I wouldn't have missed that for all the world."

Ransom looked at him, the spark of hope sputtering.

James gave him another sidelong look. "You want to ask to come with me. Where else would you go? Back to the Heath? My father is wealthy, and we need good knights in the North. Ask me, Ransom. Do you trust me to say yes?"

Something in his words, or perhaps it was the keen look in his eyes, made Ransom hesitate. He did not wish to serve someone like James Wigant, but he was desperate. And Lord Kinghorn's brusque dismissal still chafed his wounded heart.

"Can I go with you?" Ransom asked.

"Not for all the treasure in the Deep Fathoms," James replied. He paused, giving Ransom a withering look. "I've waited for this day. To see you fail. Oh, how I've waited for it! Do you have any idea how many penniless knights there are in this world? Well, at least you know how to kill. You can always kill yourself."

And with that, James walked away with a self-satisfied smirk on his face.

X

I'm at the port town of Atha Kleah, where I was waiting for Da to return from Glosstyr. All the miscreant nobles have fled back to their castles and await his return with dread. Richard Archer is not one to be trifled with, and neither is his daughter. Da is back, but the ill news he brought troubles me. We lost some good knights during this war, including some from Averanche. I heard my childhood friend Ransom was spared, thank the Aos Sí, but his luck has gone sour. Lord Kinghorn wouldn't take him into service in his mesnie, which makes about as much sense as a wingless duck.

Da said Lord Kinghorn sent Ransom home to the Heath. But when Da passed the Heath on his journey back to Glosstyr, they'd none of them heard from him. They didn't even know he was a knight, let alone one without a lord to serve. Da wished to offer him a position given all the good reports he heard about his performance in battle, but he's nowhere to be found. I'm worried about him. A knight without loyalty can quickly turn bad, as we witnessed during that awful civil war.

Da also brought word that we're shortly to get a visitor from Dundrennan. Duke Wigant's son was also made a knight. I'm already peevish enough.

—Claire de Murrow
Atha Kleah, Kingdom of Legault

CHAPTER NINE

Scarbrow Armory

The noise of birds chirping in the branches roused Ransom from his slumber. He blinked, his hand still squeezed around the hilt of his dagger, as it had been throughout the night. He hadn't set up his small tent and instead had bedded down in a grove of black pine. The smell of the crushed needles greeted him pleasantly. His stomach growled with hunger. He'd managed to shoot down a single quail for his supper the night before, and it hadn't been very filling.

The palfrey Lord Kinghorn had given him was still tethered to the tree, and it snorted at him as he sat up and slid the dagger into a sheath. His sword lay next to him. A net containing his ruined armor sat by the tree, along with the other gear he'd brought with him. Letting out a despondent breath, which came in a little puff of mist, he folded his arms over his knees, still aching from the fight and his wounded feelings.

He'd spent many nights sleeping on the ground as a knight in training. A knight had to be able to build a shelter out of branches, forage the wilderness for food, and learn how to find safe water to slake his thirst. But Ransom had always done these things with James and the others. This was the first night he'd spent all alone since he'd left the palace of Kingfountain after King Gervase's death.

Shame made his cheeks hot again. He was a landless knight who served no one. He'd been well fed in Averanche, with a training yard and peers he could joke with, but now he had nothing. His sword had nicks in it that needed a whetstone's kiss. His armor was mutilated. That awful feeling inside him persisted, and he had no idea how to soothe it.

Ransom stood and strapped on his sword belt and shook pine needles from his blanket before rolling it up. The palfrey, which was called Rust, shied from him before he loaded the armor and gear onto its back. The loss of Gemmell still blistered inside him. But he shook his head, unwilling to dwell anymore on his misfortunes, and untied the lead rope. The palfrey followed him out of the wood and back toward the road.

The countryside of Occitania looked just the same as Westmarch. But he dared not wear the badge of Averanche, which he had buried deep in his pocket. He knew from his studies of the various kingdoms that the duchy of Brythonica lay directly to the north. He'd heard rumors that the young duchess was in negotiations to marry King Devon's third son, Goff, who was several years her junior. The eldest son, named after his father, had married the sister of the Occitanian prince, but they were both still children and lived in their respective courts. The second oldest, Benedict—whom the family called Bennett—had been promised to the daughter of a Vexin nobleman. King Devon was making peace with his most powerful neighbor, while fighting off Atabyrion and Brugia, and restoring order in Legault. The Brugian defeat would give him a respite from one of his enemies, but for how long?

"Come on, nag," Ransom said, tugging at the lead rope as the palfrey balked out of pure stubbornness. Maybe the Occitanian meadow grass didn't taste as sweet. Ransom had a few coins in his purse, but it wouldn't take him very far. He might have to sell the palfrey once he reached his destination. Although the road he traveled would end in Pree, his goal was the town of Chessy on the eastern outskirts.

Sir William wasn't the only one who'd told him of the tournaments in Chessy. He'd heard boastful talk from Lord Kinghorn's knights over the years. Ransom didn't want to hope that Gervase's knight might still be there. It had been five years, after all, but Chessy was a place he could continue his training and hope to earn enough silver livres to eventually replace his ruined armor and dead steed. He'd ultimately decided against returning to the Heath. If he were to return home, it would not be to beg for money. His mother had provided his first opportunity, which he'd wasted, and he didn't trust in his brother Marcus's generosity. After the betrayal of James Wigant, he didn't know if he could ever trust anyone again.

The words the other boy had spoken still burned. But Ransom buried those feelings and hoped to get his revenge by becoming someone worthy of respect—the kind of knight any lord would want to take into service.

The journey was pleasant, and his Occitanian was put to the test. Many of the locals he met on the road asked if he was on his way to Chessy—the armor bulging in the net on the palfrey's saddle a giveaway. He responded as fluently as he could, but there was no misunderstanding his accent. Still, they were pleasant, and one even offered him something to eat, which he accepted gratefully.

He expected it would take three days to walk to Chessy, and it did. The walk was long, but he knew the palfrey would die if he attempted to ride it while it carried his burdens. How he missed Gemmell's strength.

As he approached Chessy, he saw a haze of smoke rising up from the walled fortress of Pree in the distance. While Kingfountain was built on a hill next to the river and falls, Pree was built around a river itself, the river Mer. Even from this distance, he could see the identical slate-colored spires and towers. It was a larger city than Kingfountain, with a famous sanctuary on each of the four main roads leading out of it.

Chessy wasn't fortified at all, but it was built alongside a great forested preserve called the Bois de Meridienne. The woods were part of the tournament grounds, and it was illegal to hunt there, Ransom had heard, without the express permission of the king. One of the contests the knights underwent in Chessy was hunting, and the Bois de Meridienne provided the game.

As he walked down the road, following carts and travelers on their way to Pree, he saw pavilions set up on either side. He heard the clatter of weapons and saw mounted knights with lances facing off behind a fence. Wooden stands, empty now save a few spectators, overlooked the area where the knights challenged each other. More fences separated the large yard into different sections.

The charging knights shattered their lances against each other's shields, but neither were unhorsed. A smile came to Ransom's face as he watched them ride back, fetching fresh ash lances from the young boys supporting them. He saw another match happening simultaneously, a man with a bastard sword going against a knight with a battle axe. The two smashed into each other, both heavily armored, and sought to disarm the other.

There were literally hundreds of knights assembled there, and Ransom felt like he was coming home. He didn't recognize any of the standards flapping in the breeze above the pavilions. They couldn't all be Occitanian, could they?

As he rode farther into the town, he saw a few wooden stables, but most of the structures were large tents, from which came the sound of blacksmiths hammering away and delicious scents from cooking tents. Hawkers of different ages and sexes wandered back and forth, offering their wares.

A young lass with long golden hair approached Ransom. "Would you like a confection, brave sir? From the finest penuche maker in Pree! One bite, brave sir! You will want more!"

Ransom saw the little brown square she teased him with and reached into his purse to grab a coin.

"No, brave knight! This is for free. You will want more, I assure you. Visit the tent of Master Croque!" She gave it to him and then hurried away to hand out more.

Ransom, still gripping the lead rope, looked at the morsel in his hand. It was the size of one of the gaming dice used by the soldiers. He plopped it into his mouth and stopped in his tracks as the delicious morsel began to dissolve, unleashing the most wonderful flavor he'd ever tasted. He'd never had anything like it before.

As he chewed, he stared at the knights passing to and fro. Most of them were his elders. Some were younger, mostly pages scurrying about, running errands for their masters. He listened for the tongue of his native land, but everyone around him spoke Occitanian. His training in Averanche had made him familiar with it, however, and he could make out words and phrases. He saw a pair of Brugian knights, recognizing the style of their armor, which temporarily dampened his mood, but even they spoke in Occitanian. Seeing the armor, the weapons, hearing the snort of horses, the rowdy banter, he couldn't help but grin as he wandered through the crowd, soaking it in, enjoying the flavor of the penuche still dancing with magic on his tongue.

Through the chaos of noise, he heard the clank of a hammer and anvil. For some reason, it stood out to him amidst the cacophony. Yes, he needed a blacksmith to repair his armor and sharpen his sword, although he'd given it a few swipes with his whetstone already.

Ransom led the palfrey through the crowd, trying to find the source of the noise. As he drew closer, he felt the familiar rippling sensation he'd previously only experienced during a fight. The feeling didn't come from him, though. It was radiating outward from a tent.

Ransom was confused by this, but the sensation excited him. Searching for the source, he eventually caught sight of a tent with an open circle at the top of the poles. The tent was sooty and charred in places, and smoke billowed from the opening at its peak. Ransom approached it, sensing the rush of water, the sound reminding him vividly of the noise of the waterfall outside Kingfountain.

He reached the front of the tent, where there was a display of horseshoes, a dagger, and a single gauntlet. Each was made out of a smoky metal that looked like polished silver reflecting a cloud. He'd never seen its like. His fingers lowered to the metal, and a loud hissing noise startled him. It took him a moment to realize the blacksmith inside was quenching a piece. Steam drifted from the flap of the tent.

Ransom reached to open the flap, but someone else opened it first. A short, wiry man emerged. At first Ransom thought it was a boy, but the grizzled whiskers and threads of gray in his hair belied that first impression. The man had eyes that were either green or blue, or maybe a mix. He had a hammer in his hand, and his expression was stern as he looked up at Ransom.

"Can I help you, lad?" he asked with a thick Ceredigion accent.

"You're not from Occitania," Ransom said, switching to their shared language.

"Neither are you," said the man brusquely. "You just arrived?"

"I did," Ransom said.

"In need of a blacksmith?" He looked over Ransom's shoulder at the net strapped to the palfrey.

"I am looking for one," Ransom said. The rushing sensation he'd felt earlier was fading. In fact, it had completely stilled.

"Who are you?" the blacksmith asked, his eyes narrowing.

"My name is Ransom Barton."

The blacksmith looked surprised. "You're not the kid the king almost hung?"

Ransom smiled. "That was a long time ago."

The blacksmith grinned back. "I served as a blacksmith at the palace. I worked for King Gervase. You don't look familiar at all, but you're not a child anymore. What are you doing outside Pree? There isn't a tournament for a while still. You're too early."

Ransom couldn't believe his change in fortune. He'd come here a stranger to everyone, and one of the first people he'd met was a man who'd served his king. It was as if that rushing sound had led him here. "I served Lord Kinghorn in Averanche. Can we talk inside?"

"Sure, sure. Let me tie your horse to something." He grabbed an iron hook from a metal stand near the entrance and plunged it into the turf, using the hammer he still held to drive it in like a stake. Ransom tied the lead rope there, and the blacksmith opened the flap of the tent.

"Come in." The innards of the pavilion were black with soot, and the fire blazing inside made sweat pop out on Ransom's brow.

"What's your name?" Ransom asked.

"Anders Scarbrow," the man replied. Even though he was a wiry man, his arms were corded with muscles. But he didn't look like any of the blacksmiths that Ransom had met, and he did not remember him from his time at the palace. "And what can I do for the King's Ransom?"

"I need my armor repaired," he said. "We just finished fighting the Brugians at Menonval. Lord Kinghorn dismissed me."

"Why? Did you murder someone?"

"No. That wasn't it at all. I had a rouncy that died during an ambush. The same ambush that ruined my armor."

Anders nodded knowingly. "That explains a lot. It would have cost him too much to fix your armor and buy you a new horse." He sighed. "That's unfortunate. So what you are saying is you can't afford to hire a blacksmith yourself." The interest was quickly fading from the man's eyes. "You're not even a knight yet. Boy, I can't—"

"I *am* a knight," Ransom insisted, feeling a sense of panic. "Lord Kinghorn knighted all of us before the battle."

"You have his badge?"

Ransom produced it from his pocket.

Anders sniffed and took it from him, examining it. "It's real. But you could be a squire pretending to be a knight." He gave Ransom an appraising look as he said it.

"I'm not lying. I wouldn't do that."

"Most men do," said Anders with a sigh, "although the nobles here tend to take their honor more seriously. Had a knight refuse to pay me for a sword I had made for him. Word got out, and the knight was dragged in by the Black Prince himself and ordered to pay me what he owed, plus extra as punishment, or he'd be thrown out of camp as a thief. But even so, there's a thousand ways men try to cheat me."

"I'm not asking for a gift," Ransom said, stepping forward. "I could work for you. I'm strong. Persistent. Give me the chance to earn the repairs before the next competition."

Anders frowned, cocking his head to the side. "Fetch the armor. Let's see how bad it is first."

Ransom felt a throb of hope again. He hurried out and unhooked the net from the palfrey and hefted it onto his shoulder. He went in and set it down before kneeling and starting to loosen the fastening.

"You're strong," Anders said appreciatively. "No denying that."

Ransom opened the net and pulled out the armor. Most of the pieces were battered and stained from the conflict. Ransom hadn't even bothered to clean them yet.

Anders squatted down and looked at the damage the hook had caused. He scowled and shook his head. "It's ruined," he said. "I can't fix that. It needs to be made over." His eyes fixed on Ransom. "I'm sorry, lad."

"Please." The silent feeling of desperation gnawed in his stomach.

Anders sniffed. "I'm sorry, lad," he repeated. "I'm not sure there'll be time. I have another suit of armor I'm working on for a knight."

"I'll help you with it."

"Yes, you will. I was expecting that." He paused, his gaze searching Ransom's face, then said, "If we both work together, I'll get it done faster, which means I'd have time to work on yours. There may . . . be enough time to finish it before the next tournament." A smile brightened his face. "You keep my forge glowing hot, I can work much faster. It's difficult work. It's more fun to dent armor than fix it."

The relief in Ransom's heart was fierce. "I'll do it."

"Hold on, lad. Let me finish setting the terms. You work for me half the time. You train the other half. No sense making you armor you'll ruin after your first bout. In return, you give me half your winnings. Every time. No exceptions. That means you'll be paying me twice."

"Done," Ransom said with a grin.

"You're not good at business, lad. I'm going to have to knock some sense into you. How about we limit the winnings to your first year?"

Ransom saw his mistake. "I think that's fair."

"It's not, but you'll learn the value of your coins soon enough. Everything costs something in this life, boy. But not everything is worth the cost. You need a place to sleep? You keeping that nag?"

"Yes and no," Ransom answered.

"Good. Get rid of the nag. You can sleep on the floor over there. Now go pump those bellows for me. Let's see how long you last!"

It has been almost two years since I last wrote. It doesn't feel like it, until I consider all that's happened. Da is more respected now in Legault. He travels to Atha Kleah to render justice, and his decisions are upheld. It wasn't long ago they'd argue every point, just to spite him, but he's a fair leader, and over time, they've realized he doesn't just rule in favor of the lords of Ceredigion.

I've relished riding through our lands, getting to know the villagers and their needs. There are barrow mounds and sacred sites throughout Legault. The history is rich with so many legends of the Aos Sí and the magical artifacts they made. I met an aging woman in the village of Knockcroggery who said she'd seen, in her youth, a knight with a scabbard that had the raven sigil on it. The knight could not be killed in combat because of it. I have spent many a moonlit night waiting at a pond to see if the Aos Sí would emerge and dance at midnight. Sadly, I've not seen any. But I long to.

Da thinks I should choose a husband soon, which is probably why I'm writing this from the palace of Ploemeur in Brythonica presently. We have a writ of safe conduct from the duchess for our journey to Pree to attend a tournament at a field called Chessy. Every kingdom is sending their best knights to compete. There will be much clashing of swords, shattering of lances, and likely dozens of bearded men itching to marry an heiress. I've never been to Pree before, so I'm excited to see the pinnacle of refinement, grace, and skill at arms. Da won't be fighting, but we've enough knights in our company who will take to the fields. Everyone says the strongest knights are from Occitania. Yet I wonder who else may be there?

—Claire de Murrow
Ploemeur, Duchy of Brythonica

CHAPTER TEN

Warring Legends

Ransom had never seen so many kingdoms represented on a single field before. The smart ones had begun arriving a month before the tournament, and the crowds grew worse each day. Disputes arose between rival factions, but King Lewis had provided enough guards, led by the Black Prince, his son, to quell open conflict. Prince Estian was called the Black Prince because he wore a black tabard with a silver fleur-de-lis badge, and all his knights and men-at-arms wore the same. They were quick to root out troublemakers and send them away with a writ of safe conduct lasting only one day. Ransom had seen several knights scurry away after receiving such a reprimand.

With the growing throngs, merchants from Pree were making a fortune selling food, pavilions, horses, weapons, and little remembrances they called souvenirs. After having spent two years in Chessy, Ransom was fluent in Occitanian and passed as a local, which meant he was able to purchase things at lower prices. He was eager for the tournament. Although he'd fought in many during his time in Chessy, this would be the first to bring in many of the noble houses of Ceredigion. He kept an eye out for standards he recognized, hoping to see Lord Kinghorn again, although his goal was to prove himself enough to be offered a position with one of the dukes of the realm—other than Duke Wigant, of course. His resentment against James had festered since their last encounter. But the time had come to return home. While he still didn't like Devon Argentine, he respected the stability he'd brought to the realm in only a few years. Judging by the stories he'd heard, the Argentine king was better at putting a stop to the internal squabbling than Gervase had ever been, and there was no denying he was also more successful at keeping enemies at bay.

Ransom was no longer a penniless knight. His earnings from the competitions had more than paid for the suit of Scarbrow armor that Anders had made for him. And he had his own destrier now, more valuable than a rouncy. He hadn't paid for it either. He'd won it from a noble from the Vexin, who'd lost to Ransom in a tournament. Ransom had his own tent, could afford the labor of a page, who also worked with another knight, and he was considered by many as a possible contender for winning one of the three rewards at the tournament. At least enough for people to wager on him with long odds.

The heat of the day had ended, and dusk began to fall. Fire pits made of iron were being lit to ward off the coming chill as well as to provide light. The smell of roasting meat and delicious Occitanian treats wafted in the air, stirring hunger in his nervous stomach. Ladies mingled with the knights, and the bright feminine laughter was a contrast to the times before, when the camp had mostly been occupied by warriors. The Black Prince allowed no immorality in Chessy or within the streets of Pree. Women who came to ply another trade were dismissed as quickly as knights who could not follow the rules.

"Sir Ransom!" called the voice of Tanner, his young page.

He turned, seeing the lad swerving through the crowd to catch up with him. The boy was only twelve, but he seemed younger and smaller than Ransom remembered being at that age.

"What is it?" Ransom asked as the boy caught up with him.

"Lord Kinghorn of Averanche has arrived! He came with Constable Rakestraw."

"Brilliant," Ransom replied. "I wonder if they sent anyone to secure space for them. People are starting to encamp on the road now."

"All the inns leading up to Pree are full," Tanner said. "The innkeepers are overflowing with silver livres right now."

"That they are. Find out where they're staying. I'd like to know."

"Of course! I'll do my best."

"Good lad," Ransom said, tousling the boy's hair. He watched the boy run off, dodging and weaving through the crowd again. When he turned around to continue his journey, he nearly collided with a pretty nobleman's daughter, who looked at him with a devilish smile.

"Pardon, my lady," Ransom said, bowing slightly and stepping out of her way.

Her smile grew brighter. She didn't look offended in the least, nor did she seek to pass. A knight stood next to her, an escort no doubt, who screwed up his face and gave Ransom a wary look.

"You don't recognize me, do you?" she said, and the sound of her voice gave her away. It was a Gaultic accent, one he hadn't heard in seven years.

In the dusk, he'd assumed her hair was brown, but now that he looked closer, the glow of the firelight showed its special tint.

Ransom gaped at her. It was Claire.

"I heard someone cry out your name!" she said. "And here you are!" She wore an elegantly embroidered cape over a white muslin gown with a belted girdle, arm bands, and a thin braided rope beneath her bosom. The sleeves were tight down to her wrists, with more fabric gathered higher up on her arms, slit wide so it trailed like a train. The cape was red and featured intricate needlework. He took all of her in, blinking quickly, before realizing this wasn't the little girl who had teased him playfully at Kingfountain when they were children. She had grown up.

She was examining him too, looking at his face, at the cloth tabard he wore over his chain hauberk. At the sword and dagger strapped to his hip.

"I can't believe it's you," he stammered, realizing he was gawking.

"Of course it is, you fool eejit," she said, laughing. "Look at you! I'm not sure I would have recognized you if the lad hadn't called you by name. Is this . . . is this a beard?" She lifted her hand as if she'd touch his face, before dropping it suddenly.

Ransom hadn't been to the barber yet, but had planned to, knowing the Occitanians judged those from Ceredigion harshly because of their beards, considering them barbaric and unkempt.

"I was going to see the barber soon," Ransom said, feeling self-conscious.

"Don't. I like it," she said. "Where have you been all these years?"

"I've been . . . well . . . what do you mean?"

She sighed with exasperation. "I've been looking for you."

"In the tournament camp?" he said. "How did you know I was—"

"Stop. You're not understanding me. Where have you been since you left Averanche? No one knew where you'd gone. Not even your family at the Heath. You look so sunburnt and sturdy now."

Ransom was taken aback. "You . . . you looked for me after Lord Kinghorn dismissed me?" Although he'd thought of Claire often over the years, he hadn't expected the same would be true of her—or at least not that she would have gone out of her way to look for him.

"Of course! Da wanted to take you in. You could have been at Connaught castle all this time."

"Connaught castle?"

"You keep repeating everything I'm saying. Answer me before I clout you! Where have you been?"

"Here, at Chessy."

Her brow wrinkled with disbelief. "You wanted to be a . . . a tournament knight?" Her look of interest was quickly turning to one of disappointment.

"My lady," said her escort with a subtle cough. "We should return to your father."

Ransom felt a spasm of dread. He could not stand for her to misjudge him. "That's not why I came," he said.

"Why did you come? I heard you were quite brave when the Brugians attacked Westmarch. Why did Lord Kinghorn dismiss you?"

"My lady," pressed the knight.

She turned and gave him a displeased look. "Quiet, Sir Anselm. Your interruptions are rude."

Ransom stifled an involuntary chuckle.

Claire looked him in the eye. "Tell me."

"During the war, I was . . . ambushed by fleeing soldiers who'd hidden in a barn. I was foolish. It was dark. I shouldn't have gone in there without suspecting a trap."

"They attacked you?"

"They killed my horse."

"That rouncy you used to ride with the king? What was his name . . . oh, Gemmell!"

Even now hearing the name hurt. He nodded, impressed by her sharp memory.

Her disappointment turned to hurt. "I'm so sorry, Ransom. Truly." He loved hearing the sound of her voice, the accent so familiar. He'd not dared to hope he would see her during the tournament, let alone find her wandering in the crowd. And she'd been looking for him? She'd wanted to help him all along?

"I'm doing better now," he said, forcing a smile. "I've worked with a blacksmith and have my own armor again. And a destrier."

"You worked *as* a blacksmith. I can see that. A new suit of armor is costly. So is a horse like that."

"I won the horse," Ransom said.

"A fine accomplishment." But he could tell she didn't care as much about his recent exploits as she did about their past friendship. "Why didn't you seek me out, Ransom? I could have helped you."

He felt like a fool. Like an "eejit." How he missed hearing her say that word. He couldn't tell her that his pride wouldn't have allowed it, or that it hadn't occurred to him anyone would want to help him after Lord Kinghorn's dismissal and James's callow treatment. "I . . . I . . . don't know."

Her smile was slightly mocking. "Maybe you took too many blows to the head. Well, we've just arrived, and I long to see what Chessy has to offer. Will you show me around?"

"Lady Claire," growled Sir Anselm.

She grabbed Ransom's arm. "Go find Father and tell him I'll return shortly."

"My lady, he will be *most* displeased."

"Whatever for? I am in the company of a knight, and the Black Prince's henchmen are everywhere. I'll return shortly, I promise. He's a dear friend, Sir Anselm. Now go."

It wasn't a coaxing request. It was an order.

Sir Anselm clenched his jaw and his fists and stormed away.

It felt like being in a fever dream. Ransom and Lady Claire de Murrow were walking arm in arm through the crowds of Chessy, talking as if they'd never been apart. She was curious about everything, pointing to the different stalls selling Occitanian jewelry, skewers of meat, and confections of the finest cooks in the country.

"Have you ever tried penuche?" he asked her as they approached his favorite candymaker.

"What is that, a dreaded disease? No, I've never heard of it," she answered with a twinkle in her eye. Ransom took her to his favorite confectionary and bought two of the sugary squares from the cook, who knew Ransom on sight.

"Ah, Sir Ransom, you've brought a noble lady with you this evening! How enchanting!"

"Oh? Do you usually bring your paramours here?" Claire asked with a grin, speaking perfect Occitanian.

The cook looked startled at her command of the language. "Demoiselle, no!" said the man. "Sir Ransom is a knight of true Virtus."

She arched her eyebrows, looking up at Ransom's face. "That's good to hear." Then she lifted the confection and took a little bite. "Oh my. This couldn't have been made by mortals. You have stolen it from the Aos Sí!"

The baker looked confused. "Eh, demoiselle?"

"Thank you. This is delicious." She savored another bite. Ransom smiled at the look of pleasure on her face.

They walked away after enjoying the treats.

"Do you like my necklace?" she asked.

He hadn't seen it, covered as it was by the clasp of her cape, but she pulled that aside and showed him. The necklace was made of jeweled glass. It was Brythonican—he recognized it immediately—and much too costly for someone of his means. There were merchants who sold jewelry like that in Pree.

"That's sea glass," he said. "Did you buy that here? I hope not because you would have paid too much for it."

"No," she said with a laugh. "We came through Ploemeur on the way. The duchess has a plight troth to one of King Devon's sons. Goff, I think."

"Yes. The oldest son is married. The next is biding his time. Was the necklace a gift?"

"It was," said Claire. "I visited the beach where the glass is found. It's all a lot of nonsense if you ask me."

"What nonsense?"

"The myth of Leoneyis being drowned by the Deep Fathoms. That an entire kingdom should perish because of the wickedness of its flawed king. It's all so tragic, but it's nothing but a myth. A story. A fable."

He didn't like the way she teased about it. He'd always found those stories to be utterly fascinating. Especially the ones about the Fountain-blessed. The people of Occitania revered the heroes of old, and statues throughout the realm paid homage to them.

"Why are you frowning, Ransom?" she asked, and it was only then that he realized he'd made a face.

"The stories are quite popular here. Why don't you believe them?"

"Because they don't make sense. Do you really believe your prayer will be answered if you put a coin in a fountain? It's absurd."

Ransom had deposited coins in the fountains of Pree. He felt a prickle of uneasiness.

"I know I shouldn't be so harsh," she said, tugging on his arm. "I forget how touchy people can be about this sort of thing. It's just that the traditions of Legault go back much farther. They go back even before the legends of King Andrew and Queen Genevieve. Before the stories of the Deep Fathoms caught on. In Legault, we believe in a race of beings called the Aos Sí, who are marvelous and dangerous and supremely powerful. There was a war fought between these immortals and mankind, but Wizrs invented magical relics that could harm the Aos Sí and, eventually, drive them out."

"Drive them where?" Ransom asked. What she was saying could just as easily be called fantastical as a belief in the Lady of the Fountain, but he was too polite to say so.

"Well, when the Aos Sí were defeated, the world was divided into two realms," Claire answered. "The King of Legault was to make this division. He gave the Aos Sí half of the world. The half *beneath* the water. Does that not sound to you like the source of the myths of the Deep Fathoms?" She shook her head. It was dark now, and the firelight glowed softly against her hair. "Everyone is taught to revere the

Lady. We esteem her too holy to fight unless she chooses a maiden to champion her will." She sighed. "In Legault, it is different. It would be deemed no less strange for me to don a hauberk and grab a bow than it would be for you. This . . . this *tradition* of courtliness started by the Occitanians spreads like a pox." She sighed and gestured at all the tents. "Even this tournament upholds it, makes it stronger. King Lewis may be known as Lewis the Wise, but I'd prefer to call him Lewis the Shrewd. He's remaking the world in his image. Before long, even in Legault we'll start throwing our dead into rivers. It's barmy, Ransom."

He didn't agree with her. In fact, her words troubled him. He wanted to tell her that he had experienced things he could not explain. That he could hear a rush of water every time he lifted a sword against an opponent, so long as he rested between bouts and continued to practice. The emptiness he'd felt after the battles with the Brugians had been replenished completely since coming to Chessy. Lord Kinghorn had misunderstood him all those years ago. It wasn't that he liked playing at war. He *needed* it.

He still wasn't sure what that meant—could a good man *need* violence?—but it made the principles of Virtus even more important to him. If he adhered to them, if he did what he was supposed to do and found a respectable lord to serve, someone whose judgment he could trust, surely he could use his abilities for good. Or so he told himself.

"I'm glad I found you," she said, disturbing the awkward silence that had settled between them. "Before Sir Anselm complains about me too much, I'll show you to my father's tent. I'd like to give you something when we get there."

A thrill of surprise shot through him at her words. "A gift? You didn't even know I would be here."

"So? Does it hurt to be prepared?" she said. "This way."

They left the main thoroughfare and began wandering around the various encampments where knights were gathered around fires, drinking Occitanian wine and boasting about the exploits they'd not yet accomplished.

"Where is your tent?" she asked him.

"It's behind Scarbrow Armory," he said.

"The blacksmith, of course. At least I'll know where to find you when I send for you."

He couldn't help but smile. He would love to serve Lord Richard Archer, Duke of Glosstyr. Especially if it meant being near Claire. His motivation to do well at the tournament intensified.

"Are you staying at the edge of Chessy, then?" Ransom asked, recognizing that they were nearly to the border of the Bois de Meridienne.

"Yes, near the woods. We were invited as guests of the Duchess of Brythonica."

Ransom spotted pennants with the Raven on them and headed in that direction. They were allowed in without question, and Claire walked with purpose toward the larger tent. He heard laughter and chatter in the language of the realm, and one of the voices sounded familiar.

Claire stopped abruptly. "Oh, of all the wormy vipers . . ." she muttered darkly.

He followed her gaze to the tent, where he saw James Wigant standing near some horses, looking at Ransom with all the coldness of a winter's dawn.

I believe there might be some ill blood between Sir James Wigant and Sir Ransom Barton.

—*Claire de Murrow*
Chessy Field, Kingdom of Occitania

CHAPTER ELEVEN

The Constable's Secret

Ransom's mood soured at the sight of his old companion lingering outside Claire's pavilion. Seeing the familiar face, the narrowed contemptuous eyes, brought back a rush of old feelings that he had worked hard to suppress. Yes, Claire knew him too, but she didn't seem overly fond of him. That, at least, was a partial relief.

As they approached the tent together, James managed to regain some control of his expression and offered a gallant bow to Glosstyr's daughter.

"A pleasant evening, Lady Claire. I'd hoped to see you before taking the field."

"And why is that, Sir James?" Claire responded with cold courtesy. "Were you hoping I'd bestow a favor on you?"

Ransom's heart bristled at the mention. A lady's favor was a token of some sort, something to be worn during the tournament as a mark of preference.

"I would never presume such intimacy." His eyes shifted to her companion. "Hello, Ransom. Boon companions reunited at last."

Ransom felt his hand clenching into a fist of its own accord. He was grateful to be wearing his hauberk, wondering if the viper might strike. "Good evening, my lord," he replied curtly.

"'My lord'? Why the formality?" He came forward, assuming a new guise, that of an old friend. "We were the closest friends while in service to Lord Kinghorn. No one could best Ransom in the training yard."

"Or by the stables," Ransom added, feeling anger ripple beneath his calm exterior.

James took the reminder in stride. "Or that," he conceded. He stood in front of them now, his eyes going back to Claire's. His gloved hand brushed her elbow. "Might I see you later?"

She looked down at his hand, her brow furrowing with annoyance. "I think not, Sir James." She tightened her grip on Ransom's arm and moved closer to him. "Where are you camped? If I wish to see you, I will send for you."

He smiled and inclined his head slightly. "I'm staying at an inn down the road. The Oxnard. I'll have time to spare before the tournament starts in two days."

Ransom knew it. Although he'd done well these last years, he couldn't have afforded to stay there.

"Well, have a pleasant evening, then," Claire said, tugging Ransom with her toward the pavilion's entrance.

"How can it be pleasant without *your* company?" James said. His eyes launched daggers at Ransom.

Claire ignored the comment and pushed aside the curtain of the pavilion, muttering under her breath, "I'm sure you'll buy *something* that pleases you."

As they entered, there was no opportunity to continue their conversation, for there was already one happening inside. Ransom recognized Lord Archer. Memory had enshrined him as an impressively huge man, but Ransom found himself nearly meeting his eyes. He was speaking with Lord Rakestraw, the constable of Westmarch, whom Ransom had last seen two years prior. The constable still ruled the duchy for King Devon, who had not bestowed his dukedom on anyone, instead preserving the power and authority for himself.

The interior of the pavilion was spacious, with a central main tent, where the two lords were speaking, as well as two cordoned-off sections boasting stuffed pallets and fur blankets. Chests had been arranged in orderly rows in each of these areas, and the duke's armor and sword gleamed from an armor rack on one side. Ransom also noticed some portable camp tables, one of which boasted a small coffer full of silver livres.

Both men turned their attention to the entrance as Claire and Ransom entered together. The duke's eyes looked at Claire with something akin to disappointment, and then he noticed her hand on Ransom's arm. His nostrils flared.

She released Ransom and glided forward before dropping a curtsy in front of Lord Rakestraw and her father. "Greetings, my lords! Lord Dyron—I have not seen you in several years. Allow me to introduce you to—"

"I know the lad already," Rakestraw said. He appraised Ransom with a friendly eye and a genuine smile. "Barton's second son. We met during the Brugian affair, lass. Attacked a company of knights on his own while rallying the men of Averanche. Brave and bold. I've never forgotten it."

Duke Archer looked quizzically at Ransom. "He was friends with my daughter at the palace while they were both hostages to Gervase."

"Da," said Claire reprovingly. "That's hardly the appropriate word. Neither of us were in any danger."

"That's not how I remember it, lass, may the Fountain bless his rest," Rakestraw said. He grunted. "But some of the lords didn't look on the boy fondly after the trouble with Brugia. I should ask what brings you to Chessy, lad, but that is self-evident. I don't see you wearing a badge?"

"I've been riding in the tournament circle, my lord," Ransom said. "Since I left Lord Kinghorn's service."

"A good way to keep your skills honed. Which should benefit you in the tournament. Have you captured anyone of note, young man?"

"I ransomed Lord Montignac, my lord."

"That was you?" Rakestraw said with a burst of laughter. "I'd heard he'd been taken. He's one of Prince Estian's best knights. How'd you accomplish that?"

"Is now the time for stories, Dyron?" Lord Archer said, frowning with impatience.

Claire shot a look at her father. "I should like to hear it as well."

Ransom felt the tension coming from Claire's father and decided it would be wise to make the tale as short as possible. "I snatched the reins of his destrier, my lord."

Lord Rakestraw's eyebrows lowered, and he looked at the duke quizzically. "While he was *on* the horse?"

"Well . . . yes."

The duke's look softened. "That's not an easy feat, lad."

Ransom sighed. "I knew he had a horse with armor, a destrier that had a strong reputation. It was part of a war games tournament, and I volunteered for the opposing side. I kept my eyes on him during the fighting, saw the opportunity, and rode in while he was preoccupied. After I took the reins, I led his horse away from the battle. If he'd tried to jump, he would have likely injured himself, so he offered me a ransom. I got the horse I wanted and its armor to boot. That's the story. I won't embellish it."

Rakestraw burst out laughing. "And by the Fountain, he's an honorable man and upheld his end of the bargain. The Black Prince wouldn't have allowed him to forsake his oath. Bless you, lad, that was clever. War is trickery and deceit. Ambush and evasion. Always keep your enemy off balance."

"He's lucky he didn't get stabbed by the knight's lance," Lord Archer said gruffly.

"I waited until all of his lances were broken," Ransom said.

Rakestraw guffawed. "See? Good, lad. So you've been in the Occitanian tournament circle all this time, then?"

"Yes, my lord."

"Can you speak like one of King Lewis's knights?"

"Passably."

Lord Rakestraw had an appraising look in his eye. "Good to know. Lord Archer and I were discussing business at court. There have been some vexing accounts coming from the Vexin. Ha! We've much to discuss still."

That was a veiled invitation for Ransom to withdraw.

"We can go back to visit the merchants, then!" Claire said with bright eyes.

"No, Daughter." Lord Archer's tone was determined. "I'd have you stay here."

"As you command, *Da*." Her tone was a bit flippant, and Archer bristled. "But first I must give Ransom his gift." Claire hurried to one of the ends of the tent, where she knelt by a chest. Her hair bounced down her back as she did so, and the light from the lantern made it shine its rusty hue. Aware of both noblemen gazing at him, he diverted his eyes from her, feeling his neck heat.

Claire returned to him, holding out a braided piece of leather bound with silver on each end. The pattern was Gaultic, and the silver ends had a weave-pattern design on them. He didn't know what it was at first, but when she brought it to his wrist, he realized it was a bracelet. She struggled to connect the hook to the hasp for a moment, but her eyes met his, and a small smile flashed on her mouth.

"There," she said, attaching it. "It is my favor. Wear it into battle, and it will bring you the luck of the Aos Sí."

Ransom couldn't help but notice the disapproving look on her father's face.

"Thank you, my lady," he said. "I'd better go."

"'My lady'? To you, I'll always be Claire. I'll look for you during the tournament."

Rakestraw coughed into his fist, giving Ransom a warning look to depart soon. But the man also appeared amused.

"Thank you . . . Claire."

He felt like his cheeks were burning. The tent was oppressively warm. He bowed to both of the lords and left the tent, feeling the cool night air on his cheeks. Gazing down at the favor hugging his wrist, he remembered the touch of her fingers putting it there. His heart beat wildly in his chest, and he was suddenly dizzy. But he walked out of the camp and toward his tent, grinning the whole way.

"Ransom!"

It was a harsh whisper just outside the tent. It was probably near midnight, but he hadn't yet fallen asleep, kept awake by the writhing feelings in his chest and stomach. He sat up, reaching for his dagger. The voice wasn't Anders's. Nor did it belong to his page, Tanner.

He waited, his pulse quickening.

"Ransom? This is your tent, isn't it?"

The voice sounded vaguely familiar. Warily, he untied the knots of the tent and parted it, preparing himself for attack from James or his henchmen. Even though it was late, there were still many knights out carousing. His eyes had already adjusted to the dark, and he saw a man on one knee outside the door of his tent, but his face was in the shadows.

"Who are you?" Ransom asked. He hadn't taken off his hauberk or tunic, just his boots.

"William Chappell. You know me."

Ransom recognized the name, of course, having thought of William frequently over the years. The voice was familiar, but it had been seven years.

"How did you find me?" Ransom asked with doubt.

"Lady Claire revealed it. I serve Lord Dyron Rakestraw. I'm part of his mesnie. He wants to speak with you."

Ransom couldn't believe it. He parted the opening wider, eager for a better look at his old friend, and Sir William stood, wearing a hauberk, arm guards, and a sword strapped to his waist. In the moonlight now, his face was recognizable, although much older, more rugged.

"I'm coming," Ransom said, rising. He quickly tugged on his boots, buckled his own sword on, and ran his hand over the braided bracelet to be sure it was still there.

He ducked out of the tent. As he rose to his full height, Sir William stepped back. "You're not a boy any longer. Rakestraw said you were as big as a bear. He wasn't far off."

Ransom smiled in disbelief. "I came to Chessy looking for you."

"When?"

"Two years ago. You'd said this was where you'd go."

"Well, I was here for a while, heard you ended up in Averanche. I've served Lord Rakestraw for several years now. He's a good lord. Come with me."

"Lead the way," Ransom said eagerly, amazed by all that had happened in a single day. Looking up at the sky, he saw the confluence of stars and recognized the patterns, from which he'd learned to tell the time and season. It was nearly midnight, yet sleep had never been farther from his mind.

Snores trailed from some of the tents they passed, although knights sat around dwindling fires at other campsites, warming their hands over the coals.

"Were you part of the Brugian war?" Ransom asked.

"I was," Sir William replied. "Lord Dyron told me about meeting you. When I heard Kinghorn dismissed you, I said we should bring you into our mesnie, but you had vanished. Your time in Occitania might prove to your advantage, however."

"How so?"

"I won't reveal my lord's secrets," he said, flashing Ransom a grin that only served to heighten his suspense.

It was not a long march to Lord Rakestraw's pavilion. There were knights and horses camped about it, and he felt a familiar longing to be in a lord's service again. There were two men guarding the door and several patrolling around it, which Ransom thought odd considering the Black Prince's men were the watchmen over the camp. He'd noticed them even during their brief walk.

Inside, a brazier of hot coals provided heat and some light. Lord Dyron sat on a camp stool, picking at a roast capon garnished with mint and rosemary. He eyed their arrival and took a drink from his goblet.

"Did I wake you, boy?" he asked, smiling pleasantly.

"Not really," Ransom answered.

"Oh, I imagine not. Head full of fluff and dreams. I remember being your age, Ransom, although it may not look like it. I served in the king's mesnie back when he was the Duke of Westmarch. He rewarded me well for my service, as a good lord should do. I won't sour your dreams of Lady de Murrow with the acid tonic of reality. Enjoy the smell. You'll likely not get the taste. Agh, but that's not why I called you here. Sit down." He gestured to another camp stool opposite him.

Sir William folded his arms and remained by the entrance.

The tent was dark enough that he couldn't see more than a few shadowed pallets and chests, similar to the tent he'd visited earlier. The slightly flowery scent in the air surprised him, but he didn't mention it. He listened for the sound of breathing, for the noise of others in the room. Although he saw no one else, it did not feel like they were totally alone. Only the dim glow of the coals helped him see Rakestraw's bearded face.

"Do you truly serve no one, boy?" he asked quietly, his voice sincere and deep.

"I don't," he answered without hesitation. "I have no oath binding me."

"What of the Occitanian prince? Do you serve him? Are you one of his . . . lackeys?"

"I'm not," Ransom answered. Nervous energy rattled inside him.

Rakestraw nodded, ripping another piece of the meat from the plate and eating it. "I think you're honest. Some young men are not. I imagine you are excited to compete in the tournament? Hmmm?"

Ransom shrugged. "I do enjoy competing, yes. I'm good at it too."

"I don't begrudge you that, lad. Sir William Chappell over there made a new career out of it himself, after King Gervase died. Loyalty is important to a lord . . . and a king. It was his loyalty to King Gervase that convinced me to bring him on. You were very young during that civil war." His look darkened. "One by one, Gervase's men abandoned him. They switched sides and came into Devon's service. He didn't trust them unless they earned his trust—after all, if they'd betray a king, might they not betray him if he became one? Eh? You were trained by Lord Kinghorn. He dismissed your service. Are you . . . resentful?"

Ransom wasn't sure how to answer that question or where this conversation was going. He felt as if he were in a canoe with no oars, getting dragged away by the current.

"I was . . . at first," Ransom answered honestly. "Now that I have armor, a horse, and some livres in my purse . . . I . . . I had hoped to see him again."

"I'm sure he'd take you back," said Lord Dyron. "Is that what you want?"

Ransom felt an uneasy silence after the question. What was happening? "I would be honored . . . to serve him again."

"I'm not asking about your honor. I'm asking about your ambition."

Ransom swallowed. "Are you asking if I would serve you?"

"Aye. Would you be willing to leave this dusty tent town and go riding to a better place?"

Ransom felt a smile twitch on his mouth. "I would, my lord."

"Good. Because we're leaving at dawn." He rose and spoke, his voice very low, "Your Majesty, it looks like he'll be coming with us."

Ransom's heart felt the shock of the announcement as he hurried to his feet. From the shadows came the outline of a person, and he again smelled the flowery scent.

His eyes bulged, and Ransom dropped quickly to his knee before the Queen of Ceredigion.

My maid said Sir James had come to bring me a gift, but he refused to leave it with her because of its value. Why would he do this? Does he fear I don't trust her? Or is he seeking, like the courtiers do at the court of Pree, to heighten my anticipation by suspense? If he thinks I can be bought, he's acting the maggot. I listened to the worrying news the lord constable brought from Kingfountain. The queen's land, the duchy of Vexin, has been under revolt. King Devon and Queen Emiloh continue to be plagued by small fires of rebellion throughout their realm. Lord Rakestraw said the king could not attend the tournament because he was too concerned about what would happen in his absence. Why does no one attack Occitania? It seems to me the root of these ills is festering beneath the court of the Wise King. Perhaps all the payments and rewards he disperses to knights from other realms is just a subtle form of bribery.

I am grateful, though, that I discovered Sir Ransom by chance today. He is not the boy I remember from Kingfountain. How handsome he has become. Quiet too. I think he cares for me. He kept looking at me, although I sensed something different in his gaze. I love the color of his eyes. Not quite brown, yet not green either. They reflect his moods. When Da suggested I find someone to marry while at this tournament,

I think he meant Sir James or another duke's son. It may take some time for him to accept that the decision is truly mine.

—*Claire de Murrow*
Chessy Field, Kingdom of Occitania

CHAPTER TWELVE

The Queen's Protectors

Ransom had seen Queen Emiloh years ago, when she first came to Kingfountain, but the memory had dimmed over time. Still, he recognized the slope of her nose and the slight curve at its tip, her gold hair that hung in a thousand tiny ringlets, and her strong gait—indicative of a woman who was used to the saddle. He knew she fancied falconry and took pleasure in the hunt, riding great distances with her husband. She was unusually tall as well, of a height with Lord Rakestraw and almost as tall as Ransom.

"Rise, Marshall," she said.

"Y-Your Majesty," he stuttered, unable to conceive that this was happening. She wore a cream-colored gown embroidered with flowers and fleurs-de-lis, with slit sleeves and a golden trim. Her husband's standard, the Silver Rose, was emblazed on the bodice but partly concealed beneath the cloak she wore over the gown.

"I'm grateful my presence comes as a surprise," she said, flashing him a smile. She looked too young to have sired so many sons, but then her children were all younger than him.

"We've taken great pains to ensure it," said Lord Rakestraw. He gave Ransom a sharp look. "I've not even told the Duke of Glosstyr, and he sits on the king's council. That means, lad, that you'd best keep this secret to yourself."

"Of course," Ransom said. "Why are you here?"

"Because the tournament provided a good opportunity for me to travel in disguise," she answered. "I'm returning to the duchy of Vexin to bring some of our squabbling nobles to heel. They, of course, will be here at Chessy. When they return to their castles after the tournament, they will find that I'm already at the fortress of Auxaunce, ready to call them to account for their disobedience. The king is preoccupied with rumors of other discontent. Many of our lords have caused trouble these last few years. It seems half the nobility isn't content unless they are fighting each other over a castle or grain mill. So he sent me to quell this one myself, since the duchy in question is my own."

Ransom stared at her, surprised at her candor. "The king must trust you a great deal, my lady," he said with respect.

She smiled at the comment. "Lord Rakestraw and I believe no one will take notice of a small force of knights riding to the Vexin. While I speak Occitanian fluently, I am also recognizable. We were hoping to find a young knight we could trust on this mission. An Occitanian knight, we thought, who could help throw any hounds off our scent. Your knowledge of the language makes you an even better choice. This means you will not be participating in the tournament, Marshall. But you will be well rewarded."

"I would be honored to serve my queen," he said, bowing.

"Your service is to Lord Rakestraw," she said. "He is the one my husband has given the duty of seeing me safely to Auxaunce. I think all is well, Lord Dyron. Perform the oath."

"Of course, my lady," he said. Lord Rakestraw turned and faced Ransom, putting his meaty hand on his left shoulder. "I hereby accept thee, Ransom Barton, as my sworn man, a knight of my household and due its protection and privileges. This I swear before my queen."

A tingle went down Ransom's spine. He heard the gentle lapping of waters and felt a rush of raw emotion. He reached out his right hand and put it on Lord Dyron's left shoulder. He knew the words and the pose, having seen it done before. This was the reason for the salute he'd exchanged with other knights—a knight taking an oath did so by touching the oath holder's left shoulder. The salute was a reminder of that oath and the duty of loyalty attached to it.

"I hereby swear my fealty to thee, Lord Rakestraw. I am your sworn man."

Lord Dyron smiled and lowered his arm. "We ride at dawn. Leave your suit of armor here at camp but wear your hauberk. Bring your destrier, a lance, and be prepared to ride hard. Her Highness is a skilled horsewoman. We'll be pressed to keep up with her. Once we reach Auxaunce, we'll have our gear brought to us. I'll have one of the pages collect yours. Make ready now. We aim to arrive in Auxaunce in two days."

"How many are riding with us?" Ransom asked.

Lord Dyron turned and looked at Sir William. "Eight knights, plus Her Highness. You and Sir William will ride in front in case we're stopped by anyone too curious. Your job is to convince them we're knights from Pree who were sent home by our masters after performing poorly in the early bouts."

"I will go prepare," Ransom said.

"Good. Sir William will go with you. Not that I don't trust you, lad, but I'm a cautious man by nature, and we're in Occitania right now. I don't trust them. Not at all."

An early morning mist hung over the camp—not a thick fog but thin streamers that had settled. Ransom's page had arrived to help him don his armor, but he dismissed the boy and said he was going for a ride with an old friend. He introduced him to Sir William, and Tanner murmured a polite greeting and hurried off, grateful to have been let off his duties so early. Ransom even gave him two silver livres to spend at the merchants' tables.

"It's a fine destrier," Sir William said, stroking the beast while Ransom saddled him. "What's his name?"

"Manhault," Ransom answered. He checked and double-checked the girth straps and grabbed one of the ash lances that leaned against his tent pole and deposited it into the quiver attached to the saddle. He checked his belongings and packed his coin purse. Although the bag was hefty and full of silver, he had some more coin stored in a lockbox with Anders Scarbrow in his tent. He had the urge to tell the blacksmith about the sudden change in his fortunes, but he'd promised not to reveal anything.

He checked his gear once more, earning a laugh from Sir William.

"We're not riding far, Ransom. Everything you own will be brought to Tatton Grange, I promise you."

Ransom shrugged and mounted his destrier. Sir William, who'd walked his horse to Ransom's tent, did the same. As they directed their mounts toward the road, Ransom's gaze shot down to the braided cord on his wrist, the silver tips gleaming in the morning light. How he wished he could talk to Claire, or at least send her a message. But he couldn't risk doing something that might unintentionally reveal them. He was a sworn man now, a knight who served the constable of Westmarch, the largest and most powerful duchy in Ceredigion. A giddy feeling danced up his spine.

They dodged through the camps as the knights, many suffering from severe headaches by the looks on their faces, rose to prepare for the first day of the tournament. Ransom had hoped to compete in it, to win some money and hopefully find a lord to serve. He'd never expected his fate to change so abruptly, and before the competition even started.

When they reached the road, which was thronged with carts from Pree packed with melons, pies, cooked skewers of meat, and other dishes, he spied Lord Rakestraw already mounted with several other knights. He saw the queen, disguised in a cloak and a riding dress, sitting sidesaddle as the ladies did. A scarf covered part of her face, but it was cold enough to warrant it. Her horse was an impressive animal, but it didn't stand out as anything out of the ordinary. Many lords rode to the lists with their wives or daughters with them.

As they approached the others, Lord Rakestraw nodded to both of them to lead the way, and they moved to the head of the group. Their pace was slowed by the flood of those trying to reach Chessy, but by midmorning the tidewaters of commerce had ebbed, and they were able to increase their pace significantly. Ransom knew the road to Pree very well, and while they wouldn't be stopping in the city, it was the most direct way to get to the Vexin.

At midday they halted to eat and to rest the horses, but they were soon riding again. Ransom could hear the war horses behind them, the pounding of the hooves urging him and William to ride ever faster to keep ahead of the queen. He sensed she was setting the pace deliberately, pushing the beasts past their normal limits. But her steed handled it effortlessly, clearly accustomed to the punishing pace. They passed Pree from the north, but it was too far away to see, and crossed the river on a bridge leading north to Mainz. Ransom used his Occitanian to banter with the bridge keepers, who wore the black of the prince's guard.

They rode past Mainz before sunset, skirting the city completely. The road they took was little used, and there was no one to remark on their presence save a few peasants working the land. After dark, they settled in a grove of trees and didn't make a fire. Lord Dyron sat on a fallen log and drank from his leather flask, then wiped his mouth on his arm.

"We've made good time today, lads," he said in his gruff voice. "How far to Auxaunce, Your Highness?"

"The village of Usson is not far from here," she said. "We'll be at Auxaunce after midday tomorrow."

"Are we in your duchy, Your Highness?" asked Sir William.

"We are in its southern borders, yes. But it is still not safe. The lords of DeVaux Valley are the ones causing trouble, and their lands are just to the west."

Rakestraw turned to Ransom. "Her Majesty didn't take a ship because of the recent trouble with Atabyrion. There are pirates watching the coasts, and any sizable armada would have been seen and questioned. The tournament in Chessy provided us with a good opportunity to slip through by land."

An owl hooted in the night, making many of the knights flinch and look in its direction. Ransom had hunted and camped too many times to take notice of it, and the queen didn't react either. When it became too dark to see, they all slept in their cloaks in a circle around the queen. The men took turns as guards during the night.

When it was Ransom's and William's turn to stand guard, they walked away from the camp, patrolling the perimeter, only hearing the noises of the night.

"Do you like serving Lord Dyron?" Ransom asked.

"Aye. He's a good man. He's dedicated to the king. I've never heard him complain about him at all."

"Do you think King Devon will make him the Duke of Westmarch to reward his loyalty?"

Sir William sniffed. "I doubt it. The king has too many sons. Unlike your father, he plans to bestow each of them with something. I think he'll give Westmarch to his eldest, Prince Devon. Benedict will get the Vexin. Goff will become the Duke of Brythonica. The youngest, Jon-Landon, is too young to rule, but something will be done for him."

"Where is the crown prince now?"

"Dundrennan," came the answer. "Duke Wigant's household. Having him up there has helped with the Atabyrion skirmishes, I think.

They're more hesitant to make trouble. And even though Benedict is fourteen, he's a warrior already. It wouldn't surprise me if he's ruling the Vexin within the year. After his mother tames it first." He chuckled softly. "He pleaded to come with us, or so they said. But the king wouldn't risk his wife *and* his son on such a perilous journey."

"Perilous?" Ransom asked. "The only people we've seen are peasants and bridge keepers. Were they expecting bandits patrolling the roads?"

"No. DeVaux is the risk. Men like him cause grief no matter who rules. The Vexin is far enough away from Kingfountain that he gets away with a lot because it takes so long for news to reach the court. This conflict has been brewing for a number of years. The fact that the king has sent his wife to put them in line says his patience is at an end."

They were quiet for a while before Ransom asked, "Do you miss . . . Gervase? The old king?"

Sir William was silent for a moment, staring up at the stars as if lost in thought. "Of course I do, Ransom," he said at last. "He was a good man. But . . . he wasn't a good king. All the time he wore the hollow crown, he feared losing it. Feared he had taken it dishonorably. His nobles could sense his fear, and they caused trouble because of it. I would rather wear a helmet than a crown. It's a terrible burden. Devon Argentine wears it well. It's his by right, as his mother's heir. She was the one who was chosen to rule. I think, in the end, Gervase regretted snatching it like he did. We can't undo the past, though. Can we?"

"No," Ransom agreed. But while everything Sir William said made sense, he still remembered the way the old king had saved his life. He'd had compassion for a little boy, even though he'd known that very compassion would condemn him.

Perhaps he had not been a good king, but he'd been a good man. In some ways that was more important.

They awoke before dawn and prepared provender for the horses while putting together their gear for the last part of the journey. The tournament had started back in Chessy, and Ransom couldn't help thinking about it as they passed through the village of Usson. Would Claire miss him? Would his friend the blacksmith worry what had become of him?

They did not stop, even though some of the townsfolk came out to observe the knights passing through. The looks from the villagers were wary and distrustful. Men held pitchforks or spades, wielding them like weapons in case the knights attacked.

After leaving Usson behind, the queen insisted that they hurry. Ransom knew they were getting closer to Auxaunce because of the sculpted farms they passed on the roads. Hedges along the road had been groomed to pen in sheep and farm animals. Some had openings or gates, leading to farmsteads in the distance. Plump sheep grazed within those boundaries. They passed various fruit orchards and vineyards, and Ransom was gazing at some ripening apricots in a nearby grove when he heard Lord Rakestraw's bellowed command to halt.

Ransom pulled back on the reins and did so. When he turned, his stomach lurched. Riders were coming up from behind them, the sun glinting off their armor and the metal tips of their lances. There were too many to count, at least fifty or so, and judging from their speed, their horses were fresher by far. It wouldn't be long before they caught up.

"Who is it?" Sir William asked, turning his destrier around.

"Do you recognize them, my lady?" Lord Dyron asked in a nervous tone.

The queen's face had gone pale, paler than the cream riding gloves sheathing her arms. She gazed at the approaching men, who were not far behind them. The other knights clustered around her.

"I don't see any banners. They're trying to stop us before we reach Auxaunce."

"How far is the castle?" Rakestraw asked.

"A league . . . maybe two. Our horses are winded. If it comes down to a chase, they'll overtake us."

The constable's brow furrowed with anger. "Someone saw us. Got word out."

"How could they have caught up so quickly?" the queen asked. "No one knew we were coming. We sent no message ahead of us for fear it might be intercepted by Lewis's spies."

"We can't argue about this, my lady. Ride on to Auxaunce. Send knights back to help us. We'll hold them here."

Ransom's stomach shriveled at the thought. There were at least forty to fifty riders bearing down on them.

"We can parlay with them," the queen suggested.

The constable shook his head. "Any parlay will lead to your capture and ransom. My orders from the king were to see you safely to Auxaunce. We fight them here and hold the road. If they try crossing the hedges, it'll slow them down. Go!"

The queen looked at him fiercely, then nodded. She leaned forward in the saddle and urged her horse into a gallop, launching back down the road. Ransom wanted to go with her, to see she made it safely, but he was duty bound to follow the constable's orders.

"They're not slowing down, my lord," announced one of the knights, his voice grim.

"And we're not budging," Rakestraw said. He turned his destrier around and hefted his lance from its sheath. They each had only one. Ransom pulled his out as well. His stomach churned with dread at the approaching conflict. He could see the knights more clearly as they charged forward, most of them wearing full armor. The glint of metal was not from polish. These were battle-hardened knights with mud and dirt spattered on their shields.

Rakestraw's knights formed a line, four across and two deep, blocking the road.

Ransom gripped his lance, feeling his ears tingle, his skin begin to itch. The constable's knights only wore hauberks, which would not stop the tip of a sharpened lance. That meant their only chance was to strike first and unhorse their foes with better skill.

"On the ready," Lord Rakestraw said.

Ransom saw the look of dread in the eyes of his fellows. But they faced the task without flinching. The road shuddered under the force of the stampede. Ransom licked his lips, glancing down at the bracelet attached to his forearm. He brought it up to his mouth and kissed it.

"Onward!" shouted Lord Rakestraw. "In the queen's name!"

The constable led the charge. The destriers snorted and plunged their hooves into the dirt. Ransom gritted his teeth as Manhault surged forward in the second row. He felt the lapping waters inside his chest, heard the noise of the falls in his ears. As one, the eight warriors of Westmarch charged against the larger host. Ransom's fear left him. He stared at the front row of enemies, wondering which knight he'd face first.

The two groups collided. Ransom saw the tip of a lance come through Lord Rakestraw's back as it hoisted him off his horse. He blinked in shock, unable to believe it. A man of the constable's rank would be worth a hefty ransom. Who in their right mind would kill him straightaway?

That's when he realized that they were all dead men.

X

I'm sick inside. Ransom is gone, and no one knows what has become of him.

I sought him out the morning of the tournament, hoping to spend a little time with him, but his tent was empty. His page said he went out for a morning ride with a fellow knight and never returned. When there was still no word of him by nightfall, I asked Sir James to come to our camp and demanded to know what he'd done. He looked confused, the rogue, and claimed he'd not seen Ransom since meeting him at our tent. Although he promised to have his men search for Ransom. I'd much sooner trust the knights of Glosstyr.

Da thinks I'm being foolish, but something is very wrong. Maybe someone doesn't want him competing in the tournament, afraid he will win the day. If that's all it is, I can abide such a disappointment. But if he's been wounded or killed because of this, I won't be able to bear it. What are these feelings? Why am I so anxious to see him well? It's probably nothing. But my heart whispers he has fallen into great danger.

—Claire de Murrow
Chessy Field, Kingdom of Occitania

X

CHAPTER THIRTEEN

Fountain-Blessed

ansom lowered his lance into place as the sounds of battle flooded his ears—the terror of colliding horses, the grunts of angry warriors, the strife of steel, and the splintering cracks of the lances. His own lance found a target and unhorsed an enemy knight. The man was flung from his saddle and landed with back-breaking force, but Ransom's triumph was short-lived as another knight aimed for him. He tried to swivel his lance to engage on the other side, but the lance was already coming, too hard and fast to be avoided.

Ransom felt a gut-wrenching dread that he would be impaled like Lord Rakestraw. He leaned in his saddle to dodge the thrust, but the knight had aimed poorly, and the lance struck Ransom's destrier instead. He felt the shudder of muscle between his legs as the horse took the full brunt of the charge. It was a death blow.

He knew what happened to the riders of horses who were killed.

Manhault shrieked in agony and reared up, which hoisted the enemy knight out of his saddle since he was still holding fast to the lance. Ransom pulled his leg free of the stirrup, feeling his world tilt as his destrier tumbled, blood gushing from the beast's muscled chest. Ransom felt himself falling and tried to leap free. He grimaced in anticipation, half expecting the beast to fall on him and snap his bones, but it didn't happen. Ransom managed to land on his feet, but he was buffeted by another horse charging through the wreck of men.

He stood amidst a nightmare. Swords banged on armor, and men fell all around him. To save his own life, he quickly drew his bastard sword from the scabbard at his belt and spun around. He saw the glint of dirtied armor and knew the man as an enemy since none of Lord Rakestraw's men had donned a full suit. The knight was clashing with Sir William, sword to sword, when Ransom found an opening and struck him from behind. The knight gurgled in pain, clutching his side before he slumped off the saddle. William, surprised at the sudden victory, looked down and saw Ransom there.

"Behind you!" William shouted.

Ransom whirled as a knight charged at him, lance lowered. He deflected the tip of the lance, spun around, and slashed the man's destrier as he tried to ride past. His aim was true, and he severely injured the beast.

It was a maelstrom of chaos, but Lord Rakestraw's final order had been burned into his mind. Protect the road. Save the queen from capture. Ransom fought from his feet, lunging from knight to knight through the commotion, but he felt no fear. An enemy knight charged at him on foot, armor begrimed with blood and dust. Without his own confining armor, Ransom had to be faster. Returning blow for blow, Ransom hammered against his opponent, driving him back until the knight tripped over a dead horse and sprawled backward, opening himself up for a death blow from Ransom's sword.

He heard some barked commands in a guttural language that was not Occitanian, and it struck him that he was too exposed on the road—someone could easily strike him down from behind. No sooner had the thought occurred to him than he turned and saw an enemy knight creeping up on him with a dagger. The man jumped when Ransom charged at him, and in moments, he'd disarmed the fellow with the dagger and made the knight flee.

The rushing noise of the waterfall in his ears increased. He seemed attuned to everything around him. He blocked thrusts that should have skewered him and used every part of his weapon to defend himself.

Then Sir William was there, on his feet, sword at the ready. His eyes looked fierce, and his mouth was set in an angry line. "Back to back!" he said. "Hold them off!"

The two knights stood in the middle of the road and struck down everyone who came close. Ransom felt his blood singing in his veins, pushing strength and vitality through him. Two knights attacked him at once, charging over the field of dead men. There were too many obstacles for horses now, so the enemy knights had dismounted and joined the violence on foot. Ransom glanced down the road to see if any knights had broken past the failing barrier to pursue the queen. None. He could still see her galloping away in the distance. But there was no time to get help from the castle. This skirmish would be over long before she arrived there.

Ransom felt a blow against his arm, but his hauberk saved his limb from being cut off. He kicked one opponent in the stomach, then blocked the other's overhead swing by bringing his own blade up and using both hands to hold it as he would a staff. Ransom returned the blow and struck the enemy on the helm with the pommel, which stunned the man enough that Ransom could kick him down before the next assailant arrived.

The knights continued to surge against them, roaring with frustration. Ransom didn't see any of Lord Rakestraw's other men on their feet, although he saw several lying still on the ground, their eyes open in death. He blocked, countered, and repulsed—swing after swing, blow after blow. Anyone who came near him was driven back.

Then a cry of pain sounded from behind him. Whipping around, he saw Sir William drop to one knee, his face blanched with pain as he gripped his chest with one hand. Ransom saw red and would have attacked the man who'd stabbed his friend, but William acted first—driving his blade into his enemy's armor. Then, in the space of a breath, two more knights converged and struck William down, leaving Ransom alone against the onslaught.

He knew he was about to die, but he was determined to fight on. He roared in outrage and slammed into the two men who'd killed Sir William and drove both of them back. Sensing another attack from behind, he spun around and deflected a blade aimed at his back. His instincts had protected him thus far, but it could not go on forever. The knights would close around him soon.

Then he remembered the hedge. Ransom blocked another blow and rushed to the hedge. He put his back to it, knowing it would enable him to focus only on the knights in front of him. Three came at him at once. The odds were impossible, but his sword arm seemed to move of its own will. He parried and countered with such precision that two of the three staggered back, grimacing from wounds.

There was one knight still astride a horse, and he barked at the others. He was the one in command of the group. He pointed at Ransom, shouting, and several more knights came at him, only to be repelled again. There was no weariness, no hint of pain. He knew he'd been struck several times, but he didn't feel the blows.

After knocking back his foes for the third time, Ransom stepped back toward the hedge, keeping his rear guarded. He didn't know why he was still standing. Two dozen enemy knights surrounded him. They looked amazed at his strength, his skill at arms, but they continued to press in on him, emboldened by their commander.

Ransom fought against swords, daggers, and even a wicked-looking battle axe. Yet he defended himself from each assault with cunning and skill. He was surprised that he wasn't gasping for breath. In the training yards at Averanche or the tournament grounds at Chessy, he'd fought in all manner of combinations, but never had he been so outnumbered. Still the waters rushed in his ears, inside him.

He held his place at the hedge, countering every opponent. Even the wounded returned for more, wave after wave, trying to overwhelm him. But they couldn't. He felt like a rock being pummeled by the surf. Yet the rock held firm.

"Yield!" shouted the man on horseback, speaking in Occitanian.

"Never!" Ransom shouted back, blocking again, kicking another man down.

The man astride the horse frowned and then nodded.

It was a signal.

Pain exploded in Ransom's leg.

He saw the tip of a lance puncture his muscle. The blow had come from behind him, and he realized one of the enemies had circled around the hedge and punctured it with a lance.

The gush of the waterfall began to fade, panic writhing in its wake. The pain was excruciating. The attacker yanked the lance back, and Ransom's muscles quivered as he saw blood running down his own leg. He dropped down to his hands and knees and found himself staring into the vacant gaze of his friend, Sir William, who lay amidst the other corpses. His arms trembled with weariness as he felt the draining sensation he'd experienced during the Brugian campaign. Hollowness. Emptiness. Weakness.

The pain in his leg drove away the fear of death. He hung his head, waiting for the killing blow, one that would take off his head. More orders were given. He saw the armored feet of knights standing around him. As he breathed what he felt was his last breath, he saw the braided charm still around his wrist, droplets of blood smeared on it. He thought of Claire, and the joy of seeing her smile and hearing her laugh after so many years apart. At least they'd been able to walk through the pavilions together, although his heart had longed for so much more.

Disappointment stabbed his heart. He let out his breath and collapsed, his strength utterly gone.

One of the knights asked a question. Even though it was spoken in the guttural tongue, he understood the meaning, though he didn't know how he knew it.

"What manner of knight is this man? I've never seen such a warrior."

He heard a gruff reply. "I've never seen one myself, but I've heard of such. He must be Fountain-blessed. Throw his body on one of the horses. Bring him with us."

The pain was unbearable. Yet Ransom was too exhausted to do anything other than moan when they grabbed him beneath the arms and hoisted him up.

The enemy knights had thrown Ransom's body across the back of a rouncy, securing him there with rope. He blacked out from the pain for a while until the harsh riding finally roused him again. The pressure against his chest from the bouncing was bad enough, but his leg was still bleeding, robbing his strength. None had tended to his wound in their haste to leave the scene of death.

They rode back the way they'd come, not following the queen. He didn't know why, but he reasoned that the desire to escape and survive had overpowered their need to capture the queen. Besides which, she'd gotten far enough ahead it was unlikely they'd catch up to her. The jolting blows against the hard saddle made him grunt and wish for the misery to end. All of the other knights had died. In his mind, he saw Dyron Rakestraw's death over and over again. Who would have risked such a thing? Surely the King of Ceredigion would be avenged of his foes, but why not seek a ransom from such a powerful lord? It was madness.

They rode for several leagues before turning onto another lane. They were heading into the territory of DeVaux, Ransom surmised. When they stopped, it was not at a manor or a castle but in a secluded wood.

The riders dismounted and began arguing worriedly among themselves. Their leader dismounted as well. He looked over at Ransom, who was still trussed to the saddle, and gave a command. This time, Ransom could not understand the guttural language. Two of the knights approached, released his bindings, and hefted him off the horse before dumping him to the ground. He was left where he'd fallen.

Ransom looked down at his wounded leg and saw the blood soaking his pants. He'd seen vicious wounds before but never on his own body. He turned his face away, trying not to pass out. Some of the knights drank from flasks. None offered him anything. His own thirst was difficult to bear. They spoke and debated one with another before the leader sauntered over to Ransom.

"What languages do you speak?" asked the man warily in Occitanian.

"I understand you," Ransom answered.

"Are you Occitanian, then?"

Ransom shook his head no.

"Ceredigic?"

Ransom nodded.

The man pursed his lips and nodded, looking intrigued by his captive. "Was that Lord Rakestraw we killed? He was protecting your queen?"

"Yes," Ransom said. "Why did you kill him?"

The man laughed. "It wasn't my intention to kill the constable! By the Fountain, no! I thought he'd surrender. That we'd get a fair ransom for Emiloh. But she escaped, your fellows are all dead, I lost a goodly number of knights, and now if I'm not careful, that will be my fate as well." He rubbed his mouth.

"Who are you?" Ransom asked.

"You don't know me?"

"I've never been to the Vexin before."

"I am Lord DeVaux. And you are my prisoner. What's your name?"

151

"Ransom Barton."

DeVaux shrugged. "That name means nothing to me. I thought you might be one of the Black Prince's men. I've heard one of his knights is Fountain-blessed. You fought bravely today. Such skill. It's commendable. But I won't let you go. Not without a ransom. A ransom for Ransom." He chuckled. "Will anyone pay for you, I wonder?"

Ransom didn't know. He already hated this man. His mind was whirring again, his thoughts tangled into knots.

Fountain-blessed. They think I'm Fountain-blessed.

"I'm wounded."

DeVaux shrugged. "So you are. Tend to yourself. You spilled enough of our blood—it's only proper you should lose some too. You ride with us, for we are outlaws now. We must keep out of reach of your king."

Ransom grimaced. "He's your king as well."

DeVaux scoffed. "I didn't choose him."

It was the blacksmith who told me. Ransom's tent and his gear and armor were collected by men in the employ of the lord constable of Westmarch. He was not at the tournament because he left with Rakestraw's men. I'm trying not to think of that boy as a rotten dung beetle right now for leaving without a word. I gave him my favor, and he vanished without a trace. The tournament was flawless—if you are Occitanian. One of Prince Estian's knights won the day and received the high glory and honor of the prince. Of the three champions crowned with rose garlands, all three were from the duchies of this land. And many a knight from Ceredigion will be carried home on a litter while nursing broken ribs, arms, and legs.

Da says we are leaving tomorrow. He will send me back to Glosstyr to handle his affairs there, and he will return through Brythonica to Legault as originally planned. I hope to see Ransom before I go, but no one knows where Lord Rakestraw ran off to with his knights. I feel barmy for having worried so much these last few days. I'd hoped to persuade father to take

Ransom into his mesnie, but the duchy of Westmarch has far more significance than that of Glosstyr. At least I know where he is now. That is a relief.

—Claire de Murrow
Chessy Field
(in a tent)

CHAPTER FOURTEEN

Fever Dreams

As soon as Ransom loosened the blood-soaked bandage, he saw fresh wetness well up from the gaping wound. He leaned back against the tree, panting against the pain. DeVaux's men had offered no assistance at all, and he'd had to use his teeth to bite through his tunic and rip some strips of fabric to bind his own injury. They would not even trust him with a small dagger.

Sweat and chills rippled through his body. His mind felt sluggish and preoccupied with worries of death. Even with the tight covering, the wound hadn't closed, and it bled as freely as ever. He puffed out his breath, adjusting his seat despite the agony, and tore several more strips of fabric from his tunic. DeVaux's men watched him with dark looks. He'd get no help there.

Ransom was determined to live. The thought burned in his skull alongside the growing fever. He yanked and ripped at the fabric until his strength failed him, and he slumped back against the tree to rest, breathing heavily. Then he worked at it again, until he had a long enough piece to wrap around the injury. His fingers looked grotesque with the smears of dirt and blood. He clenched his teeth against the pain as he wrapped the strip above his wound and knotted it. Then he grabbed a stick and used it to tighten the fabric until it bit into his skin. The agony was excruciating. His gasps were desperate.

DeVaux sauntered up to him, his eyes bleary from their arduous ride through the countryside. "Get up. We have to keep moving."

Ransom couldn't have spoken if he'd wanted to. Ignoring DeVaux, he wrapped another piece of torn cloth around the stick to hold it in place. The self-inflicted torture nearly made him black out.

"Get up! If you are truly Fountain-blessed, you may live. If not, there's nothing that will save you. That wound will undoubtedly fester, and you'll be dead before long. Or you'll have a stump and be a cripple all your life. We're going. Now."

Ransom struggled to rise, pushing with his good leg and using the tree to pull himself up. The bark scraped his hands, leaving splinters, which began to itch. Gobs of sticky sap clung to him. He glared at Lord DeVaux, but he said nothing. If he'd had a dagger, he would have been tempted to use his last burst of energy to attack his captor and kill him.

But he had no weapon—he had nothing but the will to live. So he hobbled to the horse and stepped onto a fallen log to mount it. His vision blurred once he was in the saddle, but he gripped the saddle horn, willing himself to stay upright. If he fell off, he knew they would leave him to die in the woods.

Another knight took the reins, and off they went again. Ransom didn't have the mental faculties to guide a horse anyway, and he had no idea where they were or where they were going. They'd slept out of doors the previous night, but he'd overheard DeVaux saying they were bound for a castle to seek refuge and supplies. Ransom slumped against the horse, trying to stifle the moans that forced their way from his mouth. His leg throbbed mercilessly.

They rode through forests, through valleys. Sometimes he'd see little farm huts. The knights would stop and pillage food before riding on. He never saw evidence of the farmers or their families. Wisely, they scurried away when armed knights came into view.

DeVaux's words throbbed in the painful mess inside Ransom's mind. He had called Ransom Fountain-blessed. But that was not how he felt. If anything, he'd been cursed by the Fountain. When he was young, he had hoped to serve King Gervase, but the king's untimely death had prevented it. Then he'd gone to Averanche to serve Lord Kinghorn, and that dream had been shattered as well. Finally, he'd thought his luck had turned around—he'd seen Claire again and been given a chance to serve Lord Rakestraw, but his lord had been pierced through with a lance. If they had ridden with armor, many if not most of the knights would have survived the confrontation with DeVaux's men. The ruse had not been worth it.

He felt his body leaning and grasped the mane of the horse with his left hand, gripping hard, trying to keep himself in the saddle. Memories of the fight rushed through his mind unbidden. He was still amazed he had outlasted all the other knights. He heard a buzzing noise in his ears, but this was not the tranquil noise of the waterfalls at the palace of Kingfountain. No, this was an angry buzzing sound, like hornets. The idea of slumping out of the saddle and landing on the scrub felt tempting to him. How long before they'd notice? How long until he died?

Ransom pulled himself back up, fighting the urge to destroy himself. He would survive this nightmare. He would be free again.

The growing fever gave him nonsensical thoughts. He imagined Claire walking through the fields of Chessy arm in arm with James. "Poor Ransom," she said with a pitying smile. "We were friends as children. Only friends."

James nodded and smiled, all sympathy and fine wishes, but as soon as Claire looked away, the look in his eyes shifted to that of a wolf hunting its prey. Ransom wanted to scream in warning. He tried to run, to pull Claire away from him, but his leg couldn't support his weight, and he fell. Blood seeped from the wound. So much blood. He was dying, drop by drop.

No! I must tell her what happened. I have to warn her.

"How long has he been like this?"

A woman's voice.

"Two days now. He's dying."

DeVaux's voice.

Someone touched his leg, and he screamed. Pain was all he felt and knew.

"I'll call for a barber. Let the wound be treated."

It was the woman's voice again.

"No! No one leaves this castle. If any of your servants slip away, you'll regret it, my lady. If he dies, he dies. But I swear the lad is Fountain-blessed. A lance wound won't kill him. You'll see. He'll recover."

"Let me provide bandages at least."

"No! Give him broth to drink and a little bread. Tend to *my* wounded knights instead. They suffer as much as he does. He's cost me a lot of men. I'll see him ransomed, or I'll throw his corpse in a ditch. Either way suits me fine, but I suspect he'll live. The Fountain-blessed do not go down so easily. Do not trifle with me, my lady, while your kin is at Chessy field."

"You would break the oath of hospitality?" she asked him.

Who was she? Where were they?

Ransom realized he was lying on a pallet filled with old straw. Was this another dream conjured by his feverish mind? He twitched. From the throbbing burn, it felt like he'd already lost his leg.

"Who gives a carp about that?" DeVaux snorted. "I killed the constable! The king will come after me himself. None of the niceties of Virtus apply to me anymore, my lady. You'd best remember that."

"Let me tend to your men," she said.

Ransom tried to open his eyes. But it took him time to force his eyelids to part, and he only caught a fleeting glimpse of her as she left. DeVaux stood over him, sneering.

"Prove me wrong," he said slyly, gazing down at Ransom. "Either way, we'll know."

He fell into an uneasy sleep, full of twisted dreams. He dreamed of his father, the big man with the eye patch and thundering voice, mocking him for lying down when there was work to be done. Even in the dream state, he knew his father was dead, but the barbs still landed. He tried to rise and couldn't walk, only hobble, which earned scorn and derision from his father. They were at the Heath, and as soon as they went outside, a huge part of the castle sloughed away and crushed his father beneath the rubble right in front of Ransom's eyes.

"You killed Father!" said his brother Marcus accusingly.

The nightmare shifted. He saw Queen Emiloh riding away from the carnage only to be shot down by an archer concealed in the woods. He screamed, trying to run to her, but his leg didn't work, and he stumbled and crashed to the ground, weeping at the loss.

Then he saw Captain Baldwin in the training yard. "What's wrong with you, boy? It's just a little pain. Defend yourself. Again. Again!" The staff swung toward Ransom's head. Too slow to stop it, he dropped to the ground, and everything in his field of vision shattered like a huge mirror.

He heard voices and realized they were real, not part of the fever dream.

"Moldy bread, my lady?" said a gruff voice.

"It's all we have left," answered the lady. He recognized her voice as the one he'd heard before. "And a cup of broth."

"Let me see that," another man said. Ransom heard the sound of sniffing. "I thought you'd brought him some spirits to dull his pain. DeVaux would have our hides if you helped him."

"Only broth," assured the lady. "Taste it yourself."

"Turkey broth."

"Indeed. No more or less."

They were speaking in Occitanian. He wondered where they were, which castle. Then he felt pressure on the bedside and smelled the broth and the faint aroma of lilac. He tried to open his eyes, but the lids were too heavy.

He felt her hand reach behind his neck and lift him up. He twitched from the softness of her touch.

"Here, can you hold this?" she whispered, bringing the cup to his lips. The smell of it made him ravenous with hunger.

He tried to ask who she was, but he couldn't speak. With the first splash of broth on his tongue, he was eager to gulp the rest of it down.

"Slowly. Shhh . . . slowly. You'll choke on it."

"He can feed himself," said one of the knights in a resentful tone. "Be gone, my lady. He's an enemy."

He felt her hand on his forehead. "I'm sorry," she whispered. "It's all I can do."

"Go on now," complained the knight.

He felt her leave, taking the smell of lilac with her. Again he tried to open his eyes. Again he failed. Grunting, he propped himself up on his elbow, holding the cup of broth she'd given him. He took another deep swallow and then drained the cup.

"She's a fair thing," mumbled one of the knights.

"Stop your lusting," said his companion. "DeVaux said not to touch any of them unless they disobey him. He'll want her for himself. I'm hungry. Go get me some food."

"What, you don't want that hunk of moldy bread?"

"No, you sod! Get us something good. Let the cripple have the bread."

The other man left, his steps echoing down the stone corridor.

Ransom didn't care that it was moldy. They'd hardly wasted provisions on their wounded prisoner, expecting him to die. He rubbed his eyes and got them to open at last. A small loaf of bread speckled with mold lay at the edge of his pallet, left there by the lady of the castle.

He wished he'd saved some of the broth to make it go down more easily. Ransom lifted the bread to his mouth and took a large bite from it. The crust was stale, and it had an unpleasant odor, but he chewed a little bit before looking down.

The inside of the loaf had been hollowed out. He stared in surprise. Strips of linen had been rolled up and stuffed inside, concealed in the bread itself. He blinked, unable to understand the new feeling that began to seep into his chest.

The lady of the castle had shown him compassion despite knowing she risked herself and those she protected.

The knight leaning against the wall stared at him, arms folded. "Enjoying your bread?"

Ransom wanted to punch him, but he shrugged instead. "Anything tastes good when you're starving."

The knight laughed. "If you say so."

"Where are we?" Ransom asked, grateful his dizziness had abated after drinking the broth. His appetite had only been teased so far.

"You think I'll tell you?" said the knight. "You've no right to know. What if you live, eh?" His look was dark. "But I don't think you're one of the blessed. DeVaux is wrong about you. I've bet ten livres on it. You'll be dead in three days. Maybe four. And you deserve it. You killed my friend." His eyes flashed with hatred. "I hope you rot and then die. Painfully."

He wasn't the first man who had wished Ransom would die. Nor would he be the last.

Ransom looked down at his wrist and found the bracelet was gone. One of his captors had stolen it from him in his delirium. The rage that filled the emptiness in his chest nearly made him start screaming accusations. It had been given to him by Claire. He wanted it back, and in that moment, he would have killed any of them to get it. The violence of his thoughts alarmed him. He was still sick, still weak. He couldn't hurt anyone. But he wanted to. He wanted to make them suffer.

Instead, he chewed on another piece of moldy bread, breathing in and out through his nose to stifle his fury. And when the other knight returned with a platter of cold meat, a wedge of cheese, and some goblets of wine, the two men sat on the floor and began to eat in front of him. Ransom turned over on the cot so that his back was to them, removed the linen from the bread. A thought struck him that perhaps the bread might help soak up some of the blood. He unfastened the bloody bandage before pressing the bread against the wound.

The lady of the castle had helped him. Knowing that secret helped him endure the agony he caused himself. He would guard her secret. As he tied the strips of linen over his wounds, he thanked her repeatedly in his mind.

He promised himself he would find a way to thank her for her kindness.

Every day I keep hoping for word, but I've heard naught but silence. It has been three months since the tournament of Chessy, and still no one knows if Ransom survived the slaughter on the road to Auxaunce. Not knowing is frightful, yet at least it allows me to hope. All the knights that Queen Emiloh brought with her were slain. Even Lord Rakestraw was slain. Peasant farmers said that one man fought against a hundred. That he was pierced by a lance from behind a hedge and taken by DeVaux.

That is all we know. Did they dump his body in the woods? What has become of him? Nothing. We know nothing. Silent, cruel, menacing nothing. Da has left for Atha Kleah to hold the courts of justice again before winter. The thought of winter coming adds to my torment. What have they done to my Ransom? And how will he survive the coming cold, if he has survived at all? I'm weeping again. How I hate to cry.

—*Claire de Murrow*
Connaught Castle, Kingdom of Legault

CHAPTER FIFTEEN

The Price of a Knight

There was a single leaf clinging to the branches of the tree. Ransom watched it, his back against the crooked trunk, wondering when it would fall. He didn't want it to. The stubbornness of the stem clinging to the twig gave him a small measure of hope. The woods were carpeted with fallen debris from the trees. A tattered cloak covered his shoulders, but it did little to warm him. Cold and hunger were his constant companions these many months.

"You try and do better," snorted Callum.

Ransom knew all their names now. He knew the moods of his guards, their temperaments. In a strange way, he was part of DeVaux's mesnie, even though he was a prisoner. He took a turn feeding the fire, which kept them all warm at night, but it would have been impossible to escape, given that multiple guards were always on duty and his leg still troubled him. Not that he would have tried to run. When a knight was being held for ransom, it was considered dishonorable to attempt an escape. And so he stayed.

He talked with the other men, bantered with them, and shared their cup of misery, which they'd all drunk from since the day they'd unwittingly murdered Lord Rakestraw.

Callum, Brett, Jonah, and Riley had come upon the notion that hurling a boulder would be a pleasant way to spend a cold afternoon. One by one, they'd hefted the massive rock, which was about the size of a miller's bag of wheat. And they'd thrown it down the hillside, seeing how far it would roll before resting. Then two men would fetch it and bring it back. So far, Riley held the record.

"I can do better than you," Jonah told another man with a snort.

"But you can't do better than Riley. His went the farthest." A dagger had been stuck tip-down to mark the spot.

Jonah brushed his hands together and swaggered to the stump. They were all of them filthy, having spent the summer and early autumn skulking in the woods, avoiding capture and threatening manors and castles alike for food and temporary shelter. The king's men had come close to them more than once, and only DeVaux's perverse luck had saved them from capture. If Ransom had had any coins, he would have cast them with his prayers into the streams of water they passed. But he had nothing of value. They'd taken everything away.

Jonah screwed up his face as they handed him the heavy stone. He stared at the mark, his eyes full of fire. Ransom rubbed his mouth, feeling the tangled beard on his jaw. His locks were speckled with bits of soot and flecks of dead leaves. He wondered if his hands would ever become clean again. But he watched the contest with amusement and secretly hoped that Jonah would best them all. He was the closest in age to Ransom, the one who'd served DeVaux for the fewest years. The others made grunting noises to try to distract him, which elicited a scowl from the flaxen-haired knight.

With a mighty heave, Jonah let the boulder fly. It landed with a thump and didn't roll at all. It was the worst of the throws and was met with derisive laughter. Jonah muttered a curse and kicked at the log.

"Don't kick it," Riley shouted. "You moved the stump, man!"

"Who cares?" Brett said with a surly frown. "We've all tried. You won. Get your coins."

No one liked to lose. Ransom had watched them bet on everything they could—throwing knives, the loudest whistle, the strongest arm. They were bored, hating the exile as much as Ransom did, and had grown petulant, even with one another.

Ransom looked up to discover the single leaf had fallen while he'd watched the contest. It caused a stab of pain in his heart to have missed such a simple scene. He'd hoped that leaf would last longer. How he felt like a withered leaf some days.

"What about Ransom? I bet he could beat your throw."

The comment from Jonah snagged his attention away from the barren tree.

"Don't be daft, he's still limping," Riley said, but he sounded concerned.

"So? You afraid of losing your winnings?" Brett added.

"I'm not afraid of him," Riley said, chuckling. "It just doesn't seem fair since he can't bet anything."

"Come on," Callum said. "It's for us to bet on. I'd risk another five livres he can beat you."

"Five livres?" Riley said, chuffing. "I'll take it. Who else is eager to lose their coins?"

"I'll bet three," Jonah said.

"It's five or nothing," Riley countered. "Are you a man or a weasel?"

"Shut it!" Jonah said with fury. "I'll bet five."

Soon they'd all agreed on the increased stakes. Riley tromped over to Ransom and cocked his head. "You up for it? I'd like to see you lose."

"Come on," Brett said encouragingly. "I'll give you my meat ration if you best him!"

They were all looking at him now, their gazes intense.

Ransom stood, and although it was painful, he exaggerated his discomfort with a pronounced wince to heighten the tension.

"He'll do it! He'll do it!" Jonah said, clapping Callum on the back.

Ransom brushed his hands together. "What do I get if I throw it farther?"

"You really think you can?" Riley challenged.

Ransom shrugged. "Hardly seems fair that I should get nothing."

"You want a share of the winnings?" Callum said, laughing.

Ransom shook his head. "No. I want my bracelet back." He looked at Riley, the one who had taken it from him and still wore it.

Riley's eyes darkened with emotion. Was it guilt or greed? Ransom had never asked for it back. He'd not said a word about the things they'd taken from him.

"Oooh," Callum said, clapping his hands. "This will be good! Come on, Riley. The boy wants his bracelet back. Wager it! Come on! Wager it! Are you a weasel?"

The others joined in, and Riley's eyes darkened more. "It means nothing to me," he said, but his look belied his words. "Throw the stone, *boy*."

Ransom was hardly a boy, but he took the insult without reaction and began to hobble to the fallen log they'd used to mark the starting point. Jonah grinned and clapped again before he joined Brett in fetching the boulder. Ransom limped up to the edge of the fallen log, but Riley kicked it with his foot, scooting it back.

Neither of them commented on it.

Jonah and Brett grimaced as they hefted the boulder back up the hill and brought it to Ransom, who stood on the other side of the log. They deposited the boulder into his arms, and the weight of it made his muscles strain immediately.

"You can do it!" Jonah encouraged, thumping him on the back. He nearly toppled over.

"He can't. He's wounded still," Riley said, folding his arms. He looked self-assured, but Ransom saw a trickle of sweat go down his cheek.

Ransom let out a deep breath, knowing his strength would ebb further each moment he held the stone. His strength had never fully returned since his capture, for he had no sword to train with. They'd taken away his hauberk and never returned it, leaving him vulnerable to attack. His muscles coiled as he prepared to heave the stone, but he sank into himself first, trying to find that spark of will. The hollow well was nearly empty still, but he could sense the ripple of water far down. He thought of Claire, just as he did every night before falling asleep. And with that thought, he felt a prickle of awareness and heard the gentle lapping of waters, even though there was no stream save the one at the bottom of the hill.

Ransom gritted his teeth as he threw the boulder with all his might. He put his whole body behind it and watched as it shot from his arms, earning a gasp or two from his fellows. The strain released, and he bent over, hands on his knees, as he watched the boulder sail. It hit the ground at a slant and began to roll. As it rolled, it picked up speed.

"Look! Look! He's doing it!" shouted Brett with glee.

The boulder went straight toward the dagger and knocked it over as it rolled farther down the incline before coming to rest. Pain shot up Ransom's wounded leg. He fell down in agony, knowing he'd reinjured himself. He was promptly surrounded by guffaws and laughter.

Although he relished the acclaim, the throbs grew unbearable, and he looked at his pants, his filthy, stained pants, expecting to see them welling up with crimson again.

"Good work, eh?" Jonah said. "Look at that! Farthest yet. Come on, Riley! Can you beat it? Can you?"

In a few moments, it became clear Riley could not. His last throw was his final attempt to beat his own record and Ransom's. And when the boulder fell short of his previous attempt, the guffaws increased, and soon coins were changing hands. Riley's purse was nearly emptied from his loss.

Ransom watched him unhook the braided bracelet. He tromped up to Ransom and held it out. "It's yours again," he said.

Taking it back, Ransom stared at it for a moment before looking at Riley's face. There was no anger there. He'd lost, but it had been his own fault.

"Thank you," Ransom said. When he was first captured, he had assumed they were all evil because of what they'd done to Lord Rakestraw's men. But he had realized they saw him the same way. He had killed many of their friends, right in front of them. He realized now that DeVaux's men were like any others, like him, even—it was a man's loyalties that determined his actions.

It made him all the more determined to serve a worthy lord.

Despite the sizzling pain in his leg, Ransom put on the bracelet and rubbed his chafed fingers against the pattern. The attempt had been worth it.

The sound of horses could be heard, and when they turned, they saw DeVaux and his other knights coming up the hill. There were only sixteen knights left. The others had died or slipped away during watch, but these sixteen owed everything to DeVaux and had tied their fortunes to him. To prevent more defections, DeVaux made them stay in companies of four, which he changed up every fortnight.

DeVaux rode to their makeshift camp on the hilltop, his breathing hard.

"What news, my lord?" Jonah asked.

DeVaux's expression was always difficult to read. He was good at keeping his thoughts to himself. But Ransom saw the other knights were grinning. It was good news for them, although he wasn't sure what that might mean for him.

With a sniff and a cunning smile, DeVaux turned and looked at the other four who had been left to guard Ransom. "It's over. We've been pardoned."

"What!" exclaimed Riley. The knights all let out a cheer.

"You mean . . . we can go back?"

"Yes, that's exactly what I mean. Full pardons, to all of us. There will be no retribution. I have the promise written here with the king's own seal." He reached into his belt and removed a scroll, which he wagged at them.

"I can't believe it," Jonah said, beaming. "He quit? He gave up?"

"A pardon isn't forgiveness," DeVaux said slyly. "I bear no illusions about that. But clearly the king has deeper problems than us. He's named his second son, Benedict, Duke of Vexin. A boy of fifteen!" He chortled. "With this pardon comes a truce for two years. I gladly took it."

Ransom's mind whirled with thoughts. He wanted to know whether he was still a prisoner. Would he be spending the winter in DeVaux's castle in a dungeon? It was better than sleeping in the woods during winter, but not by much.

"A stripling," said a knight who had accompanied DeVaux. "The prince will be no match for Lord DeVaux."

DeVaux gave a magnanimous shrug. "I will soon disabuse the prince of any notion that he can rule the duchy as he sees fit. Rest assured. We ride back to my castle, where we will feast and drink and"—he wagged a finger in the air—"keep watch on the walls in case this is a trick. But I doubt it. The king is sending someone to finalize the truce. He'll be at our castle tomorrow."

"Who?" asked Brett.

"Lord Kinghorn of Averanche. He's coming to pay the ransom."

The looks on their faces showed surprise. DeVaux would be paid for committing such treachery?

But the name made Ransom finally breathe again. A breath of relief.

DeVaux Valley was known for its grapes and for some of the best wines in the region. Not even the king, in his wrath, had torched the vineyards, for they brought much tribute and profit to the coffers of Kingfountain. DeVaux's castle, Roque Keep, was a simple one that had been built centuries before, with low mountains on the north and the south, meaning it could only be approached from the east or west. It was far enough away from Auxaunce to provide ample warning should riders come bearing arms.

When they arrived at Roque, Ransom was given new clothes, a much-needed bath, and a barber to attend to his hair, beard, and his scabs. The barber was surprised that his wound had healed so well and had not become infected. In fact, he said it was a miracle from the Fountain that Ransom was walking at all, even with a limp.

They didn't put Ransom in the dungeon, instead allowing him to enjoy the feast that had been prepared for Lord DeVaux's return. The joyful atmosphere surprised Ransom—the people were overjoyed to see their cunning lord again, and the affection with which Lady DeVaux greeted her husband in the great hall indicated his family loved him too. Why was such a duplicitous man so revered?

Ransom consumed the food with relish, savoring the fruits and vegetables more than the spicy meats, since meat was predominantly what they'd had during their wanderings. He still had no idea where their travels had taken them, although he suspected they'd left the borders of Vexin at the beginning. Nor did he know which lady had shown him compassion in a hollow loaf of moldy bread. During the feast, he tried to press Jonah and Brett for information, but they were too engrossed in the revelry to remember details, and neither man supplied what he wanted to know.

He slept that night on a pallet in the great hall along with the other knights. Dogs still rooted for food through the evening, and Ransom felt the flutterings of anticipation in his stomach. Ransom wondered whether his suit of armor was still with his blacksmith friend Anders in

Chessy, or if they'd taken it to Tatton Grange as promised. Replacing a hauberk was much easier than getting a new suit of armor.

The thought of returning to Averanche was a pleasing one. After his misadventures, he looked forward to being in the training yard again. Perhaps he'd even be called upon to help train a new generation of warriors.

Sleep came slowly, his mind too awake from the strange sounds coming from the castle. For months, he'd been lulled to sleep by the sounds of the wood and the crooning of night birds. Instead, he heard the distant clang of pans, the crunch of feet on floor rushes, and the garbled voices of cooks and servants cleaning up.

It wasn't until all fell quiet, well after midnight, that Ransom finally dozed off.

When he awoke, preparations for the guests were already underway. Ransom paced in the hall, trying to see if the pain in his leg would subside. He stroked the bracelet around his wrist, anxious to send word to Lady Claire and let her know he was well. Had she worried about him, or did she think he was dead? How would she take the news, he wondered?

With all the food he'd devoured the night before, he wasn't hungry yet, and his raw nerves made him even less so. After so many months of captivity, the wait for Lord Kinghorn was positively excruciating. He wanted to bend the knee, even his painful one, and swear allegiance to the lord.

Word finally arrived that the banners of Averanche could be seen coming up the road, and Ransom was summoned by Lord DeVaux to meet the riders in the bailey. His hands were sweating. He stood by Lord DeVaux, hating even the smell of the man. He listened with anticipation for the riders to enter, but they all stopped outside the gate, save one who rode forward leading a second horse.

Ransom squinted, trying to tell who it was. The size and bulk of the armored warrior gave him away. It was Captain Baldwin. The chain-mail hood concealed most of his features, but Ransom recognized his beard, which now had a few more streaks of gray in it. He looked displeased, even resentful, as he rode into the yard. The other knights remained outside. Ransom thought he caught a glimpse of Lord Kinghorn, although it wasn't possible to be sure at that distance.

"Welcome to Roque Keep, honored knight," said Lord DeVaux. "You have hospitality here. Bid your companions enter and rest from their journey."

"I have been instructed to decline your offer, Lord DeVaux." He looked down at Ransom impassively. Then he nodded. "I was chosen because I know Lord Barton's son."

"You anticipated trickery?" Lord DeVaux said, bristling with anger.

Baldwin said nothing in response to that question. "Can you ride, boy?" It was said in a dismissive tone. Ransom's heart began to wilt.

"Yes," he said.

"Mount up, then," Baldwin said, dropping the reins of the horse he'd guided in.

"What of the payment?" Lord DeVaux demanded. "Five thousand livres."

Ransom stared at him in shock. It was an exorbitant amount. His stomach shriveled at the thought of it.

"Half of it is in these saddlebags," Baldwin said. He leaned down and patted one of them, and the jingle of coins could be heard. "We leave them here. The other half comes once we are allowed to depart in peace."

"You dare suspect my honor?" DeVaux demanded hotly.

The captain shrugged. "Whether or not you *have* any, I don't know. But I know Lord Kinghorn does, and I know the rest of the ransom is waiting outside the castle."

"I will not forget this insult," Lord DeVaux said with a snarl.

"I don't really care," Baldwin replied. "I serve the constable of Westmarch. Maybe I should thank you for killing the previous one."

His eyes narrowed with suppressed anger. He looked ready to fight every knight assembled in the courtyard.

"Leave the coins. He may go free. I will honor the terms of the truce."

Baldwin glared at him. "I'm sure you will. Come on, boy." He didn't take his eyes off DeVaux.

Ransom eagerly complied, trying to conceal his limp as he walked. He failed at his first attempt to mount the horse, feeling a blush of shame burn his ears, but he managed it on the second try. Baldwin unhooked the buckles securing the saddlebags, and they dropped with a clinking thud to the stone floor. He looked over at Ransom and gestured for him to do the same, which he did. Lord DeVaux's eyes glittered with greed.

Baldwin nudged his destrier, and they began to back up toward the gate, the captain's eyes still fixed on DeVaux. Ransom knew the man well enough by now to believe he would not break the truce, so he turned his own horse around before following Baldwin out at a slow clop. Once they were beyond the gate, Baldwin finally gave the lord his back and gestured to two of the knights waiting for them. Ransom recognized the men from his time in Averanche and couldn't suppress a smile as they rode forward and dropped their saddlebags in front of the gate.

The wind was brisk and cold. Ransom was grateful for the cloak they'd given him in the castle, but he longed to have a sword again, to feel the protection of armor.

Five thousand livres. It was more than all the winnings Ransom had earned in his time at Chessy. Even if he wanted to pay it back, he couldn't. Dumbfounded by the situation, he rode toward Lord Kinghorn, who was still a little distance away.

"Sorry for calling you 'boy' back there," Baldwin said after coming up alongside him. "We weren't even sure you were still alive."

"I'm . . . I'm surprised that I am," Ransom said. "I'm so grateful."

"Oh, you should be," Baldwin said with a chuckle.

"Where's my armor?"

"Lord Rakestraw had one of his pages collect it months ago. It's waiting for you."

"Oh," Ransom said. "That's good to know. I am so grateful Lord Kinghorn ransomed me. I will make it up to him. I swear it."

Baldwin laughed again. "No, lad. No, you won't. He's not the one who bought your freedom."

Ransom turned and looked at Baldwin, feeling strange emotions churn in his stomach. His eyes were pleading as he stared at the captain.

Baldwin smiled at him. "The queen did. You're going to Kingfountain."

X

He is found! That wicked man Lord DeVaux of the Vexin has released poor Ransom. Da told me it cost five thousand livres to secure his release. While not a princely sum, it is still outrageous. DeVaux, the foul-smelling turtle, said his captive was Fountain-blessed, of all the nonsense. Well, however much I hate him, he has more brains than a badger, for he got his coin and also a two-year truce. From what I know of the new Duke of Vexin, Benedict is an ambitious youth with not a care for the code of Virtus esteemed by so many knights in Kingfountain. He will bring vengeance to DeVaux's valley when the truce runs out, or, if he's clever, find ways to trick DeVaux into breaking it. That's what I would do.

It seems the faeries of the Beneath have conspired to increase my happiness further. Da has said we will be traveling shortly to Kingfountain, where I might behold my friend at long last. To what purpose, might you ask? Why, there is to be a new King Devon. The son, not the sire. With all the mischief whirling around Ceredigion, King Devon the Elder

will retain his rights to rule Westmarch and crown his son,
Devon the Younger, as coruler of the vast kingdom. The only
question that remains is which man will wear the hollow
crown, for both will be kings.

—*Claire de Murrow*
(preparing to voyage, returning to Kingfountain)

CHAPTER SIXTEEN

Loyalty

Ransom had never been to Tatton Grange before, the hereditary seat of the duchy of Westmarch. It was situated in a lush farming valley that grew fields of wheat, barley, rye, and dozens of other grains, which were milled in stone huts guarded day and night by the soldiers in the duchy's massive army. Tatton Grange was a stone building that looked more like a sanctuary of Our Lady than it did a castle, with a sloping shingled roof and arrow slits instead of windows. The high walls were supported by buttresses, and the main door was twice the height of a man.

Ransom had been surprised to see how many people lived throughout the valley, with its pens full of cattle, work horses, and sundry livestock. Clusters of trees stood out within the pastures, but truly he could see for leagues in every direction, or at least until the distant hills blocked the view.

Upon arriving at Tatton Grange, Ransom was sent to the armory, where he was fitted with a chain hauberk from a vast store of them. Spears and swords lined the walls, along with an assortment of battle axes.

"You need a sword too?" asked the armorer serving him.

"A bastard sword if you have one," Ransom asked, his keen eye looking at the assortment of weapons.

"You prefer Occitanian weapons, then," said the man, rubbing his hands together. "Let me see . . . let me see . . . ah!" He went over to a pile of swords, reaching for one that was taller than its brethren. "This ought to do! And it already has a scabbard. Let me find a belt, and you can be on your way to your meeting with Lord Kinghorn."

Ransom took it, and as soon as his hand closed around the hilt, he felt a gentle thrumming begin to fill the emptiness inside. He closed his eyes, breathing it in. He drew the blade, which was speckled with stains and had a few nicks in it. It was battle tested.

When Ransom approached the open door to Lord Kinghorn's chamber, he found the man coughing into his fist. It was a scene he'd witnessed many times in the past, and he felt a measure of sorrow for the new constable. This environment was surely not one he'd have chosen.

"Come in," Lord Kinghorn said after the spasm ebbed.

Ransom stood at attention, his heart ripe with gratitude still. Lord Kinghorn took a drink of water. The table before him was overloaded with books, but there weren't yet shelves on the wall to contain them. He waited in silence until the coughing fit ended.

"How do you fare, my lord?" Ransom asked.

"As well as can be after riding so far. I was expecting an ambush, but we were prepared for one. Poor Rakestraw. He was a good man."

Ransom nodded, feeling morose again.

"You will ride on to Kingfountain, Marshall. The queen is expecting you. I will be joining shortly thereafter for the coronation."

The words startled Ransom. "M-my lord?"

Lord Kinghorn smiled. "You've been a prisoner for many months, so of course you don't know the news. Devon Argentine has been beset by difficulties ever since he took the hollow crown. One problem ends only for another to spring up. The kingship is his by right, yet he is either very unlucky or there is a deliberate attempt to undermine him."

Ransom looked at him with trepidation. "Who?"

"Who else?" said Lord Kinghorn with a steely gaze. "King Lewis has always considered these lands to be his."

"Westmarch?"

"Aye, and more. Brythonica, the Vexin. There is a history of invasions between our realms that goes back to the age of the Wizrs, I should think. Long has Lewis coveted the hollow crown, as did his father and his father before him. During the civil war, Lewis offered Devon Argentine money and troops to fuel the conflict. I think he hoped both sides would cripple each other enough that he could swoop in and win. But his machinations worked against him, and now King Devon's too powerful for Lewis to attack directly, lest he risk losing more land. And so he continues to push at him in subtle ways, funding this person and that, inciting trouble where he can. Our king is tired of constantly defending his territory. He intends to bring the fight to Lewis himself."

"How will he do that?"

"By showing King Lewis that he is not to be trifled with." Another bout of coughing seized him, stalling the conversation. After it calmed again, he continued. "King Devon is returning here, to his ancestral duchy. And he's bringing his army with him to support his interests here and make a statement to Lewis's nobles. He's decided to crown his son, Devon the Younger, as King of Ceredigion. But not the boy's queen. Noemie will be crowned later."

Ransom's eyes widened. "She's the Black Prince's sister."

Lord Kinghorn nodded. "Yes. But we still have a queen. Queen Emiloh."

Ransom winced. "The Occitanians will take it as an affront, my lord."

"The king does it deliberately. It's his way of telling Lewis that he knows he's interfering in our affairs. It's an open provocation, a challenge. Lewis believes that he will win Ceredigion through marriage alliances. Princes Devon and Bennett both have marriage alliances. Goff's is Brythonican, which again strengthens our position. The king's youngest son will be given to Glosstyr's daughter, the heiress of Legault."

The words punched Ransom in the chest. He blinked, felt his throat struggle to swallow.

Lord Kinghorn noticed. "What's wrong?"

"N-nothing, my lord," Ransom said, trying to find his breath, "but the boy can be no more than twelve."

"He won't always be so young," said Lord Kinghorn with a wry smile. "A promise is all that is needed to position for power. The Duke of North Cumbria has been trying to arrange a match between Lady Claire and his son, but that would give North Cumbria too much power."

Ransom felt sick inside. Still, he knew better than to say anything about his feelings for Lady Claire, especially when it was Devon's wife who'd funded his release. He tried to compose his face, but he feared his emotions were clear for Lord Kinghorn to see. The man was studying him closely.

"You are to report to the queen at Kingfountain," Lord Kinghorn said. "You may stop by the Heath and see your kin. In fact, I ask that you do so since you ignored my advice last time, and you will invite your brother and the rest of your family to court to attend the coronation. All of this will happen before winter." He gave Ransom a wolflike smile. "So that King Lewis and the Black Prince may spend the winter pondering and worrying about what they might expect come spring."

It was a threat of war.

"Before I go, my lord, may I ask you a question?"

"Of course you may. Go on."

"You are the most well-read man I know." Ransom swallowed. "While I was a hostage to DeVaux, he claimed that I was Fountain-blessed."

"He did. It is what made the cost of the ransom so high."

"My lord . . . am I?"

Lord Kinghorn gave him a serious look. "I don't know, Marshall. Whether it was a ploy DeVaux used to extort more livres from the queen, I couldn't say. When her knights from Auxaunce arrived on the scene, she feared all of you had been slain. But there were farmers who'd watched the battle from a distance. Men who knew DeVaux and feared him. They spoke of two knights who stood back-to-back, protecting the road and preventing DeVaux's men from going after the queen. One of those knights was struck down and killed. Sir William Chappell. I knew him." His voice trailed off, his gaze intense. "The other was struck down from behind, his leg pierced through with a lance. He was carried off. That was you." He rubbed his palms together. "I don't know anyone who could have survived what you did. They say it is very difficult to kill someone who is Fountain-blessed."

"Difficult but not impossible. What else do the legends say? I've read them too, but I've not read as much as you."

Lord Kinghorn sighed. "That is the problem with legends, Marshall. There are many stories of Wizrs and knights and magic swords. But how are we to know which of them are true and which are merely stories?"

"I suppose we cannot," Ransom said.

The constable made a sound of agreement. "In the legends, knights would leave court to seek one of the shrines of the Fountain. They would kneel in prayer and offer to serve the Fountain. If the offer was accepted, a relic of some sort would appear in the water. Some drew swords out of the water. Others would be given a gauntlet or a ring. That token was a sign that they were Fountain-blessed. And when it happened, you can be assured that every other knight in the realm would seek to challenge them to take what they'd been given. The blessing could be quite a curse. So would a wise knight ever reveal that he was Fountain-blessed? You tell me."

Ransom considered what Lord Kinghorn had said, but he hadn't survived because of magic—he'd lived because a lady had concealed fresh linen in moldy bread. True, he did have an unusual amount of success in combat, but he still wasn't sure what it meant—or even what he wanted it to.

He had yet to forget the way Lord Kinghorn had looked at him after that day at the barn or the way Lord DeVaux's men had treated him.

Maybe it didn't matter. Either way, he would serve the queen as best he could.

"But I'll tell you this." He looked at Ransom with serious eyes. "I've tried it. I've made it a point to visit as many sanctuaries as I can during my travels. At each one, I have made the same plea." He fell silent. "Nothing has ever shimmered in the waters for me to take. Not once over many years. Nor have I ever known another knight who found something."

"Thank you, my lord. With your leave, I'll be on my way home."

$$\text{Ж}$$

The stable master had given Ransom a rouncy for his mount and a mule to bear his armor and supplies. During the ride eastward, his mind was plagued by all the information Lord Kinghorn had given him. The sick feeling in his stomach hadn't abated. As he rode, he cursed himself for being a fool, for daring to hope that he might be allowed to court Lady Claire. Her bracelet was still coiled around his wrist, adding to his misery. He had no doubt that Claire and her father would both be at the coronation. Would they be able to talk? Could he dare to tell her what he knew? Should he? Or perhaps she already knew herself.

As he traveled the roads of Ceredigion a free man, he felt himself growing stronger, the ache in his leg ebbing. He'd endured a great hardship, one he would never forget. He felt he owed the Queen of Ceredigion everything for paying for his release. He would serve her until his dying day in the hopes of returning the kindness she'd done to him. His feelings about King Devon were more mottled, however. He was still the man who'd upset King Gervase, and now he was attempting to match his youngest son with Claire. In truth, it chafed to see a father provide so well for his sons—a feeling that only worsened the closer he got to the Heath.

He arrived after nightfall, having decided to save his coins rather than rent a room at an inn. The road home was familiar, and he recalled the ghost of Sir William at the crossroads, his heart burdened by the loss of his old friend.

Guiding his horse down the road, he approached the castle. It had the same general shape as DeVaux's castle, and the sight of it looming in the distance sent a rush of dread down his spine. It did not feel like home. It never had.

As he approached the gate, he was met by the porter.

"Your mount looks weary, Sir Knight," said the porter, a man Ransom didn't recognize. "As do you. Have you come seeking shelter?"

Ransom looked down at him, feeling a pang of disappointment for not being recognized. Again. "I've come to see my mother. Would you tell her that Marshall is here?"

The porter's eyes bugged. "Bless me! I didn't know! Of course. Come in. Come in straightaway!"

Lads from the stable came to attend to his horses as he dismounted. He felt weary, exhausted, and his leg pained him as he walked into the hall.

His sister, Maeg, reached him first, before he even stepped inside. He couldn't believe how tall she was or the violence of her affection as she leaped at him, weeping and smiling and hugging him tightly. The last time they'd met, he'd been a stranger, or near enough. But no doubt news had reached them about his life since he'd been away. Lady Sibyl, his mother, emerged from the lit interior of the castle then, looking older and more careworn than he remembered. She embraced him as well, and his heart was fit to burst when he felt her tears on his neck.

"You're home," sighed Maeg, hugging him again, her embrace even tighter this time. "You finally came home!"

He felt his mother's grip loosen. She pulled back, caressing his face. "We thought you were dead. We feared the worst."

"I put a coin in the fountain every day," said Maeg, stifling her sobs. "Every day."

He had tears in his eyes, but he brushed them away. And then he saw his brother, standing in the doorway, watching the scene. Ransom swallowed, trying to compose himself. He knew not what to expect.

His sister and mother peeled back from him.

And then his brother grasped him in a bear hug that took his breath away. "Welcome home, Brother!" he whispered, squeezing hard. He stepped back, grasping Ransom's shoulders. His lips quivered. And they remained that way for a moment, holding each other, unable to speak.

I've not been to Kingfountain since I was but a lass, yet it has not changed. I'm not sure it ever will. Picture, in your mind, a castle on a windswept wooded hill. There are levels of walls around it, from the base of the hill to the crest, rings of stone defenses that have held off invaders. Add in a river of rushing water, surging and violent, that ends in a waterfall that is both noisy and ferocious. To these pictures, add another: an island astride this formidable river with a sanctuary as old as the legends of the Fountain itself. I think it was built by the Aos Sí, for no mortal could ever construct something so grand. On each side of the river, imagine a town that has grown upward where it cannot grow wide, with thatch roofs, timbers, plaster, and flowerbeds nailed outside windows. Next, add in the merchants lining both sides of the street, offering their wares of sizzling sausages, crumble pies, and honeyed wafers so sticky that even the bees are deceived.

That is the scene that awaited us as we rode into Kingfountain in preparation for the coronation of Devon the Younger. When we arrived at the palace, no less than three knights approached us and swore lifelong fidelity to me if I would but grant them a nod, a wink, even the promise of a kiss. Thankfully, the knights of Glosstyr aren't so dramatic.

Sir James didn't try such foolishness with me. In fact, he was appropriately aloof, which was surprising, yet pleasing.

The palace is the place of dreams. Yet where is he? I've yet to catch sight of Ransom.

—Claire de Murrow
Kingdom of Ceredigion, Palace of Kingfountain

CHAPTER SEVENTEEN

The Fount of Blessings

A wooden palisade had been built behind the castle of the Heath to hold the stockyard animals that provided food and milk for the inhabitants. Ransom leaned against the wooden posts, listening to the lowing of the cattle and smelling the offal. He saw an orchard of peach trees, but it was too late in the season for any fruit, although his mother had said there were jars preserved in the cool storage rooms beneath the castle.

The evening before, he had sat in front of the blazing hearth with his family and told them stories about his life. Training in Averanche with his mother's cousin, Lord Kinghorn. Fighting the Brugians. Competing in the tournaments at Chessy. But the tale they were most interested in was that of his capture and confinement with DeVaux's men. They were all shocked to hear how much the queen had paid for his release.

"Five thousand livres," his brother had whispered in awe. "Our lands don't produce that much in five years."

His brother had three knights in service, and they'd all listened to Ransom's stories along with the members of his family. As a mesnie, it was very humble, and it confirmed Ransom's decision not to return home to seek help, although at the time he'd stayed away because he'd feared his brother would not *want* to assist him.

His sister, Maeg, stood near him now, staring at the beasts. "I'm grateful you came home, Marshall. I feel as though I know you much better now."

He smiled, giving her a tender look. "I wasn't sure whether I'd be welcome. The last time I came . . . I was only too grateful to leave."

"Father was a hard man," Maeg said. "He always worried about whether there'd be enough. Enough food. Enough protection. Enough livres. He fretted and worried his whole life, trying to protect us."

Ransom didn't talk about his childhood memory of being offered as a human sacrifice to King Gervase. It still ached, but he didn't wish to burden his sister.

"Was it painful when Father died?" Ransom asked Maeg.

"Of course," she said, frowning. "When they brought his body back, I couldn't believe it was him. I don't think I ever saw him sit still for very long. I kept expecting his corpse to jump up and get back to work on the castle." She shook her head, and her dark hair flashed in the autumn light. "He was a harsh man. An unfriendly one. We put his body on a bed of rushes and sent it floating onto the pond. No one came, it was just Mother and me and Sir Kace, who had brought the body back. No one wept, although we felt miserable. The Deep Fathoms didn't claim him. The wolves did."

The thought made Ransom's stomach clench. "He left a dowry for you, though?"

"Two hundred livres for both of us," she said. "It isn't much, but it is better than pigs or cows."

"I should hope so. Are there any young knights that you fancy, Sister?"

She gave him a wary look. "Mother keeps asking, but I don't dare tell her."

"Thankfully, I am not your mother," Ransom quipped.

"Sir Kace," she said with a sigh, resting her head on her arms while leaning against the barrier. "He's always been so kind to me. So thoughtful. But he's bashful by nature. He would never have dared to ask Father for my hand."

"You are young still," Ransom said. "Give him time."

"What about you?" She turned, grinning at him. "Is there a fair lady who has won your heart?"

Ransom looked down at his braided bracelet. "Perhaps."

"Perhaps? This sounds interesting. What is her name? Is she Occitanian?"

"No."

Her eyes dancing, she tugged on his arm. "Tell me."

As he looked at his sister, it struck him that she was only a few years older than the age Claire had been when they'd left Kingfountain. Part of him wanted to reveal his heart to her, but he didn't want to sound like a fool.

He knew Claire de Murrow was not for the likes of him.

Before arriving at the palace, Ransom had stopped in one of the villages on the outskirts and paid a blacksmith to help him don his armor. He didn't wear his helmet because he wanted to feast on the sights and smells of the palace city.

As he rode into Kingfountain—one hand loosely holding the reins, the other resting on the pommel of the sword he'd gotten from the armory in Tatton Grange—many vendors flocked to his horse. Other passersby asked for his name and what lord he served, but he didn't answer their questions, only nodded amiably and continued at a leisurely clop through the streets. When he reached the bridge that crossed over the falls, the sound of rushing water filled his ears, and he thought about all the times he'd heard it since leaving. The waters of the river had a pure smell—it was difficult to describe, but the scent of wet rock was overpowering and memorable.

As he reached the gates leading to the sanctuary, he turned his horse and rode into the courtyard, feeling an overpowering sense of tranquility as he did so. He approached the large pool outside the massive structure and reached into his purse to retrieve a single silver livre. He tossed it toward the center of the pool, watching as the coin plopped into the water. He stared at the statue of the Lady of the Fountain and nodded to it, offering a small prayer in his heart.

Thank you, Our Lady, for sparing my life.

A prickle of warmth went down his back, making him feel restless and uneasy.

Was it his imagination?

Gooseflesh tingled down his arms, nearly making him tremble. He stared at the statue for a moment longer. Lord Kinghorn was a Vox knight who had tried for years to hear the voice, but he had never heard an answer. Lord Kinghorn was one of the most honorable men in Ransom's acquaintance—if he had not been deemed worthy, what hope did Ransom have? None whatsoever. Besides which, the creeping anxiety he'd felt while talking to the older man returned at the sight of the Lady. What would he do if he *did* hear the voice of the Fountain?

What if it told him that he'd gotten everything wrong?

He turned his steed and exited the gate, aware of the constant stares that came his way. No one recognized him, but then again, why would they? He'd left as a lad, and the city saw many knights coming in and out.

As his steed climbed the hill, memories of his youth at Kingfountain came rushing back. Claire was in most of them. He let out his breath slowly, trying to tame the nest of hornets in his stomach. He was worried about talking to her, afraid he'd come across as a fool, yet he needed to see her. Truth be told, he was also worried about seeing Queen Emiloh. How could he thank her for paying for his release? No simple words could suffice.

When he reached the gates, the soldiers on duty asked him to identify himself.

"I am Marshall Barton come from Tatton Grange. Lord Kinghorn sent me."

"You are expected, Sir Ransom," one of them said. "Enter the courtyard. You'll be met by Sir Acostel, who is greeting the visitors. He will direct you."

"Thank you," Ransom answered and continued on. The mule balked before passing under the portcullis. Ransom wondered if the animal feared the gate might suddenly come down, cutting it in half. It was a strange thought to have, and he shook his head at himself and continued in.

Sir Acostel had long, flowing, light brown hair—balding on top—and a trimmed goatee. He wore a fancy tabard with the silver rose badge on it and gripped a leather-bound book as he stood waiting for Ransom to approach. A page stood by him with a quill and a bottle of ink.

"Greetings, Sir Ransom," he said after the introduction. "The queen has been eagerly expecting you. You have two horses in your possession and your armor, I see. Your other baggage will arrive from Tatton Grange, I presume?"

"Yes, I believe so," Ransom answered, feeling a tickle in his throat. He coughed to clear it.

A stable hand arrived with a mounting block, and Ransom swung down from his saddle and thanked the boy.

"Sir Graun!" called Acostel. A knight approached quickly. "This is Ransom Barton. The queen wished to see him at once upon his arrival. Please escort him to Her Majesty."

They entered the palace, and as Ransom walked alongside the fellow, he took in the sight of the familiar rooms, noting how much they had changed. During Ransom's final days at the palace, so many servants had abandoned Gervase that the halls had felt desolate. Now they were festooned with garlands and thronged with people in fancy livery and servants carrying an assortment of dishes, although none were laden with food. Was this just a preparation for the coming coronation?

"I fancy your armor," said Sir Graun. "Where'd you get it?"

"An armorer in Chessy," replied Ransom.

"It must have cost a fortune. Were you ever a tournament champion?"

"No, although I did win some events."

"Funny how all the champions tend to be Occitanians," he sneered. "Have you met the Black Prince?"

"In passing."

There was a little more small talk before he realized that the knight was escorting him to the king's chamber. He'd expected to go to the great hall. The rest of the walk was made in silence, nervous on his part and companionable on the knight's end.

"This is Sir Ransom, come on the queen's orders," said Sir Graun once they arrived outside the guarded door.

One of the guards knocked on the door and opened it. He said something, and out came the chamberlain, a silver-haired man in a velvet tunic, with a chain of office around his neck. Coming behind the chamberlain was Lord Archer, the Duke of Glosstyr. Ransom recognized him immediately and felt his stomach clench with dread when he saw the duke scowl at him. The man said nothing as he passed.

"Welcome, Sir Ransom. Please, come in," said the chamberlain with a bright smile. "I am Sir Iain. I've served Her Majesty for many years. Oh, don't mind the gruff duke. He's always surly like that. You are very welcome."

Ransom entered the chamber, expecting to see only the queen, but when he stepped farther inside, he caught sight of King Devon leaning against the wall, cradling a goblet in one hand. Ransom's knees began to tremble.

"There he is," said Devon with a shrewd smile. He pushed away from the wall and started pacing the room with a restless energy. His free arm gesticulated. "The lost sheep has been found. A rather expensive sheep, I daresay."

"Husband, be kind," said Queen Emiloh, rising from a sofa on the other side of the room.

"I'm always courteous, if not always kind. Welcome again to Kingfountain, Sir Ransom. Your reputation for needing saving precedes you."

The words were a blow, but Ransom didn't flinch.

"Devon, please. Be civil."

"I *am* being civil. He cost five thousand livres. I wouldn't have paid half that for one of my own sons."

Ransom stared at the king in surprise, trying to tame his surging feelings of humiliation and dread when he saw a smile flicker on the king's mouth. He realized that the man was toying with him, trying to get a reaction.

"I'm certain Your Majesty would have paid ten times as much for one of his own sons," Ransom said, bowing slightly.

The king beamed, striding toward him. "See, Emiloh? I knew he could handle my jests."

"You didn't know. You've never met him before," she said with a sigh. "My apologies for my husband's rude sense of humor."

"It's not rude, how dare you suggest that! I'm offended."

"If you're offended, then I'm a duckling," she said. As she approached him, Ransom knelt before her, and she held out her hand with the royal ring on her finger. Ransom kissed the gem.

"Rise, Sir Ransom," she said.

"Yes, on your feet," said the king. "I can't bear such tedious formalities behind closed doors. I may yawn to death. He's here, and we've shooed away Lord Archer to speak with him. Best he knows why and soon."

"We will finish talking about Lord Archer later," said the queen. "He has a right to be concerned."

"I don't give a fig about his right to be concerned," said the king in a dismissive manner. "He has a duty to be loyal. If it were not for me, he never would have won Legault, and his daughter wouldn't have the right to choose her husband anyway. I gave it to him, and so he owes me his allegiance. It's really quite simple; I don't see why he's so upset about it."

Ransom's stomach shriveled. So the rumors were true—they intended to pressure Claire into marrying their youngest son.

"It's still too soon," the queen said. "Jon-Landon is but a boy."

"Is there not the same gap in age between my lady and myself?" Devon said. "I was no more than Sir Ransom's age, I declare, when I wooed you for myself."

"You make it sound so romantic," said the queen with flaring nostrils.

The king set his goblet down, folded his arms, and approached Ransom. "What? Would it have been more romantic if I'd laid siege to Auxaunce? If I'd starved your populace into surrender? You are so bloodthirsty, my lady." He gave her a knowing smile.

The queen arched her brow. "The business at hand, my lord?"

"Ah, yes. Sir Ransom." He stroked his beard, appraising Ransom like he would a destrier. "You are young, handsome, and well trained, which I've been assured of by Lord Kinghorn himself. A capable man. Has an eye for these things. You are not prone to outbursts, which we've just proven. Circumspect, I like that."

"Husband . . . there are pressing matters still to attend to. Just tell him what you intend."

"I'm getting to it, I'm getting to it," he said with a dismissive gesture. Ransom felt his insides squirm, but he maintained a calm expression. He wasn't sure what he'd expected, but the king and queen had very different personalities. He seemed more hot-headed, she cool and careful. "You're here to be of service, lad, are you not?"

"Y-yes, my lord," Ransom stammered.

"You do feel a sort of obligation, do you not? Five thousand livres is quite a ransom . . . Ransom." The king grinned.

"It is."

"Are you Fountain-blessed?"

"I don't know, my lord," Ransom answered.

"Of course you aren't," the king snapped. "That's a myth. It's . . . it's a fable from the ages." He snapped his fingers. "There are no Wizrs anymore. No magic rings. But I care not about that. DeVaux believed you were. That is why he insisted on getting his full recompense. If people continue to believe that you are, then you will be valuable to me, worth more than five thousand livres." He glanced at his wife. "Stop glaring at me, Emiloh! On with it, then. You were summoned to Kingfountain, Sir Ransom, to serve the King of Ceredigion. To be part of the king's mesnie. From what Bryon has told me, you're quite lethal with a blade. You fought well in the Brugian campaign, you've done well at Chessy, and most importantly, you saved me from paying an even heftier ransom for my dear wife. I owe you at least forty-five thousand livres for that!"

Ransom blinked in surprise. "I'm to serve you, my lord?"

"Not at all!" he chortled. "I said the King of Ceredigion. You will serve our eldest son. Your duty is to keep that feckless young man alive!"

Why does loyalty always demand such a heavy tax? I am furious right now and have already shattered one of the palace mirrors. I was aiming for the wall. King Devon, may the Fountain drown him, has demanded of Da that I marry his youngest son, that sniveling little prince. His eldest brothers have been given kingdoms and duchies, so why not find something else for the royal brat? Of course, the king stooped to remind Da of the help he offered us in reclaiming Legault, my hereditary right. Yet does not that very hereditary right grant me, the daughter of a queen, the right he seeks to wrest from me? Why irk a man and his daughter so? Why try to strangle their consciences? Even according to the precepts of Virtus, which I despise, a lady is to be wooed by a knight who proves his worth through deeds of valor. The prince is still pinching his own pimples. Why did we come to court? Now I just desire to go back to Legault. This court is poisonous. I want nothing of it.

—Claire de Murrow, Daughter of the Queen of Legault
(in case anyone has forgotten)

CHAPTER EIGHTEEN

The Queen's Charge

Ransom's mind was awhirl at the change of events as Sir Iain led him away from the king's chamber to another where he would be dressed in the royal regalia in preparation for his meeting with Devon the Younger. He learned during the walk that Devon had earned the title "the Younger" because once, as a child, he had demanded entry into his father's royal council by announcing that he was like his father, only younger. They'd laughed at his boldness then and admitted him, and the name had stuck ever since.

Ransom was given a silver-and-blue velvet tunic embroidered with the royal insignia of the Silver Rose. The cloth was the softest he'd ever felt. He'd observed since coming to Kingfountain that most of the men in court wore their hair long, to the shoulders or longer, as if they were competing with the women, but they also had beards. It was not the fashion in Occitania, and Ransom wondered if his visit to the barber had been the right move. He wasn't clean-shaven, but his beard was cropped close. Sir Iain's was pointed at the chin.

"After the coronation, you will live wherever your master goes," said the chamberlain. "You will travel with the king or do the errands he bids you."

"Which king?" Ransom asked.

Jeff Wheeler

Sir Iain gave him a sidelong look. "The younger, of course. Naturally. And he will go on doing the work his father the king bids him."

"So there will be two kings ruling Kingfountain? The father is not giving up his authority?"

Sir Iain chortled. "Why would he?"

"Not any of it? What will his son be king of, may I ask?"

Sir Iain looked at Ransom's tunic critically and nodded. "It fits well. To answer your question bluntly, Sir Ransom, he will be a king of ceremonies. Royal events, greeting visitors and dignitaries."

"How is he a king, then?" Ransom asked, feeling a growing unease at this news. Would the son chafe in such a role? A title with no power was not much of a title at all.

"He is a king in waiting," said Sir Iain. "There is no doubt that he will rule his father's vast holdings. No argument over succession. The lad has been trained in war, wisdom, and the faith. His young wife is one of the daughters of King Lewis of Occitania. What more could a man ask for? This is the way of court, Sir Ransom. It is not your place to second-guess His Majesty's will."

Ransom heard a little clicking noise, and the wall nearby swung open, revealing Queen Emiloh. Her sudden arrival startled Ransom, especially her use of a concealed door.

"Your Highness!" he said in alarm, preparing to drop to his knee, but she forestalled him with a dismissive wave of her hand.

"Please, Ransom, save such demonstrations for the great hall."

"My lady," Sir Iain said with a sigh, "it's not fit for the queen to make use of the escape tunnels."

"I appreciate your advice, Sir Iain, but a queen may do whatever she wishes. And I wish to speak privately with this young knight."

Sir Iain sighed again, more openly this time. "Which is my command to withdraw. My lady, I feel it is my duty to advise you this is highly improper. Please lock the door after I exit. There are enough rumors wagging through this castle as it is."

"I will, Sir Iain. Come back to my chamber to discuss the coronation."

"As you command," he replied, without even bowing, and went to the door. After he was gone, Queen Emiloh bolted it.

Ransom's insides twisted. He felt the pressure of the moment, of being in an unexpected private audience with the queen. Her look was serious, even worried, and she stood by the door a moment, bowing her head, her brow furrowed. At last she turned and looked at him.

"My husband's displays of pride and candor take some getting used to." He judged by her look of concern that she didn't like them. "You are new to the Argentine court, Ransom. It is different from how it was under King Gervase's rule, from what I've been told. You would know better on that score." She dipped her head to him, as if acknowledging his superior first-hand knowledge. He felt humbled by her manners, and the tight coil in his stomach began to loosen. "I came here merely to offer my counsel, if you'll have it."

"Of course, my lady."

"Please. Call me Emi as the knights who serve me do. How I tire of such formalities." She gave him a gracious smile. "But let me be candid with you, Ransom. I have brought you here to serve my son. Of course, I had to arrange it so that my husband thought it was *his* idea. He has forgotten that everything we've achieved has been done *together*. His memories of the past have become shaded by pride, I fear. He believes in his heart that he did it all alone. Sadly, that is a failing of most men. And one, I'm afraid, my son will fall victim to as well." Her lips pursed, and from the way her fingers worried at each other, he could tell anxious thoughts nagged at her.

"The king asked me to keep your son alive," Ransom said. "I believe the word he used was 'feckless.'"

"'Reckless' might have been less insulting. Devon, my son, has always been impulsive, daring . . . adventure-seeking. When he trained in Dundrennan, he snuck away from the castle with the other squires, roaming the town during the night and causing mischief. Drinking to the point of excess and being unfit for duty the following morning. When he returned here, he showed some decorum . . . for a few days. But now he roams the city, only this one is much bigger and . . . not everyone is grateful that an Argentine rules. There have been some altercations."

Ransom let out his breath. "He needs a protector."

Queen Emiloh looked him in the eye. "He needs an *example*, Ransom." She stepped closer to him, then reached out and took his hand in both of hers. "I fear Duke Wigant's son has not been a wholesome influence on him."

"Is Sir James here?" Ransom asked, dreading her answer.

"Yes, but only for the coronation. And then I've made sure that he'll be returning to Dundrennan to learn how to be a proper duke. It would not be fitting for a duke's son to be part of the king's mesnie." She squeezed his hand. "It is my hope that your influence on him will help guide him. We forbade Duke Wigant from knighting our son in Dundrennan. Devon feels the stigma keenly. But his errant ways have not qualified him for the honor of knighthood. You earned your rank the eve of your first battle. I think he will look up to you, will come to admire you. Your influence will help mold his character." Her fingers dug almost painfully into his hands. This was a mother's plea of desperation. "Be loyal to *him*, Ransom. That should supersede any loyalty you feel to his parents. I chose you because you did not abandon me in my hour of need. Nor did you abandon Lord Rakestraw after his murder. And you did not abandon King Gervase either." Her voice softened in tone. "I remember you as a boy. I was too preoccupied then with my own brood of children to take pity on your situation. But I felt a desire to help you if I could. I regret that I did not. I was too drowned in politics and trying to outmaneuver my own husband to secure his throne."

The handle of the door jangled, followed by a curt knock.

The queen released his hand. She touched his face tenderly and said the next in a whisper. "If my son believes that you serve my husband or me, he will not trust you. He is seventeen and thinks he knows everything about the world already." Her smile turned sad. "But heed my words. Be loyal to him, Ransom. Help him become the king that Ceredigion will someday need."

Her confidence in him made his heart beat stronger with determination. "I will, my lady."

She arched her eyebrows.

He licked his lips. "I will, Emi."

The smile she flashed him showed she was pleased. She quietly slipped through the hidden door and gently closed it behind her as the knocking grew louder.

Ransom was given a new sword from the armory at Kingfountain, a bastard sword with the royal crest engraved on the hilt, and a dagger to be used for cutting meat during meals as well as another one for fighting in close quarters. Sir Iain introduced him to the palace cooks, to the chief steward who would pay him his wages, and to a squire who had been entrusted with his belongings, which had been retrieved from Tatton Grange. These visits took up the remainder of the afternoon, but he was brought to the prince's chamber as Devon and his knights ate the evening meal.

When he was admitted, there was no doubting which of the young men assembled at the table before him would be called the Younger King.

Devon was tall, nearly as tall as Ransom, and while he was more slender in build, he was fit and strong and had an aura of command. The ribbed velvet tunic he wore had a high open collar and was the color of pomegranates. Ransom had never seen such a vivid color before, and it stood out from what the others were wearing. Devon's hair was dark with streaks of gold, thick and wavy and trimmed above his shoulders, and he had a goatee that seemed to be trying too hard. The resemblance to his father was unmistakable. As soon as he caught sight of Ransom, he chuckled something to the four other knights gathered around him. All eyes turned in unison to look at him.

It came as little surprise that one of the men was Sir James.

"My lord prince," said Sir Iain, who had escorted Ransom there, "I should like to introduce you to Sir Ransom Bar—"

"No need for an introduction, Sir Iain! I can tell who he is just from looking at him." He set his goblet down on the table and approached Ransom in a friendly manner. Several knights stopped eating, wiping their hands on linen napkins, before rising to their feet. Devon tapped his own chest with his thumb in a knight's salute before reaching out and grasping Ransom by the shoulders. "Sir Ransom! You are just as James described you." His blue eyes were intense, piercing, and he gazed at Ransom with a mixture of delight and wariness.

Sir James rose from the couch and came over, standing by the prince's shoulder. "You look a little shrunken, Ransom. I take it they didn't feed the prisoner very well."

"He's big enough!" said the prince with a laugh as he released his hold on Ransom's shoulders.

"It's my honor to serve you," Ransom said.

"Oh no, it is *my* honor to have you in my service," said the prince. "What do you make of him, James? You were friends once."

Ransom kept his expression guarded, but in his mind he heard James disavowing him. *I've waited for this day,* he'd said. *To see you fail.*

"I've always been more than a little jealous of him," said James, putting his arm around the young king. "He was better than all of us. He's a tad boring, though. I always had to persuade him to go carousing. I wonder if that's changed?" His look was challenging.

"Has it?" the king asked, a grin threatening to burst through.

Ransom felt tempted to punch James in the stomach, but he knew it wouldn't be wise. He'd clearly formed a powerful connection with the young Argentine.

"Sir James's desire to go carousing certainly hasn't changed," Ransom said, giving him a bold look. "In fact, we were out together the night the Brugians invaded. It surprised us to see all of Lord Kinghorn's knights in town, buying things to prepare for war instead of sausages and wine." He smiled and nodded to James. "We were among the first to know. And Sir James was the first among us to be knighted."

"Oh, I like him already!" said Devon. "He tells stories! Is it true, Ransom, that you've fought in the tournament circuit at Chessy?"

"I have."

"I've so wanted to bring my knights there. Is it true that the Black Prince competes in events?"

"He does on occasion."

"Yes!" said the prince eagerly. "You will have to train us, Ransom. All of us, except for James. The poor sod has to go back to Dundrennan. I pity you, truly. Come spring, we will ride to Pree to fetch my wife, and we will stop by Chessy. Oh, how I've wanted to go!" His eyes were lit with genuine enthusiasm and determination. Ransom wondered if he'd even considered that his father was deliberately provoking the King of Occitania by having his son crowned without his wife.

A look of anger brooded in James's eyes. He'd never liked for anyone to do anything interesting or challenging without him. "Perhaps I could convince my father to let me go," he said.

"Both of us have to persuade our fathers, if we can," said Devon. "At least I have an excuse to go. Oh, what honor we will win! But first, introductions are in order. Sir James, you already know. Poor man can't help how ugly he is, but what can be done about it? Here is Sir Alain of Yvescourt, a town in Westmarch."

Sir Alain nodded to Ransom, who nodded back.

"This is Sir Talbot from the Vexin, my mother's lands. Here is Sir Robert Tregoss of Stowe. He's a beggar on a horse, I tell you! I don't know anyone who can ride or joust better than Tregoss. A fair warning, his destrier will take a bite out of you if you get too close." Sir Talbot had light brown hair, down to his shoulders, and a close-cropped beard, and Sir Robert was dark in hair, eye, and beard. "And finally, here is our good friend Sir Simon of Holmberg. He keeps my purse, pays for our food and drink, distributes our largesse for such worthy deeds as drinking copious amounts of wine, and is the man who begs coins from father's steward when we run out! Sir Simon! Hail to thee!" Sir Simon was the shortest of the group, but he had a friendly smile and a goatee that was similar in style to his prince's, only it was fuller since he was older.

"Shall we go out again tonight?" James asked, clapping Robert on the back. "The coronation isn't for two more days. I'm sure we can sleep it off by then. If you're too tired after your journey, Ransom, you can wait for us here."

Ransom knew it would take time to win trust among these fellows. But it was clear to him that they took their moods from the Younger King and especially from Sir James. He had no intention of leaving them.

"Do you have a favorite place to go?" Ransom asked, looking at the king, signaling his willingness.

"I suggest the Broken Table," said Sir James. "Remember that brute of a man who likes to start fights?" He glanced at Ransom. "I wonder how our new knight of fellowship would hold up against someone like him?"

A sour feeling rippled through Ransom's stomach.

He has been chosen to serve the Younger King. Why did this surprise me? But I confess that it did. I thought perhaps he would serve the Vexin queen, as some call her, since she paid his ransom. But word has spread through the palace. Gossip does fly on quicksilver hooves. I tried to find Ransom today, but he was being moved from place to place, never still for more than a moment. I might not see him until the coronation itself, and even then, will I have the chance to greet him? I don't know.

My maid from the palace, her name is Genevote, such a pretty name, informed me that Ransom joined Prince Devon for supper. Sir James was also in attendance, along with the rest of the prince's knights. That particular news made me determined not to go. How awkward that would have been. He's written five letters . . . or was it six? They're all full of courtly nonsense. I haven't responded to any of them, nor will I. I wish I could get a message to Ransom. The wind is cold tonight. I'm restless. I must be patient, but it is so hard. Genevote is asking what I'm writing, so I should hide this book. I wouldn't want her to read it.

—Claire de Murrow
Kingfountain Palace
Eventide

CHAPTER NINETEEN

The Anvil's Thrum

The Broken Table was not what Ransom had supposed, a seedy tavern with dilapidated furniture, the skeletons of chairs in piles on the floor due to drunken brawls. Far from it, it was jovial, and the name came from the legend of King Andrew and his Ring Table. The proprietor made the dubious claim that his furniture had been made from the famous wood of that high court, long since lost to the mists of history. A fire raged in a hearth fashioned from stone blocks.

The brute mentioned by James was the huge man in charge of keeping the peace. His name was Gimmelich, and he sat in the corner with a huge tankard, keeping an eye on the customers. A scrawny minstrel played a lute on a barrel, singing a little ditty and encouraging participation from the half-sober crowd. The Younger King joined in the merriment, raising a cup as he belted out the lyrics in a surprisingly melodic voice. Sir James stood alongside him, although his pitch was off. They had all come wearing deep-hooded cloaks, which they'd doffed upon entering the establishment.

"You're not drinking," said Sir Simon, scooting his chair closer to Ransom's.

"It's best if at least one of us keeps his head," Ransom replied. "It's hard to protect a man if you can't walk straight."

"Very true," replied the knight, taking a small sip from his cup. "It's usually me that remains sober. Glad I won't be alone this time."

"Where is Holmberg, Sir Simon?"

"It's in the duchy of Southport. A coastal town." Sir Simon was modest in size, but he had a look of wisdom in his eyes. He glanced around the room repeatedly, keeping aware of his surroundings. There was a wariness to him.

"Are you nervous?" Ransom asked him.

"No, just trying to keep track of how much everyone is drinking. Here comes Sir Robert with his third cup. Some of the tavern keepers try charging us extra for our drinks. I hate it when the prince decides to pay for everyone's. Sometimes I don't have enough coin with me."

Ransom could appreciate the quandary. "He's just showing his generosity, as a good lord should."

"Oh, he's generous," said Simon under his breath. "If only his father were."

"The king is wealthy, is he not?" Ransom said. "With the revenues from all his lands, his worth must rival that of King Lewis by now."

"Wealthy he is. Generous he is not."

Sir Robert slumped down in a chair at their table, stifling a belch. "Where is your cup, Sir Ransom?" he asked, giving him a hearty thump on the back.

"I think you're drinking for both of us tonight," Ransom said.

"That's commendable, thank you," said Sir Robert with a lopsided grin. "However, Sir Simon would disapprove. And I already owe him money for the trinket I bought that lass before leaving Dundrennan. She will mourn me, I fear. Poor lass." His words didn't ring true.

"Since you brought up the topic of your debt," said Simon, "shall I remind you that you were to reimburse the royal purse after the steward paid you?"

"I haven't seen the steward yet. After the coronation." He tipped his cup and drank some more.

"It better be, or I'll charge usury."

"No one likes a miser, Simon."

"Or a debtor either," said Ransom. "A knight pays his obligations."

Clapping started up in the center of the room as the minstrel began plucking a dancing tune on his lute. Someone joined with a flute, and soon a wheel of people had formed in the center of the floor for the dance. James and Devon were quick to join it. More patrons continued to flood into the establishment, the crowd so thick it made Ransom uneasy. Word must have spread that the Younger King would be present tonight.

"And you would know all about that, wouldn't you?" said Sir Robert with a taunting look. "Five thousand the queen paid for you, was it not? What did she ask in return?"

Ransom could see he was already drunk, or nearly so. Men tended to say things they regretted later when less than sober. Sir Simon's eyes widened at the insult, and he slowly leaned away. He clearly expected some sort of reprisal to be exacted, and Ransom did imagine punching Sir Robert on the jaw. His cup would spill, and the scrap would likely bring Gimmelich over in a hurry. But then he let go of his anger, choosing to ignore the insult instead. As a prisoner among DeVaux's men, he had learned some patience.

He'd use words instead of fists. "She told me that the Younger King's knights need a little discipline. I can see she was right."

"I am a knight, just as you are," said Sir Robert, his face twisting with anger.

"Prove it with your deeds," said Ransom, then turned away and folded his arms. He wondered if Robert might be foolish enough to start a fight with him. The matter was quickly decided when the bout of dancing ended and Devon and James returned to the table, both of them laughing and breathing hard.

Devon lounged in a chair, his long legs stretched out. He looked around for something to drink, then nodded to Simon to get something. The long-suffering knight set off to do so.

"Do you dance, Sir Ransom?" Devon asked between breaths. The collar of his pomegranate tunic had been tugged open even more.

"My leg is still healing, my lord. But I know a few Occitanian ones," he answered.

"I should like to see them. You are so serious, I cannot picture you in a reel. I'm still trying to take your measure."

James grunted. "Why, he's taller than me but not so tall as Your Grace."

"I don't mean measure him like a horse," said Devon, chuckling. Simon returned to the table with a serving maiden who carried a couple of full cups. Devon took one of them and thanked her before taking his first gulp. He winced, shook his head. "Not the finest grog tonight, I'm afraid. Sorry, lads. I think they are saving the better stuff for after the coronation."

"And a fine celebration that will be," James said, accepting a cup from her as well.

Devon set his down, shifting his body to face Ransom, putting his elbows on the table. "I heard from my mother that DeVaux's men had to use a lance to bring you down. That they speared it through your leg."

"That they did," Ransom said. "And the scar will prove it."

Sir Robert rolled his eyes and looked away, but Devon was clearly interested. "I'm surprised you didn't lose it. A normal man wouldn't have survived such a wound."

"He's Fountain-blessed," said James with a wry smile.

Sir Talbot joined them at the table. He had a questioning look. "Who's Fountain-blessed?"

"They're saying Ransom is," said Simon. "I'd wager it's true."

"Are you?" asked Devon with interest. "Is that how you survived?"

"I survived because of the generosity of a lady," Ransom said softly.

"Now this I must hear," James crooned, leaning forward.

The others did the same. Even Sir Robert turned around.

Ransom saw their attention, their interest. They wanted a story. They craved one. He wondered if they were bored with the riches and finery of court—it certainly seemed so from their level of interest. "After I was captured, they tied me to a nag and dragged me through half of the Vexin and who knows where else. I was still bleeding the whole time, though they refused to treat me. I had to rip part of my tunic with my teeth to bind my own wound." Sir Alain, who'd joined them shortly after Ransom started speaking, began to look a little greensick. "Soon it was soaked in blood. I had to rip more of the cloth and reapply the bandage. It wouldn't stop bleeding. I was sick and fainting from the pain. I knew if I didn't help myself, they'd leave my corpse in a ditch."

Even James was listening closely now, and some of the other patrons were edging forward, trying to hear.

"We reached a castle. I don't know where. The lord of the castle was at the tournament at Chessy. His wife or kinswoman offered hospitality to DeVaux, but under the threat of violence. They threw me on a pallet in some dungeon. I was so fevered, I could hardly think. But the lady of the castle came down with a loaf of mold-ridden bread. The knights guarding me didn't want it, so I was allowed to eat it."

"That's disgusting," Sir Robert said.

"Food is food to a starving man," said Devon. "Go on."

"The bread, I discovered, had been hollowed out. The lady had stuffed linen bandages inside it. Those bandages and that moldy bread spared my life. I never knew her name."

"She was the Lady of the Fountain, I daresay," said Sir James with a facetious smile.

"I've seen that done before," said Simon eagerly. "I saw a barber do it once after a knight was injured in a duel. The cut was deep. The barber pressed moldy bread on the wound after he'd cleaned it."

"You're daft!" said Robert. "Bread?"

"I saw it! I swear it's true!" Simon objected.

"Is that who gave you the bracelet?" Sir Talbot asked. "It's a lady's favor, is it not?"

Ransom and James exchanged a glance. "No. I got it at Chessy."

"Who is the lady?" Devon pressed, lifting his cup. "The design looks Gaultic."

"Lady Claire de Murrow gave it to him," said James. There was something in his voice, in his earnest gaze, that made Ransom wary.

"Lady Claire?" Devon sputtered, pulling the cup away from his lips. He looked from James to Ransom and back again. "Oh! Oooh!" Then he slapped the table, laughing hard.

The others joined him in laughter, relishing the ill humor between Ransom and James.

"Well, you must both be good to your new king," said Devon, lifting his cup again. "For in all likelihood, I will be the one who permits her husband to marry her and become the new duke of Glosstyr as well as a queen's consort!"

"Isn't she promised to your youngest brother?" Sir James asked evenly.

Ransom's stomach twisted with disgust as he awaited the answer.

"That's the thing about promises from my father," said Devon with a hint of bitterness. "They can take many years to be fulfilled. I'm married to King Lewis's eldest daughter. Yet we've seen each other no more than a dozen times. We must wait until spring to be reunited." His gaze drifted off. "Ah, but what spring? When? Always a promise, then a truce. Then another promise." He shook his head. "I grow weary of it."

"At least he is fulfilling *this* promise," said Sir James. "He's crowning you king."

"Yes, and that deserves a toast," said Devon, rising. "Good master of the tankards! A drink for all who have come. Drink to your new king!"

A chorus of cheers lifted up in the now full establishment. The excitement was for the ale, aye, but the people seemed to harbor a genuine fondness for their prince—soon to be their second king. He had a talent for making people feel both heard and valued. Simon hung his head as the cups were poured, and then he and Ransom exchanged smiles and shrugs.

The mood in the Broken Table was one of exuberance and excitement, yet a strange sense of disquiet stole over Ransom as the evening wore on. There were cups clattering, shoes stomping on the floorboards, men yelling, yet he could hear the rush of the falls in his ears. It was an ever-present sound in Kingfountain, but this feeling, deep in his bones, was more than the echo of water. He felt a warning prickle down his back. He felt the presence of danger.

Involuntarily, he got to his feet, his hand coming down to the hilt of his sword. The feeling inside him reminded him of the vibration he'd felt while beating metal with a hammer, something he'd done at the forge with Anders. It was a tremoring noise that was silent yet still discernable. He cast his eyes around the room, looking at the cheering faces of men and women. Everyone else seemed oblivious to it, their faces showing no acknowledgment of anything but good cheer. The sound of the waters in his ears grew louder.

A throb of pain shot down his once injured leg, which made him grit his teeth. He closed his eyes, focusing on the pain, trying to understand what he was feeling.

The threat was not inside the tavern. It was coming.

"What's wrong, Sir Ransom?" Simon asked him.

Ransom opened his eyes and saw the look of concern on Simon's face.

Without answering, he started moving through the crowd toward the door. There were so many people he had to push his way through some of them, and the tone of the vibration grew stronger. It was both a warning and a commandment to investigate. He'd experienced this sort of feeling in battle, but never in a place like this, where no one was armed. If they had been, he feared he would have started cutting them all down in response to the conviction in his heart that something was coming, something dangerous.

As he approached the front door, he sensed someone's presence. That was the only way to describe it. A matching thrum of hammer and anvil. As the two forces joined, he knew that the person was approaching the tavern. He then sensed them abruptly turn and depart.

Ransom shoved past those blocking his path, forcing his way to the door. Worried that they were under attack, Ransom shoved against it with all his might, and a person on the other side stumbled. Then he yanked the door open, exposing himself to the crisp night air, and saw a man sprawled on the street.

"Oy! Whaddya do that for!" he said, rubbing his backside.

This was not the person he sought, but he could sense them still, moving swiftly, walking away from the tavern. Ransom stepped out into the air, surprised to see fluffy flakes of snow coming down. It was too soon in the season for snow, so he momentarily wondered if they were ashes from a burning fire, but one landed on his cheek, and he felt the cold.

He started walking after the person, hand still gripped around his hilt. Darkness and shadows swathed the world around him. He caught sight of a figure in a cloak, staying close to the wall. Slender, sure-footed. Ransom increased his speed and began to gain ground. The cloaked figure turned its head toward him, and he caught a glimpse of long, flowing hair in a sudden flash of moonlight. It was a slim figure, and the gait was not that of a man. Then shadows smothered her again.

He could sense her now, feel her trying to outdistance him. This was the threat he had sensed inside the tavern. He couldn't explain it, not to himself or anyone. But there was something that connected the two of them.

She darted into the next alley, and Ransom started to jog, the snow beginning to whiten the edges of the rooftops and the seams within the cobblestone street. As he reached the dark alley, he felt another pulse of warning and knew, without a doubt, that she was not alone. His senses screamed at him.

Ransom stopped and drew his sword. The black maw of the alley seemed to yawn at him. Memories of the barn flooded his mind. It had been a mistake to ride Gemmell into it without caution, and he would not make such an error again. A strong feeling of dread came over him. The Younger King was in danger.

Ransom turned and marched back to the Broken Table. He shoved open the door just as the first salutes were expressed. Everyone had a cup lifted high, and Devon bowed with a triumphant grin.

"Long live the king!" they shouted in a hazy stupor.

Ransom muscled his way directly to Devon and grabbed him by the arm. "You're in danger," he hissed in his ear. "We must go at once."

X

We awakened to find it winter. How much it snowed the other night. The castle and hills were transformed, and the servants bustled to shovel the courtyard and the steep road leading down to the city below.

The coronation was splendid. Ceremony is an interesting concept, even if the traditions differ between kingdoms. The Younger King looked very dashing in his finery and appeared solemn and alert. Another crown was fashioned for him, a duplicate of the hollow crown in style, although smaller. Was that deliberate? His father's advisors will be tutoring him in statecraft. He was even granted his own seal of authority, which, again, is smaller than his father's. Queen Emiloh looked ill at ease. And, I must admit, so did the Elder King. This action ensures a stable transition should any harm befall the sire. I wish I knew what they were thinking or why the snows have come so early this year.

I was able to see Ransom amidst the entourage. He had a limp, which he tried to conceal. But it was an absolute relief to see him so hale. And yes, he was conspicuously wearing a bracelet. It made me smile.

—Claire de Murrow
Sanctuary of Our Lady
Coronation Day

CHAPTER TWENTY

Two Kings, One Lady

The warmth from the fires within the great hall was quite a contrast to the chill morning outside. Servants carried enormous dishes with racks of meat, a variety of pears and plums, and an abundance of Occitanian wine. Ransom saw some of the palace dogs rooting beneath tables for fallen scraps.

Dancing and music created a lively atmosphere, but his eyes were fixed on the two kings of Ceredigion, locked in a heated argument beyond the main tables where the feast was underway. He didn't know what had started the row, but the situation was heating up quickly based on their angry looks and rising voices. It saddened him to see conflict so soon. Queen Emiloh abruptly pushed away from the table and strode toward her husband and son.

Ransom approached them surreptitiously, keeping along the walls where the servants were mingling, some of them openly watching the scene unfold.

"Be about your business," he reprimanded. The servants who'd been eavesdropping quickly scattered, especially when they saw the badge on his tunic.

As he drew nearer, he began to hear their voices.

"You are both making a scene," the queen scolded. "Cannot this wait?"

Devon the Younger's face was flushed. "I was giving my lord father the *courtesy* of sharing my plan to travel to Occitania in the spring to fetch my wife. She should have been here for this event, and I seek to heal any breach this may have caused with King Lewis. I don't understand why I must be lectured on statecraft when Father manages to botch it completely on his own."

Ransom wanted to cover his face. He felt a little guilty for listening in, especially since he'd sent the servants on their way for doing that very thing, but in order to protect the Younger King, he needed to understand what was going on within the royal family. He had never seen Gervase's son, Bertram, speak to his father in such a way. But then again, the prince had been much younger when he'd died.

"You may wear a crown," said the Elder King in a voice strangled with rage, "but you understand little about the cost."

"Oh, I do understand, Father, since you are so quick to boast about how much these feasts and fetes do indeed cost!"

"This is unseemly," said the queen. "This is supposed to be a celebration, and you are both arguing like fools."

"I did not choose my bride, but neither did I argue or seek to thwart the match—"

"You were a child," snapped his father. "You still are!"

"I am a man," said the Younger King in a cool voice. "Did not your own father trust you with a command when you were but fifteen? Were you not knighted by then as well? You hold me back because you're afraid I will become more powerful than you have ever been."

"Son," said the queen warningly.

"Oh, let him speak his mind," said the father. "Tell me all about how you've been so mistreated. I've given you a kingdom! No one gave one to me!"

"Mine is a false crown, and we both know it. You've made it abundantly clear that I cannot rule in my own right. You've given Bennett authority in the Vexin. Goff will have power in Brythonica when he weds the duchess. But you're telling me that I cannot even go and fetch my own wife, that I must instead entrust the task to one of my knights? Why would King Lewis seek to harm me?"

"Oh, he wants you on the throne, my boy," chuffed the Elder King, "but he will see you destroyed the moment you have an heir. Lewis desires the crown for himself and his heirs. You have no idea how subtle he is."

"Yet you bound me to his daughter, did you not? Let me bring her to Kingfountain myself. As a man. I'm not afraid of going to Pree. You are."

Ransom saw the pained look on the queen's face as she glanced between her husband and son, unable to move either man. Her hands had clenched into fists, and unshed tears glistened in her eyes.

The Elder King's voice was raw and throbbed with anger. "You will get your chance to rule. When *I* am dead. You will inherit a realm at peace, her borders swollen to bursting. Her enemies cowed and humbled. I have not worked this hard for this long to see it all crumble away because of your vanity. You will not go *anywhere* unless I command it. Is that clear?"

The younger Devon's eyes looked molten with hatred. "As clear as the moon," he snapped and strode away in a fury.

The confrontation left a sour feeling in Ransom's stomach. He wondered if he would be given the task of fetching the Occitanian princess in the spring. He didn't relish the thought. He couldn't help but wonder how Lewis would react to the slight of the coronation.

He saw the queen reach for her husband's hand, but he jerked his away.

"Sir Ransom?" said a familiar voice from behind him.

Ransom turned and saw a man he recognized as the dock warden of Kingfountain, Sir Hugh. The man was responsible for safety in the wharves and within the city of Kingfountain itself. Standing next to him was Sir Iain, the queen's chamberlain.

"Have you met Sir Hugh before?" asked Sir Iain.

"I have not. A pleasure, sir."

"I wanted to thank you, Sir Ransom," said the warden, "for the warning you relayed to Sir Iain the other night. I personally interviewed the tavern keeper at the Broken Table as well as some of the other places the prince—I mean, the Younger King—was known to visit. I asked if they'd noticed any unfamiliar sorts lurking about recently. Several made mention of a lady in a cloak. Sometimes she was alone, other times accompanied by several knights. She paid in the coin of our realm, so her presence didn't stand out, but I thought it curious that they identified her as a lady."

"If you asked them if they'd seen a lady, might that not have influenced their answer?"

"What sort of warden would I be if I gave such information freely?" said Sir Hugh with a smile. "I'm not a fool, Sir Ransom. I asked if there was anyone unfamiliar lurking about. They mentioned the lady, which fits with what you told us. There was also a report of the night watch being attacked recently. It seems this lady or her escorts are rather hostile to forms of authority. There's a warrant out for their arrest. We also tripled the guard for the coronation ceremony at the sanctuary." He gave Ransom a nod. "Well done, Sir Ransom. Your warning was timely."

"Thank you, Sir Hugh." Ransom wondered if the lady had come with the intention of vengeance against Ceredigion for past and present slights. Or was she merely a spy, come to gather information?

"If we capture this mysterious lady or her servants, I'll send word to Sir Iain. Even though you only caught a glimpse of her, your testimony may be useful. You were also very clever not to pursue her into that alley."

Ransom shrugged off the praise. "Thank you for letting me know. I'll advise the Younger King to stay in the palace for now."

"That would be for the best," said Sir Iain. The two men excused themselves, and Ransom continued to walk in a circuit around the great hall. He saw his new master in conversation with Sir James and frowned at the friendship and intimacy between them. It would take time to earn the Younger King's trust. But he felt gratified by the warden's news— although he didn't savor the thought that his new master was in danger, he now knew that he could trust the pulses of warning he felt. He noticed King Devon the Elder and Queen Emiloh had returned to their seats, one sulking, the other at least pretending nothing was amiss. It was so stifling in the hall—even more so because of the tension he saw and felt everywhere—that Ransom could hardly bear it. Memories of being at Kingfountain as a child came back sharply, reminding him of King Gervase, the father he had lost. His heart swelled with longing. He wanted to serve someone honorable, like Gervase had been. So far, the Argentines were a bit of a disappointment. The ache of loss prompted him to leave by one of the side doors, and he walked through the corridor, going through the maze of passages until he reached the doorway leading to the royal docks.

As he walked outside, his boots crunched in the snow. The noise from the celebration faded, and he felt the tension ease from his shoulders as he soaked in the sound of the rushing waterfall. He walked down the stone path leading to the dock where the knights of King Gervase had dumped his body into the river in a canoe. Memories of that day were vivid, but the scenery had changed completely—night instead of day, snow instead of fair skies. He thought of his friend Sir William Chappell, and wondered how the stalwart knight would have handled such a duty, where loyalty was knotted with conflicts. Snowflakes came down on his hair, his arms, but the cold had not penetrated him yet.

He reached the edge of the dock and stood there for a moment. It was empty, for all the boats had been taken inside for storage. Standing there, he wrestled with his feelings, trying to get them under control again. But before they had fully settled, he heard someone approaching from behind. For an instant, he had a warning to step away from the edge of the dock, knowing that if anyone shoved him in, he'd perish not just from the frigid waters but from the plunge off the falls.

When he turned, he saw a young woman approaching him. It was dark enough that he couldn't see her face at first, and for a moment, he worried it might be the cloaked woman he'd seen two nights previously. He approached, wanting to reach for his sword, but he didn't—his senses were all heightened, prepared for an ambush.

"You are Sir Ransom," said the girl.

"Yes," he answered. "Who are you?"

"I am Genevote," she said. "My lady saw you leave the banquet. She wishes to speak with you."

"Who is your lady?"

"I serve Lady Claire de Murrow."

Surprise jolted him at her confession. He'd seen Claire of course—his gaze always found her when she was present—but he hadn't thought he'd have the opportunity to speak with her privately. Even if they had met by accident, what could he have said, knowing as he did the king's plans? "Where is she?"

"She was wise enough to stop and fetch a cloak before going out into the cold," said Claire, stepping out of the shadowed archway, smiling at him. "Unlike some barmy knights."

"My lady!" gasped Genevote.

"I grew impatient," said Claire. "But thank you for finding him anyway. You may go."

"As you wish, my lady," said the maid. And she hurried back inside, leaving them alone together.

A familiar ache filled Ransom's heart as he looked at Claire, her cloak's cowl covering her lovely hair, the dark velvet fabric splotched with snowflakes.

"Do you want to go back inside?" he asked her.

"Are you trying to escape me already?" she replied with a laugh. Her accent sounded delicious in his ears.

"No, but it's cold out here."

"I'm not cold yet, Ransom. I was afraid you were going to bed early or something. You didn't even look for me in the hall."

He sighed. "I did notice you, but you were talking to others. I didn't want to be rude."

"I would much rather have been talking to you," she said, looking up into his eyes and tilting her head slightly. She breathed out a little mist. "You don't know the rules of the game, do you?"

His brow furrowed. "Game?"

"The game of courtiers, Ransom. You are one now, whether you believe it or not. You serve the Younger King. You have a position of influence. You'll hear gossip. People will ask you for favors. Do you really not know what I'm talking about?"

He hung his head, feeling abashed as they walked back toward the edge of the dock. "I've not been here for very long."

"Well, let me teach you the rules, then, since you are clearly a dolt in such matters. It is the fashion here to set your sights on a lady who has a higher rank than you do. Like Queen Emiloh, for example. Or your master's wife, whenever she comes."

"Why would I want to do that?" Ransom asked in confusion.

"It is part of the game of courtiers," she answered. "You fight in her name. You prove your valor and all that rubbish and nonsense. You try to earn symbols of your beloved's affection. And then, of course, you brag about your exploits to others in your mesnie. It sounds fantastic, doesn't it?" Her tone of voice indicated she found it quite the opposite.

He let silence fall between them. Was she accusing him of setting his sights on someone else? Could she be jealous? They reached the spot of trampled snow where he had stood alone moments before. The river glided by peacefully but felt dangerous.

"Say something, Ransom," she said, staring at the water.

"What do you want me to say?"

"If I told you what to say, then it wouldn't come from your heart. It would come from mine."

What did that mean? Now he felt utterly confused.

"Are you angry with me?" he asked her.

"Not yet. But you're acting like a barmy eejit. Are you so completely ignorant of these things?"

"I think I am," he said, feeling acutely uncomfortable. "When I was training to be a knight in Averanche, there were . . . some . . . who wanted to practice wooing. I practiced with swords and lances instead."

"You mean Sir James?" she asked, looking at him directly.

He stopped himself before the accusation slipped out, but her eyebrows arched expectantly. She looked so beautiful in that moment it took his breath away.

"Say it, Ransom. Say the truth."

"Yes," Ransom said, turning away, feeling his cheeks growing hotter despite the cold.

"He's shown a lot of attention to me," she said, turning to face the river again. "It did seem a little . . . rehearsed. He can be quite charming."

A horrible feeling grabbed at his stomach. He'd have been tempted to throw Sir James in the river had he been present.

"He is . . ." Ransom swallowed, trying to regain his composure and failing. "He's a miscreant."

"Oooh, that's a strong word, Ransom," she said, eyes shining. "Try being more blunt. He's worse than a pig's fart in a tent."

Ransom chuckled. "Is that a Gaultic insult?"

"We are masterful at them," she said proudly. "I should teach you some. You need to practice more." She smiled at him then, which was why the question slipped out of him.

"But how can I when you're not around to teach me?" he asked.

"'Tis true. I wish Da had paid your ransom, Ransom—oh, it never gets old saying that!—and that you'd come to work for us. Then again, there is something honorable about serving a king. At least, a partial one. The father and the son are at odds. That puts you in a difficult situation, doesn't it?"

"I should think so," Ransom admitted. "But I serve the Younger King. He is my charge. He has my loyalty."

"He's handsome, affable, and quite good at dancing, or so I've heard. I've never had the pleasure of being his partner. But he's a brainless badger, Ransom." She looked him in the face. "You know that, I hope."

"I made mistakes when I was younger as well," Ransom said. "Nearly got myself killed."

"True. You've always been a bit of an eejit yourself." She touched his arm. "But you survived. And you learned. It's good to see you again." She lowered her hand. "I worried about you. I truly did."

The wistful look on her face told him that she was hoping for something. Something he feared he could not give, however much he wished it were otherwise. But he could at least give her the truth. Reaching down, he rubbed the braided bracelet she'd given him at Chessy. He saw her eyes go down to it.

"I'm not really a courtier," he said, bending his elbow and bringing it up higher. "I've nearly died twice. Games don't amuse me. I wear this because you gave it to me. And I'll always wear it until you ask for it back."

"And why would I do that?"

"Because you may not have any other choice," he said. "I've heard the Elder King wants you to marry his youngest son."

"The brat prince. Yes, I know."

He swallowed. "They told you?"

"Da says that I should. But I don't want a prince or the spoiled son of a duke." She looked as if she were about to say something, but stopped herself. She looked down.

"What is it?"

"You're being an eejit again."

"Claire . . . I can't ask for something I have no right to expect. I serve the king now and will likely serve him for many years. I'm not at liberty."

"And you think I don't know that?" she asked, blinking at him. "They cannot force me to marry any of them, Ransom. It's a Gaultic custom for the woman to choose. Try to remember that, all right?"

She turned, the hem of her cloak swirling some snow, and walked back down the dock.

The ache in his chest hurt worse than the one from his injured leg. He knew how to treat wounds from a battlefield. He had no idea how to cure this one.

At last the winter has ended. A robin has been fetching thatch and building a nest in a nook in the wall here at the castle of Glosstyr. I've been trapped here for months, the onset of snow preventing either Da or I from crossing to Legault. We spent the midwinter celebration in Ceredigion. I missed the Gaultic celebration—the haunting melodies of the songs and the strange lights that glimmer in the woods, reminding us of the Aos Sí and their strange ways.

The Elder King asked Da if Jon-Landon might stay with us in Glosstyr during the season, and he could hardly disagree. What a strange boy he is. His brothers all have gold in their hair, but this lad is dark, brooding, and rather sullen. I'm grateful the petulant child didn't attempt any wooing. That would've been unbearable. No, he seemed ill at ease among us, and I did pity him, but not enough for pity to turn into any sort of fondness. I received a midwinter gift from Sir James. Nothing from Ransom. I was frustrated by our conversation following the coronation. Did he understand what I meant when I said that I have a choice? Does the fool man know I've already chosen him? Maybe I should have written a confession of feeling on a note, bound it to an arrow, and shot him in the heart from the palace walls. He may not understand anything more subtle.

—Claire de Murrow
Glosstyr Keep, Duchy of Glosstyr

CHAPTER
TWENTY-ONE

The Trial of Flags

The warming air had reduced the snow in the training yard to graying mounds that diminished each day. The air was brisk, but only a few icicles remained in the shadowed corners of the yard. Ransom gripped the blunted sword, breathing slowly to calm himself, his vision limited by the iron helmet. Even in a war game, he felt the urge for violence. He feared losing control of himself again.

"We need a strategy," Devon said, standing shoulder to shoulder with him, watching as the rabble of knights began to approach.

"Aye, don't let them take our flag," said Sir Robert Tregoss.

There were four corners within the square training yard, and a flag was posted in each. The game ended when all four flags were in the possession of one band of knights. It was a game that left bruises, twisted ankles, and often concussed skulls. Duke Benedict's team was edging toward them on the right. Prince Goff from the left. The Elder King's knights stood directly across from them, although they were holding back. For now.

"Who should we attack first?" asked Devon.

"Benedict is the most determined to win," said Ransom.

"Just call him Bennett like the rest of us. There's something about being the second in line, isn't there?" said Devon with a grunt. "What would you call it, Ransom? Jealousy?"

"Poverty," Ransom replied. The Younger King was good at banter, and they had gotten to know each other well these last months.

A throb of warning touched his mind, and he felt the familiar stirring of the waters. Each of the princes wore a tunic identifying him as one of the Elder King's sons. Yet as Ransom stared at the figure that should be Benedict, he had the sudden impression that the prince had switched tunics with one of his knights. With everyone wearing helmets, there was no way of seeing the faces.

"Eyes on Bennett's men," Ransom blurted out.

"What is it?" Devon said.

That was all the warning he had time to give. All five of Benedict's knights charged them at once, leaving their flag undefended.

"On the ready!" Devon shouted. *"Dex aie!"*

It was the battle cry the Younger King had chosen. As one, his knights shouted it in response as they prepared for the onslaught. Ransom led the attack, feeling his heart thump in his chest, and confidence sing in his blood. It was like a dam bursting whenever he went into battle. But to his surprise, all five of Benedict's knights singled him out. They weren't trying to bludgeon past them to seize their flag— they wanted to take him out of the competition. He crossed swords with the first, deflecting a blow, and then kicked the knight in the chest, knocking him down on his back. Three more charged him, screaming in rage, trying to barrel him to the ground.

"They're after Ransom!" shouted Simon.

Ransom spun around, bringing an elbow into the visor of one attacker, while using the length of his dulled blade to block a thrust aimed at his side. He clenched his blade with both gloved hands, then swung the hilt like a mace into the helmet of another attacker. Someone kicked at his leg, but Ransom didn't flinch, even when he felt the pain.

He swung his blade around again, knocking another man down before reversing it, bringing it down hilt first. A fourth knight charged at him, swinging like a man gone mad. Ransom sensed it was Benedict—even though he couldn't see any visual indication of it, he knew it deep in his bones.

Benedict came at him like a reaper on a field, making long sweeps with his sword, trying to get close enough to deliver a stunning blow. Ransom blocked the first two and counterattacked, putting the prince on the defense. He advanced, swinging blow after blow, testing the prince's defenses as he'd done throughout the winter months. One of Benedict's knights, the one wearing his tunic, tried to hit him from the side, but he sensed it and ducked, countering with a slash that knocked the blade from the fake prince's hand. The real prince tried to surprise him with a clubbing blow to the helmet, but Ransom caught Benedict's forearm on his, kneeing him in the stomach as he did so. When the prince crumpled, he wrested the sword from his hands and, for good measure, shoved him down on his back.

He stood over the prostrate prince, holding two swords instead of one, then nodded to the young man before turning. Goff's men had attacked them while Ransom was preoccupied, and Devon was nearly surrounded. Ransom rushed to him, kicking down a knight who had encircled behind the fight to strike the Younger King in the back. The kick sent the knight down on one knee before Ransom clubbed him on the helm with a pommel. He saw another knight trying to get back on his feet again and gave him a boot to the ribs to dissuade him from rejoining the fight.

The contest ended as all the previous bouts had ended, with the Younger King's knights prevailing. Only three were standing by the end, Robert, Ransom, and Devon himself. But they had all four flags in their hands, and the courtyard was full of moaning, prostrate bodies. Focused as he was on his own role, Ransom had barely noticed what was going on around him.

Devon ripped off his helmet, his face streaked with sweat, and his eyes blazing with triumph. He grinned and pounded Ransom on the shoulder with his fist in celebration. Ransom removed his own helmet and dropped it on the ground. His arms and shoulders were weary, the rush of the waterfall beginning to fade. But he was full of energy still, could have gone on even longer. The contest had not even begun to tax his full strength.

"The Fountain was with us again," Devon crowed. He wiped his mouth on his arm, panting hard, but he grinned with pride and exuberance.

Prince Goff flung his helmet down on the ground in a rage and stormed off, cursing under his breath.

Ransom walked over to Prince Benedict, who sat glumly on the ground, the helmet next to him. He had long hair and a short beard that matched his father's, except it had bits of gold and red to it. Benedict took pride in the fact that he'd never shaved so far, determined to grow a truly intimidating beard by the time he reached twenty. It was not like Devon's goatee, meticulously trimmed by his barber.

When Ransom made it to the prince, he reached down to help him up.

Benedict glowered at him but grudgingly took his hand and rose.

"Did you know it was me?" Benedict asked darkly.

"What did you hope to gain by your deception?" Ransom asked, not answering the question.

"I've always wondered if you held back," said Benedict. "During our fights in the training yard. If you treated me delicately because of who I am."

Ransom wondered at the question. "And what do you think now?"

"Just answer me, man!" Benedict blurted. "Stop being the philosopher!"

"When you ask me to train you, I set out to do just that. I never hold back, my lord. It wouldn't help you, and it would shame me if I did."

Benedict swore vehemently. He glared at Ransom, his eyes shining with anger.

"That angers you?" Ransom asked in concern.

"I'm furious that I can't beat you," Benedict said. He kicked his helmet and sent it tumbling away. "I'm leaving for the Vexin, and I *so* wanted to humble you before I went."

"You're only sixteen, my lord," Ransom said. "I'm sure you will someday. Keep practicing against better men."

Devon approached the two of them, and the condescending look on his face was sure to rile Benedict even more. Devon was only a few fingers taller than Benedict, but in a brawl between the two, there was no doubt in Ransom's mind who would win. Benedict looked like he'd worked a forge. He was naturally athletic, and he trained harder than anyone else in the castle, in Ransom's opinion.

"Don't say it," Benedict growled, pointing an accusing finger at Devon.

"What? I was going to ask if you wanted to borrow Ransom for a season and take him with you. I see you do not, Brother."

"Are you serious?" Benedict demanded.

"By the Fountain, no! The best knights should stay with their king."

"It doesn't gall you that he's better than you?"

Ransom was grateful that Devon was more even-tempered than his brother. "Did not King Andrew have a knight that was better than him? Did it make him any less of a king?"

"Are you saying you believe those old legends?" Benedict scoffed. "You're more of a fool than I thought."

"I know you think me a fool. But we are brothers still. Let us not part ways breathing ill words. It was a bold move, I should say. Rushing my most powerful man all at once. Bold, but stupid. It's fortunate none of you need a barber to mend a cut." He wrapped his arm around Benedict's neck and gave him a hug. "See me before you go," he said in a low voice. "There's something I wish to discuss with you. But take a bath first. How you stink!"

"I bathed last week," Benedict said, showing affront before grinning in reply. He hugged Devon back. The brothers laughed and clapped each other on the back. Then Benedict looked at Ransom, his rage having melted like some of the ice in the yard. He thumped his chest in a knightly salute, and Ransom mirrored it.

Devon folded his arms, watching his brother go. "He wants you to knight him, you know," he said.

Ransom raised his eyebrows in surprise.

"He admires you, Ransom. By the waters, we all do! They all attacked you as one, and you knocked them down as if they were a stack of spears! Did you know it was going to happen?"

"I just had a feeling," Ransom said. "Like that night before the coronation. I could tell Benedict wasn't wearing the royal tunic."

"The lad is brave, no doubts there," Devon agreed. "Another victory. I've never won so many times before. Sir James was a pleasant fellow, and a clever thinker, but none of that matters when it's time to fight. You are unstoppable. It's usually Bennett who's difficult to beat. My brother's envious as well as admiring." He clapped Ransom on the back, and they started walking back to the castle while the pages picked up the fallen weapons and armor.

"What do you need to talk to the prince about?" Ransom asked him.

Devon smiled. "He knows I'm going to try and persuade Father to let me go to Pree. He wanted me to send a message to his betrothed in the Vexin."

He flashed a conspiratorial smile, but Ransom knew in his heart the Younger King had just lied to him.

☩

Ransom had been at the castle long enough that he'd witnessed more than one shouting match between the two kings of Ceredigion, but he still hated to see the ill blood fester between father and son. Worse yet was the pained look on Queen Emiloh's face as she watched two men whom she loved deeply bicker with each other.

Most of the servants had already fled the hall at the onset of the argument, but Ransom, who stood as a mute witness, felt he had no choice but to stay. He hadn't been dismissed, after all, and he was being used as part of the Younger King's argument.

"And I do not see why I must send my *knight* to fetch my own wife! It's humiliating, Father! Not to mention a cause for gossip."

The Elder King was no longer on his throne, but he stood next to it, his arm propped on the back of it. The queen sat on hers, her fingers gripping the padded armrests so hard her knuckles were white.

"Of course you don't see it," snapped the angry father. "Because the roads have been safe since you were a child. They were made safe by *my* laws! By *my* force! I know King Lewis. I know what kind of man he is. I do not trust him."

"Yet you married me to his daughter," came the quick reply, an argument that had been made multiple times already. "I never once refused or demanded my own choice. You picked her, not I! All I am asking is for the chance to get her myself. And Ransom will come too! He has the might of a dozen men, at least, and we'll bring other knights too. A hundred, five hundred, however many you insist we bring. Why are you so stubborn?"

"Stubborn? Do you even hear yourself?"

"I trust my safety to Sir Ransom Barton," the Younger King insisted, stabbing his own chest with a finger. "You gave him to me, and I thank you for it. Let him do his duty and protect me as he would my bride and anyone else he is charged to protect. Let me go!"

"And what does the queen think?"

Ransom could see the frustration, the impassioned feelings of the first Argentine king. The look he gave his wife had not softened, but at least he was seeking her counsel.

"He is eighteen now," said the queen patiently. She looked at her husband with pleading eyes. "He should be allowed to make his own decisions."

"Even if they are foolish and flawed?"

"How is my reasoning flawed?" the younger Devon demanded hotly.

The king held up his hand to his son, his jaw clenched and his eyes sharp as daggers. He looked back at the queen.

"Even so," she answered, "I don't think Lewis will harm him. He wanted the match very much. He's wanted it consummated for some time now."

"Of course he does," said the Elder King. "Can you not see it? Either of you? He wants to take Ceredigion and turn it into a duchy. *His* duchy. If we allow it, he'll carve us up like a midwinter turkey. I do not feel it is prudent to send you there, my boy. Can you not trust my judgment? My experience?"

Devon folded his arms. "Does Sir Ransom believe there is danger awaiting us?"

The Elder furrowed his brow. "What are you saying?"

"He knows, Father. Somehow he knows of danger before it happens. Even today, in the training yard, he knew Bennett had switched tunics with—"

"Bennett switched tunics?" the Elder King roared.

The queen buried her face in her hands and sighed.

Ransom felt a squeeze of guilt on his heart and wished his master hadn't mentioned the ruse from the game so publicly.

"My sons are all insane," the king said with a rasp, shaking his head. "What did Goff do? Strum a lute and sing during the fighting?"

"Father, you're being unreasonable."

The queen lowered her hands and shot her son a warning look.

The Elder King circled around to the front of his throne, hands on his hips. "Is it not *unreasonable* that a father should be countermanded by his son? That a king's orders should be argued against as if they were not firm decrees?"

Ransom swallowed, prepared for another emotional storm.

"I didn't mean that," said Devon, hands up placatingly. "I just ask for this boon. This favor. This . . . mercy. Let me fetch my wife myself. Let me reveal the wonders of our land to her. I'm . . . I'm too jealous to give that opportunity to another. Send whatever escort you require to ensure my safety. Enough of a host that it will make King Lewis and the Black Prince cower in fear. Please, Father. You have no idea how much this means to me." He swallowed, his face solemn and pleading. His hand was outstretched just so. Ransom admired the artlessness of his plea. He wondered if it would be enough to soften the Elder King's stubborn heart.

The Elder King looked at his wife again. She nodded to him encouragingly. Then he turned to Ransom, his grave expression showing his resistance had indeed cracked.

"Some lessons must be learned through suffering," he said with a sigh. "The Lady of the Fountain knows I've made my share." Ransom felt the weight of the king's eyes on him. "Is it true? Can you sense danger?"

"I suppose it is," replied Ransom meekly.

The king snorted. "Maybe you are Fountain-blessed after all. Do you agree with my son and my wife? Should I let the newly crowned king of Ceredigion go amongst his enemies in Pree?"

Devon, his friend and king, shot him a pleading look as he bit his bottom lip in anticipation. When Ransom turned back to the Elder King, the man was staring at him intently.

It was a moment that made Ransom feel torn in two. Each of them wished for his support, but no answer he could give would satisfy both men. He had to choose between them.

"Well?" the Elder King prodded.

"I do think he should go," Ransom answered truthfully. "I would not want anyone else fetching a wife for me." As the words left his mouth, he felt a growing sense of loyalty to the Younger King. That feeling triggered a surge of conviction that shot through his body, strengthening his limbs and sharpening his mind. Something wonderful and strange was happening to him, almost like when he stepped onto the battlefield.

The Elder King's lips pursed. He knew the look of a defeated man. The father nodded reluctantly. "Five hundred knights is a sizable escort," he said. "Go by way of Tatton Grange and inform Lord Kinghorn of your mission. I command you to return to Tatton Grange within a fortnight, with or without your bride. I shall await you there. Should Lewis attempt to detain you, show him you are his equal, and set your own terms. Promise me, Son."

"I swear it," said Devon, grinning broadly. "Thank you, Father."

"Make your preparations, then," said the king, slumping down onto his throne, his eyes full of anguish. Ransom wondered what he was thinking, what caused him such grief.

He suspected that the answer lay in the future. In the royal city of Pree.

A rider came to the castle today wearing the king's badge. I could not specify which monarch the man represented, for they both wear the Silver Rose. However, Da showed me the writ and the seal, which was the larger seal, the one for the Elder King. He ordered Da to stay in Glosstyr. To stand ready for any circumstances that might befall the realm. When I asked Da what this meant, he said that before we left Kingfountain, Devon the Elder had advised him to be prepared to go to battle. The king was uneasy about something, but he would say no more on the subject. Da said that he will be sending me back to Legault. I should be grateful, but I am worried about departing now.

—Claire de Murrow
Glosstyr Keep
(during the intrigues of men)

CHAPTER
TWENTY-TWO

The Court of King Lewis the Wise

Ransom had visited Pree many times during his years in the tournament circuit, but he had never been inside King Lewis's palace, nor had he been on the island fortress at all. Pree was split in two by a massive river, the Mer, but unlike in Kingfountain, there was no waterfall, for the river cut through a fertile valley full of orchards, fields of grain, and woods preserved for hunting by the king's men. The city expanded on each side of the river, but the islands within the river were also used, many of them by the royal family, as they could be walled in to provide protection from attack.

The palace occupied half of the largest island, and from his window in Devon's room, Ransom could look down at a vast courtyard, servants' quarters, and an intricate mazelike series of gardens, all contained by a massive wall that formed the shape of a ship's prow. Riding land and stables occupied the farthest point. Down in the courtyard, he could see the small figures of people walking to and fro below, like so many ants scrabbling on rocks. Their room was in the upper section of one of the many turrets in the palace, offering a view that was breathtaking. The interior buildings were narrow but very tall with steeply slanted rooflines, gabled with windows for row after row of guest rooms. Ransom guessed that the palace held five times as many visitors as Kingfountain could. The five hundred knights who had accompanied them on the journey had been absorbed effortlessly into the space.

He heard the door handle turn and backed away from the window as Devon's wife, Princess Noemie, walked in with two of her maids. Her dark chestnut hair was braided into thick knots on each side of her head, covered in white silk adorned with beads. Her crown, with the fleur-de-lis points, nested above the gauze, but there was another thin veil that settled over the tines of the crown and framed her lovely face. Her gown was the finest Occitania could produce, and the jewels on her wrist, fingers, and neck were worth more than anything he'd seen before.

Noemie had a proud look, that of a woman well aware of her beauty and rank, and she noticed Ransom as the only inhabitant of the room.

"Is that you, Sir Ransom?" she asked with a haughty voice, speaking in Occitanian instead of the language of her husband.

He bowed at the waist. "Yes, my lady."

She walked up to him, her two maids trailing in her wake, and offered her hand for him to kiss her royal signet ring, which he did. Her hand was cold.

"You speak Occitanian well, for a foreigner," she said. "Say something more to me."

"What would your ladyship like to hear?"

"Praise me." The command had been delivered in a bored, offhanded tone, but he felt a knot of concern twist in his stomach.

"My lady has minstrels and poets for such talk. I'm but a lowly knight."

"Where is my husband?" she asked, looking at him impatiently.

"He and your brother have taken to the steam rooms below the castle," Ransom said. "I'm expecting their return shortly."

"You do not enjoy a steam bath yourself?"

"It's an interesting custom that I am not acquainted with yet myself, my lady." He wanted her to leave. Although they were not alone, he felt slightly uncomfortable in her presence. She turned and walked to the nearest stuffed couch, but instead of sitting, she touched some of the decorative pieces on a table next to it.

"You have been in Pree for three days, Sir Ransom, and have already bested our most accomplished knights," she said in a stern manner. "Did you come here to mock us?" She gave him an accusing look.

She was incorrect. He'd bested five of their favorites, one of them a duke. He didn't think it would be wise to correct her.

"We came to bring you to Kingfountain," he replied. "I was challenged. I accepted. It is the way of knights."

"If you wish to please me, Sir Ransom, you will lose your next challenge." She stared at him as she said it—the look in her hazel eyes a different kind of challenge.

He listened for the sound of others coming, hopeful his master would arrive soon, but there was nothing other than the whisper of wind in the turret above them. In that moment, the sound seemed almost menacing.

"My lady, when I became a knight, I suffered the last blow I am required to endure without striking back. I have not sought to shame your people. If I am challenged, I will fight and do my best, as I've always done."

"I am your queen," she said archly. "Obey me."

"You are my king's wife," he answered. "You have not been crowned yet at Kingfountain."

Her lip curled in anger at his rebuff. "And if my *husband* ordered you to fail?"

"Who is it you do not wish me to defeat?"

Noise from the turret, the sound of marching steps, announced the arrival of Devon. The princess turned, hands clasped together, as the door opened to admit her brother and her husband. They wore comfortable royal tunics, both in the fashion of Occitania, and they sauntered in as if they were the best of friends.

The princess offered a kindly smile and inclined her head to both of them, her expression transfigured to one of gentle kindness. Ransom had seen behind her mask.

"We were just looking for you!" Devon said, coming to her and kissing her cheek. "But we were told you'd climbed all the way up here." He glanced at Ransom in confusion, as if silently asking how long she'd been there.

Ransom shook his head, squinting a little to indicate it hadn't been long.

"Why should I not wish to be with my lord husband?" she said, her accent thick as she switched to speaking in his language. "I grew miserable without my fine men." Then she went to her brother and offered her cheek to him as well.

Prince Estian wore his typical black tunic, decorated with silver fleur-de-lis embroidery. He was a handsome man, perhaps only a few years older than Ransom. Not as tall as Ransom, or even Devon, he had a darker complexion and a clean-shaven jaw, as was the custom in Occitania. His hair was slicked back, still damp from their time in the steam rooms. He gave his sister an affectionate hug. She looked at him with a protective gaze, and although she had not answered Ransom's question, he realized that his next challenge might be coming from the Black Prince himself.

"I have an exquisite idea, my love," said Devon to his wife, coming and taking her hand and kissing it. "It was your brother's idea, actually, but I'm not ashamed to take credit for it. Let's ride to Chessy this afternoon."

"There are no tournaments this day," said Noemie.

"We will make one," said Devon eagerly. "You will pick the prize."

The princess looked troubled by the request. Her eyes went to her brother and then to her husband. "But . . . but Papa is holding a feast tonight in your honor."

"The feasts here start so late. We'll be back in plenty of time."

Not with five hundred knights to rouse and muster. That alone could take half a day. Ransom had given orders for them to be on their guard and alert, not to be deceived by cups of wine offered with smiles. How many of the knights had obeyed, though?

Noemie looked worriedly at her brother. "I think it a fine thing to have a tournament. But why must it be today? There is one scheduled in a fortnight."

Devon looked disappointed. "But I must be home by then. *We* must return to Westmarch. Surely we can go there and back if we travel lightly."

Ransom's insides twisted with concern. He wasn't sure if he should speak up or not, but he recalled the concern in the Elder King's voice as he urged his son to reconsider the voyage to Pree. He decided his silence would not benefit his master.

"My lord," he said after clearing his throat.

Devon looked at him, brow furrowing.

"I would not advise going to Chessy today."

"Why not?"

Ransom glanced at the siblings and back at his lord. "I fear it would take too long to ready your knights."

"Then we go with those who are ready. We're not going to be ambushed, Ransom. Estian's men will be with us as well."

Ransom looked at the Black Prince. "I don't think it wise, my lord."

"It *is* wise to be cautious," said Prince Estian, meeting Ransom's gaze. "While I agree you will be perfectly safe, Devon, there is tension between our kingdoms. Someone else might try to exploit that opportunity."

Devon's countenance fell as he looked back and forth between the two of them.

Princess Noemie gave Devon a coaxing smile, running her fingers through his damp hair. "Shall we not go to Chessy another day, Husband? Surely your father will permit you to attend the tournament in a fortnight?"

Devon put his hands on his hips and sighed. "Frankly, no. I don't think he will."

"Are you not his equal?" asked the princess, and Devon flinched. Ransom wondered if she'd said it deliberately.

Devon's cheeks flushed. "Do you not also seek to please your father, the king?"

"Of course," she said, giving a pretty smile. "But when I am your queen, it is my duty to please *you*. He will not be the king forever. We will have our turn. Hopefully, while we are both still young."

It was said in a teasing way, and she rested her hand on his chest, looking into his eyes adoringly.

But Ransom had already seen her duplicity. He didn't trust her at all. The Elder King had been right—they were in a den of vipers.

The royal feast was attended by all the major lords of the kingdom of Occitania. And given the copious amount of wine the guests were drinking, along with the feast of strange-smelling cheeses smeared on round biscuits and legs of meat dripping with grease, Ransom wondered if anyone else in the room was sober but himself. Devon laughed and seemed to be enjoying himself, surrounded as he was by nobles who were going out of their way to praise him and insinuate themselves in his favor.

Servants kept circling around Ransom like carrion birds, offering goblet after goblet of wine, all of which he refused. He paced throughout the decorated hall, weaving between the swirl of dancers moving to intricate music played by court musicians. Although he had no present feeling of danger, he feared he was missing something. Had the cloaked lady followed them perhaps?

He searched for glimpses of her in the hall, but the only people he recognized were from his group. The hour grew later and later, and some guests fell asleep in their chairs.

After making another circuit around the hall, Ransom noticed that King Lewis was sitting closely with Devon, speaking in a low voice. The boisterousness of the earlier hours had waned. Ransom approached the two monarchs discreetly, straining to hear their conversation. When he was close enough, the words became audible to him.

"He does not treat you with trust and respect," said Lewis, a distinguished man with graying hair. He had a kindly hand on Devon's shoulder, a fatherly gesture. "Already you feel like my son, Devon. I wish you had been allowed to spend time at my court. Instead, he sent you to the icy wastes of Dundrennan. We are not the enemies you've thought us to be. Surely you realize that now."

Ransom felt a strong tug of warning. He didn't look at the two rulers, instead letting his gaze wander across the hall while he listened to their talk. This was just what the Elder King had feared.

"I love your daughter," Devon said. "Noemie is a treasure, truly. I want her to be able to come back here, to see you again. So that you might know your grandchildren."

"Of course! Do I not wish it as well? I promised her to you in order to heal the ancient breach between our kingdoms."

"Father thinks you put DeVaux up to his schemes," said Devon. "To sow discord in the Vexin."

Ransom felt a powerful need to interrupt the conversation, to pull Devon aside and encourage him to use discretion, but he knew it was impossible. He could only listen.

"Men like DeVaux are naturally greedy, my son. And so was your grandfather. He used the civil war to increase his lands and doubled the size of La Marche."

"You mean Westmarch?"

"Naturally I would prefer to speak of it after my own tongue." Lewis smiled warmly. "The border wars have done so much damage between our realms. Let us end the fighting once and for all. My son, Estian, will be king after me, and you will rule Ceredigion. You have brothers enough, Devon, but can you find room in your heart for one more? I have two daughters and one son, a blessing from the Fountain in my old age. I want to see peace between our people, but you know it cannot be while your father rules."

Ransom closed his eyes with dread, feeling powerless to stop the scene from unfolding—which was when he felt a hand descend on his shoulder. He opened his eyes and found Prince Estian was the one there.

"May I have a word with you, Sir Ransom?" he asked.

He could think of no pretext to refuse, and so he nodded and let Prince Estian lead him away from the conversation that he desperately wanted to hear. He saw Princess Noemie's hazel eyes fix on him, a look of alarm spreading across her face as she watched her brother escort him across the hall. She was sitting amongst other ladies of court, not within earshot of her husband's conversation.

"There has been some talk going about the palace," Estian said, his eyes probing. "Rumors."

"That is typical at a royal palace, I should say," Ransom replied evenly.

"True. Might we speak in Occitanian? You are comfortable in that language, I understand?"

"I am."

"Good," he said in Occitanian. "I am concerned sometimes that I may use the wrong word, and I don't want to be misunderstood."

Ransom swallowed as Estian turned and faced him. The princess rose from her seat, her eyes fixed on the two of them. Her hand squeezed the arm of her chair. She was too far to hear their conversation.

"I'm afraid that the rumors may be exaggerated," Estian said.

"And what rumors are these?" Ransom asked, wanting to end the conversation quickly, fearing he was about to be challenged by the other knight. Only a coward would refuse.

"That I intend to challenge you to a test of prowess. Everyone is talking about you right now, Sir Ransom. There are some ugly individuals, I would say, who may even be wagering on the outcome. The knights of your company, for example, spread such rumors. There have even been a few brawls between our men. I would like to put the rumors to rest."

Ransom felt like he was about to step in a huge mound of stinking manure. He said nothing, just looked at Prince Estian with a neutral expression, trying to tamp down the frenzied feelings inside him.

"I did not intend to challenge you, Sir Ransom. Now is not the time to test each other's skill. You came here with your king to fetch my sister. I am certain that someday we will cross lances or swords on a tournament field. But not soon, I hope." He patted Ransom on the shoulder. "Is it your intention to challenge me? If so, be done with it. This is your chance."

Ransom felt a surge of relief. "I came with a duty to fulfill. I do not seek a fight, nor will I turn away from one."

"I thought as much," said Estian with a handsome smile. He clapped Ransom again. "Let the rumors die, then. You have my word as a knight."

"You have mine as well," said Ransom. They saluted each other, thumping a thumb against their breasts.

Estian walked away from him, joining a group of men who were chatting amongst themselves. Ransom regarded Noemie and saw a look of relief on her face. She sighed and gave him a smile, a sincere one possibly. So, she had come to him earlier because she worried about her brother's reputation. How pointless the rumors and the worry had been.

When Ransom turned to go back to Devon and King Lewis, he saw Simon hurrying toward him, a flustered, worried look on his face.

"What's wrong?" Ransom asked when they were close together. Ransom looked over Simon's shoulder, seeing the deep conversation still in progress.

"I overheard something," said Simon in a low voice, rubbing his chin. "I don't think the two drunken lords realized I know enough Occitanian to be dangerous." His eyes flashed with concern. "They're preparing to invade."

Ransom narrowed his eyes. "Who?" he asked softly.

"Westmarch," Simon said with agitation. "They've been preparing all winter."

"The Elder King is at Tatton Grange as we speak," Ransom said.

"I know," said Simon urgently. "They know it too."

The seas were not calm on the way back to Connaught castle, but they were nothing compared with the ill feelings in my heart. The castellan was surprised that Da had not come. They were expecting us together. During our winter's absence, several issues of concern arose, and many of my people are on their way to the keep to air their grievances. I am the lady of the castle now, and it is my judgment they will receive. I should be excited for this opportunity to act in my future role. Yet doubts continue to whisper in my ear. I know Ransom is in Pree. Will I feel safe until he makes it back to Kingfountain? I think I was too harsh with him when last we met, and I regret my tone. Can he help being ignorant of how to please a woman? Or should his very ignorance strengthen my regard for him?

—*Claire de Murrow*
Connaught Castle, the Fair Isle

CHAPTER
TWENTY-THREE

Oath of Rebellion

Captain Issoudun's face pinched at the news. "Have you shared this with the king?"

Ransom shook his head. "He's surrounded by Occitanians at the moment. But I shall tell him as soon as he returns to his chambers. I came to you, Captain, to begin preparing the knights for a hasty departure. Be ready to ride. How many men are fit for a battle, do you think?"

"All of them," said Issoudun stiffly. "I assure you, Sir Ransom, they can be ready to leave at once should the order be given. But let it be given by the king."

Issoudun was one of Queen Emiloh's knights and had been selected to lead the host because of his experience during the wars with King Gervase. He was twice Ransom's age and not a man of pleasant humors, but he was a capable and trustworthy soldier.

"Naturally," said Ransom in an undertone. "Be ready."

"We are more ready than you think," said Issoudun before turning and approaching some of his men. Ransom left them to confer and plan, and went back to the great hall. Night had fallen over the palace, and the torches cast shadows along the walls as servants continued to supply food and drink for the feast. King Lewis was seated alone, sipping from a jeweled goblet. Devon was gone and so was the princess. Indeed, many of the revelers were departing due to the lateness of the hour.

Ransom had not been gone that long, but it had taken some time to find Captain Issoudun. He didn't see any of Devon's mesnie remaining, which meant the king and his wife had likely returned to the turret room. Ransom hurried out of the hall, only to be intercepted by the Black Prince.

"You seem troubled, Sir Ransom. Is anything amiss?"

There was a suspicious air about the prince now, and Ransom bridled the urge to knock him down.

"Nothing that concerns you, my lord," he replied quickly, trying to move past him.

"Can I have a moment of your time?"

"Tomorrow, perhaps. I must attend to my king."

Prince Estian smiled graciously and gestured for him to proceed. "By all means." But there was a strange look in his eye as he said it. Ransom didn't know what it meant, but he didn't like it.

He took the stairs two at a time, hoping he'd overtake Devon and Noemie or at least some of the knights, but he didn't. The entire way up the darkened stairwell, he listened, trying to hear the echo of steps on stone. Because of the few torches hanging from sconces, it would be the perfect place for someone to ambush him. Ransom drew his dagger and plunged ahead, open to every sound, every shadow. He dreaded sensing the presence of the hooded lady in such a place, and his worry and the steep incline soon caused sweat to streak down his ribs and his breath to come in hard puffs.

He reached the upper floor without incident and went into the room. The knights of the mesnie slept in the sitting area, some on couches, others on pallets that had been provided. The royal bed had long velvet curtains surrounding it for added privacy.

Devon was talking with Sir Robert near the couch, his tunic open. His sword belt hung across the back of a chair. He turned when Ransom entered.

"What in blazes is the matter with you?" Devon asked in concern, seeing the way Ransom was panting, the dagger still clutched in his hand.

A maid had removed Princess Noemie's head gear and jewels, but her hair was still braided, and she still wore her gown. Everyone turned to look at him in bewilderment.

"My lord, I must speak with you," he said, trying to catch his breath and failing. He slid the dagger back into his scabbard.

Devon stifled a yawn. "It's late, Ransom. Can we not speak on the morrow?"

"It's urgent, my lord."

Devon sighed. "What is it? You have our attention."

Ransom saw the Occitanian servants were looking at him, as was the princess. Her eyes narrowed with suspicion.

"In private, my lord," Ransom said, walking over to the windowed balcony on the north side of the chamber. He turned the handle and opened the glass door, stepping out into the cold spring air. Stars were so thick in the sky it felt like he could scoop some in his hand if he reached up. The gardens below were darkened, but there were still lights from torches being carried down in the courtyard below. A stubborn horse let out a noisy grunt.

Devon stepped out on the balcony, followed by his wife.

"What is it?" the king asked with growing concern.

Ransom pressed his lips together tightly, looking at the princess as she sidled up next to Devon, gripping his arm.

"Your knight looks so worried," she said. "What news could have possibly alarmed him so?"

Did she already know? It wouldn't surprise him, but the darkness of the balcony limited his ability to gauge her expression.

"Could I speak with you alone, my lord?" Ransom asked.

Devon shook his head. "Whatever you have to say can be said before my wife. I shouldn't have to tell you that, Ransom."

It was too important for him not to disclose it. He had to take a chance. "Simon overheard two Occitanian lords boasting about preparations to invade Ceredigion. They're going to strike while your father is waiting for you at Tatton Grange."

Devon stared at him, dumbfounded for a moment. "I take, by your demeanor, that you believe it to be true."

"I asked Simon to point out the men he overheard. One was Count Hardle and the other, the Duke of Bayree. It wasn't idle gossip from servants."

Devon looked at his wife, and she looked at him.

"My lord, I took the liberty of notifying Captain Issoudun. We could ride out of Pree this evening, while everyone is going to bed."

"That is a sensible idea," Devon said.

Ransom expected Noemie to deny it, to accuse him of lying. But she didn't say anything. Her face was calm. Knowing, even.

"I'll await you in bed, my lord," she said, kissing Devon's cheek. "Perhaps you should tell him alone."

Ransom's stomach experienced a jolt, leaving behind a feeling of sick suspicion. He watched the princess exit through the balcony door. When Devon turned around to face him, Ransom saw her look back through the glass, a sly smile on her mouth. She was enjoying the moment.

"You already knew," Ransom said.

Devon chuckled, folding his arms. "Of course I knew. I planned it."

Ransom's chest hurt. He blinked, trying to master the feeling of shock and surprise. "You're betraying your parents? What did King Lewis promise you?"

"You think I'm just doing this because of some hasty promises spoken over cups of wine? No, my friend. I enlisted *his* help. It serves both of our interests."

Ransom felt like the turret balcony was spinning. He wanted to grab the railing for fear of falling.

"I wondered how long it would take for you to realize what was going on," Devon said. "Simon didn't know either, but Robert, Talbot, and Alain do. We've been planning it for a while. And you helped, Ransom. For which I'm appreciative. Without your counsel, Father might not have let me come to Pree. So let us be honest with each other at last. Are you ready for the truth?"

Ransom's skull began to throb with the enormity of the betrayal. He knuckled his brow and then nodded. "Your parents will be devastated, Devon."

The Younger King shrugged. "One of them will be. The queen is part of the plan. My mother . . . just to be clear."

Ransom gazed at him in open surprise.

"Bennett is going to lead the forces from the Vexin. Prince Estian will lead forces to join ours. James will come down from Dundrennan with a host, and the queen will hold Kingfountain for me. Father will be surrounded in Westmarch. I think the plan is simple enough. But history tells us simple approaches are often the best."

Devon rubbed his arms. The chill from the balcony was overcoming the warmth from the banquet. "The question that remains to be answered, Ransom, is what role you intend to play in this. Mother thought you could be trusted. She felt you would be loyal to me and was an instrument in persuading Father to assign you to me. I've tried to take your measure, man. You swore allegiance to me. You serve in my mesnie. Or do you? Who holds your loyalty?" He inclined his head to one side, regarding Ransom closely.

Ransom's hands were trembling. He felt unprepared for what had happened—a turn of events he had not once anticipated. But he remembered the Elder King's first order, that he try to keep his son alive.

"Before you answer," said Devon, holding up his hand, "let me be clear that no evil consequences will befall you. While I cannot permit you to leave Pree to warn Father, I will not force you to serve me in duplicity. If you are loyal to him, you will remain here at Pree until the fates have decided which of us will wear the hollow crown. I intend to depose my father, not murder him. You can continue serving him or not. You deserve a castle of your own, at the least, and I will see that you get one. If you serve *me*, on the other hand, realize that your future rewards will be much greater. I know you fancy Glosstyr's daughter. So does Sir James. It would be within my power to reward one of you with her hand. She's rebuffed all of James's attempts at wooing, but I think she might be more positively inclined your way."

"Is Lord Archer allied with you?" Ransom asked, finding his voice at last.

"No," said Devon. "I wasn't sure which side he would take. Father sent him back to Legault, so his involvement in this will be limited. It may be over before he gets wind of it. No matter. He's pragmatic. He'd bend the knee, I should think, when it comes time. So . . . Ransom . . . I know you're surprised. Not even you are clever enough to disguise yourself with me. If you are loyal to my father, I hold no grudge. You've been doing your duty. But I hope my mother was right. She thinks you're the type of man who will risk everything to protect the one you serve, that you'll put your life on the line for me, as you did for her."

Ransom felt a little numb. "I'm still reeling from the news, my lord."

"You should be. It's been a carefully guarded secret."

"May I ask why? Just to be sure I understand your motives. Your father gave you a kingdom."

"But he shouldn't have," said Devon. "That's not how *he* earned it. He won Ceredigion. He defeated King Gervase, although he didn't kill the man to do it. He negotiated a transition of power, became his rightful heir. I wear a crown, but it's a band of gold. It's worth nothing!" Devon's expression became more heated, more agitated. "He gave it to me because he didn't want everyone fighting over succession. But Father is young, and he would never willingly pass his authority to me. Not even a portion of it. Without it, the title is empty. The people prefer me to him—you've heard the man's sharp tongue, and he's miserly besides—and he's content to use that to his advantage. But if I want real authority, I have no choice but to take it. That is how things are done in this world. With allies and with strength. It's like the game of Wizr, which is so popular here in Occitania. Father detests the game, but I'm grateful to have learned it. This is my move, Ransom. My threat on the board. One side cannot have two kings." He folded his arms again. "Which side will you be playing on?"

"Your father suspects you," Ransom said. "That was why he wanted to send me to fetch the princess."

"He is paranoid in the extreme," Devon said. "But while he doesn't trust me, he doesn't suspect his wife. That's how I know we will succeed. By the time he learns of her betrayal, it will be too late to react to it. She's tried, Ransom. She's tried to help him understand that his decisions are alienating his sons. He's too proud to trust us with the same authority his father gave him when he was a young man. Instead he gives me the peel and keeps the whole fruit to himself. He should have listened to his queen."

It made sense now, why the princess had been so cautious about her brother's health. Why she worried Ransom would challenge him or something would force them into conflict with each other. The princess wouldn't want anything to get in the way of the rebellion that, if successful, would increase her power and authority, making her a real queen instead of a fake one.

"I trust your word as a knight," Devon said. "Whatever you tell me, I will believe. If you are loyal to my father, there is no shame."

"One more question, my lord."

"Of course. But make it quick. I'm getting cold."

Ransom smiled, remembering the shivering nights he'd spent while a captive with DeVaux's men.

"What if your father wins? Have you considered that?"

Devon pursed his lips and shrugged. "I find it unlikely, but you're right. It is wise to consider all possibilities." He rubbed his goatee and paced a bit. "Will my father execute me for treason? Lash me with ropes inside a boat and send me into the river? I think not." He stopped and faced Ransom. "Actually, I think he would respect me more for having tried and failed. But let's be honest, Ransom. He's facing the combined might of the Vexin, North Cumbria, five hundred knights under me, and the King of Occitania, including . . . which you so adroitly learned this evening, the support of the Duke of Bayree and Count Hardle. Both of whom deserve a flogging for not being more discreet."

"When did you plan on telling me?"

"Before we left Pree," Devon said. "The only way you were to go with us was to pledge your loyalty anew. Now, it's cold out here, and my wife is awaiting me in bed. Have you decided yet?"

It was a heavy decision to make. And a painful one. Ransom didn't want to be disloyal to either man. But Devon the Younger had made his decision, and now Ransom needed to do the same. He couldn't be loyal to both father and son.

In this moment, he did wish he could hear the voice of the Fountain, if only so he could know what was right. He did not wish to fall in with the Occitanians, but Devon was the man he had agreed to serve, and there was no denying the king had used his son as a sort of prop—a figurehead. The Younger King had, at least, the cunning to be a king.

But Ransom was the one who had to decide, no one else. He found himself thinking of that first meeting with the king and queen, and in it he found his answer.

"I never deceived you," Ransom said. "Your father did not suborn me to betray you. He asked me to serve you, and I agreed." He dropped down to his knee. "I am your sworn man, and I will be so long as you'll have me."

As he said those words, he felt the ripples within him grow stronger. His pledge strengthened him somehow, just as it had before their journey to Pree. Devon's hand touched and then squeezed his shoulder.

"Thank you," Devon said huskily. "I know you mean it. And, as your liege lord, I swear to protect and defend you. And to reward you for your good service."

Ransom looked up, meeting the Younger King's eyes, which looked wet with tears.

"If you're going to fight your father, my lord, you'd best do it as a knight."

"Do you mean it, Ransom?" His eyes gleamed as he said it.

"I do. I was knighted before my first battle, my lord. I think you should be as well. King Lewis could do the honors."

"No, Ransom. It will be you who cuffs me with your gauntlet. Only you. That will be my greatest scar and my deepest honor." His smile was so broad, so thankful. He looked like a king.

It gave Ransom some measure of comfort. But he couldn't shake the sinking feeling that victory would not be easy.

It might not even be possible.

King Devon Primus (called Devon the Younger or just the Younger King) has come out in open rebellion against his father, Devon Ursus (whom they call the Elder King). I did not want to believe it at first when word arrived from some merchants, but Da has sent me notice that this was why he remained at Glosstyr Keep. There has already been fighting in the borderlands of Westmarch. Da is riding forth with his warriors, coming at the command of the Elder King. All is in turmoil. These few years of peace have passed like shadows. How many must die before this foolishness ends? Da has ordered me to secure Connaught and be wary of nobles who would take advantage of the unrest. It is wise counsel, for stupidity is unfortunately contagious.

What is Young Devon expecting? Will a lion give way to a cub? The fool. The ignorant fool. If he had brains, he'd be dangerous. He'll learn the true nature of the powerful. Brainless badger.

—Claire de Murrow
Connaught Castle
(not yet under siege)

CHAPTER TWENTY-FOUR

Siege of Arlect Castle

Smoke abounded. It stained the skin, tainted the water they drank, and gnawed at their armor and swords. The smell of it reminded Ransom of his boyhood, of the siege against his father's castle. This time he wore armor, which had blackened with soot. The taste of ash was in his teeth. He wondered if he looked hard enough through the vapors, whether he'd find that lost boy, waiting to be hung for a crime not his own.

From the haze surrounding Arlect castle, he saw Captain Issoudun's grimy face appear. The two met, and the captain gave him a knightly salute.

"Ho there, Sir Ransom. It's nearly dawn. You think we'll crack this castle today?"

"We'd better," Ransom said, wiping his mouth. He hadn't slept much in the last few days of war, but he felt alert and full of vigor. The fighting they'd experienced had strengthened him instead of draining him.

"I think we will," said Issoudun.

"What gives you confidence?"

Issoudun put his hands on his hips. "They say there are only three ways to breach a castle, lad. You know them, I'm assuming?"

Ransom knew the theory, but this was the first test of it. Thankfully, men like Issoudun had had years of practice during the civil war.

"Surround it and cut off reinforcements," he said. "Breach the walls with siege engines. Or dig a tunnel beneath one of the walls and then build a fire so strong it collapses the earth and breaks open part of the foundation."

"Aye, but there be a fourth! Trickery. Never underestimate its usefulness. You trick the inhabitants into opening the gates. The lad's father is a master of that. We'd best be wary."

It was good to know. The defenders of the castle had retreated when attacked. Some had argued to the Younger King that he should pass by Arlect and drive deeper into Westmarch to encircle his father's forces and keep them from retreating into Ceredigion. But Devon had won his first battle in the field outside the town of Spurring, and he wanted another victory to keep the momentum going. Leaving an armed castle behind would limit his ability to maneuver, especially since they didn't know how many men had holed up inside it. Ransom had been one of those who had argued they should take the castle. But if the siege took too long, it would blunt their offensive, giving the Elder King more time to retaliate and gain allies.

War was indeed like a game of Wizr, an endless one.

"How is Captain Stafford doing with the tunneling?" Ransom asked. Without siege engines, one of their options had been removed, so Devon had decided to undermine one of the walls. Knights had already cut down a tree to make a battering ram, but that was a diversion, to make the besieged knights inside believe they were going to try to breach the gate by force. Meanwhile, sappers were digging beneath the corner wall of the castle. The smoke was there to hide their movement from those guarding it.

"I think he'll be done today," the captain responded. "If they figure out what we're doing, they'll bring archers to that wall, and it'll slow us down. But all this smoke helps hide our intentions. I think we have the castellan plenty confused."

"Who is it? Do you know him?"

"Sir Jude of Wentland."

Ransom knew the name. "One of Lord Kinghorn's knights."

"Oh, you know him?"

In his mind, Ransom could picture the scowling face. "Aye. I trained with him at Averanche."

"You know Kinghorn, then?"

"Aye, and he's my kinsman too."

"Pfah! You don't say! Mark my words, I think the walls will fall today."

"I hope so. I'm back to report to the king from the night watch."

"Well enough. Until later."

Ransom saluted him, and they parted. Issoudun had been privy to the secret all along, and when he'd learned that Ransom would stay true to the Younger King—and, indeed, had knighted him in Pree—his friendliness toward him had increased. It had turned into outright regard after the first battle, when Ransom had single-handedly unhorsed ten other knights and claimed bounties from each without killing them. Many lives had been lost that day, many dead to be buried, but Ransom had kept it from being a slaughter.

Although he did not regret his decision to stand behind the Younger King, it didn't feel right battling his own countrymen. It troubled his conscience.

Ransom found Devon's tent in the haze and approached it. Sirs Simon and Alain were on guard outside.

"Is the king awake?"

"Aye, go in," said Simon.

Ransom parted the canvas door. Devon sat at a table within the tent, already wearing a hauberk and a smoke-stained tunic. His face was sooty, but he smiled at Ransom, beaming with pride at his conquest. Princess Noemie sat abed, holding a blanket to cover her nightclothes as she read from reports. The sight of her chestnut hair streaming down her back, unbraided, caused a tightening in his chest, so he looked away. She glanced up at him, then went back to reading.

"How was the night watch, Ransom?" Devon asked eagerly.

"I found one man asleep at his post and gave him a thrashing before sending him to his captain," Ransom said. "But all the rest were alert. Discipline is good."

"I'm glad you were hard on him. Fear will keep them awake. Do you think the defenders of Arlect will try and attack us at night?"

"Not likely," Ransom said. "We probably outnumber them. No, they're hoping reinforcements will arrive or we'll move on."

"Which is precisely why we need to end it before help comes," Devon said. He pored over a rudimentary map on the table in front of him. "Come look at this. Advise me."

Ransom gazed at the map, which looked like it had been scrawled by a court scribe. It was all written in Occitanian. Instead of Westmarch it said La Marche. "You got this map from King Lewis?"

"Yes, but I wonder if it is accurate. Isn't there a castle here?" He pointed to a spot to the east of their location.

"Yes, one built during the civil wars. It's not in our path."

"Father's maps are more accurate, then. That gives him an advantage. I should have spent less time in the North. I don't know Westmarch as well as I should."

"Ransom looks tired," said the princess. "Let him rest. If they breach the wall today, he'll need his strength for the fighting."

He glanced at her again, wondering why she'd said such a thing, although it was, of course, true. He was impressed that she'd come on the campaign instead of remaining behind in the safety of Pree. Her advice throughout the situation had been both useful and well thought out, and yet his instincts warned him not to trust her. Her behavior was different when her husband wasn't there.

"You haven't slept, have you?" said Devon, looking at Ransom's bleary eyes. "She's right. Get some rest. We'll wake you if anything exciting happens. All this soot and smoke. It makes it hard to breathe."

"This is war," said Noemie.

"By your leave, then," Ransom said, nodding to them both. He left the tent and found himself lost in the smoke for a moment, but then he remembered his tent was behind the king's. All of the mesnie slept around Devon, a final circle of defense. A page helped him remove his armor, but he wouldn't take off his hauberk, and he slept with the pommel of the sword the Elder King had given him in his hand. He stared at it, feeling guilty still for what he was doing. But exhaustion made him succumb quickly to sleep.

He dreamed that he and Lady Claire were walking together at the tournament camp at Chessy. They were laughing joyfully—the kind of laughter only possible for the unburdened. He could see the streaks of crimson in her hair, illuminated by the dazzling torchlight. He wanted to touch her hair. Would he dare do so, even if he knew it was a dream?

He smelled flowers. Did dreams have such strong smells? His eyes blinked awake, and he realized the smell was hovering over him. A hand jostled his shoulder.

The princess's voice whispered to him through his half sleep. "Wake up, Sir Ransom. The king summons you."

He twisted, finding Noemie bending over him, her hand on his shoulder. She was dressed in a riding gown besmirched with soot, but her hair was braided and tethered back, a narrow gold band across her brow. She'd never come into his tent before.

The grogginess he felt left him instantly, and he sat up quickly.

"You could have sent a page," he said, rising fast.

She gave him a mocking smile, but it was nothing like the kind that Claire gave. This one was more predatory.

"There were none, and you were nearby. It's no trouble. We must all do our part. Come quickly."

She rose and went to the tent door. He could only tell that it was still daylight, not how long he'd been asleep. Her presence in his tent unnerved him, but he tried to shake it off as he hastened to put on his armor. He'd finished the lower half when a page arrived and helped him finish it. He thanked the lad, strapped on his sword, and went to join the other knights inside the king's tent. When he entered, several of the others gave him the knightly salute.

"Ah, he's here!" said Devon. "Captain Stafford has finished the tunnel and filled it with brush. The tunnel is supported by log beams along its length. When we set fire to it, the whole thing will collapse and, if our luck holds, so will the eastern corner of the wall. That means we can attack through the rubble and gain the castle before they make it inside the inner keep, which will be harder to breach. We've made a show of getting ready to use the battering ram tonight, and from what we've seen, they've gathered all of their men to defend against it."

"They won't know what's hit them," said Sir Robert Tregoss with a smirk. "My lord, I beg the privilege of leading the attack on the breach!"

"No, Sir Robert. I've chosen another to lead it." He looked at Ransom. "I want you to do it. Bring me the castle."

Robert's face flushed with animosity, but he didn't say anything else. Some of the knights scowled as they noticed Robert's reaction. The majority looked at Ransom with approval.

"By your leave, then," said Ransom. He looked at Robert. "I want you at my side."

"By the Fountain, let's finish this!" Robert said, smiling at the unexpected rapprochement.

They ate food, had something to drink, and prepared to assault the castle walls. Torches were handed out to the few men who were preparing to launch a battering ram against the castle gate. Darkness combined with the smoke, and after the sun set, Ransom gathered the knights who would join him in the charge into the breach. He picked fifty of Issoudun's men, thinking that more would only make it harder.

They waited in the dark by the rear of the castle, wearing cloaks to conceal any glint from their armor. When his men were in place, and darkness had fallen, the order was given to Captain Stafford to light the fire. With so much smoke, the additional output wasn't readily observable.

"I hope this works," Robert grunted in the darkness, crouching near Ransom as they waited.

Soon they could all hear the crackling noises of burning twigs and branches. The noise grew louder and louder, and they felt heat coming from the ground. Even more smoke began to drift up, blowing in the direction of the wind.

When the cave-in happened, they all felt it. The ground thumped and shook like a drunken man. The sound of cracking stone rent the air, and part of the wall sagged and then burst like a broken jar. The eastern tower didn't fall, as planned, but the wall to the left of their position did, bringing up a plume of chalky stone dust that mixed with the smoke. Shouts of alarm sounded from the tower, a lone warrior crying out in panic.

"Into the breach!" Ransom ordered, unsheathing his bastard sword. *"Dex aie!"* He led the way, with Sir Robert at his heels. Their knights swarmed over the broken bits of rubble, hurrying to get inside before the defenders could arrive. Within, he saw a dead man's arm poking from beneath a huge collapsed section of the wall.

The cries of alarm carried, traveling from one person to the next, and suddenly, the knights of Arlect rushed to defend the breach. Ransom felt the surge of energy inside him, felt the rushing sound in his ears. He blocked the first one and banged his pommel on the man's helmet, knocking him down in one blow. Sir Robert screamed in rage and cut down a man to Ransom's left. The other knights joined the fight and drove deeper in.

Howls of dismay came from the ranks of the defending knights. They'd been caught completely unprepared. Ransom's knights pushed in, and he saw the rampart leading up to the keep. He barreled past two knights, disarming them both with quick, jabbing thrusts, and then placed himself before the rampart steps, blocking the retreat into the keep.

"To the stairs! To the stairs!" shouted Sir Robert before he was suddenly knocked down.

A knight in battered armor stood over him, bringing up his sword to skewer the man, but Ransom charged the attacker and deflected the blow.

The knight turned against him instead, screaming in rage, and Ransom recognized the armor. He'd seen it often enough. It was Sir Jude.

The two clashed with their weapons, Ransom blocking a relentless attack as the older knight strove to kill him. Although he did not share that goal, he matched the man's energy, moving fast, coming at Jude in a series of sweeps and cuts. They'd faced each other on the training yard so many times. And Ransom had never lost to him then either.

Jude backed away, panting, half sobbing. "It's you! I know it's you! Traitor!" he screamed, filling the air with a mournful cry as he swiped his sword again, his goal to end Ransom's life.

Ransom stopped the downward thrust, twisting his own hilt to trap Jude's, and then shoved him hard, knocking him down on his back. The knight's blade clattered on the stone.

Stepping forward, Ransom leveled his blade at Jude's helmet. "Yield," he ordered.

Sir Jude, on his back, wrenched his visor up. He looked up at Ransom with fear and undisguised grief.

"Traitor!" he croaked.

"Yield!" Ransom barked. "I'll not ask again."

A look of misery crossed Jude's face. Misery and humiliation.

"Do it," ordered a voice from behind Ransom. "I order it." It was a voice he recognized. It belonged to his kinsman, the man who had trained him. A feeling of horrible guilt swelled in Ransom's breast.

It was Lord Kinghorn's voice.

Sir Jude's mouth twisted with agony. "I yield," he said stubbornly, tears streaking down his cheeks as he collapsed back onto the ground.

Ransom turned and saw Lord Kinghorn coming down the rampart steps. His sword was out, turned upside down. He offered it to Ransom.

"And so do I," he said solemnly.

A riot began in Atha Kleah as soon as word of the rebellion reached it. The Hall of Justice has been seized by the rabble, but our knights escaped with their lives, and they brought news of the attack to Connaught. Although we know not who will win the civil war in Ceredigion, the rebels in Legault see it as an opportunity either way—if the son wins, my father will be weakened by his connection to the Elder King. Even if the Elder King is victorious, his focus will be on his own kingdom, giving them an opportunity.

If Da hadn't taken so many of his knights with him, I would have ridden to Atha Kleah to put down this rabble myself. The castellan has urged me to secure the castle, but I don't want to act like I'm frightened of them. I'm not. We will watch the roads and see if anyone dares march against Connaught. Everyone in the castle is worried and nervous, but I am not. Yes, I'm the daughter of a chieftain king. But I'm also an Archer. I'll defend my keep with a bow.

—Claire de Murrow
Connaught Castle
(first day of the riots)

CHAPTER
TWENTY-FIVE

Four Roads

Ransom escorted Lord Kinghorn through the haze and mess of soldiers to Devon's tent. There was even more smoke billowing about, and men carried torches to avoid running into each other. He heard the wheezing coming from his prisoner's chest, which reminded him of how the haze had bothered Lord Kinghorn back in Averanche. The memories added to Ransom's already festering guilt.

The knights wounded during the taking of Arlect were being treated for their injuries, some of which were serious and would prevent them from riding on. But they'd captured the castle easily enough. It was not even midnight yet.

Sir Simon looked at Ransom curiously as he watched him appear through the thick air, and his eyes bulged in recognition when he saw who was coming. Simon hurriedly poked his head into the tent and alerted the occupants to the arrivals. The flaps were tied open already, and Ransom ducked slightly before entering.

Devon was already beaming when he saw Ransom come inside, and his grin only widened at the sight of Lord Kinghorn. Noemie's look had a hint of intrigue as her eyes went from one man to the other. She folded her arms, the jewels around her bodice glittering in the torchlight as she stood next to her husband.

"Who is this?" she whispered to Devon in Occitanian.

"Darling, this is Lord Bryon Kinghorn, the constable of Westmarch," said Devon with a satisfied grin. "I'm impressed, Ransom. I sent you fishing for a castle, and you brought me a more excellent catch."

"My lord," Ransom said, bowing slightly. "I was trained under Sir Bryon in Averanche. He has surrendered himself and asks that you spare the garrison at Arlect. There are twelve dead, and a dozen more injured in the fighting."

"It could have been much worse," said Devon. "Well done. Sir Bryon, welcome. This is an unexpected honor."

"Unexpected to be sure, Your Highness," came the reply. "I'd anticipated you'd bypass Arlect. We were hoping to surprise you from behind."

Devon nodded, his smile looking even more pleased. "Some had advised me to move on. If I recall, Sir Ransom was not one of them."

Ransom felt sweat trickle down his back beneath his armor. He flushed with the praise but said nothing. He didn't like seeing Lord Kinghorn humbled like this.

"Where is the Elder King's army?" Noemie asked, her jaw lifting slightly. She had a queenly expression and the tone of command.

"I do not intend to be disrespectful, my lady, but I cannot answer you. Duty bids me remain silent."

"If you kneel and swear loyalty to me," Devon said, stepping forward, "then your duty would alter. Ride with us, Bryon. I would value your advice and your leadership."

Ransom's heart tugged when he saw the pained look on Lord Kinghorn's face. His lips pressed together, the anguish of the choice apparent.

"I cannot, my lord."

"Let me persuade you," said Devon, his eyes shining with the hope that he might yet turn the constable into a strong ally. "You've served my father as the constable of Westmarch since Lord Rakestraw died. I would make you the Duke of Westmarch, part of my royal council. The lands would be yours for your eldest son, Dalian, to inherit. You've been a wonderful custodian. Swear loyalty to me, and I will invest you on this very day. You're a capable man, Bryon. You won't get this opportunity from my father. Please . . . consider it carefully."

Ransom swallowed, seeing the look of temptation in Lord Kinghorn's eyes. It was more than just a generous offer. It was a magnanimous act, and if the constable accepted it, it could turn the tide of the rebellion. If they knew the Elder King's plans, his whereabouts, they could respond quickly and decisively. Yet it would be an act of betrayal. One that would haunt Lord Kinghorn for the rest of his life. Ransom looked at the princess's face, saw her narrowed eyes, her cunning. Yes, she wanted Bryon to give in as well, but for different reasons. She was judging his worth as a pawn.

A man who betrayed his lord once might be inveigled to do so again.

Lord Kinghorn blinked quickly, glancing around the tent. He met Ransom's eyes, and the young man felt a twist of dread in his stomach. Although it would undeniably work in the Younger King's favor if the man succumbed, Ransom did not want him to compromise himself. It felt *wrong*.

"My lord, I am your prisoner," he said, his voice thick. "If I broke my vow to your father, then you would forever worry that I might break faith with you as well."

Devon's smile flattened, and a dark look, bordering on anger, flashed in his eyes. Relief shot through Ransom, though, as did respect for the man he'd once served. He wondered if he might have been in Arlect, on the other side of the castle walls, if he'd only been given the chance years before.

"I don't agree with your decision, Sir Bryon," Devon said flatly. "But it is yours to make. Provide him with a tent and all the comforts due his rank. If this war ends in my favor, my lord, you will find that my next offer will not be so . . . generous."

Lord Kinghorn's nose flared, but he stood firm and said nothing in reply. Ransom escorted him outside and around the tent to his own. "This is mine," he said, gesturing to it. "Get some rest. I'll find a page to attend to you."

Lord Kinghorn turned, his eyes watering, and he coughed deeply into his fist.

"I have your word you won't try to escape?" Ransom asked.

"You do," said Lord Kinghorn. "But you already knew that." His look turned sad, regretful. "Perhaps that's something *you* should be worried about for yourself."

Two days later, Ransom sat on his destrier, pondering Lord Kinghorn's words as he waited at the crossroads with Devon and the other knights in the mesnie. The road split into four directions, and a wooden beam planted in the weeds bore dyed-black planks pointing in the various directions. The words carved into them looked bone white from the color of the wood. They'd come up the western road, and the marker pointed back to Arlect as well as the ranks of knights who were coming down the road like a long metal snake. The eastern road went to Beestone castle, which was on the way to Kingfountain. To the north, the marker said Blackpool. The southern road bore the name Southport. Which direction they would take depended on what lay down each road.

The Younger King shifted in his saddle, the chain hood down around his shoulders. It was a fair day, and lazy clouds drifted above.

The wind came from the east, bringing the smell of the pasture grasses. There were no travelers on the road. They'd seen no one at all.

Devon wiped his goatee with a gloved hand. "Where is Issoudun?" he murmured, gazing north. "I don't want to stay here all day. We should be riding by now."

They'd sent the captain ahead with riders, but he had not yet returned with news from their allies to the north. Both Sir James and Benedict were supposed to be moving down from that direction. Nor had they heard from the Black Prince, who was attacking down near Southport. It made no sense to keep going east, which was where they suspected the Elder King's forces to be.

A horsefly came and landed on the unarmored neck of Ransom's steed, and he waved it away. They all wore their full armor, which added to their discomfort.

"Do you want to send out another rider?" Ransom asked him.

Shouts rose up from behind them, and both men twisted around in their saddles. Knights were pulling off the road to allow a rider from the west to come through, with people shouting "Make way! Make way!"

A tingle of concern went down Ransom's spine. Why was the rider coming from the west? He turned his horse around, and so did the Younger King, whose face became grave with concern. The rider bypassed the others, and they recognized him as Sir Tibult, one of the princess's knights.

He was dripping with sweat when he arrived, his armor bearing the sigil of the fleur-de-lis. Ransom stared, knowing he was from the princess's guard, who were with her and the supply horses and the rearguard of the army. She'd ridden in the back because it had been deemed safer, but this man's presence suggested otherwise.

"My lord!" he said, half choking. His eyes were wide with shock.

"What is it, man?" Devon asked, his voice throbbing with agitation. "Why aren't you with Noemie?"

"I b-barely escaped," sputtered the knight.

"Escaped what?" asked Devon in confusion, eyes widening. "You should have stayed with her, man!"

"It was too late! She's been captured." He spoke in Occitanian, his breath coming in quick gasps. "They almost caught me. I had to kill two knights to make it out. They shot arrows at my back, tried to kill me and my horse!"

"Who? Who did this?"

"The king's army. Your father! He's coming from behind us!"

At that precise moment, the Younger King's horse began to drop clods of manure onto the road. The smell of sickening fumes wafted from the heap.

Devon looked stunned, as if someone had struck his skull with a mace.

"Behind us?" he asked.

They'd been expecting to face him in front, joined by the forces from the north and south. They were their most vulnerable at that moment, with just the knights Devon had brought with them. The Elder King must have known as much and hung back rather than pressing forward. He must have discovered the betrayal went beyond Devon.

Ransom looked at Sir Robert Tregoss, who mouthed a word of dread, having gone pale.

"The princess was taken, along with *all* of the hostages from Arlect, who have now been freed. The king knows the size of our force. They're riding hard behind me! We must go at once!"

Devon looked at Ransom, eyes bulging with panic. "Which way do we ride? North or south?"

"We should ride south, of course!" said the Occitanian knight. "Prince Estian's army is that way. He will help free his sister."

Devon scowled. "She's my wife," he snapped. He swore beneath his breath, then turned back to the sign of the crossroads. Three roads. Three choices.

"Ransom, which *way*?" Devon shouted in agitation.

Lord Kinghorn's words came back to his mind. He felt the panic of the situation, the overwhelming urge to start galloping away, any direction but west, but he tried to calm his thoughts. If he had to choose between Estian and Benedict, he'd choose the latter. His instincts told him that even if the Black Prince helped them win, it would be a win for Occitania, not for the Younger King.

"North. Let's find your brother."

"Prince Estian's army is bigger!" complained the other knight.

"But it will scatter to the winds if things go poorly," Devon said, nodding in agreement with Ransom. Looks of terror were showing up on faces. Word of their predicament was spreading quickly.

"Let's ride, my lord," Ransom said, turning his horse around.

"We cannot leave my lady behind!" said Tibult in despair.

"You already did!" growled Devon.

They followed the marker to Blackpool, going north at a hard pace. Ransom led the way, and the road shook with the thunder of the hooves of their army. Five hundred men. It was not enough to face a king's army. Not by any means.

They were all completely bewildered by the turn of events, but it was important not to let the shock of the moment rob them of good sense. At least they'd had a warning. If the Elder King's army had come up from behind and caught them unaware, it would have been a disaster. Although their army would be weary and road-worn, perhaps Estian would be able to attack the Elder King's forces from behind, and they could trap the army between them. It was a desperate situation, but it was still possible to win.

They rode for two leagues, passing villages along the way. No one came out, but as they passed, Ransom saw fearful faces peering at them from gaps in the windows.

They paused at the next village they found so their horses could rest and slake their thirst from the troughs in the village square. A soldier came bearing the news that they were being pursued. The king's army was about a league behind them and riding fast.

"Clever old man," Devon said with a grimace. "Ride on!"

Away they rode, knowing the Elder King's knights were putting an equal amount of strain on their animals. They rode another league, and still there was no sign of Issoudun and his riders. Dread blossomed in Ransom's chest as he realized the awful truth. Something must have happened to him, or Benedict was too far away to help them.

The answer came before dusk.

There was a bridge ahead, one made of stone. Four knights sat astride their chargers across its length. On the other side, a host of warriors had assembled, all mounted and waiting.

Ransom reined in, realizing instantly that it wasn't Benedict's army. Devon slowed and came up next to him, eyeing the armored warriors waiting silently for them. Ransom noticed that one of the knights on the bridge held up a standard, announcing the allegiance of the force.

These were the Duke of Glosstyr's men.

Devon heaved for breath, his chest rising and falling quickly. "Richard Archer's men," he said, then he swallowed.

"And he's waiting for us," Ransom replied, looking at him. The Elder King's army came hard on their heels. Although the Black Prince's army might yet help them, they were now trapped between the two forces. "This means Bennett isn't coming."

"That's what it looks like. This . . . this isn't going the way I thought it would."

Other knights rode up and halted. Horses nickered angrily at the sudden stop. Ransom looked back down the road the way they'd come. There seemed to be fewer men following them. He saw one knight on a destrier suddenly break ranks and flee into a field. He was joined by a few others.

Devon had seen it too. "They're fleeing? Well, can I blame them? This is bad, isn't it?"

Ransom breathed in through his nose and then let out the breath. "I think they've got us."

"We could fight Archer, though? Couldn't we?"

"He has three or four times as many men as we do. And they're rested."

Devon turned back, looking at the bridge. His expression darkened. "I didn't want it to end like this."

"Your father may forgive you," Ransom said. He felt an unexpected tingle of relief. Part of him was grateful they'd been outmaneuvered. The prospect of the rebellion had never felt quite right for him, but he'd pledged his loyalty, and loyalty bound him.

"When I said that before, I didn't think it was going to happen this way. This is awful. I don't see how it happened. We had everything in our favor."

"Such is the nature of war, my lord. Some will fight, but I think if you try and press it, men will die in vain."

"Are you saying surrender?"

"I'm saying we can't win this. But I'll do as you command me, my lord. If you want to fight our way through the duke's men, give the order."

Devon turned at the hips, then looked back at their dwindling ranks. "I wish this were over already. You're right. There's really only one thing to do." He licked his lips, and his shoulders slumped. He turned his head to look at Ransom. "Would you be so kind, Sir Ransom, as to ride ahead and surrender to the Duke of Glosstyr? If I'm going to lose, I'd rather it be to him than to my arrogant father."

The tingle of relief turned into gall. The last person Ransom wanted to see at that moment was Claire's father.

✕

This isn't a riot. It's a revolt. The scouts have said they are approaching from the north, the west, and the south. I can see the line of torches from the tower. At least ten thousand are coming to siege Connaught castle. We had to raise the drawbridge after some fighters pretending to be peasants came in on a wagon and suddenly tried to ambush those guarding the gears. They were slain on the spot, but it showed our vulnerability.

The castellan ordered the bridge to be lifted. We have stores of food and enough knights to hold the castle for a time, but he's worried that we are susceptible to treachery from within. Someone might already be here who will deliver the castle into their hands. I don't know how long Da will be away. The castellan thinks I should flee by ship after sunset. If I'm caught here, then I'll be abducted and hidden away at some noble's keep and tortured until I consent to marry. I don't know what I should do. Da would want to keep me safe. But I want to protect his interests here in Legault.

Word just came. One of the knights patrolling the wall was shot by an arrow and killed. What should I do? I cannot *abandon these men who have been so faithful to my father. I wish this castle stored some ancient magic of the Aos Sí.*

—*Claire de Murrow*
Connaught Castle
(the siege begins)

CHAPTER
TWENTY-SIX

Confronting Shame

Night had fallen. Ransom gripped a spear with the banner of Devon the Younger fluttering from the tip as he approached the stone bridge, his heart afire with emotion. He kept his expression somber as he approached the guardians alone.

"Hoy there, Sir Ransom," said one of them. "Have you come to fight or surrender? We've been watching your lord's men slip away in the dark. How many of you are left?"

"Enough to fight still," Ransom answered gruffly. "I've come to speak a truce with the duke."

"How about you join us instead," said the knight, grinning in a wolfish way.

Ransom stopped his destrier at the edge of the bridge. His senses were sharp and alert as he studied the knights of Glosstyr. Would they attempt to seize him and drag him to Lord Archer as a prisoner, a defeated knight? The flowing sound of water came to his ears, and the feeling of alertness sharpened. If they tried, he'd use the spear first and then grab his sword to fight them on the bridge, perhaps providing

Devon with an opportunity to escape. As he stared at the ranks, he felt their weaknesses, their vulnerabilities to his skill.

But he heard something else. The subtle chime of a bell. It came from the woods on the other side of the bridge. He sensed the cloaked lady he had last encountered before the coronation. Turning his gaze, he looked into the woods, but it was too dark to see her. It didn't matter. He knew she was there, and somehow he knew she could also sense his presence. Was she on foot or on a horse? Were her protectors with her?

His gut told him she was as much of a threat as Glosstyr's troops, if not more.

"I would like Lord Archer's word that I can come and go," Ransom answered, shifting his attention to the antagonists in front of him. His instincts screamed a warning. She was so close to his own king as well as the duke. What was her aim? Her goal? He wanted to go back and warn Devon, but he dared not turn his back on these knights.

"You don't trust us, Sir Ransom?"

"Not at the moment," he replied. "I want his oath before coming over."

The knight sighed and tugged on the reins, swinging his charger around and heading back over the bridge. The horseshoes made a sharp clicking sound against the stone. Ransom gazed at the woods again, feeling the presence of his opponent still. She hadn't moved. Did he intimidate her as she did him?

In short order, the knight returned. "Lord Archer gives his word you may cross the bridge safely. Both in coming and going. He'd like to speak with you." He cocked his head. "Is that enough, Sir Ransom? Or do you need it in a writ of safe conduct?"

"I trust his word," Ransom said. His destrier started forward, and the knights backed away, giving him room to pass. As he crossed the bridge, he felt the presence of the lady to his left. Despite the sea of mounted warriors in front of him, he swiveled his neck and gazed in her direction. Now that he was awash in torchlight, he wondered if she could see his face, could tell he was staring at her. His muscles bunched with energy. How he wanted to charge into the woods and find her, but he knew such a move would rile up the men of Glosstyr. Still, an uneasy wariness festered inside him as he approached the line of men.

"Sir Ransom," said a voice on his right, and he looked over sharply, recognizing the voice as Prince Benedict's.

He saw Benedict astride a horse, and for a moment he wondered if one brother had betrayed the other, but no—the Duke of Vexin was only wearing a chain hauberk and tunic. He had no sword, and he rode a palfrey rather than a warhorse. The knights on either side of him wore Glosstyr's badge, and one of them held the lead rope of Benedict's horse. So he was a prisoner himself.

"Good evening," Ransom said, nodding to him. One brother captured. The other to be shortly.

The look of subdued anger on Benedict's face showed that he was not enjoying the moment either.

Let's get this over with, Ransom thought to himself glumly as he approached Lord Archer, who sat astride a massive destrier. His armor was fluted with an embellished design that gave him the look of a dangerous boar. As Ransom approached, the duke removed his helmet and cradled it in one arm. Claire's father looked weary and concerned, but despite the gray streaks in his beard, Ransom could sense his strength and skill, his energy. He could also sense pain in his left leg and a swollen foot. On foot, Ransom could have easily beaten him. Mounted, though, Archer was a formidable knight. His dark eyes narrowed with suspicion beneath his bushy eyebrows.

"I wondered if this might be a trick," Lord Archer said, "but I recognize you."

"And I you," Ransom replied. "I come on behalf of my king."

"So do I. The true king." His look sharpened with anger. "While I fight here, my own lands in Legault are being ravaged. Believe me,

I would like to end this as quickly as possible. What message do you bring me?"

"My lord, I am sorry about your troubles. Truly I am. I hope your daughter is well."

"I don't know myself," he snapped curtly. "If Devon the Younger seeks to negotiate, you're wasting my time. I have orders to arrest him and bring him to the king."

"That should not be difficult to fulfill. I believe he is coming up the road behind us."

Lord Archer's bushy eyebrows furrowed. "Then why have you come?"

"He wishes to surrender to you. Not his father. His wife, the princess Noemie, was captured already. I just saw his brother among your retinue, so there's no hope of help from the Vexin. We're surrounded."

"Indeed you are," Lord Archer said. "Glad you've realized it would be folly to continue. You gave your lord bad advice, Sir Ransom."

The accusation stung, but Ransom absorbed it by saying nothing. He sensed the presence of the lady still. She hadn't moved, nor did it seem she planned to. Still, he worried she might cross the river while he was distracted with Glosstyr.

Lord Archer met his gaze and held it, weighing his words. "Is this a trick, Sir Ransom?" he asked at last. "A deception?"

"No, my lord. My king is prepared to surrender himself immediately."

"Disarm your men and bring him to me. Lay down your weapons, and we will cross the bridge and accept the surrender."

Ransom looked at the knights surrounding Lord Archer, and he could not help but wonder what it would have been like to encounter him under different circumstances, whether they would have come out victorious. He sighed at the lost opportunity, but his heart hung on Lord Archer's words. He feared for Claire's safety. "Very well. I will bring your instructions to the king."

"Do so at once. If this is a trick, Sir Ransom, your honor is at stake."

"I wouldn't have come if it were a trick, my lord," he replied. "I am loyal to my king, but I value my honor more."

Those words had a visible effect on Lord Archer. His glare softened noticeably. "I'm glad to hear it. We'll watch and await your surrender. You may keep your weapons, Sir Ransom. I grant you that exception to prove I bear you no ill will."

He felt a surge of gratitude in his chest. "Thank you, my lord."

Lord Archer nodded to him.

Ransom turned his horse around and started back toward the bridge, his heart feeling a little lighter, yet the sickening feeling of defeat still lingered.

As did his awareness of the woman hidden in the woods.

It was after midnight when they reached the camp of the Elder King's army. Ransom had told Devon about the cloaked lady in the woods and his suspicion that she might be an Occitanian spy. To which Devon had promptly replied that if she *were* Occitanian, she was there to look after him, not hurt him. He'd said it with a touch of rebuke, as if Ransom should know better than to distrust his allies, but his dismissal of the danger had not settled well with Ransom. It still bothered him now as they entered the king's camp.

Why did the Younger King put such trust in Ceredigion's enemies? It was what had gotten them here, was it not?

No one was asleep. Cooking fires were going, and the men and knights were celebrating their success. When Lord Archer rode into camp, a cheer went up for Glosstyr and his men, and the sting of shame burned hot on Ransom's neck. Devon, his king, tried to look gracious in defeat, but Ransom could see the stress lines around his eyes, the false smile on his mouth. His brother, Benedict, looked sullen and humiliated, and he gazed at his victors with repugnance.

They reached the royal pavilion at the center of camp and dismounted. Ransom saw Archer stiffen with pain and favor his left leg. It was subtle, but it aligned with what he'd noticed earlier. This ability to detect others' weaknesses had developed over the last years and grew stronger every day. He didn't fully understand it, but it had started during his time in the tournament circles and had served him well on the battlefield.

Lord Archer grimaced as he walked toward the tent, disguising the pain remarkably well.

Benedict and Devon both dismounted, and as they walked toward their judgment, side by side, Devon put his arm around his brother's neck. "We do this together, Brother."

"What do you think he will do to us?" Benedict asked worriedly.

"Forgive us," said Devon with a grin. "What else can he do?"

"He can name Goff his heir," said Benedict angrily. "Or worse, Jon-Landon."

"I don't think he will," Devon said, clapping him on the back. Ransom followed them into the tent, where he found the Elder King pacing. He wore a fur robe over his hauberk and the hollow crown atop his head. Lord Kinghorn stood near him, sipping from a jeweled goblet. The constable nodded when he caught Ransom's look of recognition.

"Well, well, well, the lost lambs have been found," said the king, putting down his own goblet. His eyes were twinkling with his surprise victory, but there was a dark look on his face. A look of revenge that instantly put Ransom on his guard. Lord Archer found a camp stool and eased himself down on it. Kinghorn fetched him a goblet of wine.

Being called a lamb made Benedict bristle with anger, but Devon took it with a tired smile. "I underestimated you, Father," he said by way of apology. He looked around the tent. "Where is Noemie?"

"On her way to Kingfountain, of course," said the Elder King with a smug look. "Along with the other *traitors* we captured."

"You call it treason? How can it be when I am an anointed king?"

"Because of who *gave* you the crown!" the Elder King raged, his eyes flashing with wrath. He knocked over his goblet, splashing the wine, and walked up to Devon and smacked him hard across the face.

Ransom felt a knot of pain inside his chest. He saw the mark of the palm against the Younger King's cheek, who could have blocked the blow. Maybe he'd been tempted to. But he'd let it happen in spite of his knightly prerogative not to. Because, despite everything, Devon Argentine was his father. And maybe he also knew he deserved it.

Benedict didn't cower. He glared at his father, as if daring the man to strike him as well.

The Elder King gave his younger son a withering look of contempt. "Did I not give you both enough? You ungrateful wretches. A dukedom was not sufficient for you, Bennett? Hmmm? And was not Kingfountain a splendid gift? What a negligent father I am."

"You know that's not why we did it," Devon said to his father, his look of humiliation raw and bleeding. "A kingdom isn't a gift, Father. It must be earned. It's what *you* would have done."

The Elder King glared at him. "Keep telling yourself that, Son, if it makes you feel better. I didn't rip Kingfountain out of Gervase's hands like . . . like a scepter. I knew his health was failing. I could have driven him into his grave. But no. After he named me his heir, I agreed to remain the Duke of Westmarch until he died. I was *patient*, boy!" His lips quivered. He turned away, trying to control his raging emotions.

Ransom's heart felt rent in two again, just like it had that night in Pree. He felt sorry for the king. He felt sorry for the brothers. The pain inside the family was immense.

"What are you going to do with us, Father?" Devon asked softly.

"I'm going to teach you . . . patience," the Elder King growled. He turned around then, his eyes fierce once more. "You are hereby confined to the palace of Kingfountain. I revoke your authority to govern. Lord Kinghorn will rule in my absence as I continue to punish Lewis for his treachery. And *you*," he said, glaring at Benedict, "will be confined to Dundrennan for a time. How long will depend on how quickly you learn your lesson. Your ally, Sir James, was discovered some time ago and confessed the scheme. I scarcely believed my wife was involved. I didn't *want* to believe it."

Benedict's eyes widened with shock. "What will you do to her?" he demanded.

"I've prepared a nice, cozy tower—the tallest one—as her new quarters at the palace," said the Elder King with a vengeful voice. "Yes, your mother will be imprisoned as well, and I swear on my soul that she will rot in that castle until her dying day. I believed both of my sons capable of such an act of perfidy." His eyes were wet. "But not her. You turned her against me. I never want to see her face again."

"That is unjust, Father," Devon said, his voice throbbing with emotion. "Give that punishment to me instead. I deserve it!"

"Oh? Now you understand how poorly you judged your chances of success? You should have thought through the consequences before you began listening to that eel of a man in Pree. He's not your friend. He's not your father. I am! You owed *me* your loyalty. Instead, you would have both put me in confinement for the rest of my life. Prove to me you have learned your lessons, you unworthy curs, you . . ." He seemed about to say more, but his words choked off. He calmed himself slightly. "Perhaps my youngest is the most fit to rule after me. Goff is only fit to rule a purse. We shall see. Take nothing for granted, boys. You must prove yourself worthy to replace me now." He turned and looked at Lord Kinghorn. "Take them away. I cannot bear to look at them any longer."

Lord Kinghorn set down his chalice. His expression was one of shared misery. "Away we go. Back to Kingfountain. I relieve them from your custody, Richard."

The Duke of Glosstyr nodded, rising painfully to his feet.

As they left the tent together, Ransom heard the strangled sound of tears coming from inside. They'd not walked ten paces before a heart-rending cry split the air behind them. The soldiers' celebration fell silent. Men stood on their feet and faced the Elder King's tent. They stared, smiles fading, as they listened to the agonized keening of a king.

Ransom's heart ached as he listened to the sounds of the death of loyalty. A chill wind began to whip through the camp, scattering ashes and blowing cinders.

X

Has it only been two years since I last wrote? It feels like so much longer. I've tried to write dozens of times, but every time I picked up the quill and dabbed it in ink, I would burst into tears. I didn't have the strength until today. Why today? I don't know. The ache hasn't gone away. The pain is still there. The sadness never leaves. But today my hand is strong enough. Today I can write the words.

Da is dead. He returned to Legault following the Younger King's rebellion with an ache in his leg, his foot. He fell sick in Atha Kleah. The treacherous nobles had fled his coming, fearing the retribution. And then he was gone. It happened so quickly. I don't even know how he injured his foot. He never spoke of it, but I saw him wince in pain. He said not to worry. I believed him, but I shouldn't have.

It's not the tradition in Legault to tie a corpse into a boat and release it into the river. But I did it for Da because he would have wanted it. Through my tears, I knew that I would have to leave Connaught castle. When word came of his death, they swarmed it like maggots on meat. I took a boat to Glosstyr, crying the whole way there.

I wasn't long in Glosstyr before the Elder King summoned me to Kingfountain. He held a ceremony for my father, recognizing him for his loyalty, for his faithfulness. He said he felt as if his right arm had been struck from his body. I never knew the king felt that way. When it was over, the king took me aside and said that he was claiming wardship over me, as King Gervase once did when I was a little girl without a mother. I was surprised. I told him that I could do him more good if I were at Glosstyr myself, ruling in my father's place. No. That wasn't to be. Being warden over me gave him the right to confiscate Da's treasury. It also gave him the right to name a new duke of Glosstyr. He cannot force me to marry against my will, which my Gaultic heritage prevents, but he's tried many times to give me away. Some are older men, twice my own age. One of them is his youngest son. I refuse them all. He cannot force me. I've told him whom I wish to wed. But he will not allow it. He wants nothing to do with his renegade heir or the knights still sworn in his service.

King Devon Argentine the Elder is now the richest man on the continent. He hoards silver livres like a miser and uses them to summon armies of mercenaries to fight on his behalf. His second son, Benedict, has come to terms with his father, hoping to be named his heir. He travels around the realm with these hired killers, punishing those who are disobedient to the king's wishes. But not Devon the Younger. The people still adore him and pity him, but not as much as they pity his mother. I'm one of the few allowed to see Queen Emiloh. I'm her maidservant, you see, her lady-in-waiting. It's lonely in this tower. So very lonely.

—*Claire de Murrow*
Queen's Tower, Kingfountain Prison

CHAPTER
TWENTY-SEVEN

The Tournament at Chessy

hy are we still holding back?" Devon demanded impatiently as the clash of blades continued to ring out through the churning dust of the tournament field. Some horses writhed in pain on the field, having met an ill turn of luck during the live combat. Knights bashed against each other in dreadful rage, seeking to win the most prestigious part of the program.

Ransom looked through his visor at the melee, the words of the king almost a whisper through the roar of the waterfall surging in his ears. He looked to the side, where he saw the Black Prince and his knights gathered at the edge of the combat, observing the chaos on the field. But something nagged inside Ransom's chest. The prince was wearing full armor and so were his men. They were bystanders now, yes, but he had a deep suspicion they were about to enter the fray.

"Estian is going to join the fight," Ransom said, keeping his eager animal in check. It wanted to charge into the thick of the battle.

"His banner was not among those presented at the beginning," Devon said. "He's just watching."

"Trust me, Devon. He's waiting for others to fall first. Hold back."

"There is no glory in that," Devon carped. "We're so close to winning this tournament. I want this victory, Ransom. I want it so badly my teeth hurt!"

Yes, Devon wanted it. He wanted to shove it in his father's face, to prove that he was worthy of something.

"Devon's right," said Sir Robert on the other side. "It'll be over if we wait much longer. Let's get in there and finish it."

"Oh, a nasty blow!" Devon said. A groan went out from the audience as a knight was bashed in the helmet with a flanged mace and fell off his horse backward.

The groan was replaced by a sudden cheer from the wooden stands. Ransom turned just in time to see the Black Prince and his mesnie charge into the tumult. The surprise attack caught the others off guard, and soon knights were spilling from their horses right and left. Some held up hands, offering to yield and pay a ransom.

"By the muddy Fountain, how did you know that would happen?" Sir Robert said in astonishment, turning his neck and visored helmet toward Ransom.

"Now!" Ransom shouted, urging his destrier forward. *Dex aie!* Sir Simon had already been knocked out of the match, but that still left Talbot and Alain in the mesnie. As one, they barged into the melee, swinging their swords.

Ransom buffeted one of the Black Prince's knights from behind, knocking him off his saddle. He swatted the man's empty steed to clear it away and went straight for Estian himself. Claiming the prince as a prize would be worth a hefty sum indeed.

Prince Estian swiveled in the saddle and met Ransom's bastard sword with one of his own. The man stared at him through the slit in his visor, eyes full of determination. Estian and his knights were the regular champions at the tournaments in Chessy. Ransom had often wondered if they won so many times because people let them win.

He certainly didn't plan to do so.

Ransom deflected the counterthrust, and the two knights were suddenly knee to knee, deflecting and parrying each other, their blades ringing out as they clashed in the air.

"Get him, Ransom! Get him!" shouted Sir Talbot.

Ransom felt the prince's weakness. He was a skilled swordsman, but he was weaker on his left side. Ransom used his legs to guide his destrier to rear up, hooves flailing. The prince's steed backed away, screaming in rage, and when Ransom's horse came down again, he'd shifted position to the prince's left side. He directed his destrier forward and started hammering against Estian's armor. The prince blocked two blows, but he failed with the third and fourth.

A preternatural warning came, and he sensed someone coming at him from behind. Ransom jerked his elbow up and caught the blow of the flanged mace on his elbow instead of his helmet. A blind blow like that would have knocked him senseless.

Then Estian redoubled his assault from the other side. On the defensive, Ransom swiveled his blade through the air, propping the tip on his other gauntlet, and held it up as a staff to ward off the rainstorm of blows. The man with the mace hit his shoulder this time, the blow of metal against metal ringing like a bell. Ransom kicked his destrier to move forward, but he felt someone yank on the edge of his armor. The horse kept going, and Ransom fell off.

His stomach clenched with the rush of air, and he landed flat on his back. A horse stepped on his helmet, twisting it around sharply before dust blinded him.

Ransom's heart was racing, and he knew he'd be trampled if he stayed on the ground. He couldn't sit up, so he rolled to one side, hearing the thump of hooves against the dirty yard. The fall had not knocked the air out of him, and somehow he was still holding his sword in one hand. He dragged himself to his knees, and when he started to stand, a mace glanced off his helmet.

He heard the crowd cheer as he reached up, grabbed the mace, and pulled the knight right off his horse. Still gripping the man's arm, Ransom knelt and raised his sword with the other hand.

"I yield!" shouted the knight, his voice hoarse and thick with dust.

Ransom let go of him and rose. He couldn't see anything. His helmet was askew, leaving him with only peripheral vision from one eye. He turned around in a circle, finding himself in the midst of a sea of horses and fighting men. He caught a glimpse of another knight and reached up and grabbed him next, yanking him off his horse. Another cheer went up from the crowd. He didn't know why at first, but then he saw the black armor of the fellow he'd unhorsed. One of Estian's men.

A warning feeling came from behind again. Ransom pivoted on his heel and raised his blade defensively.

"Yield, Ransom," said Prince Estian. The words came from above. "You can't even see."

"I respectfully decline, Your Grace," he said, his breath coming fast and labored.

He sensed the downward thrust of a sword. And, despite his temporary blindness, he blocked it. Prince Estian struck at him again, but Ransom parried the blow. He sidestepped, hearing the hot snort of the destrier just in front of his face. He went to the prince's left side and stabbed at him. His sword hit armor, and he heard a grunt of pain.

The mount swung about, its rump coming straight at Ransom. He heard the noise of it, his mind filling in the details, and he backed away as the horse spun around. Someone came up behind him, and Ransom swung around in a full circle. His blade struck the attacker, shearing through armor and hauberk. The crowd screamed in excitement.

Despite his inability to see, Ransom's other senses felt stronger, and the water rushing in his ears imparted a calming sensation. He turned back just as Estian charged at him. Ransom jumped at the horse, grabbing the bridle with his left hand, tangling his fingers in the straps of leather. The force of the mount toppled him, but he clung to the harness and beat on Prince Estian with his sword until there was nothing left to hit. He heard a crunch of armor and a gasp of dismay from the crowd.

The destrier, still in his grip, slowed and stopped, stamping angrily. His rider was gone, and Ransom controlled the bit in his mouth.

"Easy there," Ransom said in Occitanian to the beast. He stroked the flank, but the horse turned and bit his arm, its teeth glancing off his armor.

Ransom swatted the destrier on its rump with the flat of his blade, sending it off running. Turning his head, he thought he saw the prince lying on the ground nearby. He approached, listening for any sounds of danger. He heard Devon laughing. It was then he sensed a presence in the throng before him. The woman he had encountered in the past. She was not near him, but she was somewhere in the crowd. He turned to the side, trying to catch sight of her, but his helmet blinded him.

Prince Estian tried to sit up, struggling to breathe, and Ransom used his boot to knock him down on his back. He put his sword to the prince's chest, running the tip of the blade higher until he reached the edge of his helmet. He twisted his shoulders until he could somewhat see the prince below him. He could feel the woman coming closer.

Was she here for Devon? Or was she merely keeping watch, as she had done in Ceredigion? For all he knew, she was simply there for the show. This could be proof that the woman was, in fact, Occitanian.

Although he doubted Devon was ready to hear it.

"Are you going to kill me, Sir Ransom?" Estian asked.

"Yield," Ransom said, his voice echoing inside his own helmet. He didn't know if he'd spoken it loud enough, so he shouted it. "Yield!"

No one had defeated Prince Estian before. Not in a tournament.

He knew what it felt like to be humiliated, so he could imagine what the prince must be feeling. Would his sense of honor prevent him from submitting in defeat? Ransom worried about leaving Devon unguarded for very long.

"I yield!" the prince finally thundered.

Ransom backed up a few steps, lowering his sword arm, feeling dizzy. Then Devon was there, still astride his destrier and laughing with joy. They'd grown even closer after the rebellion. Ransom considered him a true friend. And while Devon was prone to emotional decisions, something Ransom attempted to steer him away from whenever possible, he was a good man. He turned again, trying to catch a glimpse of the elusive person he could still sense. But she had not come closer—indeed, she was slipping away.

"We did it! We won the melee! Well done, Ransom! Is your neck broken? Can you even see?"

Ransom felt for the king's horse and the shushing noise of the waterfall began to recede. He wanted to tell the king about the woman, but he suspected Devon would be no more ready to hear it now than he had been two years ago. He was protective of his wife, and he wouldn't take kindly to the supposition that her father was scheming. He would have to think more on it before he approached his friend. "I can't see a thing," he said. "Get me to Anders. I need a blacksmith to get this helmet off."

※

"The dent in this thing is the exact shape of a horseshoe," Anders said, chuckling, while wrenching with a pry bar.

"Just get it off," Ransom said, kneeling on the dirt floor of the forge tent, his head extended sideways on the anvil.

"I saw the fight," Anders said. "Most of it. You kept calm after falling off your mount. Most knights panic when that happens."

"I *was* panicking."

"It didn't look like it. The crowd . . . I've never seen them so lusty. They were cheering for you, even though you're a knight from

Ceredigion. Even though you bested their prince. Mark my words, today you were a hero."

He groaned. "Just stop talking and get this helmet off me."

Ransom felt the strain on his neck. What if the helmet was too badly damaged to be removed, and he had to walk around with a crooked helmet on for the rest of his life? It was a ridiculous thought and made him start to laugh.

"You think this is funny, Ransom?"

"No . . . I was just picturing going back to Kingfountain like this."

"You think you'd make it that far? You'd ride into a tree."

"The horse can see even if I cannot."

The metal groaned, and Ransom winced as he felt yet more strain against his neck.

Another voice sounded from the tent door in Occitanian. "Where's Sir Ransom Barton?"

"Do you think this suit of armor I'm wrestling with is empty? This is the man."

"The helmet still isn't off?" asked the newcomer.

"Would you like to have a go at it? I'm trying not to break his neck."

"You must hurry. They're all waiting."

Ransom gripped the horn of the anvil and tried to turn so he could hear better. "Who's waiting?" he asked.

"Sir Ransom, you've been named the champion of the tournament! *Everyone* is waiting!"

It felt like a thunderclap had struck him. Ransom blinked in the darkness of his helmet, not sure he had heard correctly. Not daring to believe it.

"If that's the case," Anders said with a grunt, adjusting the pry bar, "you can afford a new helmet! Our deal still stands, doesn't it? Half your winnings belong to me?"

The shell of the helmet bent, and Anders pried it off. Fresh air filled Ransom's lungs. Sweat streaked down his face. Dizziness washed over him. Looking up, he saw a herald wearing the fleur-de-lis of Occitania. The *royal* herald.

"I'm coming," Ransom said, rising slowly, hoping he didn't faint.

The herald beamed at him and dashed from the blacksmith's tent. Ransom looked at Anders. They'd been friends for years, but their deal had ended years ago.

"How many knights from Ceredigion have ever won a tournament here?" he asked softly.

Anders smiled smugly. "None that I've ever seen. And I've been here a long time."

Ransom put his hand on his sword pommel. He gazed at the tent, remembering the years he had spent there, working the bellows for Anders to earn back the price of his armor. On his wrist he still wore the braided bracelet Claire had given him the last time he'd been in Chessy. It was dusty and coming loose in places, but he still remembered the night she'd given it to him. He would never forget it. Every time he passed the castle courtyard in Kingfountain, he would look up at the tower window, hoping for a sight of her. Only once had he been lucky enough to see her looking out. He didn't know if she had seen him as well.

Anders put his hand on Ransom's shoulder. "Go claim your prize, Ransom. You earned it. No one has defeated the Black Prince except his personal sword master. After today, everyone will know who you are."

A sickening feeling clutched at his stomach, but with it came a surge of triumph he'd never experienced before.

"They're waiting for you," Anders said, giving him a push toward the opening. "Get out there."

Ransom walked out of the tent and headed toward the stadium, where the crowd of nobles were sitting. Wooden palisades fenced off the lower-class folk. As soon as they saw him coming, a tumult began, and the cheering was deafening. Knights who had participated in the events saluted him as he plodded on, and the crowd opened so that he could enter the fighting yard. He saw banners congregated at the front of the stands, showing the different crests of those in attendance, including many of the noble houses of Occitania. At the very front, a series of steps had been put in place, leading to wooden platforms for the awarding of the prizes. The center one was vacant, and Ransom swallowed his nerves as he approached it. Prince Estian was not standing on any of the platforms. Since he'd been defeated, he wasn't entitled to pride of placement. He turned, his black armor spattered in dust, his helmet off. He watched Ransom approach without emotion.

Standing before the platforms were the highest noble ladies in attendance, including Princess Noemie. She held a wreath of silver laurel leaves. The victor's crown. She betrayed no emotion as she watched him approach, but Devon grinned at him from Noemie's side. The victory of Ceredigion was an accomplishment worthy of boasting.

The shouts grew louder until Ransom reached the steps and started up them. When Ransom reached the middle of the platform, about a dozen trumpeters raised their long horns and let out simultaneous blasts, which quieted the crowd.

A giddy feeling swelled in his stomach. The champion prize was usually significant, around five thousand livres, depending on the event. This might double what he already had from the ransoms he'd received during the short-lived rebellion. Lord Kinghorn had paid his ransom as promised, even though Ransom had been on the losing side of that conflict. A knight was no knight if he did not honor his pledges. Which meant he could expect something from the Black Prince as well.

Simon now borrowed funds from *him* instead of asking for money from the Elder King.

The blast of the trumpets ended. The herald of Occitania then stepped forward. "Presenting the victors of this tournament of Chessy!

In third place, and winner of two thousand livres, is Sir Rasten D'Orchard!"

Cheers swelled from the audience as the noblewoman standing next to Noemie placed her silver crown on the victor's head. She kissed him on the mouth before withdrawing. Ransom had forgotten about the Occitanian tradition of kissing the victors. It had totally slipped his mind.

Sir Rasten wiped tears from his eyes. He gazed at the noblewoman with adoration and gave her the knightly salute, which won a throbbing cheer from the crowd.

What do I do? Ransom wondered, feeling a growing sense of dread. Devon's wife had spent the last two years trying to make him fall in love with her. Sometimes she treated him like dirt. Other times, she flirted with him and hinted that she admired him. Still others, she spoke to him with undisguised coldness. He didn't trust her, or trust being alone with her, but in his duties for the mesnie, he was often assigned as her protector. It bothered him that she manipulated everyone around her so much, especially her husband.

"The second-place victor, winner of five thousand livres, is Sir Combren of Brugia, third count of Erfrut!"

Another cheer came as a second lady stepped forward to place a crown on Sir Combren's head. Ransom had beaten the man in the contest of swords. The other knight favored overhanging guard attacks, holding his sword above his head, blade pointed down. It took a lot of arm strength to pull off such a move once, let alone repeatedly, but it gave him a stylistic flair that had won him a lot of praise during the tournament. Until Ransom had disarmed him effortlessly.

When the noblewoman leaned down to kiss Sir Combren, he met her lips with relish, gripping her cheeks as he did so. He held the kiss for too long, earning a boo from the crowd. Sir Combren didn't seem to care and rocked back on his heels with a gloating smile. The lady flashed Ransom a wicked grin and winked at him. His insides roiled.

He looked at Devon pleadingly. *Don't make me do this,* he wanted to say.

Because he knew who would be delivering *his* crown.

Devon's grin only broadened, and he gave him a look that said, *Enjoy it while you can.*

The trumpets rose again and sent out another blast of notes, which calmed the restless crowd.

"And now," declared the herald when silence reigned once more. "The champion of the tournament of Chessy, blessed by our Lady of the Fountain, winner of ten thousand livres and the castle of Gison!"

A surprised gasp came from the audience. Ransom blinked in wonderment. A castle was part of the prize? He'd never seen that happen before.

"Sir Marshall Barton of the court of Kingfountain, also known as Sir Ransom!"

Cheers exploded in the air, sending waves of feeling through Ransom's body. He was conflicted, yet he couldn't deny this was probably the greatest moment in his life. The faces around him looked joyous, not contemptuous.

Then Princess Noemie came forward, holding the silver laurel crown in her hands. She tried to look proud and disinterested, but the noise and exuberance had an undeniable effect. A small smile cracked through. She stood before him, dressed in an expensive Occitanian gown, her hair in braids and coils beneath her silk veil.

She set the crown gently on his head, and its pressure was lighter than a breeze compared to the helmets he was used to wearing.

"Well done, Ransom," she said, her voice barely heard over the ruckus. She seemed to be enjoying herself, her face relaxed and eager, as if this moment meant something to her. "Thank you for not killing my brother."

"I wasn't going to," he said softly.

Her eyebrows arched. "Oh? It seemed as if you might."

She flashed him a radiant smile as she bent down to kiss him. His heart hammered like an earthquake. It felt . . . wrong. Disloyal. Her eyes closed as her face lowered to him.

Ransom was tortured by conflicted feelings. Suddenly, instead of savoring his triumph, he wished he were anywhere else. In fact, he wished he were in the queen's tower at the palace, a place he was forbidden to go. A place no one wanted to go but him.

A place where he could see Claire.

At the last moment, he turned his head slightly so that her lips brushed the edge of his mouth. He felt their softness, and it was a dangerous sensation that stirred emotions he didn't want to feel.

Because of her veil, perhaps no one saw what he did.

But when she opened her eyes, pulling back, he saw that his action had greatly offended her. He'd refused her kiss. From the look she gave him, he wondered if she would make a scene and force a kiss from him in front of everyone. He felt a trickle of defense go up his spine, his instincts warning him of her intentions.

He gave her a look that told her not to.

Her flawless knuckle came up and wiped her bottom lip as she stared at him in wonderment, in fury, yet she clearly knew there was still a crowd to please.

It was a look that promised revenge.

X

I must admit that it felt good to start writing again. Emiloh asked me about the book, and I shared portions of it with her yesterday. It led to a very deep conversation, one in which she spoke of her past, her youth in the duchy of Vexin. Her father died when she was fifteen. For some reason, I hadn't remembered that. She cherished him, so she could understand how I felt about losing my father. It's been difficult picturing her as anything other than the Queen of Ceredigion. But she knows fear, loss, and the uncertainty of the future. I asked if she had ever been in love before marrying the Elder King. Her look showed that her mind went far away. She nodded but said nothing more.

Ransom has returned to Kingfountain with Emiloh's eldest son. Apparently, the fool eejit won the tournament of Chessy, and if the rumors are true, he nearly killed the Black Prince. We saw them ride into the courtyard, but the tower is too high to see very well. I should like to see him again, but if fancies were horses, even beggars would ride. I don't know where I've heard that saying before. Things are so different now. But I wish him well. I truly do. Even if it means we cannot be together.

—Claire de Murrow
Queen's Tower
(a fair summer's morning)

CHAPTER
TWENTY-EIGHT

The King's Contempt

The queen's throne had been removed from the royal hall of Kingfountain, which was a sorry sight that still made Ransom cringe inside. The king's was empty, for the man could hardly bear to sit still and usually paced in front of the dais, as he did now, listening to the report of their victory.

"I wish you had been there, Father," said Devon the Younger. "We won honor for Ceredigion."

"It sounds like Sir Ransom did the brunt of the work," quibbled the father, giving Ransom a sidelong look and a somewhat approving smile. "They gifted you a castle, did they? Which one?"

"Gison castle, my lord," Ransom answered.

The king pursed his lips and nodded appreciatively. "That was probably intended for the Black Prince, whom they expected to win. That they gave it to you instead? Curious."

Devon the Younger flushed with anger. "It would have been dishonorable to do anything less."

"Don't patronize me with talks of honor, lad. Maybe they seek to bend our famous knight to their will. Gifts are quite an inducement."

"We all shared in the glory, Father. The celebratory feast was quite liberal. Even you would have thought so. The best wines, berries from Brythonica, and the meat . . . I've never tasted better."

"Oh, Lewis knows how to throw a party," said the king with disdain. "Was he there?"

"Of course not. We were allowed to compete on the condition neither of you would attend. He wouldn't go back on his word."

"I think he would, if it suited him. Well, there's enough of that. I'm off to the North tomorrow to hear justice. Be a good lad and try not to ruin the peace whilst I'm gone?"

"What is that supposed to mean?" Devon demanded.

The Elder King stopped pacing and gave his son an accusing look. "Your penchant for Occitanian wine might tempt you to carouse in the city again. I've permitted it in the past, even though I wish you wouldn't. I don't mind if you go hunting or hawking, something to divert your boredom, but I'd rather not have one of my sons stumbling around drunk in front of my people."

His son looked as if he would argue but reined in his temper and, after a brief struggle, maintained his equanimity too. "Of course. I will respect your wishes, Father."

The king lifted his eyebrows in surprise. "My son acquiesces? A true miracle worthy of the Lady."

But again, Devon didn't rise to the bait. "There is another tournament, Father. One that will be held in the duchy of Brythonica. Midsummer's Eve, I think. I should like your permission to attend that one as well."

The king screwed up his face and tilted his head. "Is that why you're being so agreeable?"

"No! Not at all. If you say no, then I will stay here and . . . hawk." He stared at his father with pleading eyes, with a look that barely concealed his desperation. It was clear from his tone that he thought the art of falconry beneath his contempt.

A look of wariness was on the king's face. "Brythonica, you say? A chance to see your brother Goff as well?"

"Yes . . . yes, of course!" said Devon. It was obvious he hadn't even considered that.

The king sighed. "Very well. I'll reward your forced humility with magnanimity. You have my permission to go, on the same terms as before. Lord Kinghorn sends his knights to escort you there and back."

"Thank you, Father!" Devon burst out excitedly.

"I wasn't finished. I'll inform Lord Carlson to provide ample funds. Your mesnie are champions now, and I want them to look the part. Fresh royal tunics, flourishes for the horses, that sort of thing. A new banner with the Silver Rose. He'll entrust Sir Simon with a thousand livres to spend liberally. Flaunt it, my son." He closed his hand into a fist. "Show them the *power* you represent."

The younger's eyes widened with eagerness. He was so grateful for the news that he didn't question his father's motives, but Ransom saw something beyond the words. The Elder King was turning their victory at Chessy into a political statement. But all Devon could see was the possibility of jingling coins and fame.

"You are . . . most generous, Father," said Devon, his exuberance spilling out. "Thank you. Thank you!"

"I don't usually squander my coins, lad. There is a purpose behind everything I do. Don't squander my goodwill."

"I won't. I promise you! Thank you again!"

The king gestured for them to leave and turned to approach Lord Kinghorn, who sat in one of the councilors' seats adjacent to the throne, along with the other members of the king's council.

Devon turned to leave, grinning eagerly at Robert and Simon before clapping them both on the back. Ransom stayed where he stood, hoping he'd have a moment to petition the king himself while his courage was high.

Lord Kinghorn noticed Ransom still standing there. He must have mentioned it in a low voice because the king abruptly turned around and gave him a quizzical look.

"What is it, young man?" asked the king. A look of annoyance flashed across his face. "Speak."

Ransom bristled at being called *young man*. He was almost twenty-three, but he didn't want to be peevish. "I wondered if I could have a word with you, my lord?"

"A word only? Very well. I grant you one."

Ransom wasn't sure if he was teasing or not, but he approached the king, who met him halfway.

"What is it, Sir Ransom?"

"Claire."

The king blinked. "You took me at my word, didn't you? One word. Well, I'm afraid I must ask you to elaborate on your intentions." Wariness crept over his expression. "If you're asking to marry one of the wealthiest heiresses in the kingdom, I'll save you the trouble with a definitive and unyielding answer of *no*."

"No, my lord, I wouldn't presume—"

"You would, actually. But go on. What do you want with her? I'm very busy. Speak plainly."

"I should like to see her. But I understand that no one may visit . . . the tower . . . without your express permission."

The king stroked his beard and then scratched his neck. His look of annoyance increased. "To what purpose?"

"We were childhood friends, my lord. We both grew up here at the palace. I should . . . I should . . ."

"Don't stammer! Say it."

"I should like to see her again. That is all. Her father died. I wish to give her my condolences."

The king threw up his hands. "I would be an ungrateful king indeed if I denied such a meek request. To the tower you may go. The password for the guards is *'perfidia.'* An hour only. Such can be spared for the victor of Chessy." He ended it with a laugh, showing he didn't think highly of the accomplishment.

"Thank you, my lord."

"Go on, get out. Enjoy your sport whilst the men in the kingdom work." He turned and walked back to Lord Kinghorn.

Ransom slipped away before the king could change his mind.

There were too many steps leading up to the queen's tower. It was the tallest tower within the palace, and Ransom had admired it from below many times. But climbing the spiral stairwell winded him, and his anxiety increased with every step. A few torches hung from rings in the walls, but the arrow slits were narrow, and it was dark. Wind whistled through the gaps, and it was colder than he'd expected. He ran his hand over the rough stone bricks as he headed up.

By the time he reached the top of the stairs, he was gasping for breath and put his hand on the window casing as he paused a moment to catch it again. The guards at the foot had allowed him to pass after his declaration of the king's password. He had seen no one else.

While Ransom was still bent double and panting, the door to the chamber opened abruptly.

And there was Claire de Murrow.

"I heard someone coming up the steps, but then it went quiet and . . ." Her eyes widened in recognition, and her speech trailed off.

"I'm sorry . . . I didn't announce myself," he said breathlessly.

"You're not supposed to be here, Ransom," she said, her expression showing worry. "You'll get in trouble."

"The k-king . . . granted me permission . . . to see you."

Her hand came up to the edge of her bodice as she blinked in surprise. "You asked to see me?"

"I did. I was given only an hour. May I come in?"

"Of course!" She turned. "Emi, look! Look who it is!"

As he entered the chamber, he took note of how small and close the space felt. Even so, this wasn't a normal prisoner's quarters. There was a curtained bed against the far wall, framed in golden wood with little filigree designs carved into it. A mirrored wardrobe was built into the foot of the bed, the door ajar. A fire burned in a hearth decorated with marble pillars. The floor, cut from diagonal slices of wood, was picturesque as well, although a rich red rug concealed most of it.

By the only window sat a sturdy desk and two chairs, and he saw several small books stacked on it, as well as one that was open with an inkwell and stained quill nearby.

Queen Emiloh rose from the bed, wearing a simple but rich gown. She was just as tall and regal as he remembered, and he dropped to a knee in reverence.

"Oh dear, no," said the queen with a smile. "I'm in disgrace. No need for that. Come, Ransom. Please. We are friends."

Claire had walked to the table and gently closed the open book, scooting it toward the edge. He wondered what was written inside it, and why she'd so deliberately moved it out of the way.

"You are still my queen," Ransom said, feeling a surge of gratitude for her—thick and warm and delicious. He'd never forgotten the way she'd paid his ransom when he was captured by DeVaux's men. The last he'd heard, DeVaux had been humbled by Benedict and the mercenaries.

"I have no rings for you to kiss anymore," Emiloh said. "So good of you to climb up here. Claire and I do not get many visitors."

"Not many at all," said Claire with an impish smile. "But we're never lonely."

Ransom gazed around the room again, looking at the trappings and the shape of the tower, and felt a strange sense of familiarity. As if he'd been there before. But of course he hadn't. He would have remembered climbing all those steps. Still, something about it thrummed inside him. He heard the gentle lapping sound in his ears, but it wasn't a premonition of danger. Something in the room had triggered a part of him. He didn't understand it.

"We've heard about your victory at Chessy," said the queen. She gave Claire an encouraging nod and a significant look.

"We did!" said Claire, a little breathlessly. "Well done, Sir Ransom! I wish we'd been there. Of course, we couldn't have been there, naturally, but both of us should have . . . liked to have . . . been." She bit her lip, her cheeks flushing.

"Thank you," he said. "I didn't come to boast." He felt his feelings tying themselves up in knots. "Your Highness, I'm sorry that you are . . . that you are imprisoned here. Is there anything I can get for you? Anything you need?"

"Just my freedom," she said sadly. "It's been two years. That feels a long time, but it has gone by quickly. Thank you for offering. Lord Kinghorn makes sure that our needs are met."

"He's a good man," said Ransom.

"Indeed," said the queen, who gave Claire another imploring look that Ransom didn't understand.

He sighed. "I'm sorry about your father, Claire." He looked at her, feeling her loss keenly. "I met him . . . well, I should probably confess that I surrendered to him on behalf of the queen's . . . son. He had already captured Prince Benedict by that point and blocked a bridge. I did notice he seemed to be injured."

"His leg, was it?" Claire asked, her countenance falling.

"It was his leg, yes," Ransom said. "I heard that he died at Atha Kleah shortly thereafter."

Tears welled up in her eyes. She quickly brushed them away. "Yes. Yes, I know."

"I'm sorry to bring you pain. I respected him. It's a grievous loss. I'm sorry, Claire."

She squeezed her eyes shut, nodding briskly. He hated how helpless he felt. How he wished he could do something to help her, to soothe her grief.

"Your Highness," he said, turning back to Queen Emiloh. "There is something about that night that I haven't told anyone. I feel a bit foolish, but it needs to be said, I think."

"Go on," said the queen, looking at him seriously. Claire's eyes shot open, and she looked at him in confusion.

"After I crossed the bridge, when I was going to see Lord Archer, I felt the presence of . . ." His words trailed off. "Forgive me. This won't make sense unless I go back further. Remember the night I first began serving your son? I reported that there was a lady in a cloak."

"Yes. Of course I remember. You brought my son safely back to the palace. The dock warden never found the woman or her guards."

"Your Highness, she was there that night. When we surrendered to Lord Archer."

The queen's brow furrowed. "She was among Lord Archer's knights?"

"No," Ransom said. "She was in the woods nearby."

The color leached out of Claire's face.

"How did you see her?" the queen asked.

He sighed again, hesitant to explain himself, given he could not offer a rational explanation. And yet . . . what he'd seen and felt that night had haunted him in the long months since, even more so since the tournament. "I didn't. Nor did I get a good look at her that first night in Kingfountain," he said. "I didn't just stumble upon her in that alleyway. I went looking for her because I could sense her presence. I don't know how to describe it, only that I knew she was coming to the tavern. I felt her coming. And she . . . felt me. That was why she turned and fled. I sensed her that same way in the woods by Lord Archer's knights."

"Did she harm my father, do you think?" Claire asked pointedly. "Was his death more than a happenstance? 'Twas that very night he formed a pain in his foot."

Ransom's stomach clenched with dread. He'd never considered the possibility before, if only because he'd assumed the lady had been there for Devon—to watch him or perhaps even protect him if Devon had it right. It had never occurred to him that she might have come for revenge, but it made a sick kind of sense. If she really were an Occitanian spy, surely she would be inclined to murder the person whose presence had ensured the Elder King's victory.

"I don't know, Claire," he finally said, meeting and holding her gaze. "I only know that his foot was injured that night. I saw him limp, but it went deeper than that. I *knew* he was injured. I could sense his pain."

"Sir Ransom . . . are you indeed Fountain-blessed?" the queen asked.

"I don't . . . really . . . know."

"Have you had this feeling about others? Or was this lady the first?"

"The first. They say one of the Black Prince's knights is Fountain-blessed, but I've never gotten such a feeling from him. It's just talk."

The queen began pacing. "I've long suspected you might be. Lord DeVaux insisted that you were, which is why it cost so much to save you."

"I was saved by a loaf of moldy bread and bandages," Ransom said.

"Isn't it possible the Fountain might work its miracles by simple means rather than grand gestures? The legends of the Fountain-blessed go back to the reign of King Andrew and his court. This palace," she said, gesturing to the room, "was built in emulation of it. No one knows where he lived. Some say the original is in Occitania. Others claim it was in Brythonica. There are so many legends about them, the men and women and Wizrs of the court." She gazed at him. "It feels like the world keeps returning to these stories. That they must be real because they keep happening, over and over again. Sir Ransom, if you *are* Fountain-blessed, then the legends say that you need to seek a sign of it."

He swallowed. Lord Kinghorn had said a similar thing years before. He'd thought of it many times since, but he had been too afraid to pursue the possibility. Afraid of losing control of himself. When he had felt the Fountain's influence on him, he hadn't always liked the violence he'd done. He felt he needed a cause to serve, a way to bridle it. It was part of the reason he'd prefer to be in service to a lord than to start his own mesnie. "What do you mean?"

"There are sacred shrines dedicated to the Lady of the Fountain. Not the little pools that people toss coins into. The ancient ones. They say that those who are Fountain-blessed can make a pilgrimage to one of these shrines and seek a sign. If they are truly one of the blessed, the Lady will give them a gift from the waters. Sometimes a ring. Or a cape. Or a scabbard."

Ransom felt troubled. Lord Kinghorn had also tried that—and failed. He gazed at Claire and saw a look of consternation on her face. It was clear that she didn't believe a word of what was being said.

"I still serve your son, Your Highness," he said. "We're going to Brythonica next. Are there any shrines there?"

"Yes," said Emiloh. "It is an ancient kingdom. Visit the sanctuary of Our Lady of Toussan. If I were still the queen, I would send you there now."

"Should I tell the king?"

She shook her head. "He doesn't believe in such things, but they say the very crown he wears was once a gift from the Fountain. There is no record of when the hollow crown was made or by whom. It has strange powers, Ransom. I urge you to do this on your journey to Brythonica. I believe it will help you defend my son."

"I will, Your Highness," Ransom said, although he still felt conflicted about his capacity for aggression and violence. His gaze returned to Claire. "I feel like my time is near an end, but I don't want to leave."

Claire's face brightened. "We go for walks every day if the weather is fair," she said, turning to the queen.

Emiloh's expression darkened. "He would get in trouble, Claire."

"No one goes there," she said. "There's a little garden in the courtyard above the cistern. Lord Kinghorn lets us walk there, to see the sun and feel the breeze. You could find it, Ransom. You could meet us there."

He wanted to, but he also feared the repercussions. More so for Claire and the queen than for himself. "I will see if I can."

"Please do," Claire implored. She lifted a hand as if to touch him, but then let it fall. "I should like to see you again."

"So would I," Ransom said, giving her a smile.

Going down the stairs was much easier than going up them had been. He felt a foolish grin on his mouth the whole way down and became more determined to find the small courtyard with the cistern. Claire had described the location to him and how to access it. They were usually escorted by one of Lord Kinghorn's knights. Ransom would need to go there first. It was a risky proposition, but perhaps he could convince Devon to come with him—he could visit with his mother, and Ransom could talk to Claire.

When he reached the bottom steps, he felt a prickle go down his back. He knew the guards were supposed to be stationed on the other side of the door, but he sensed that they were gone. Then he felt someone behind him, and he whirled, his hand wrapping around the hilt of his sword.

"So this is where you went," Noemie said, emerging from the shadows beneath the stairs. The look on her face was raw and angry. Offended.

He stared at her for a moment, then released his grip on the weapon. For a moment, he'd feared it was the lady in the cloak.

"Why are you here, my lady?" he asked her warily.

"*Your* lady?" she said, walking up to him, her eyes burning with emotion. "Don't mock me, Sir Ransom. Not when you avoided my kiss. You shamed me in front of everyone. At least now I know why. But I still don't understand it." He saw tears of fury glisten in her eyes. "*I* am to be your queen. Your devotion should be to me. Not to her. Not to that Gaultic girl. They say you love her. Is it true?"

He felt the hairs on his neck stand. "Why are you here?"

"Because I'm jealous! You want me to admit it? Why do you torture me like this? This is not the way it is supposed to be, Ransom. You are supposed to love *me*."

He took a step toward the door. "You are Devon's wife."

"Yes! Queen Genevieve of the legends fell in love with her husband's best knight. You aren't doing what you are supposed to do. Why? Why do you torture me? This is supposed to be *our* time, Ransom, but it doesn't even seem like you care." She wiped a tear on her sleeve.

He stared at her in total confusion. Her meaning escaped him, but he felt wary of being alone with her. "I have no idea what you're talking about," he said, then hurried to the door and opened it, leaving Noemie behind in the shadows.

Ransom was as good as his word, although that shouldn't have surprised me. He found his way to the cistern courtyard and brought Devon with him. He's done it thrice, and each time, I am grateful for the chance to talk. He seems worried about something, but he will not reveal what it is. Whenever I ask, he just glances at Devon and then shakes his head. I can see the wrinkles of worry on his brow. How I wish I could ease them.

The queen has chided me that I am too reticent around my knight. She said a popular saying in the duchy of Vexin is that a woman must show more affection than she feels or else the poor, daft man she fancies will never take the hint. While it is true that men are poor and daft when it comes to love, I do not want to be the hunter but the hunted. The problem is that I long for what eludes me, not what is offered to me. If I bend to the Elder King's will and marry a man of his choosing, I can escape this prison. I can return to my homeland, my beloved Legault, which I can only reclaim with an army behind me. But my heart is with Ransom. He is being celebrated as a champion, a knight without peer. It is only a matter of time before other maidens will attempt to conquer him.

I wish he weren't going to Brythonica for the tournament.
I wish he'd stay here, where he is nearby. But I know I'm being
a reckless fool. Go win another tournament, Ransom. Show
them your worth.

—Claire de Murrow
Cistern Courtyard
(Fare thee well.)

CHAPTER
TWENTY-NINE

Whispers from the Fountain

Noemie's words itched inside Ransom's mind, festering like a dirty wound. He did not trust her, not in the smallest degree, yet her actions, especially since that interlude in the shadows of the tower, seemed to match her words. Whenever he was in the same room as her, she would often look his way. The moment their eyes met, she'd look down, her hands trembling, her conversation distracted. Everything about it felt wrong, and the knowledge of how she felt—or claimed she felt—clashed with his sense of honor, his sense of himself, and his feelings of duty to his king and his friend. And the ache he carried in his heart for Claire.

He did all that he could to stay away from Devon's wife, to not let her trap him into conversation as she had done in the tower. She didn't touch him, or give him any outward show of kindness. But those eyes, pleading and raw, unsettled him. And her words were a mystery he could not comprehend. She'd made it sound as if their love had been preordained somehow. He was mystified by it, feeling as if he were walking in a fog. The stolen moments with Claire and the queen were the only times when he felt his mind was clear.

Devon's entourage rode their horses to Brythonica, armor bright and polished, banners fluttering in the air. Noemie rode alongside Devon, her jewels glittering in the sun, the silk scarves wrapping her headdress, trailing in the breeze, her posture elegant atop the strong chestnut she rode. He saw her laughing and talking with her husband. But every once in a while, she would look back at Ransom, and he would look away, pretending to enjoy the scenery while he felt that awful tugging sensation in his chest, one that pulled him between attraction to the beautiful princess and his deep misgivings about what she intended. Why would she deliberately try to tempt him when he showed no interest in her at all?

He sensed a horse approach alongside him and turned to find Sir Simon of Holmberg there in his shadow.

"Are you looking for money to borrow, Simon?" he asked, smiling at his fellow knight.

"Not yet, of course," replied the knight. "Actually, the king's steward has more than compensated you for the previous loans. Not to mention your first payment arrived from your new castle in Gison. You are becoming a wealthy man, Ransom, for you spend very little of what is your own. The other knights in the mesnie squander their income. You and I are the only ones who seem capable of keeping our heads when it comes to debt."

"Life is a harsh and foul-smelling bill collector," Ransom said. "I never want to be a debtor to that foul onion again."

"Have you been to your new castle yet?"

"No, but I hope to visit it after this next tournament. My father's castle was always in a bad state of repair. I hope the one in Gison doesn't cost me more than it's worth."

"With that attitude, you won't be taken in easily," Simon said approvingly. Then he lowered his voice. "Do you consider me a friend? Or, if that is too strong a word, an ally?"

Ransom turned his head and gave Simon a confused look. "We've known each other for a long time now, Simon. I do consider you a friend."

"Can I offer you a friend's advice, then? Even if it is something you'll not want to hear?"

A concerned lump formed in Ransom's stomach. "Of course you can."

"I've overheard Sir Robert talking to some of the others. He's jealous of you, Ransom. Surely you know that."

"If you thought that would surprise or offend me, you're mistaken," Ransom said softly, his insides throbbing with sudden anger.

"Wait until you hear what he says behind your back. What he says to Talbot and sometimes Alain. He said you're playing Devon for the fool. That you and the princess have been meeting secretly."

The injustice of the accusation stung him. "That's not true," he said, his temper flashing.

"Whether or not it's true," Simon said, his voice suddenly pleading, "be careful. Robert is watching you, determined to find you out or find something incriminating. I've seen her look at you, Ransom. Something's changed. She used to look at you with indifference or scorn, but not anymore."

Ransom closed his eyes, the anguish increasing. He wasn't the only one who had noticed then. He opened his eyes and turned to look Simon in the face. "I swear on my honor I've done nothing wrong." He held up his wrist and rubbed the braided bracelet that Claire had given to him. "I already wear a lady's favor for all the world to see. And I would *never* betray the king."

Simon looked at him, his expression neutral. "I believe you. But be careful, Ransom. Be very careful."

They arrived in the beautiful seaside city of Ploemeur, and servants brought them up a winding cliff to the palace built atop a jagged mountain crest. It was a beautiful country with fields of ripe berries being harvested by farmers who lived in quaint cottages. The fortress was impressive and secluded, its strategic position atop the ridge making it unassailable by sea, and the switchbacks offered it protection from armies on foot or horseback.

They were greeted at the palace by Prince Goff and his wife, Duchess Constance. They appeared to be quite well matched despite the fact that she was several years older than the prince, who was now in his seventeenth year. The young couple enthusiastically proclaimed that Constance was with child. A troubled look crossed Noemie's face, but she was gracious in her response, even though her expression seemed to indicate that she was repressing great pain.

The Argentine siblings had always bantered with each other, but not today. Devon's mood soured immediately, and they were shown to their accommodations within the palace. While their luggage was brought up from the baggage horses, Ransom caught sight of Devon on his knees, trying to comfort Noemie, who was sobbing. It was clear the prince's news had upset both of them, likely because Noemie's womb had not yet quickened. He quietly withdrew, not wanting to intrude on such a private moment.

He walked the palace grounds, admiring the decorations and the breezy air gusting in from the huge open windows. His senses reached out in yet another attempt to detect the presence of the cloaked lady, but he did not feel her. The palace had a restful feeling about it, a sense of harmony with the Fountain. They would be safe here.

One of the glass doors led to an opulent balcony, so he wandered out there to take in the view. He watched as the waves crashed onto the beaches far below, which adjoined the town at the base of the ridge. From the heights, he could see the sanctuary of Our Lady of Toussan. It was an impressive structure, with tall towers that gleamed in the sunlight. As he stared at it, he recalled Queen Emiloh's admonition to go there. The sanctuary of St. Penryn was farther east, but it was invisible in the distance—although he did get a sight of Averanche.

Ransom was still standing there, soaking in the atmosphere and the salty air of the sea, when he was found by the chamberlain of the castle.

"Some of the knights of the mesnie are interested in visiting the town below," the steward said, smiling. "Shopping for trinkets. Would you care to join them? I was sent to find you."

"Is my master planning on staying here?" Ransom asked. He wanted to be sure that someone was guarding Devon at all times.

"He would like to stay with his wife at the palace, I believe. Are you interested in joining the others?"

Confident Devon would be safe and under guard—even more so because of the peaceful feeling he got from the palace—Ransom said, "I should like to see the sanctuary of Our Lady of Toussan."

The steward beamed. "That is a commendable place to visit. If you'll accompany the knights, I will send an extra servant to bring you to the sanctuary to pay your respects."

"Thank you," Ransom said. "I would be grateful. Is it the oldest sanctuary in Brythonica?"

"Oh yes," said the man with enthusiasm. "It is quite remarkable. I hope you enjoy your stay with us, Sir Ransom."

"So do I," he replied. Perhaps he'd also find a gift for Claire while he was here. He recalled the necklace she'd shown him years before. He'd like to get her another one—a token she could wear, much like the bracelet still on his wrist.

The sanctuary of Our Lady of Toussan was even more impressive up close when one stood beneath the tall arches and gazed up at the imposing spiked towers. Gurgling fountains surrounded the grounds, and Ransom enjoyed watching the visitors approach them with a coin or two. In approaching the sanctuary, he'd witnessed several children, some as young as two, kiss their coins before throwing them into the water with a shriek of delight.

He had to ascend a mountain of stairs to reach the sturdy doors to the inner sanctum, and his anticipation built with every step. Once he stepped inside, a worshipful silence engulfed him. Only whispers were spoken here. He felt a sense of solitude as he entered the space, the speckled stone more aged than that of Kingfountain, but it was a strangely comforting feeling. His runaway thoughts finally eased their grip. The sexton at the doors greeted him with a benevolent smile that Ransom acknowledged with a nod.

An oval-shaped pool of clear water sat at the exact center of the enormous hall with its black-and-white-tiled floor. Many knelt around it, he counted nearly a dozen, hands clasped and heads bowed. Some looked into the waters. Some looked up to the interlacing buttresses in the ceiling overhead. Brilliant, multicolored light sparkled in through stained-glass windows. At the apex of the hall stood an enormous statue dedicated to the Lady of the Fountain. A pair of young people stood in front of it, hands clasped, gazing adoringly up at it.

Ransom felt strange and a little out of place. Out of everyone kneeling around the main fountain, only one was a knight like himself. A few of the other visitors had taken note of his presence, but Ransom overcame his feeling of self-consciousness and knelt by the stone ridge of the pool. Something didn't feel right, however, and he had the impulse to wander a bit more. Trusting in the sensation, he rose and started walking.

In his exploration, he found a small anteroom with a little stained fountain bubbling within it. It was a confined space, not at all as striking as the huge hall, and the stone of the fountain looked worn away from the constant pressure of the water. It smelled old and dank, but it *felt* better. No one else was in the anteroom, and so he entered it and walked around the fountain, watching the water burbling from the spout at the top and listening to the splashing noises it made as it fell.

The rim of the fountain was wide enough to form a bench seat, so he sat down on it, immediately feeling the cold through his clothes. A few coins lay at the tiled bottom, nearly black with stain. How long had they been sitting in the waters?

In the solitude of the room, he planted his palms on the cool stone and bowed his head. He tried to summon the feeling of the rushing waters. Nothing happened. Was this what had happened to Lord Kinghorn?

He waited, trying to wrestle through his feelings. He felt unworthy, even a little ashamed of his act of reverence. Feelings of angst and self-delusion stole over him. What was he doing there? Who was he to think that the Fountain would speak to him? That he might be Fountain-blessed? No, he was the second son of an insignificant lord who was dead and gone. He was a knight with too much blood on his hands. When he died, his corpse would be buried in a mass grave after some tragic battle, not decorated like King Gervase's and sent into the river.

He remembered the funeral, the solemn knights carrying their king to the edge of the water. The sound of the falls seemed to whisper to him that he would never be a great man like Gervase.

"May I help you?"

With the noise of the fountain, he hadn't heard any footsteps approach. Ransom's head snapped up, and he stared into the eyes of the aging deconeus, the gray-and-white robes revealing his office.

Ransom stood quickly, embarrassed to have been discovered there. "Pardon me, Deconeus. I meant no disrespect."

"Of course you didn't," said the man in a kindly way. "You come from Ceredigion. I recognize the badge on your tunic. You are one of the king's knights, I presume? A guest at the palace?"

"Indeed, sir," Ransom said. "If you'll excuse me."

"Tarry, if you will," coaxed the deconeus. "I don't often find many visitors here. Most say their prayers around the large pool over yon."

"I didn't know it was off-limits," Ransom said.

"It isn't, but few people come here. Why have you come, Sir Knight? To pray for victory in the tournament?"

Ransom felt unsure of himself. The dark feelings he'd experienced had rattled him. "No."

"Then why have you come? Why to *this* fountain in particular?"

Part of him wanted to trust the old man. Part of him feared what the deconeus might say. His reluctance to seek out the voice still churned inside him. He wrestled within himself.

"I see you are reluctant to speak," said the deconeus. "Then I will. While I was going about my duties, I heard a whisper from the Fountain to come here. And so I came. And then I found you. I could have ignored that whispering. Many do. But I've learned over the years to heed it. I was supposed to find you, although I know not why. Perhaps you do?"

Ransom blinked in surprise at the deconeus's words. "The Fountain told you to come here?"

"It did, sir, although it was more of a feeling than a request made in words. I imagine it brought you here as well. Why did you come? What are you seeking?"

He still wasn't sure if he should trust the old man—he felt vulnerable here, as if he'd gone into battle without his armor—but the deconeus's story was compelling. And Queen Emiloh had sent him here with a purpose.

"I seek a blessing from the Fountain," Ransom said softly.

The deconeus squinted a bit and nodded. "Ah. I thought so. You will not find that here. Try St. Penryn. That sanctuary is even older."

His feelings of confusion intensified. Why hadn't the Fountain whispered its directive to him rather than the deconeus? But perhaps this nudge was all that he needed. St. Penryn wasn't that far. A boat could get him there and back in a day.

He sighed with frustration and stepped out of the anteroom. When he returned to the large pool, fewer people were there. But one stood out to him. A lady knelt at the edge, her silk veil concealing her face. But her braided chestnut hair was familiar to him, as was the fine dress she took no pains to conceal.

It was Noemie, kneeling in prayer.

He felt something inside him lurch. A sound filled his ears, although it was not that of the fountain but the dissonance of stone grinding on stone. Dizziness washed over him, and he had to put his hand on a pillar to keep from swooning. The feeling left as quickly as it had come, but it made him feel sick inside.

Noemie lifted her head and raised the veil. She turned and looked at him.

Her eyes widened with shock, and then a look of hope filled them. She rose and started walking toward him.

He looked at the door, wanting to run.

"You came," she whispered excitedly when she neared him. "I prayed that you would."

The Elder King's resentment has not waned. Someone reported to him that we had been seen near the cistern. I was brought before the king's council and interrogated on who was there and what was said. They suspect another bout of treason, at least that is what the questions led me to believe. I've witnessed nothing of the sort. Just a mother who loves her eldest son and a son who wishes to spend time with her. They asked me if Ransom was behind the meeting, but I took responsibility and said it was my idea. They seemed almost disappointed it wasn't more insidious.

How long will this confinement last? The Elder King's will is implacable. He still hates Emiloh. But there is something more than the rebellion of her sons. This hurt goes deeper than that. I wish I knew what lay behind it. A wound can be healed if it is treated in time. This one still festers.

—Claire de Murrow
Queen's Tower
(guilty of meddling in the affairs of kings and queens)

CHAPTER THIRTY

Shadows Unseen

oemie reached out and touched his arm, making Ransom recoil from her touch. His cheeks burned with consternation, and he took a step backward.

"It was not your prayers that brought me here," he said in a warning voice. "I must go."

"No!" She clutched his tunic instead, her fingers curling into a fist. "No, please . . . not yet."

"This is unseemly, Your Highness," he said, wondering if he should break her grip himself. People were already starting to look their way. If news should reach Sir Robert or Devon himself . . .

"Don't you dare walk away from me," she said, her voice throbbing with emotion. "Please. If you are suffering even a small portion, admit it now."

"I admit to nothing," Ransom said. "You are mistaken if you suspect feelings that are not there."

She looked around the assembly, and then she unclenched her hand and released his velvet tunic. "This is not the time or place, but we must talk, Ransom." Her voice dropped low. "You must understand that Devon's *life* is at stake."

He stared at her in surprise. Was she speaking of the cloaked lady, or was this merely a new tactic to control him? He suspected the latter, although he took any threats against Devon seriously.

"Meet me tonight," she whispered. "In the corridor by our rooms there is a pillar with the raven mark leading to an anteroom with a small fountain. I will meet you there at midnight."

She turned, rubbing her hands together.

"I will not," he said brusquely.

She looked over her shoulder. "Then you do not value the life of my husband. Midnight."

Ransom began to walk fiercely toward the main door of the sanctuary. As he exited, the light from the sun was so blinding he had to shield his eyes with his hand. He nearly walked into a man.

"Ransom?"

It was Sir Robert Tregoss.

Ransom gave him a wary look. "I thought you were with the others?"

"I came with Princess Noemie," he said. "Were you . . . meeting her?" His voice dripped with suspicion.

"No," Ransom answered bluntly and marched off, taking the downward steps two at a time.

A seabird's cry split the air overhead as he jogged down the steps. Many of the birds had gathered around the visitors, some pecking at fallen crumbs. The princess's words had been burned inside his mind. They whispered in his ears as he returned to the market to look for a piece of jewelry for Claire. He found a necklace with four glass beads woven into a Gaultic knot made of silver. He bought it and didn't even haggle over the price. He felt as if Noemie's eyes were following him. Every time he caught a glimpse of dark braided hair or a silk veil, he wondered if it was her.

And that night, when he heard a bell toll the midnight hour, he still lay awake on his pallet, gripping the necklace in his hand, feeling the edges of the silver mark his skin. He'd passed the raven mark after returning to the castle. Heard the splashing of the water.

He knew Noemie would be waiting for him there. Moonlight came in through the silk curtains. It felt as bright as noon. A fever burned inside him. She claimed to know something, perhaps about the cloaked lady. The knowledge teased him, tantalized him, but he lay still. He would have to seek the information another way. To meet her in private would be beyond dangerous.

How long would she wait before she realized that he wasn't coming?

The tournament held in Ploemeur had brought knights from nearly every kingdom. And Ransom went through them all like a farmer scything his field. The agitation he felt because of the impossible situation with Devon's wife seemed to fill him with limitless energy. He felt the churn of the waterfall before each match began, and there was no diminishing of it after the contest ended. He unhorsed every opponent effortlessly. And one-on-one, he was peerless.

His last victim was Sir Terencourt, the champion of the Duchess of Brythonica. Ransom battered him down again and again, instinctively knowing the knight's weaknesses. Each attack from the knight was suspected, anticipated, and blocked. He went down for the third time, barking in pain and clutching his armored leg.

Again Ransom stood over him with his bastard sword, the thrum of energy still at its peak. "Yield."

The knight leaned forward, panting, and then clambered back to his feet. He looked at Ransom with fatigued eyes. There was a dribble of blood on his forehead.

"I . . . will . . . not," the knight rasped.

Ransom stepped back, feeling it was almost a mockery to fight a man who was clearly winded and suffering the humiliation of pending defeat. He glanced at the crowd, saw the eager looks for this last bout to be over.

The thought came that the knight was only pretending to be winded, that he would leap and attack with sudden fury and vengeance.

Ransom turned his head just in time, the warning coming to his aid.

The knight launched his attack at that very moment, sword arm raised high to bring a sweeping blow down on Ransom's helmet. The ruse would have worked had Ransom not sensed the attack.

He felt a surge of energy, an emotion like rage, and spun around, swinging his own weapon. His sword cut off Sir Terencourt's arm as it was descending in a downstroke. The knight, his eyes bright with shock, fell to his knees. The limb clashed to the ground, still gripping the sword.

A gasp went up from the stands.

Ransom couldn't believe what had happened. He hadn't intended to maim the man—he'd moved on instinct. Sometimes the rage of battle just made him lose all control.

Sir Terencourt fell forward, holding himself up with his remaining arm. "I yield!" he croaked in pain.

Ransom backed away from him, shock and horror making him dizzy as he watched men drag away the champion of Brythonica. Someone shouted for a barber. He shifted his gaze to the crowd, taking in the expressions on their faces. Fear. Horror. He'd not only bested their champion, he'd ruined the man. Dizziness washed through him, and he felt he would stumble. But he took a deep breath, sheathed his sword, and forced himself to return to Devon's pavilion.

When he got there, he was alone for a moment, left to wrestle with self-recrimination and the fear of what he was capable of—of what he could become if he were not careful. Memories engulfed him. He recalled the time he'd stood alone against DeVaux's men. The same thing had happened during the Brugian invasion. What was he becoming? A butcher of men? What would Lord Kinghorn say if he saw him now?

He heard voices outside, and Devon and Noemie entered the tent. The look she gave him wasn't one of horror, it was a look of awe. She gazed at him with undisguised adoration.

Devon looked a little greensick. "By the Fountain, Ransom," he said, shaking his head. "I thought he was going to strike while you were distracted, but you spun around and took off his arm. Remind me never to get on your bad side!"

Sirs Robert and Talbot came in next.

"How much did you win?" Talbot asked.

"I bet against Ransom," Robert said, grimacing. He gave him a look of jealousy and disappointment. "You took off the man's arm!"

"You're only sore because you lost," Devon said. "It was foolish of you to bet against Ransom. I knew he'd win. Just . . . not like *that*. Well, it's the risk we all take when we become knights. Some poor fellow was so concussed today he says the same phrase over and over again, like a mule kicked him in the head."

Sir Simon came in, juggling a coin bag with a bright smile. "That was unexpected, but we're now the favorites for winning the tournament. The last event takes place in two days. Everyone needs to recover . . . everyone who *can*, I mean. I think we'll win this one, my lord."

"Oh, we will," Devon said, clapping Ransom on the shoulder. "They'll all be too afraid to charge against our mountain!" He turned to Sir Simon. "Have we spent all of the livres Father gave us yet?"

"No, there's still quite a bit left," Simon said.

"Then give each man their due, and we'll spend the rest of it tonight! They may be angry that we bested their champion, but only a fool begrudges a man liberal with his coin."

The knights of the mesnie crowded around Simon, hands open eagerly for coin, except for Ransom. He still felt sick inside. He had no desire to wander the town again, especially as word of his victory spread. The locals would hate him. Once the livres were handed out, the knights of the mesnie left the tent, leaving Ransom alone with Devon and Noemie. She stood by a little pedestal with a spherical bauble on it, picking it up and toying with it.

"Go enjoy yourself," Devon said to him, looking confused by Ransom's reticence.

"My lord, I'd like to beg your leave to go on a journey."

Devon's brow wrinkled. "What?"

"I would like to leave Ploemeur."

"Impossible. I need you for the last event, Ransom. We're going to win this one too and wipe that smug grin off my brother's face."

"I'll be back in time for that," Ransom said. "I'd like to go to St. Penryn."

His request seemed to baffle Devon even more. "St. Penryn?"

"I'll need use of a boat, but I could probably be back at the palace by midnight if I leave soon."

When he said the word *midnight*, Noemie flashed him a pained look.

"First you wanted to see Our Lady of Toussan, and now St. Penryn. Whatever for?"

He wasn't sure what to say. Noemie stood within hearing, so he could not possibly share his fears about the Occitanian spy, not given the way Devon had reacted in the past. He also did not wish to announce for everyone's ears that Queen Emiloh had given him the charge, and while Devon knew Ransom could do things most men could not, he had never expressed a true belief in the Fountain. It was unclear how he would react.

"I feel I need to go," he said simply.

Devon pursed his lips. "Are you all right, Ransom? You look troubled."

He stared at the Younger King. "I'm troubled by what I did to that man."

Devon nodded and put his hand on Ransom's shoulder. "Guilt is unpleasant. Thankfully, I find solace from it in a cup of wine. Maybe you find yours in a better place. I did want your advice, though. Yesterday, while we were spending my father's money so wantonly, I came across an old friend who is here for the tournament."

"Who?" Ransom asked.

"Sir James Wigant," Devon said. "When he heard you were fighting, he decided not to join in. He wanted us to have the glory. He can be pragmatic about some things."

"What advice do you need?"

"Well, Sir James is chafing under the restrictions my father has put on him as well. He cannot leave the kingdom without permission, and he owes the king a loyalty debt he'll be paying off for years. He's right sick of them, to be honest. Feels we're beating cheated of our rightful inheritances. He warned me that if I don't do something about Bennett, my brother will be named heir instead of me."

Ransom frowned. James was always scheming, and his schemes rarely turned out well for anyone involved. "And?"

"And I want to know what you think. Should I . . . cause some trouble for my brother?"

"What good would that do?" Ransom asked.

"Father respects someone who fights for what he wants. He's not impressed by knightly tournaments. Although he's glad for the reputation they give us, I know how he truly feels. He thinks them a waste of time . . . and money. He's proud of what Bennett has done to assert his authority throughout the realm and his own duchy. I think Father will only be proud of a son who defeats him. I have to start somewhere."

"This isn't the time to risk your father's anger," Ransom said. "Nor is it wise for Sir James to do the same."

Devon smiled and patted his arm. "I thought you'd say that."

The tent door ruffled, and Devon's brother Goff stepped in, his face mottled with anger.

"Ah, Brother," Devon said, feigning cheerfulness. "We were just talking about siblings."

Goff gave Ransom a threatening look. "May we speak, Devon? Privately?"

"Yes, yes—we shall. Ransom was just asking for a boat to visit St. Penryn. Could you arrange it? It would be much faster than going by horse."

Goff sneered. "The tide is out now and comes in this afternoon. It would be foolish to send a boat out now. Perhaps tomorrow?"

Devon sighed and turned to Ransom. "You'll have to postpone your journey until after the final bout of the tournament. I don't want to risk losing you before our moment of glory."

"I'll go back to the palace, then," Ransom said, feeling disappointed. The trip to St. Penryn was important, and he didn't wish to wait. "I don't think it would be wise for me to wander the streets of Ploemeur."

Goff snorted. "You think not?" His lips trembled with rage.

Devon put his arm around his brother's shoulders and gave Ransom a slight nod and a grin. The message was clear: *Get going.*

Ransom started toward the door when he heard Noemie speak. "I'm feeling unwell. I think I'll go back to the palace with Sir Ransom and rest."

Devon looked at her in concern. "When did this come on?"

"Just suddenly," she said with a tired sigh. "A little rest is just what I need."

Devon looked from her to Ransom and back again. Ransom clenched his fists, trying to master his growing feeling of dread.

"Brother," Goff snarled.

"Go with Ransom," Devon said to Noemie. "There's no one I'd trust more to guard you."

There is excitement in the air about the tournament in Brythonica. From what we've heard so far, Devon's mesnie has done well. Ransom won the joust and the individual combat. He defeated the champion of Brythonica in a rather gruesome way. Is it true or just an exaggeration? It's hard to tell, as rumors can never be fully trusted. If they win the war challenge, which takes place in the royal hunting woods south of Ploemeur, then we will sweep the laurels for the entire tournament. Everyone in the palace is talking about Ransom, admiring his prowess as a knight. I've even heard that the Elder King will reward him with some lands if he wins this tournament.

I'm happy for him, truly. But how I wish I were there to add my voice to the cheers. He is winning such a brilliant reputation for so young a knight. I'm so very proud of him.

—Claire de Murrow
Queen's Tower
(pining . . . yes, I'm pining)

CHAPTER
THIRTY-ONE

The Sickness Inside

The horses for the knights in the competition were kept in a paddock on the tournament grounds, but the palace had opened its stables to the royal visitors so that the guests had transportation up and down the mountainside. When Ransom and Noemie reached the stable master, he said he would bring a palfrey for the princess and a rouncy for Sir Ransom.

"I'm not feeling well enough to ride," Noemie said. She held on to Ransom's arm as if to steady herself. "I will ride up the mountain with him."

The stable master saw the wince on Ransom's face. "I can provide a wagon for you, my lady, if you're feeling unwell."

"That would take too long," she demurred. "Fetch the horse."

Ransom's stomach clenched with dread. When the stable master bowed and went to secure their mount, Noemie squeezed his arm. "Thank you for not denying me. I do feel unwell, just not in the way they think."

He chose not to comment.

The horse was brought, and Ransom mounted it. The tail flapped, and one of its ears twitched. He gazed down at Noemie, seeing the look of expectation in her eyes as she waited for him to help her mount. Honor and dignity demanded he accompany her to the palace, but he didn't relish the task. It felt as if she were a spider spinning him deeper and deeper into her web.

Ransom assisted her in mounting the saddle behind him, and she immediately wrapped her arms around his waist. He felt sick inside, but with no other recourse, he twitched the reins and started at a gentle walk to the road leading back up to the palace above. The stable master watched them go with an envying look.

"Why do you hate me?" she asked once they were finally alone on the road, the horse grunting as it plodded up the path.

"I do not hate you," he said simply.

"I think you enjoy watching me suffer. Do you take pleasure in that?"

"I do not wish to cause you pain, no. But what you keep asking is impossible."

"Nothing is impossible for two determined souls, Ransom. This is the way of things. The way of the world. Even the way of your queen."

Ransom wanted to shut his ears, to stop listening. He hated feeling helpless, but he didn't know how to extricate himself from this situation. It only seemed to get worse. "Do not speak of the queen that way," he said, growing angry.

"Is it the truth you cannot bear? There were always rumors about Queen Emiloh. When she was the young duchess of Vexin, younger even than I am, she fell in love with one of her knights and carried on an affair with him before she married Devon's father."

His mind blazed with rage that he was listening to gossip intended to injure the queen. He urged the horse into a trot, which made them both start to bounce in the saddle. She gripped him more tightly to keep from falling off.

But at least it stopped her from speaking, from filling his mind with doubts. He pushed the horse to the edge of its endurance, wanting the ride to end as soon as possible. Noemie just clung to him, pressing her cheek against his back. He wore his armor still, but he could feel the pressure of her, and his willpower failed him enough that his mind conjured wild imaginings. He shoved them aside, one by one, determined to honor his promise to himself and to Devon.

The horse was lathered by the time they reached the palace, exhausted by the punishing pace of the ride. There were a few servants awaiting them in the courtyard. One of them tried to help Noemie off, but she collapsed in a faint as soon as her feet touched the ground. The servants murmured worriedly as Ransom swung off the saddle.

"I'll send for a healer," one of them said.

"No, no," the princess said, blinking rapidly. "I merely swooned. Sir Ransom will take me to my rooms."

"Are you certain you don't want a healer?" the servant asked. "It would be no trouble at all."

Ransom stared at her with a feeling of disgust.

"I am weary, that is all. I will be well soon enough. Sir Ransom will take me." She looked at him with an expression of defiance. It would be beyond rude of him to deny her—indeed, he could not do so without creating more gossip—and she knew it.

She swayed a little as the servants helped her back to her feet, which nearly made Ransom snort. Then she gripped his arm and began to walk tentatively.

The servants took the horse to the stables as they shuffled forward. "I don't believe any of this," he said in a low voice.

"I really do not feel well," she said, grimacing.

He shook his head, feeling pricks of doubt in his chest. Was she playing with him? Or was she truly feeling unwell? Distrust battled with real concern, the dichotomy making him feel even more ill at ease.

With Noemie gripping his arm as if she might faint again—or for the first time—at any moment, they walked side by side down the corridor. They didn't pass a single servant, but perhaps that was not so odd. Most of them were probably enjoying the festivities of the tournament. The marble tiles shone with the warm sunlight spilling in from behind silk curtains. When they reached the door, he opened it for her. Her pace slowed, and he noticed a sheen of sweat on her forehead. Could such a thing be faked?

"Help me to the couch," she mumbled.

As they started to shuffle toward the couch, her legs gave way again, and she sagged against him. Her head lolled, and he noticed her skin had become pale. Worry began stabbing him more earnestly.

"I'm getting a healer."

"It's too late for one," she said, panting.

Ransom lifted her up effortlessly, and this time her head sagged against his chest. He carried her to the couch and set her down on the cushions. The feelings of dread intensified.

What if Noemie died on his watch?

What if she was an even better actress than he'd thought, and this was all a pretense?

"Get me a cloth, dip it in cool water," she whispered. "I'm . . . I'm burning up."

He rose and looked around the room. He'd planned to leave the instant they arrived, but he couldn't walk away now, not when she seemed so ill.

He knew there'd be a pitcher of water in the adjoining bedroom, so he hastened to retrieve it. There was also a bowl, empty, and a towel. He poured water into the bowl and picked up the towel with his other hand. As he heard the waters splashing against the ceramic, a trickle of power shot through him. A warning.

He turned his head just as Noemie followed him into the room and shut the door behind her, blocking his sight of the chamber beyond. She slid a bolt into place. Her eyes looked feverish and dangerous.

"I've barred the other door too, Ransom," she said, her strength remarkably improved. "The servants won't come. We're alone."

He crumpled the little towel and tossed it aside. It clearly was not needed. He set down the pitcher of water.

"You will not reject me this time," she said, leaning back against the door, shaking her head.

He still wore his dust-spattered armor and had yet to remove the sword strapped to his waist, but he'd never felt so afraid, so helpless. The pulse of warning began to fade. He turned back and poured more water from the pitcher, filling the bowl. The sound of it was soothing. He breathed out slowly.

"I order you to do this," she said. "Trust me when I tell you that it will save your king's life."

He squeezed his eyes shut and set down the pitcher. It had all been another ruse, a lie—even her talk about the threat to Devon.

Turning, he looked at her. "Trust you? I don't, Your Highness. What you ask of me is wrong. I am loyal to your husband."

She pressed herself against the door, shaking her head. "If you are loyal to him, you will do this. I command it. The guilt be on *my* head, not yours."

She was blocking the only exit. He already knew the balcony attached to the room was suspended over a cliff. There was no other way out. He started walking toward her, intending to bodily remove her from the exit if need be.

"You could not take away my guilt," he said. "I am his sworn man, his knight. Loyalty may mean something different in Pree. I begin to think that it does. Devon trusts me. Even with you." He shook his head. "It would be treason to break that trust."

361

Her eyes flashed with rage and despair. "You'll kill him. I swear it on the Fountain. This is the only way to keep him alive!"

She had chosen her words well. Devon's safety was paramount in Ransom's mind. "Who threatens him?"

"I will tell you. But you must sit down and listen to me. Sit down, on the bed."

He didn't trust her reasoning or her attempt to delay him further.

"Get out of my way," he said, reaching her.

She shook her head. "Why must you be so stubborn! Why must I be the one who begs! There is no one here! No one will know!"

"Get out of my way," he said, his tone becoming darker.

She curled her hands into fists, and tears started streaming down her cheeks as she pummeled her fists against his breastplate. He gripped her by the arms and lifted her aside. Then he unbolted the door and opened it. She let out a primal scream of anguish as she tried to throw herself in his path.

But he wouldn't let her prevent him from leaving. He sidestepped her and marched across the room, listening to the keening of her voice as she raged against him, cursing his name in Occitanian, filling the air with blistering oaths.

Ransom felt relief when he reached the other door and turned the handle.

And found Sir Robert Tregoss standing on the other side. His face was flushed as if he'd been running.

Ransom flashed him a menacing look, and the knight took a step back.

"The princess is sick?" he asked worriedly.

Ransom felt certain he had been set up. To be caught in a compromising situation. He nearly attacked Robert, but he feared what might happen if he allowed his anger to escape. He might not stop punching until Robert was dead.

Noemie let out another shriek of rage. Robert's eyes widened with concern.

"Her only sickness is inside," Ransom snarled, "but you knew that." Then he shoved Robert against the wall and walked past him, looking for a place of refuge, a place to hide.

They won the tournament.

Cheers of acclaim filled the air as Ransom took the victory stand again, and the Duchess of Brythonica gave him a laurel crown made of gold with seven pieces of jeweled glass. She kissed his cheeks, one on each, as she'd done with the other champions, and proclaimed that he'd won ten thousand livres and the rank of viscount, which came with a small manor on one of the hills in Ploemeur.

Sir Terencourt approached him after the ceremony, his stump wrapped in bandages, and offered his congratulations as well as an apology for not conceding earlier during their match.

"I was too proud," he told Ransom. "I knew I should have yielded, but I couldn't bear the shame of it. It's not your fault. You could have killed me, and I would have deserved it. Instead, I only lost my arm." He smiled weakly, showing that he was far from recovered. But his kindness eased at least a portion of Ransom's guilt.

Even Devon's brother Goff congratulated him, albeit reluctantly. The revenue from the manor would not be as substantial as what he earned from his castle and lands in Occitania, Goff said, but it was also nothing to scoff at.

The celebration was to continue in the town of Ploemeur. Several knights invited Ransom to join in the carousing, but he rejected them, feeling numb in his heart. He knew he had to tell Devon about the incidents with Noemie and also his suspicions about the cloaked lady. The conversation would be a difficult one, however, and he decided it would be best to wait until they returned to Kingfountain. He did not wish to cause a scene in front of Goff. Besides which, the princess hadn't been able to meet his eyes since it had happened. She ignored his presence entirely with an air of indifference. With any luck, she would continue to do so.

Sir Simon approached him during his wanderings and said that Devon had asked to see him, so they walked together past the merchants' stalls.

"Have we spent all the livres the Elder King gave us?" Ransom asked Simon.

"It's actually harder than I thought," Simon replied. "There's still a bit leftover after last eve. I might just give the rest to you instead of wasting it here."

Ransom chuckled. "Just spend it. Give whatever is left to the king's other son."

"Now that you are richer than King Lewis, you can afford to be so generous," said Simon.

That sort of distinction had its own troubles, though. During the tournament, many knights had attempted to capture him, hoping to receive a handsome ransom. But none of them had successfully challenged him. He'd never felt so strong, so quick, so confident in what he could do.

After passing more well-wishers, they found Devon's pavilion, bright with torchlight against the encroaching evening. Revelers walked in groups down the streets, cheering and greeting each other noisily. Ransom and Simon entered the tent and found the mood within quite altered.

Ransom felt a sudden chill go down his spine when he saw Sir James next to the Younger King. He held a goblet, his smile feral. There was no sign of the princess or any of her maidens. It was just the king's mesnie and Sir James.

When Ransom looked at Devon, he saw his friend's countenance had completely altered. The jovial camaraderie from earlier was completely gone. His eyes were red-rimmed, as if he'd been weeping, and there was no mistaking the accusation and anger with which he regarded Ransom. All was not well.

Ransom's chest constricted. Sir Robert stood right next to Devon, arms folded imperiously, his eyes full of hatred. Of *victory*. Ransom's heart sank.

"You summoned me, my lord," Ransom said, his voice sounding thick.

Devon glared at him. His eyes were like daggers. "Yes. I did."

Ransom took in James's smugness. Why was he even there? Why was he always there when Ransom was humiliated?

His gaze shifted to the other knights of the mesnie. Sir Talbot looked disappointed, and Sir Alain couldn't even meet Ransom's eyes—he just kept looking at the floor as if ashamed for him. No servants were present. But Noemie's absence seemed even more conspicuous now.

The feelings thrashing around inside Ransom's stomach were dark and savage. The silence grew uncomfortable. Then devastating.

"I am here, my lord," Ransom said simply.

Devon took a step forward, his eyes flashing with rage, and Ransom wondered if his friend, his king, would strike him. No man had that right. Would he let him?

"Take your winnings," Devon said. "Enjoy them. You will not be returning with us to Kingfountain."

It felt like a hammer stroke ringing on an anvil. His heart ached in his chest.

"My lord?" Ransom asked in confusion.

"Was I not clear, Sir Marshall Barton? You will not be returning with us. I release you from my service. You are no longer a member of my mesnie. You have all the time in the world now to visit any sanctuary you would like to *appease your guilt!*" Devon's eyes blazed with fury, with betrayal. "May the Fountain wash your stain. Get out of my sight."

The pain wrenching Ransom's heart was worse than anything he'd ever felt before. He was being dismissed, dishonorably, for something he'd never done. Oh, the look on Robert's face said it all. So did James's sneer—he suspected it was no accident the man was here to witness his downfall.

The injustice of it stung worst of all. He could only imagine what lies Noemie and Sir Robert had spewed about him. And now he would have to leave Devon in their clutches—at the mercy of whatever the Occitanians had planned for him.

Devon had a trusting heart but sometimes lacked discernment. He'd heed their advice, to his detriment.

A small voice in the back of his head also wondered what Claire would think of him.

What would she believe?

He wanted to speak, to defend himself, but he did not. He would not accuse the princess in front of these men. His ears burned hot, and he felt on the verge of violently expelling everything he'd eaten that evening.

"Why are you still standing there?" Devon asked with withering contempt.

"You are in danger, my lord," he forced out, his tone urgent. "Please hear me out."

"I don't want to hear another word from your lips. Get out."

Ransom bowed his head to the Younger King and then turned and walked out of the tent and into the night. Tears threatened his eyes, but he willed them back. As he walked, a half-drunken noble fell in alongside him.

"I wish you'd never been born," the Brythonican said, burping, laughing. He clapped Ransom on the back, then staggered off drunkenly.

The words stung. He'd already felt guilty about the manner of his victory against the Brythonican champion—about his violence—and the man's statement struck him down to his core.

You're not worthy. Even serving Devon loyally could not make it so.

Suddenly he felt like that little boy again, standing on a barrel with a hangman's noose dangling before him. In his mind's eye, he saw himself turn and look back at King Gervase.

The grinning king nodded to him, gesturing for him to put his head through the noose.

X

It can't be true. Has everything I've hoped for been a lie? The Younger King returned. Everyone is saying that Ransom is in disgrace for trying to seduce Devon's wife. The rumors are so ugly. They say that his heart turned proud after he won his second championship. That his fame and success sent him the way of the heroes of legend. The stories have left me with an aching heart. Part of me believes it is true, and part of me questions whether they've all gotten it wrong. Has some bout of madness overtaken the realm?

I don't know what to think. All I know is it hurts to breathe. It hurts to think. It hurts to grieve. Some stains cannot be washed clean. Oh, Ransom. Were you acting the maggot in Brythonica? Are you just like other men? I cannot hold Noemie entirely blameless either. Perhaps she bears a degree of fault for this transgression. I can usually find some comfort in tears. But not this time. This time they burn my eyes.

—Claire de Murrow
Kingfountain Palace
(heartsick)

X

CHAPTER
THIRTY-TWO

The Sanctuary of St. Penryn

Ransom rode his destrier against a stiff wind, leading the packhorse burdened with his supplies. He had a heavy heart, which grew even heavier as he glanced at his lance. No pennant flapped in the breeze, for he was once more a knight without a lord.

The coastal road was choked with scrub, a sign that the sanctuary had few visitors. Most of the trees grew at sharp angles from the consistent push of the sea winds.

Ransom had the trophies from his victories and enough silver livres to start his own mesnie should he want to. But he could not think of the future, he could not think beyond the shame of having been forsaken by his king, a man to whom he'd shown unshakable loyalty. After this journey was done, he had decided to return to the Heath and see his family. They, at least, deserved to know the truth about his infamy. He could never return to Kingfountain.

Memories tormented him. What could he have done differently to avoid this fate?

Sir Simon, at least, had been sorrowful at his departure. He didn't believe the tales. Having one person not think ill of him was better than none, but Ransom knew his reputation was tarnished irrevocably. People would believe the worst, especially since the story was so lurid. That was the nature of life. He sighed, enduring the chafing wind. It was nothing compared to the emotions abrading his heart.

It sickened him to think of Claire learning the news. There was no way to get word to her, for she was one of the Elder King's wards. Any correspondence to her would go through Devon the Elder first, although his lackeys read his correspondence before he did, so it likely wouldn't even get that far. No, he would proclaim his innocence in person, face-to-face. How that would happen or when, he didn't know, but he would not rest until it did.

Although Ransom tried not to dwell on his misfortune, it felt like his life was a never-ending series of setbacks and failures. He wanted to serve someone and to serve them faithfully. It was part of his character now, forged during his misadventures and trials. Yet he'd once again been wrenched away from his master without warning. This was more than a mere disappointment. Part of his soul had been wrenched away. He felt empty, as if his secret well of strength had been ruptured.

In the distance, he finally spied the sanctuary of St. Penryn. It jutted out of the rocky cliffs with all the luster of antiquity. It was not as grand as some of the other sanctuaries in the realm, but what it lacked in adornment it made up for in resilience. In truth, he'd never felt less worthy of a distinction from the Fountain, but he'd told Queen Emiloh he would heed her charge, and this, at least, was something he could do.

He reached the sanctuary late in the day, passing a few windswept villages on the route. As he drew near, he could hear the crash of the surf against the lower cliffs. The ocean seethed within its foamy depths, sounding as unsettled as he felt inside. He rode up to the grounds with a heavy heart and dismounted. There were no servants about. The sanctuary felt abandoned. He tied his destrier to a mounting post and then secured the packhorse as well. Gazing up at the ancient stone walls speckled with lichen and moss, he wondered whom he'd find inside.

After climbing the steps, he approached the iron door of the sanctuary and pulled at the handle, which opened with a loud groan of metal. The noise of the wind and waves was muffled as he ventured inside and shut the door behind him. A few torches sputtered, and the interior was chilly and uncomfortable. A statue of St. Penryn stood at the front of the space along with a dark pool of water. His armor rattled as he walked toward it, and his footfalls were heavy—if someone was here, they would surely notice him. Cobwebs clung to the corners of the vaulted windows, and when he reached the edge of the pool, he saw heaps of rusting coins. He stared at them, wondering how long they'd been spoiled by the waters. These looked even older than the ones he'd seen in the secluded pool at the other sanctuary.

"May I help you?"

The words, spoken in Occitanian, came out of nowhere, and Ransom turned in surprise, seeing the gray cassock of the deconeus, who wore light leather shoes and approached with soundless steps. He had no beard, which was surprising, although he had a mane of snow-white hair atop his head.

"I don't know, Deconeus," Ransom answered bleakly.

The deconeus gave him an affable smile. "I saw your two horses out front. Looks like all your worldly possessions came with you. Are you in need of money? I hope you didn't come here to rob the sanctuary."

Ransom had plenty of coin to spare. "No, Deconeus. I'll not rob you."

"You wouldn't be the first who has tried," said the man with a grin and a glint of humor in his eyes. "Your accent says you're from Ceredigion. Am I right?"

"You are."

"Why have you come? Most knights are drawn to the grand sanctuary palaces in Pree, Brythonica, or better yet . . . Kingfountain. Yet you came here."

There was no one else present, at least none that could be seen. The kindly deconeus seemed a pleasant fellow, yet Ransom felt embarrassed to make his request. He feared earning the other man's scorn.

And yet, what difference could it possibly make? Could he fall any lower? He sighed again and looked the deconeus in the eye.

"I came here seeking answers. For many years, I have harbored the idea that I may be Fountain-blessed."

The warm smile on the deconeus's mouth drooped to a thoughtful frown. "Indeed. That is a rare thing these days. Who sent you?"

"I was encouraged by Queen Emiloh to seek out the oldest sanctuaries."

"The imprisoned queen? Interesting. That you know her means you are one of her household knights, then? One of the ones the king dismissed, perhaps?"

"No. I served her son."

"Which one? She has many."

"The Younger King."

"Ah. This is quite unusual. It's been a few years since anyone has come here seeking such a boon."

"Others have come?" Ransom asked.

He nodded. "Although few enough. This sanctuary was built by the King of Leoneyis before his kingdom was swept into the sea."

Ransom studied the old man carefully. "That's just a legend, is it not?"

"Yet here you are, come all this way, asking if you have special powers and gifts. I think people are drawn here because the king of Leoneyis had a Fountain-blessed knight who served him. An Oath Maiden."

Ransom's brow furrowed. "A woman?"

"Yes. She was not the first, nor will she be the last. She served her king dutifully, but he betrayed her in the end."

A jolt of feeling went through Ransom's heart at the words. The familiarity of the situation was unnerving.

"I've never heard of this before," Ransom said.

"Of course not. There are records here, written on pages of vellum in ancient ink. One gets lonely after a while, being in such a secluded place. Reading is a good way to pass the time. Are the stories of King Andrew and his Ring Table merely that? Stories? Or are they records of a time long since past? You came here seeking to know if you are Fountain-blessed, but I'm afraid you will not find that answer here."

Ransom felt a pang of disappointment. He'd hoped to finally have his answer, whatever that might be. "Why not?"

"Because in all the stories, those who are Fountain-blessed go on a pilgrimage. They travel far away, to the East Kingdoms. It's a journey that takes a year each way. It's a sacrifice of time that few nobles are willing to grant, especially to those who serve them. I daresay the Younger King would grant you permission to visit St. Penryn, but he would not be so keen to send you on such a long and perilous journey."

It struck Ransom deeply that such a journey was now entirely possible. He had no one left to serve.

"If I were to undertake such a pilgrimage, where would I go?"

The deconeus huffed a laugh. "The last person to ask me that was a young woman of Occitania. She didn't like the answer, and I doubt you will either."

Ransom's eyes widened. "Who was she?"

The older man shrugged. "She never told me her name. This was about six or seven years ago. I don't believe she was married, but she looked to be roughly the age at which women marry. She wore a cloak and a hood."

Ransom started. Was this the lady he had sensed and seen?

"Do you know her?" the deconeus asked, looking at him with open curiosity.

"I may know of whom you speak. There is a lady I have noticed . . . one whose presence I could sense."

"That is a trait of the Fountain-blessed," said the deconeus, eyeing Ransom with interest. "Did you know that? It's in the writings."

"And you do not know her name? She was from Occitania, though?"

"She spoke in Occitanian with an accent not from Pree, but . . . then again, you have a trace of accent yourself that is not from these parts. She said she'd gone to many sanctuaries seeking wisdom about how to know if she was one of the blessed. I will tell you what I told her. In all the stories, when one is blessed, they are given something from the Deep Fathoms. A treasured gift. Sometimes they're given a choice of what to take, although the gifts are not always what they seem. Some are curses. King Andrew was given a sword and a scabbard. Yet the Wizr Myrddin told him the scabbard was more powerful than the sword."

Ransom nodded, his attention riveted. "Where did you tell her to go?"

"There is a desert far to the east that separates us from the East Kingdoms. In the middle of the desert is an oasis called Chandleer. That is where I told the young woman to go. There is a fountain in the desert, a spring of pure water. That is why the caravans stop there. But it is a difficult journey. And dangerous."

An itch had begun to quiver up Ransom's spine upon hearing the man's words. The words gave him a spark of hope. Something to focus on instead of hiding away. Perhaps the situation would improve if he left on this quest. Much could happen in two years. The furor might ebb; the truth might reveal itself.

"Did the young woman ever return?" Ransom asked.

The deconeus shook his head. "I never saw her again. Only the Fountain knows if she went on her quest."

"Thank you, Deconeus. You have given me what I needed."

"You will seek the oasis, then? That is your pilgrimage?"

"I believe so. May I borrow some parchment and ink? I need to pen a letter before I go. Is there a courier I can hire to send it?" He'd decided to write his warning to Devon before leaving. The letter might be read, but he was determined to plead his innocence and warn the king about the dangerous lady who was always lurking beyond sight. Especially since Noemie was perhaps aware of her.

The deconeus nodded grimly. "Of course. I'll make the arrangements. But first I must ask you something. The records tell us that the Fountain-blessed glean strength from acts of self-discipline. They form habits, if you will, which strengthen their abilities. Because of their devotion to their craft, they are blessed with abilities beyond the ken of normal men and women. In the records, they call this magic. But it is more than superstition. They do not quit when challenges bar the way, and they are driven to feats that could be seen by some as truly miraculous. Have you experienced such as these before?"

Ransom had no hesitation. "Yes, Deconeus. Yes, I have."

The deconeus pursed his lips. "Then I wish you the Lady's favor on your journey. If you succeed, I would be most honored if you'd return and tell me more of what you faced. Two years may seem a lifetime to one so young as you." A smile lifted his lips. "I just wish I had been brave enough to try it myself."

Spending time with his family at the Heath had done Ransom some good. Yes, word had reached them before he did. But they hadn't lost their good feelings for him, and when he explained the truth of what had happened, they were relieved to learn that his conduct had not been dishonorable.

His sister, Maeg, was a handsome young lady now, with a fair share of suitors, although she was still interested in one of the household knights. Marcus, his elder brother, had gained a lot of weight during his time overseeing the affairs of the castle. Since the Elder King preferred to hire mercenaries these days, many of the nobles had not kept up with their training. Sibyl, his mother, continued to pet Ransom's hand while he ate or when he shared stories of his adventures. They all loved hearing his stories, especially the one about the tournament he'd won despite being nearly blinded by his helmet.

He'd only planned to spend a day at the Heath, but his family encouraged him to lengthen his stay, and their warmth convinced him to do so. He enjoyed walking with Maeg and discussing the affairs of the court with his brother. One afternoon, sitting by the hearth, his mother asked for his permission to send a letter to Lord Kinghorn informing him of the truth of the matter. But Ransom refused her.

"No, I sent one to Devon myself. I don't think he's ready to heed me, but I needed to warn him anyway. I fear he's put himself in a dangerous situation. Perhaps things will change for the better while I'm away."

He went on to ask if she would oversee his income from his properties in his absence, and she readily agreed. With tears in her eyes, she thanked him for his trust in her.

"I have means now," he said, embracing her. "When I was young, you helped me find a position with Lord Kinghorn. I wouldn't be the man I am today if you hadn't sent me to him. I should like to help you in return. Can I help with Maeg's dowry?"

His mother grinned at him, and he could tell the offer pleased her. "It would mean very much to us all. Thank you." She squeezed his hands. "We're blessed to have you."

They made a feast for him on his final night staying with them. He'd been to feasts at Kingfountain and Pree, but this one was different. He didn't feel like he needed to watch his back or be wary of anyone approaching him. His sister was quite a storyteller herself, and he enjoyed listening to her talk and even sing, which he responded to with enthusiastic applause. While he was with his family, he felt a gentle throbbing inside his empty well. Yes, he had been rejected by his master, but he could be loyal to his family. Perhaps that was enough.

It was near the end of the meal when a courier arrived. It was one of the Elder King's heralds, and the sight of the man's badge—the Silver Rose—caused a prick of envy in Ransom's chest. He rose to greet the herald, but the man went directly to Marcus instead.

"What news?" Marcus asked the man, taking a sealed scroll from him.

"The king wishes you to be ready," he said curtly, then his gaze shifted to Ransom sitting as one of the guests. He clearly recognized him, but it didn't disrupt his composure.

Marcus broke the seal and quickly scanned the note. He let out a whistle of surprise.

"What has happened?" Sibyl asked. Maeg looked worried.

Marcus lowered the scroll, his face full of dread. "Duke Goff invaded the duchy of Vexin. Two of the king's sons are fighting each other."

"Aye," said the herald. "The Elder King's ungrateful sons will never be at peace with one another."

Ransom heard the words, but a memory sparked in his mind. Goff had asked for a private conversation with Devon during the tournament. A sour feeling twisted in his gut. At the time he'd assumed the meeting was about the fate of Sir Terencourt, but now he wondered. Was Devon part of this outburst? Had he been talked into something he would regret? Was James now the one giving him advice? Ransom had no illusions about the outcome of a fight between Benedict and Goff. Benedict was more ruthless and more determined.

The sickly feeling inside him grew worse. Things were not as they seemed.

A log in the hearth exploded in a crackle of thunder and a shower of sparks.

He could not help but think it an ill omen.

⋊⋉

I continue to be astounded by the feckless nature of men. Are they all eejits? I am aghast at the latest news coming to the palace. The Younger King was behind the treachery in the Vexin. Somehow he persuaded his brother Goff to start the trouble. But it was a ploy, a diversion from his true aim, to depose his father, the king. Again. There was to be a talk of a peace in Westmarch, but Goff had concealed men there in the hopes of ambushing the Elder King. But their father was too canny for them, and the men were discovered and driven away. When his treachery was revealed, the Younger King fled toward Brythonica, but his escape was cut off.

Young Devon is holed up in Beestone castle, the castellan of which was sympathetic toward him, and his father is preparing to besiege the castle and bring his son to heel one more time. The barmy catastrophe could have easily been prevented. It wouldn't surprise me if Duke Benedict attacks Brythonica in retaliation. Such witless fools. The father gave a kingdom to his son, although it wasn't freely given, and the inheritance would have been the work of a lifetime. That future end wasn't enough to satisfy the Younger King's ambition. And now he's barricaded himself inside a castle that, some say, is without peer. Yet somehow, I don't imagine it will take long for the Elder King to bring the walls down.

—Claire de Murrow
Queen's Tower
(disgusted with the kingdom)

CHAPTER
THIRTY-THREE

Death Watch

Gison castle was small but formidable. It was one of the rewards Ransom had received for winning the tournament of Chessy. He liked it well enough, even though it did not feel like home. The only place that had felt as such was the Kingfountain of his childhood. The main hall was smaller than that of the Heath, but the timberwork on the interior was sturdy and the walls in good repair. His steward, a man named Lamere, had just finished going over the revenues with him, and Ransom had given the order that Lady Sibyl was to handle the finances moving forward.

Night had settled, and the few servants within the castle were lighting the interior torches. Ransom sat at the dining table, his meal complete, brooding about the journey that lay ahead.

Word of Devon's attempted insurrection had already reached him, and he was grateful to be nowhere near Beestone castle. He picked up the goblet and saw the cup was already empty before setting it down again.

Lamere strode back into the dining hall, a confused look on his face. "My lord, you have a visitor."

Ransom started in surprise, then pushed back the chair. Who would think to visit him here? He'd told none but his family he intended to make the journey. "Who is it?"

"Sir Simon of Holmberg," said Lamere. "Do you know him?"

Suddenly Ransom remembered telling Simon about the castle on their journey to Brythonica. He'd forgotten all about it during the upheaval in his life. "I do. Send him in at once," Ransom said, his confusion growing. Concern gripped him, and he began to pace while Lamere left to fetch the visitor.

Simon strode swiftly into the dining hall, his hair windblown and his face weary from an arduous journey. The panicked look on his face struck Ransom forcibly. So, too, did the fact that his skin was paler than chalk.

"What's happened?" he asked with dread.

"You need to come with me," Simon said. "Right now. This very night."

Ransom gripped the edge of his chair and cocked his head. "Where?"

"To Beestone castle."

"If this is your idea of a jest, Simon . . ." Ransom started, but one look at his friend's face silenced him.

"Devon is dying," Simon said softly.

The news struck Ransom like a staff to the ribs. He took a couple of steps toward his friend. "I don't understand."

"I don't know what news has reached you, but I will be brief. He sent me to get you. He told me to kill as many horses as necessary and *bring you back* to him. He was wrong about his wife. It was Sir Robert who was carrying on with her. When Devon found out . . . he . . . I've never seen him so distraught. Noemie fled the castle. She's probably back in Pree by now. She won't stand by him when he falls, not again. She won't be a prisoner like Emiloh. Then Devon fell sick. He's been coughing up blood. He sent Talbot to tell his father that he surrenders.

And he sent me to get you. He feels horrible about what he did to you. He wants your forgiveness . . ." His voice cracked. "Before he dies."

Ransom stared at him in disbelief, feeling the shock of the situation down to his bones. The sudden sickness could be no coincidence. He grieved for Devon, but he also felt the sinking sensation of having acted the fool. Noemie had told him that Devon's life was at stake. He'd believed it to be yet another ploy to sway him into her trap.

The words the Elder King had spoken to him years before came back with haunting prescience. He could hear the voice ringing in his skull.

Your duty is to keep that feckless young man alive!

"How far is Beestone?" Ransom demanded.

"I left there this morning. My horse nearly died getting me here."

"Are you fit to ride?"

Simon nodded, but his exhaustion was apparent.

"Get some rest. You can have a horse from my stables. I'll leave at once. Lamere!"

The steward, who had been waiting just outside the door, entered with an expectant look.

"I want the fastest horse from the stables prepared. I'm leaving at once. When Sir Simon has recovered, you will provide him a fresh mount and send him after me. Everything I wanted for my journey, I want you to send to Beestone castle. My armor, provisions, everything. Send them to Beestone." He gripped Simon's shoulder. "Refresh yourself, and join me as soon as you can."

"I'm coming now," Simon said.

Ransom shrugged. "I'm not waiting for you."

Before the candle had burned past another notch, Ransom was wearing his hauberk and a cloak and galloping out of Gison into the night.

X

As Ransom rode, his thoughts twisted into knots full of revenge and self-loathing. He'd been played a fool by the cloaked lady. With Ransom out of the way, Devon had been left totally unprotected. Who was a part of the plot? Sir Robert, surely, and Noemie had known. Did that mean the Occitanian king was the snake?

The woman had been watching Devon for years. Why kill him now?

No other travelers strayed across his path all night. When dawn came, he stopped to water his mount at a stream before pushing onward again. The rouncy was bred for stamina, and it sensed the concern and worry of its rider and responded with surprising resolve. His stomach growled with hunger, but he didn't stop to feed himself. Each league increased his anxiety to arrive in time.

Ransom had been to Beestone before, during his journeys throughout the realm. It was one of the largest strongholds between Kingfountain and Tatton Grange and had withstood invasions in the past. But Devon had few resources, and Ransom wondered if the Elder King would beat him there. He vowed to himself he would not allow it to happen.

By midmorning, he finally saw Beestone on a hill in the distance, a small town nestled at its base. When he arrived, his horse was lathered but still enduring. He looked for evidence of the Elder King's army, but the people were going about their business. Some glanced at him, but few paid him much notice.

Ransom's horse clopped up the road leading to the gates of the castle. As he arrived, he recognized Sir Alain standing guard.

"You made it!" Alain gasped in astonishment. "I thought you'd be here this evening by the earliest, if at all!"

Ransom looked down at him from atop his exhausted mount. "Does he live?"

Alain nodded. "He's . . . he's very sick. He's been calling for you all night."

Ransom nodded and guided the horse into the bailey. There was a well in the middle of the yard, and he saw a few young men drawing water from it. As he approached the well, he sensed the presence of the cloaked lady. The realization did not surprise him. He'd expected he would find her nearby, although it surprised him to feel her presence pulse from the well itself. Ransom reached the edge, and one of the boys looked up at him in awe and admiration, much the way he might have regarded a knight when he was younger.

"Water my horse," he told the boy.

"Yes, my lord."

Ransom dismounted and stood by the rim of the well. Something struck him, a strange feeling that he had been there before and that she had been there with him. He looked at the lad, who was probably eight years old.

"Have you seen a lady here?" he asked the boy.

"Pardon?"

"Have you seen a lady here at the well?" he asked. His hand gripped the hilt of his bastard sword.

The boy looked around. "No, my lord. Not since the princess left."

He knew the lady in the well could feel him too. That meant she was waiting for something, but what? And how was he to reach her? Was she really crouched down in the well? He carefully leaned over, looking down into the darkness. That strange sense of recognition thrummed inside him again, and he heard the distant roar of the waterfall in his ears. He felt the power pulse inside him, although it was much depleted.

"I'm here," he called, hoping his voice would carry down the shaft.

He waited for an answer, but none came.

Ransom backed away from the well and started toward the fortress. She had done her damage, and it was likely too late to reverse it. He could at least see his king. The rest could be handled later. As soon as he entered, he saw Talbot leaning against the wall, hands covering his face as he tried to control his grief. Ransom walked up to him and gripped his shoulder.

Talbot's face crumpled when he saw it was Ransom. "It's *you*," he said in a choked voice. "Go to him. I can't bear to see him like this. He's wasting away before our eyes. I've put twenty coins in the well as prayers he'll recover. But he keeps getting worse!"

Ransom dug his fingers into Talbot's muscle. "Simon said you were sent to deliver the surrender. What happened?"

Talbot nodded, then started sobbing. "The king thought . . . it was a trick. He trusts his son not at all. I swore on the Fountain, by the Lady of the Fountain, that it was true, that Devon wishes to see him before he dies. But the king sent me away. I can't bring myself to tell him, Ransom. He wanted to beg his father's pardon before he died. He's afraid . . . he's afraid of going to the Deep Fathoms. It was Robert who turned Devon away from you. I don't know why we believed him. He was jealous of you from the start."

"Where is Robert?"

"In the dungeon," said Talbot with malice. He broke down weeping again. "I can't do it, Ransom. I can't. You have to tell him. His father won't come in time. He won't see his mother either, or his brothers."

Ransom stared at Talbot, feeling himself ready to break down. Why was it up to him to deliver the dark tidings? Devon had dismissed him from his bonds of loyalty, and yet they existed still within his chest. They felt like chains. Seeing Talbot so distraught had withered his remaining hope that Devon might yet recover.

"I'll do it," he said.

He was brought to the chamber where Devon lay dying. The healer, a barber from the village below, wrung his hands and shrugged helplessly as he looked at Ransom. His bushy black-and-gray beard, so full compared to his balding head, made him look almost comical, but no levity was possible at such a moment. Ransom bit his lip as he gazed at the almost corpse on the bed.

Devon had shrunk since Ransom had last seen him. Blood seeped from his eyes, staining his pillow. His teeth were yellow and his lips chapped. The smell of filth permeated the chamber in a nauseating mist. Ransom nearly choked on it. He stared down at his friend, his king, and all feelings of resentment vanished, replaced by pity.

"Ransom," Devon croaked, the sound otherworldly.

The knight approached the bedstead, and the barber fled the room. Even though the hearth was blazing, Devon trembled as if frigid. His eyes were closed, scabbed, but he'd still sensed Ransom. Or could he see him?

"I'm here," Ransom said, coming to the edge of the bed. He knelt by it, still perceiving the presence of the cloaked lady beneath the castle. He took the king's hand in his own.

"Is it really you, my friend?"

"Yes. Simon came and told me. I rode all night."

The chapped lips tugged into a smile. "I don't deserve . . ." The words failed as a coughing fit started. Bloody spume came from his mouth. Ransom dabbed his lips with a soiled towel that lay near the bed.

Devon struggled to quiet the rattling in his chest, but his breath came in agonized fits, each gulp of air a struggle. The pain the Younger King endured was horrific to behold. Ransom closed a fist and pressed it against his mouth, trying not to weep.

"I don't . . . deserve . . . your loyalty," rasped the young king. "But I thank . . . you . . . for it."

"You will always have it," Ransom whispered. He felt tears trickle down his cheeks. His heart throbbed with compassion and concern, and his restored loyalty to the king brought him strength. It filled the well inside him.

"It was . . . Noemie. Her lies . . . drove my actions. She's gone. Back to her people." He swallowed, wincing.

"I should have told you," Ransom said. "She tried . . . but I never wanted it. I wanted Claire."

"I know. That pains me still. I knew it, but I was so jealous. It blinded me . . . to the truth. My father was right . . . about Lewis. I see it now. Father is always right." His labored breathing began to slow. "He's not coming."

Ransom squeezed his hand. "Talbot tried. But there is no trust left."

Devon swallowed again, grimacing once more in agony. "I hoped . . . but you're right. I betrayed him every day. In my heart. Ransom, tell him . . . for me . . . that I'm sorry. He hates me."

"He *loves* you," Ransom said thickly. He remembered the horrible noise the Elder King had made after they left his tent years ago. It was a cry of anguish from a man whose beloved eldest son had disappointed him.

"I'm such a failure," Devon gasped. His breathing became shallower. "I wanted so much . . . to be the king."

"You are *my* king," Ransom said, the tears flowing freely now.

"I was only a pretend one," Devon whispered. "I should have done more. Tell Mother . . . love . . . her."

Ransom squeezed his hand again.

"Father . . . have mercy."

"I'll tell him," Ransom said, wishing he didn't have to witness the Younger King's death or relate the news to his family. But such was his fate. Such was the cost of loyalty.

"Ransom . . ."

"I'm here," he said, half-blinded by tears. He waited, listening, aching, his heart swollen with grief.

"Forgive . . . me . . ."

Ransom hung his head, still gripping the Younger King's hand. "I do."

The gentle grip on his hand failed, the last wheeze of a breath coming out like a sigh. And then he was gone. Heat scorched Ransom's eyes as he stared down at the waxen face. It looked so little like his friend. Gone was the man's ever-present smile, his good-natured camaraderie, and his ambition too. All that was left was a husk.

Ransom released his grip, and Devon's arm fell onto the sheet.

"If I cannot serve you any longer here," he said, making it a vow, "then I will serve you next in the Deep Fathoms."

He rose from the bedside and walked to the door. Opening it, he saw Sir Alain and Sir Talbot waiting there. They looked at him eagerly, hopefully, but he shook his head, communicating with his silence that the king was dead.

Talbot broke down in tears.

Alain shook his head, his grief obvious, but he could still speak. "Someone will need to tell his father." He looked at Ransom pointedly, while Talbot shook his head in horror.

"I will do it," Ransom said. "Have a horse prepared for me."

But he had a visit to make first.

$$\text{X\!X}$$

The dungeon below Beestone castle lay at the bottom of a winding, cramped stone stairwell. In one hand he carried a torch, which he'd fetched from a rung on the wall, and the other gripped the hilt of his sword. As he went down, he sensed the presence of the lady. She was heading toward him.

When Ransom reached the bottom steps, he saw a single guard sitting on a chair by the iron door.

"Open it," said Ransom.

The man looked at him lazily. "No visitors," he growled. "On orders of the Younger King."

"The Younger King is dead," said Ransom darkly.

The sentry rose and brushed off his legs. "Then my task is finished. He's all yours."

The man walked past him and started up the stairs, and Ransom slid the dead bolt free and opened the door. The dungeon was lit from within by torchlight. He sensed the presence of the lady, the nearness of her as she approached him, but he could not see her. Where was she coming from? He could only tell it was from somewhere ahead, within the prison, not behind him.

Ransom drew his sword and entered. The light made shadows on the floor, showing a diagonal form of the cells' barred doors. He smelled moldy straw and urine. There was only one prisoner, Sir Robert Tregoss, standing against the bars.

"Hello, Ransom," he said, his face twisting into a leer. "Come for vengeance?" He didn't appear worried.

Ransom walked deeper into the dungeon, moving the torch from side to side to illuminate what he saw. Robert turned away from the glare, his eyes unused to such brightness.

"Who is she?" Ransom asked.

"Who is who? Am I supposed to read your mind?"

"The lady in the cloak. The one who came to the tavern that night. The one who killed Lord Archer. The one who killed our king."

Sir Robert shrugged. "Why don't you ask her yourself?"

Ransom sensed her presence more strongly now. He heard a little scrape of stone coming from the far end of the corridor. A throb of warning struck him. Danger. She'd come here for him. He lifted the torch.

Sir Robert reached suddenly from behind the bars, seizing Ransom's arm, the one with the torch, and yanked him hard against the metal.

The news is such a shock that I cannot bring myself to believe it. Devon the Younger is dead? Can this be true? The knight who brought the morning meal said he had heard it directly from Lord Kinghorn. Beestone castle has been reclaimed. How could Devon have fallen ill so quickly? This is no ordinary malady. In fact, I'm suspicious that he was poisoned. Princess Noemie was not at Beestone. She fled back to Pree the instant her husband became ill. What madness is this?

Lord Kinghorn has a son, several years younger than me. He has greeted me several times in recent days. I wonder if this is yet another of the Elder King's ploys to sway me in the hopes that I will consent to marry at last. But I will not yield. My heart is still broken, and I will not let him force me to marry. Still, it galls me that the Elder King bleeds my inheritance away from me, coin by coin. He uses none of it to punish those horrid nobles in Legault who pick over the scraps like carrion birds. The king is a greedy man. But he'll find I'm a stubborn woman.

—Claire de Murrow
Queen's Tower
(written resolutely)

CHAPTER
THIRTY-FOUR

The Hour of Crows

Ransom collided with the bars, the impact briefly stunning him. Sir Robert wrenched against his arm with both hands, trying to pull his limb inside the cell. Ransom dropped the torch involuntarily, and it spun when it struck the ground, sending a dizzying flare of light in circles, revealing a cloaked shape emerging from the far end of the corridor. The figure held a cranked crossbow.

"Come on, you favored crow!" Robert snarled, trying to bend Ransom's arm. "It's your hour to die now!"

Ransom pulled with all his strength, slamming Robert face-first into the bars. The man grunted in pain but held fast. Ransom tried to maneuver the tip of his sword through the bars to stab the other knight, but it only clanged against the metal. Left with no other options, Ransom pulled the other way as hard as he could, wrenching his shoulder uncomfortably as he did so.

The twang of the crossbow sounded, and in the blink of an eye, he felt the bolt pierce his leg, the same leg that had been injured before. Pain shot through him, not just the feeling of the bolt embedded in his muscle, but the memory of the injury that had come before. Ransom gasped with anguish, looking down to see the shaft, the fletching, and the blood already spilling from the wound.

He needed the Fountain's power—*now*—or he'd die in this dank dungeon.

Whatever you ask of me, I will do, he thought in silent determination. *This I swear to you as a knight. Please help me now, as you've done in the past.*

As soon as the thought went through his mind, he heard the roar of the falls amidst the cacophony. Strength filled him, mixed with firm determination and purpose. He hoisted Robert off his heels, slamming him into the bars again. This time he used the hilt of his bastard sword instead of the tip, clubbing Robert on the temple with it.

With a groan of pain, Robert released him and stumbled backward, holding his hand to his face. Freed from the grip, Ransom stumbled and went down. His sword fell from his grip as he caught himself on his arms. The pain in his leg was overshadowed by the rush of what must have been magic. He squeezed his leg above the wound but felt only numbness. He looked up, seeing a dagger in the lady's hand. She threw it at him.

Ransom twisted his shoulders, and the blade whistled past him, barely missing him. He lunged for his blade and grabbed it, but as he tried to lift it and rise, the lady swept forward and kicked him in the face, knocking him on his back.

The numbness in his leg shot up to his hip. A fiery, tingling sensation burned beneath his skin. Poison. Ransom grabbed the bolt protruding from his leg and ripped it out, yelling in agony as he did so.

"Let me out of here!" Robert bellowed.

Ransom saw the woman standing over him, drawing another knife. He saw an oily substance on the blade. Ransom used his uninjured leg and hooked his boot around her ankle, but she sidestepped and then dropped atop him, the blade coming down toward his neck. Ransom lifted his arm, blocking the strike. He could only see part of her face hidden behind the cowl, but he saw streamers of golden hair that looked strangely familiar.

He felt the life and energy inside him draining. The roar of the waterfall dimmed as whatever poison she'd used on the crossbow bolt infiltrated his blood. He had to act quickly. He deflected another dagger strike and grabbed the front of her cloak, clutching it with all his remaining strength as he rolled, bringing her sideways and then beneath him. The numbness stretched up into his stomach, then his chest. He felt every heartbeat begin to slow.

Trembling as his strength failed, he grabbed her wrist with his other hand as she tried to stab him again. He squeezed it hard, trying to force her to release the dagger. She did not yield, but he still had a grip on her wrist. She pushed and bucked against him, trying to free herself, but he was far heavier. His fingertips went numb and began to spasm. The sound of the waterfall reduced to a whisper, and she pulled her dagger hand free.

It was now only a matter of time before she finished what she'd started. The hauberk he was wearing would help deflect the blow, but it wouldn't save him. His ability to defend himself melted away. Ransom swayed, desperate to live, to survive the fight. He looked down at his own arm, the one still grasping her cloak and bodice, and saw the braided charm that Claire had given him. He focused on it, gathering strength from it. If nothing else, he wished to know who his enemy was before he died.

She tried to pry his hand away, but she couldn't. In a last burst of strength, he broke the clasp of her cloak, and the hood fell away.

It was Emiloh.

He blinked, his vision swimming. No, it wasn't the queen. But it was someone with an uncanny resemblance to her. The same golden hair, slightly crinkled. The same eyes in a younger face. A face much closer in age to his own.

He felt the dagger tip against his chest.

"Will you let go of me now?" she asked, her voice calm but insistent. Her eyes flashed in warning.

Ransom's surprise took away the rest of his resistance. The poison felt as if it were crushing his heart, rendering him incapable of fighting. He slumped to the ground, his vision beginning to blur, but it had been clear long enough to capture her face. Emiloh's daughter. It had to be. She was older than Devon, probably Ransom's age or older. Where had she been? Were the sordid rumors about the queen having a lover—a knight—more than just gossip? Confusion and disbelief clashed within him. He rolled onto his back and could move no more. Even breathing became impossible.

"Just kill him!" said Robert impatiently.

He saw blurry shadows, but the dark violet of her coat stayed in focus, almost dazzling his senses.

"Be silent, Sir Robert . . . or face the king's justice," the woman said.

The numbness had paralyzed him. He stared at her, at the light shining on her face from the sparse torches. She looked down at him, a half smile on her mouth.

"I didn't come to kill you, Marshall," she said. "But Devon had reached the end of his usefulness. Your leg will heal as it did long ago. When I last tended your injury. Put some bread with mold on it first, then wrap it in clean bandages."

He listened to her in shocked silence, his heart spasming again in recognition. The lady in the castle. It was her? The knowledge filled him with a strange conflict. Who was she? What was her name?

What could explain her behavior?

He felt her fingers graze through his hair. Then she stood abruptly, and as she passed by him, he felt the fringe of her cloak brush his cheek. The iron door creaked and groaned. He was blind now, unable to breathe, yet still alive.

"I want to kill him." It was Sir Robert's menacing voice.

"Try, and you'd die before your blow could fall," said the woman. "Let's go."

He could sense her leaving, back down the corridor from whence she'd come. The grinding of stone could be heard. The feeling faded away while he lay helpless, suffering keenly but still alive.

※

Ransom swayed on the horse, clutching the reins tightly, trying to keep from fainting. His injured leg had been treated and bandaged by the same barber who had failed to keep Devon alive. The paralysis of the poison had eventually passed, and he'd found himself alone in the dungeon. He'd crawled up the steps, almost falling at least half a dozen times before a servant found him. The lady had not reclaimed the poisoned dagger she'd thrown at him, and he'd kept it as evidence to bolster his story.

He'd learned after reviving that the Elder King was in the next town, less than a league away. So even though he was badly injured, Ransom was determined to fulfill his promise to bring tidings of the son to the father. As he rode and kept himself in the saddle, he thought of the face he'd seen. He heard her voice over and over in his mind. She'd killed Lord Archer. She'd killed Devon Argentine, her half brother. She'd killed others too, he had no doubt. But she hadn't killed him. Why? Perhaps it was because she'd tended his injuries, using her skill to heal instead of destroy. Or maybe some other reason had stayed the killing blow.

He had a firm conviction that she was the same lady who had visited St. Penryn years before him. She'd clearly learned enough about her powers to use them proficiently, while he was just a novice.

As he drew closer to the town, he heard the thunder of hooves before he saw the knights riding toward him. He slowed his own horse and tried to seem steadier than he felt. Looking down at the bandage wrapped around his leg, he saw blood seeping through it already. Another bout of dizziness came upon him.

He was no stranger to the men who approached him, having beaten all of them in the training yard. Looks of immediate recognition rose on their faces. The foremost gave him a knightly salute.

"Sir Ransom! What are you doing here?"

He responded to the salute in kind. "I came to see the king. And bring him tidings of his son's death."

His words shocked them, but they offered no argument or discussion. They fell in around him and took him back to the town with them. Even though he no longer wore the badge of the Silver Rose, he felt he belonged there. His responsibility was a dreadful one, but he was determined do it.

They arrived at the home of the mayor of the town, where dozens of horses were stationed out front. Ransom winced as he swung his leg over the saddle. As soon as he touched the ground, he had to grab the saddle horn to keep from collapsing. He squeezed it hard, summoning his courage and his strength. He then limped after the knights as they led the way into the mayor's home.

The Elder King's face turned ashen when he saw him. "Leave us," he ordered curtly.

Once the room had emptied, Ransom attempted to kneel with his good leg, but the king waved at him in annoyance. "I see you're wounded. None of that. Did my son send you?"

"My lord, your son is dead."

The Elder King's eyes widened with the shock. "He wasn't . . . it wasn't trickery? He did lay dying?"

"Yes, my lord. I was there at the end, gripping his hand as he passed beyond to the Deep Fathoms. He charged me with bringing you the tidings."

The king groped for a chair and sat down, his expression dumbfounded. Grief and shock battled for dominance on his countenance. "Is this all true? Surely it is, for you wouldn't lie to me." He looked at Ransom imploringly. "You wouldn't do that to me, would you, lad?"

"No, I would not. He was murdered, my lord. Poisoned. Like Lord Archer."

The king stiffened. He stared at the hearth, rubbing his lip, his hand trembling. "Poison, you say?"

"Yes. The same person who had stalked your son in the city. I met her, my lord. She nearly killed me."

"Sit down, Ransom. Sit before you fall down."

Ransom complied, the injury grieving him, but he ignored it. "Do you know who she is?"

"I don't," said the king. "I'd heard that Lewis had someone in his employ. Someone who removed his enemies." His lips pulled back into a snarl. "She's fled, then?"

"Yes. Along with Sir Robert Tregoss, who is a traitor to your son and to you. I took the liberty of sending some riders out to try and cut off their escape."

The Elder King glanced at him, a small smile appearing and then fading. "Did you now? That was clever, Ransom. You've always been clever." Raw emotion battled across his countenance.

"I'm sorry to bring you this news, my lord. Truly. If I had been there, I might have prevented it. I would have died trying."

The king blinked quickly, trying to suppress tears. He stroked his lip silently. "I didn't believe the accusation, you know. About you and Lewis's daughter. I didn't want to believe it, but I also thought it beneath you. He dismissed you. Foolish, foolish boy!"

"We were all misled. But his biggest regret was his disloyalty to you. He begged me to tell you that he was sorry for it."

The king's face crumpled, and he covered it with his hands and began to weep. Ransom had already wept for Devon. He watched the king suffer, knowing he could offer nothing to appease his grief. So he waited in silence until the bout of terrible anguish had passed.

The Elder King lowered his hands, shaking his head disconsolately. "I've been stitched and wrapped and fed yarrow root and thyme. But there is no poultice to apply to the wound caused by an ungrateful son. I did not believe that I would outlive him! He looked like a king. The people loved him more than they ever loved me. But how many thank the butcher for the cut of meat they enjoy? No, they thank the cook, who had the easier task." He sighed, squeezing his knees. "Oh, Devon," he said with deep emotion, "I would have given the Fountain my life for yours. I'm getting old. It's in my bones now." He looked Ransom's way, his eyes serious. "You will be there when we send his body to the falls. You were part of his mesnie."

Ransom nodded. "I would be honored."

"Some people may hate you, for even if told the truth, they will always prefer a lie, but you should be there anyway. I demand it. The gossipers and naysayers will have their day for a season. But I exonerate you. And so will those who want my goodwill."

Ransom's heart ached. "I will come. I would like to bring the news to the queen. May I?"

A black look came on the Elder King's face. His face twisted with anger. "Never. Not until the fountains run dry and the world becomes a desert. Let her rot in her tower till then."

The king grieves in an unnatural way. Whatever betrayal he feels, he lets others suffer tenfold plus six. Emiloh is not permitted to attend her son's funeral rites. She told me that I could go, but I will not leave her alone during her mourning. Something tells me that she suffers some secret grief beyond the death of her son. I wish I could understand it. But she bears her wounds alone.

The city is draped in black. It is quite a different scene from the celebration of the Younger King's coronation. So much has changed. It reminds me of when I was a little girl. I watched them tilt King Gervase's boat into the river. I didn't believe it would happen again until the Elder King died. None of us can see the future, for there are no longer any Wizrs who possess that awful gift. Or maybe they never existed.

They send Devon on a boat in the hopes that his body will be reunited with his soul in the Deep Fathoms. But the Aos Si rule that realm, and they mock our mortal traditions. My beliefs would be heresy here in Kingfountain, of course. I must keep them to myself. Above all, the people of Ceredigion prize loyalty. They would not welcome this son who betrayed everyone around him. That is the problem with our world. Loyalty has died.

—*Claire de Murrow*
Cistern Garden, Kingdom of Ceredigion

CHAPTER
THIRTY-FIVE

Into the Falls

Ransom tried not to limp as he carried the canoe holding the body of the Younger King, tightly gripping the staff that supported it. Memories flooded him—the king's easy laughter, his excitement about the tournaments, his tireless desire to prove himself. He'd been such a charming man, one who could win over anyone in the world except for his own father. And, apparently, his own wife.

But while those memories were fresh in his mind, the past conjured others no less potent. He'd watched Sir William Chappell perform this very feat for King Gervase. And now Ransom stood in his place, his old friend and mentor long since dead, killed on a bloody road to protect the queen. And for what? Now she sat in a different kind of prison.

He heard the falls because of their proximity, but he strained to hear the noise inside his soul. He felt empty, bruised, and forsaken. Once again, he had no one to serve. Part of him had hoped the Elder King would ask him to stay after he'd revealed his plans for the pilgrimage. The Elder King had only shrugged and said to do what he must.

Ransom had been watching the queen's tower, hoping to catch a glimpse of Claire one last time before he left. But there was nothing to see. The tower looked empty and desolate. He still had the necklace he'd bought her. But there was no way to get it to her.

Directly across from him, holding the other length of the pole, stood Sir James. Ransom avoided his gaze, feeling nothing but contempt and loathing for the man. Some of those involved in the rebellion had fled to Occitania. But not Sir James. No doubt he'd tried to pass his share of the blame to someone else, most likely the Younger King himself. But Ransom respected most of the other men seeing Devon to his rest. Sir Simon and Lord Kinghorn were among them, and so were Sirs Talbot and Alain.

They reached the end of the dock, and the deconeus of the sanctuary gave a brief speech. The Elder King stood there wearing a sable cloak with a wolf-pelt trim. The hollow crown was fixed on his brow, his eyebrows nettled with pent-up emotion. But he looked grim, angry, and defiant. Standing by him were his three surviving sons—Bennett, Goff, and Jon-Landon. Bennett and Goff each stood on opposite sides of the king. Their enmity for each other was plain to see in their dark brows and twisted frowns. Jon-Landon looked bored and disinterested in the events. He wasn't much older than Ransom had been when he'd left Kingfountain to make his way in the world.

Crackles of thunder sounded overhead, even though the sky was barren of clouds. Ransom looked up and saw thunderheads emerging from the northern skies. The season had been calm and beautiful, but it appeared they'd have a storm.

At the conclusion of the rites, Ransom and James hoisted their staves higher, forming a ramp so the canoe would tilt and go down into the waters. He felt the release of pressure from it, and watched and heard the scraping sound of wood against wood. Then the canoe splashed into the swift-flowing river. Ransom stared at the waxen face of his friend, his king, as the canoe bobbed in the water before the current took it away. He made the knightly salute as a token of farewell.

Sir James released the staff and sniffed. Ransom clutched the pole, unable to bear looking at the man.

"I heard you're leaving on a journey," said James at his shoulder.

"You're glad I'll be gone," Ransom said with a tone of rancor.

James chuffed. "Yes. Don't hurry back. I've heard Kinghorn's son has hopes of marrying Claire. Maybe she'll finally say yes to someone. She wouldn't want a gimp anyway."

Some people were skilled with the poison of words.

Ransom turned his head, and the smug look on James's face made it obvious how much he relished sowing discord. He'd done the same with Devon—and it had led the Younger King to his death.

Ransom swung the staff into James's stomach, knocking the wind from him, then cracked it down on his head, which made him collapse in stunned silence and pain. Shocked murmurs rose from the crowd, and the king's eyes blazed with wrath. Ransom handed the staff to Sir Simon, nodded to him, and then walked purposefully away, still trying to conceal the limp. This time, he hoped, he'd never return to Kingfountain.

The time had come for Ransom Barton to be his own man.

EPILOGUE

The Secrets of Lewis the Wise

King Lewis sat on an overstuffed chair in his private chamber, his swollen foot resting on a padded stool, yet still the pain knifed through him. His barber had suggested cutting off the foot, insisting the disease would only spread up his leg if he let it continue, but he refused to give the disease such a victory. Bowing his head, he focused on the pain, so he didn't hear the door squeak as it opened.

At the sound of the door shutting, he lifted his head and opened his eyes. His only son, Estian, stood by the entrance. Seeing his boy caused him a mixture of grief and pride.

"Were you asleep, Father?" asked the prince. It was late afternoon, but sometimes Lewis was so exhausted by then he couldn't keep his eyes open.

"It hurts too much to sleep, my boy," he answered. His hips were aching as well, and he shifted to try to get more comfortable. Estian crossed the room, his build and physique that of one who'd carefully trained for knighthood. Lewis had once been that pliable. It felt a long time ago.

When Estian reached his side, he paused to look at the Wizr set sitting in an open box on the small table next to the chair.

"Two pieces are missing," he said, his brow furrowing. He looked to his father for an answer.

Lewis grimaced as he shifted again. "I know. She has finished her mission."

Estian sighed. "I liked Devon very much. He was not always prudent, but he was a good fellow. A friend even."

"It is not wise to make friends of your opponents, Son." He reached out, and Estian took his frail hand in his strong grip. "The game must be played. Only one side can win."

"I know, Father."

There was a pained look on his son's brow. Lewis squeezed his hand. "I am doing what I must to make the game easier for you, to ensure *you* are the victor in the end. Devon Argentine is doing the same thing for his sons. But when I am gone, he will turn his gaze on you. He is a ruthless opponent, my son. Do not underestimate him."

"Will he name Benedict his heir?"

The king sniffed. "Yes, but not yet. He made mistakes with his eldest son. Mistakes he will not be quick to repeat. If he knew how sick I was, he would attack with all his might. You must be ready for him, Estian. You cannot let him win. It would destroy Occitania."

"I won't let him win," said the son. "I swear it on Mother's soul."

Lewis nodded. He heard the subtle click coming from a large framed tapestry mounted against the wall. The weaving depicted a castle in the duchy of Bayree with emblems of fish around it.

"I need to try and rest, my boy." He released his grip on his son and let his own hand fall slack on the chair.

"I'll check on you later," Estian said. Before he left, he looked at the Wizr set again. "What of the other missing piece?"

"Oh, he probably tried to interfere with her mission," said Lewis with a smile. "It saddens me, for there are so few Fountain-blessed among us."

"Do you think he really was?" Estian asked with interest.

"She told me he was," he answered, knowing his poisoner was lurking behind the frame, listening in to their conversation. "That is why your sister tried to turn him to our side of the board. Well, better that he should die than work against us."

Estian gave him a long look, then nodded before he walked back to the door and left.

As soon as he was gone, the frame opened, and she emerged from her hiding place, her cloak still protecting her identity. She went to the door and slid the latch into place first, a necessary precaution. His toes felt like they were on fire.

She came to him, lowering the hood, and withdrew a small vial and handed it to him.

It was a tonic for the pain. It wouldn't heal his debilitating sickness, but it would lessen his agony. For that he was grateful, and he greedily twisted off the end and swallowed it all quickly. He breathed out in a pleased sigh, eager for the potent combination to bring him relief and then blissful sleep. He handed her the vial and cap and watched as her nimble fingers fixed them back in place.

"I didn't want Sir Ransom to be killed," he told her. "I wanted him *turned*."

Her brow wrinkled. "I didn't kill him," she said, then she touched the rim of the box with the Wizr set and examined the pieces with a look of concern.

"Devon's piece disappeared first. Then Ransom's," he said. "Not on the same day."

"I shot him in the leg, but that shouldn't have killed him," she said. "The poison I used disabled him. Sir Robert wanted him dead, but only out of vengeance. He came back to Pree with me. But I see he's not on the board either."

The tincture she'd given him was already beginning to work. The fiery pain in his foot was fading, and he felt a calm euphoria that would soon overwhelm his unease. "If he is dead, he is dead. So be it. But be sure. Find out what happened. That is your next mission. If he lives, do whatever you must to turn him."

"If Noemie failed—"

"It was her pride," he said, interrupting her. Then a giggle burbled out of his mouth, and he was ashamed at his loss of self-control. "She thought it would be easy. You are more clever than her. I command it. This illness is killing me. My son will rule in my place, and you will be loyal to him. You are . . . you are . . . very special to me." He felt his eyelids begin to close.

As they shut, he wished he could fight the sleep longer. There was more he should tell her before it was too late.

Too late.

AUTHOR'S NOTE

History has a way of speaking to us, like voices whispering from the dust (Isaiah 29:4). While I was writing The Grave Kingdom series, I had three more ideas for new series to write. Sometimes I just can't turn my imagination off . . . not that I'd want to. But out of those ideas, I kept hearing the voices from Kingfountain whispering for me to come back, to gaze into the past and explore the world more deeply.

The First Argentines is intended to be a four-book series and has been from the start. When I pitched the idea to my then editor Jason and to my new editor Adrienne, they were both equally excited to hear about this new Kingfountain adventure. Adrienne and I share a love of medieval history, especially the historical fiction novels of Sharon Kay Penman.

This is the story of Ransom Barton, and it will be told over several books spanning many, many years. As with most of my novels, there are real historical nuggets that inspired the tale, but I'll hold off on revealing those until later. You've probably seen archetypes and shadows of previous Kingfountain characters in this story already. If you think you know what's going to happen, think again. I never tell the same story twice. I also continue to be inspired by the Arthurian legends of the past and how they have infiltrated history over the centuries. I love taking ideas like these and twisting the legends and real history into new and interesting configurations.

Thank you for joining me on this journey and for enduring the painful gaps between publication dates. Thank you for the kind notes and generous reviews, which I always take the time to read. I hope Ransom's story inspires you to find loyalty within your own life. It's easy to hold on to it when things go well. The real challenge is maintaining loyalty when life gets hard. And it always does.

ACKNOWLEDGMENTS

I knew my new editor, Adrienne Procaccini, and I would get along when she announced her fandom of one of my favorite authors, Sharon Kay Penman. Her love of medieval history (and Jedi light-saber dueling) gave us an instant bond. Thankfully, that's the only change to my team this time. You, lucky readers, still get to benefit from my ongoing partnership with Angela, Wanda, and Dan, who help get my books shipshape and Bristol fashion. I'm grateful they have all been involved in my writing for a while, which is especially useful going back to the world of Kingfountain that I love so much.

For this book, I'm grateful to everyone at 47North and Amazon Publishing who have invested so much in my success as a writer. To my first readers who wait with bated breath for each book to finish so they can provide helpful feedback—thank you, Robin, Shannon, Travis, Sunil, and Sandi. And to the amazing Shasti O'Leary Soudant, the amazing cover artist who helps people judge a book by its cover and judge it for the best! Also, to Kate Rudd, my amazing narrator, who has partnered with me ever since she voiced Lia in *Wretched of Muirwood*—you are spectacular!

Mostly, I'm grateful to you for reading this story and sticking with me for so many years. Thank you!

ABOUT THE AUTHOR

Photo © 2016 Mica Sloan

Jeff Wheeler is the *Wall Street Journal* bestselling author of *The Immortal Words*, *The Buried World*, and *The Killing Fog* in the Grave Kingdom series; the Harbinger and Kingfountain series; and the Muirwood, Mirrowen, and Landmoor novels. He left his career at Intel in 2014 to write full-time. Jeff is a husband, father of five, and devout member of his church. He lives in the Rocky Mountains and is the founder of *Deep Magic: The E-Zine of Clean Fantasy and Science Fiction*. Find out more about *Deep Magic* at https://deepmagic.co, and visit Jeff's many worlds at https://jeff-wheeler.com.